PRAISE FOR *THORN*

"Delightful and heartfelt, *Thorn City* whisked me through the streets of Portland and twist after twist of a perfectly plotted thriller! This debut delivers a satisfying meal better than any Michelin-starred food truck." —Elle Marr, Amazon Charts bestselling author of *The Family Bones* and *The Alone Time*

"The rich backstories of these wealthy characters make them come alive. Come to the party for the secrets and gossip. Stay to see if they survive the mayhem." —Cate Holahan, *USA Today* bestselling author of *The Widower's Wife*

"Pamela Statz simultaneously celebrates and gleefully skewers her hometown of Portland, Oregon, in a delightful, madcap thriller with enough punchlines and plot twists for half a dozen novels. *Thorn City*'s larger-than-life cast—from ambitious, amoral city executives to sweet but wayward twenty-somethings, from a struggling ad man to a chameleon-like tattoo artist—keeps the comedy and tension unwaveringly high, against a backdrop of hipster food cart pods, boutique ad agencies, and the hallowed corridors of City Hall itself. Portland truly is weird, and every page of this fast-paced, hilarious debut sparkles." —Emily Raymond, bestselling co-author, with James Patterson, of *Expelled*, *The Girl in the Castle*, and *Tell Me Your Best Story*

"With an insider's eye, Statz takes the reader through the nuanced underbelly of the City of Roses. This debut page-turner is a terrific addition to your crime fiction shelf." —Suzy Vitello, author of *Faultland* and *Bitterroot*

"*Thorn City* captures exactly what's special about Portland, from the ubiquity of our food carts to the ever-present undercurrents of social and geological upheaval. Still, the characters and their struggles are universally relatable—and so realistically written that I wouldn't be surprised to run into them one day at a mayoral event, kebab stand or local emergency room!" —Jennifer Hanlon Wilde, author of *Finding the Vein*

"A page-turning romp with Portland at its center, *Thorn City* is part who-dunnit/part coming-of-age saga with city politics, tech bro culture, economic disparities, and drug dealing thrown in to round out the experience. A fast-moving, thoroughly enjoyable read." — Margaret Juhae Lee, author of *Starry Field: A Memoir of Lost History*

"Pamela Statz has weaved an intriguing novel with a cast of characters to love and root for, and those to love to hate! A complete immersion into the Portland culture, *Thorn City*, is a complex, and twisty ride that unveils its multiple layers of lies and secrets at a perfect pace, not letting go until the very last page. Bravo!" —Mary Keliikoa, author of the award-winning *Hidden Pieces* and *Deadly Tides*

"Statz delivers a sneaky and addictive gem by captivating readers in this cleverly written thriller. In *Thorn City*, appearances are not what they seem. Those holding corrupt power will kill to keep their secrets safe and maintain status in Portland's high society." —Erica Blaque, author of *Among Wolves*

THORN CITY

Thorn City: A Novel
© 2024 Pamela Statz

ISBN13: 978-1-947845-49-7

Ooligan Press
Portland State University
Post Office Box 751, Portland, Oregon 97207
503.725.9748
ooligan@ooliganpress.pdx.edu
www.ooliganpress.com

Library of Congress Cataloging-in-Publication Data
Names: Statz, Pamela, author.
Title: Thorn city : a novel / Pamela Statz.
Description: Portland, Oregon : Ooligan Press, [2024]

Identifiers: LCCN 2023027542 | ISBN 9781947845497 (trade paperback) | ISBN 9781947845503 (ebook)
Subjects: LCGFT: Novels.
Classification: LCC PS3619.T3827 T46 2024 | DDC 813/.6--dc23/eng/20230613
LC record available at https://lccn.loc.gov/2023027542
Cover design by Isabel Zerr
Interior design by Savannah Lyda

References to website URLs were accurate at the time of writing. Neither the author nor Ooligan Press is responsible for URLs that have changed or expired since the manuscript was prepared.
Printed in the United States of America

THORN CITY
A NOVEL

PAMELA STATZ

Ooligan Press | Portland, Oregon

For Justin

PROLOGUE

He stood vigil, watching and waiting. A van pulled into the driveway, and two men emerged dressed in black, their faces concealed by ski masks. They approached the house with dark intent, their breath visible in the chill morning air.

He had to stop them.

Rushing to the front door, he reached out to turn the lock, but he was too late. The door opened, and the men entered. They motioned for him to stay silent. One pointed toward a staircase leading to the second floor and waited for an answer.

He lowered his eyes and nodded. Ashamed, he retreated to the kitchen.

He listened. Low voices, then a cry of protest followed by piercing screams. Almost as startling came silence, then heavy footsteps on the stairs. Was it over? No.

She burst into the kitchen, her face shifting from fear, to confusion, then rage as she realized the truth.

Already knowing he'd fail, he made a final protest. He would have fought to the death if he'd known it was the last time he'd ever see her.

CHAPTER 1
THE GALA

The city bus lurched to a stop and coolly exhaled two twenty-somethings clad in sequined mini-dresses. As the pair stepped onto the pavement, the summer heat rose in waves around them, and the air had the unpleasant odor of a city street gone too long without rain. Jamie flipped back her hair, squared her shoulders, and started down the sidewalk at a quick clip. Lisa followed, her ponytail wilting in the humidity.

"How much farther is it?" Lisa asked. "I can barely walk in these heels."

"Then take them off," said Jamie over her shoulder.

"Go barefoot?" Lisa scowled at the grimy sidewalk. A homeless man catcalled her from a partially collapsed tent. She hurried to catch up with Jamie. "I thought this was supposed to be a fancy party. Why hold it in the Park Blocks?"

"Because it's very Portland chic to have fancy parties in shitty parts of town."

"Did you bring band aids?" Lisa asked hopefully. "I think I'm getting a blister."

"Of course," said Jamie, as though offended Lisa had to ask. Still walking at a rapid pace, Jamie opened her purse, rooted around, and handed Lisa two bandages. "One for the back of each foot. I also have mints, antacids, aspirin, tampons, lip balm, tissues, sunglasses, gum, lipstick, condoms, concealer, a flashlight, and an emergency candy bar."

"You're a mobile drug store," said Lisa, reaching for the chocolate.

Jamie slapped Lisa's hand away. "Does this look like an emergency?"

"Yes, Jamie. Yes, it does."

Jamie snapped her purse shut and glanced at her watch. "He's expecting us at seven."

Lisa rolled her eyes. "Nigel's parties suck whether or not we show up."

"True, but fuck Nigel, I'm doing this for the money," said Jamie. "I want to find him before the party starts so we can get paid."

The light changed at the corner of Burnside Street and Eighth Avenue, but Lisa didn't budge. "Can't we just rob a liquor store, then go home and binge watch something on Netflix?"

"That's a super fun idea, Lisa, but no. We can't afford Netflix." Jamie grabbed Lisa's hand and pulled her across the street. "I know we promised ourselves we'd never work another party, but rent's due. I don't want to have to ask my parents again."

"I know," said Lisa with a pang of guilt. The money she had inherited from her father covered her tuition and most of the rent, but not much else. A girl had to eat. She could ask her mother, but that option was infinitely worse than working at one of Nigel's parties.

Lisa followed Jamie toward the stretch of green that made up the North Park Blocks. Usually the domain of homeless and meth heads, tonight the park had been transformed with white party tents, flower-laden tables, and thousands of tiny lights strung across towering Dutch elms.

Jamie made a beeline for a slim man in a pale blue linen suit, who stood talking with a bouncer near a silver and white balloon arch.

"Hey, Nigel. We made it," said Jamie breathlessly.

"It's about time," Nigel said as he motioned to the bouncer to let Jamie and Lisa through. He looked them over with a critical eye. "What on earth are you wearing?" he asked Jamie.

Jamie was encased in a ridiculously short, shimmering green cocktail dress. She twirled, almost tripping in her strappy sandals. "It's new. I ordered it on Bimbos-R-Us."

"Wherever you got it, it's perfect." Nigel turned to Lisa and motioned for her to spin as well, but Lisa just crossed her arms over her gold sequined number and shook her head no. Nigel didn't press the matter. "Now, girls, you both know the drill. It's not about just standing around looking pretty."

"We know," said Jamie. "Be the first to dance, the first to karaoke, and don't forget to talk to the socially inept about their hopes and dreams for the future."

"And no drinking. If someone offers you one, dump it discreetly." Nigel mimicked pouring out an imaginary cocktail behind his back. "Like so."

Jamie groaned. "How are we supposed to tolerate this if we can't drink?"

"If this is because I vomited on that guy's shoes . . ." Lisa said, glaring at Nigel.

He glared back. "I'm not paying to replace another pair of suede wingtips."

"Fine. No drinking," said Jamie, giving Lisa a warning look.

Nigel smiled. "Thank you. And next time catch a ride over, and make sure it's a car with air conditioning. You're both all shiny. Go powder your noses."

He tried to shoo them away, but Jamie stood her ground and held out her hand. "There's still the matter of payment."

"Of course, how could I forget?" He pulled a wallet out of his back pocket and counted out six one-hundred-dollar bills. He handed three to Jamie and three to Lisa. "Now go pretend to have fun," he said, waving them off.

Lisa and Jamie headed across the party grounds, following signs for the ladies' room. Other than staff, they appeared to be the only attendees.

"Where is everyone?" Lisa asked.

"The party is for some tech conference. Guests should start showing up soon. I assume it'll be the usual bullshit," said Jamie.

"Totes," agreed Lisa.

They walked past waiters prepping hors d'oeuvres and stocking bars with liquor, beer, and wine. In tandem, tattooed hipsters readied trendy food trucks that would give the party that signature Portlandia vibe. Signs advertised culinary mash ups like the Korean Kabab, the Prussian Pierogi, and Double D Donuts.

Under the trees, the summer air felt cooler. The sky was still bright, just hinting toward twilight. For a moment, Lisa let herself pretend that she was an actual guest at the party, that she could relax and have fun.

"Does Patrick know where you are tonight?" asked Jamie.

The spell broke.

"Nope. And he's not going to. He hates it when I work parties." Lisa pulled her phone from her purse. There were three new messages, each with a tiny photo of Patrick's face. She clicked. "Oh no."

"Has he been arrested? Tell him we can't cover his bail."

"It's so much worse," Lisa said, handing Jamie her phone. "He got a tattoo."

Jamie squinted at the photo, a close up of Patrick's arm. "Does that say, 'Lisa Forever'?"

Lisa nodded vigorously.

"That is amazing," said Jamie. She started laughing, almost losing her breath. "This dress is too tight."

"You're not helping," Lisa said. "Maybe it's a joke." She took the phone back and zoomed in on the photo. The tattoo looked fresh, the skin angry and sore. She suddenly felt nauseous. Tapping quickly, she texted back, 'WOW' with a red heart emoji, hoping it would be vague enough until she had a chance to fully absorb the latest expression of her boyfriend's devotion.

"Lisa Forever," sang Jamie, still laughing. "Lisa Forrreeeverrrrr."

"Shut up," Lisa said. "Anyway, he loves me. What's wrong with that?"

"Maybe it's time to look for some friends who aren't from a school for troubled teens."

"Um, hello," Lisa said.

"My situation is completely different," said Jamie. "I chose to attend the Lost Lake Academy."

"After your juvenile court judge strongly suggested it," Lisa said.

Jamie shrugged. "Regardless, I'm here to act as your emotional support animal. Whereas Patrick is a little bit confused and a lot fixated on you."

"He's not fixated," Lisa said, her hands on her hips. "He's just stuck. Anyway, you introduced us."

"Sorry."

"And maybe it really will be Lisa and Patrick forever," Lisa said with a shrug. Even as she spoke the words aloud, she wanted to snatch them back. Patrick and Jamie had pulled her through some dark times at the Academy, but they were years beyond that now. Lisa and Jamie were in school, Lisa was working on a degree from the College of Art and Jamie studied political science at Portland State University. They had plans. But Patrick liked his job at the bike shop, and he seemed perfectly content sharing a dumpy apartment with three other guys. Lisa figured he would grow up someday, but she was losing patience with his inability to commit to anything other than her. She couldn't solve all his problems. She had too many of her own.

"And if not forever, there's always laser tattoo removal," said Jamie with a smile.

As they walked past the row of food trucks, Lisa spotted the ladies' room—a massive trailer that looked distinctly portable. "A port-a-potty? You have to be kidding."

"Oh no, this is a Presidential Potty," said Jamie with reverence.

"A what?"

"Presidential. My cousin rented one of these for her wedding. They're super nice."

"Whatever." Careful in her high heels, Lisa followed Jamie up three steep steps to a steel door marked "Ladies."

The interior was sparkling clean and quite luxurious with four bathroom stalls, all empty. Lisa shrugged and made herself comfortable in front of a large mirror. She'd overdone her makeup. Her eyes were lined with black pencil, and her sparkly gold eyeshadow matched the color of her strapless dress. Her lashes held a thick layer of mascara, and her pert lips were a deep pink. She should have plucked her eyebrows before leaving the apartment, and that blemish hadn't quite cleared up, but it was nothing Jamie's bag of tricks couldn't fix. She picked through her friend's purse and pulled out a stick of concealer.

Jamie stepped into a toilet stall and returned with two disposable seat covers. She handed one to Lisa.

"What am I supposed to do with this?" asked Lisa, holding the thin tissue with the tips of her fingers.

"Blot."

"No."

"Yes. See?" Jamie started patting the tissue against her skin, and like magic, her face went from shiny to matte. "Better than those fancy-ass blotters from Sephora. And they're free."

"I like free," said Lisa, following her friend's lead and pressing the tissue to her face. "So, what's the plan?" she said, her voice slightly muffled.

"A few rounds of mingling, then assess the catering options."

"What about the food trucks? Korean Kabab's here," said Lisa. She crumpled up her toilet seat cover and tossed it into the trash. "You know how much I love their kimchi burritos."

"Your obsession with fermented vegetables is disturbing," said Jamie.

"I blame your grandmother."

"Grandma Kim does make the best Bibimbap this side of the Pacific," said Jamie. "Okay, Korean Kabab it is. We need to keep up our strength. At nine, we hit the karaoke stage. We'll do one together. I'm thinking we start strong with . . ."

"Not Journey," interrupted Lisa, as she touched up her lipstick.

"You're so good, though. You sound just like Steve Perry."

"No. I'm singing 'Rebel Girl.' I don't care if Nigel complains."

"Are you sure we shouldn't stick with something a little more conventional? You know, like the B-52s, Britney, even Bon Jovi."

"It's our duty to musically educate these tech bros."

"Fine. Are you ready?"

"As I'll ever be."

They looked at each other's reflections in the big mirror and practiced their smiles. "Don't let me do anything stupid," they said in unison, and laughed.

CHAPTER 2
GEORGE GETS HIS FIX

George Green arrived at the party dressed in his signature look—a light wool navy blazer, ironic T-shirt, distressed designer jeans, and vintage Nike Cortez sneakers in black with a white swoosh. The touch of gray at his temples lent him gravitas, but his face retained a youthful vigor that, from a distance at least, still read hipster.

Tonight's party was the culmination of a conference sponsored by the city and various local pillars of industry, George's company included. Advertising agency Burnam & Green occupied a full block of prime real estate in Portland's trendy Pearl District and had satellite offices in the usual hotspots of Beijing, London, Rio, and Tokyo. The company's Portland-based mothership was an architectural marvel of reclaimed Douglas fir, raw steel beams, and open workspaces outfitted with the finest furniture Design Within Reach had to offer.

Earlier that evening George had delivered the conference's keynote speech to thunderous applause. A quick scan of social media assured him that the crowd had found it brilliant despite its notable absence of original content. His delivery was outstanding, his voice deep and soothing with a touch of grit, the residue of a youthful smoking habit. Though his words lacked real substance, twenty years of ad campaigns had polished them to a fine and appealing gloss.

Now, with the party at full tilt, George held court with a glass of Kentucky bourbon in his left hand, his smart phone in his right. He was flanked by groupies: eager young men—and a token woman—all pitching ideas, grasping for opportunity, desperately hoping George would help launch their careers.

George should have been in his element. The chance to flaunt one's power in Portland was rare, but a restless unease deflated his mood. The reality was that Burnam & Green was poised on a knife-edge. The company had been hemorrhaging clients since the retirement of George's older and wiser partner, Henry Burnam. Fortunately, no one but George and his CFO knew how bad things were.

For the moment, George tried to push aside his worries and do his best to pontificate. "You need to get to the sharp point," he said. George's admirers absorbed his words as eagerly as their watered-down gin and tonics. "Break down the silos and focus on the north star of your creative ideations." The sea of heads bobbed. Even with this show of adulation, George felt his anxiety grow. At any moment he could pass into obscurity and irrelevance. He was forty-five after all, and admittedly in the full flush of a midlife crisis. Right now, he needed something stronger than bourbon to take the edge off. Across the crowd, he saw the woman who could give him that something—Sheila.

George excused himself and started to wade through the throng. He was greeted on all sides by associates known and unknown. No one let him pass without enjoying a moment in his orbit. Some merited a handshake, others an air kiss, a few received a hearty pat on the back, and he always replied with a modest "thank you" to their words of praise for his excellent speech. As he advanced, he kept a close eye on his target.

Finally, George shook off the last hanger-on, only to face disappointment. Sheila was deep in conversation. He couldn't see her expression, but he recognized the man with whom she spoke. Unlike the rest of the attendees, who shared the damp, flushed cheeks of their second or third drink, Victor Smith was sober and angry.

Victor had a lean and handsome face, framed with a full head of deep gray hair that must have been black when he was young. Dark rimmed glasses gave him a slightly professorial look, and people were easily taken in by his natural charm, only to be later stunned by his complete lack of empathy. One of Portland's most notorious slum lords, Victor had started his career tearing down historic buildings and replacing them with cheap apartments, parking garages, and strip malls. In the last few years, Victor's company, Victor Smith Construction, had shifted focus. VSC cranes and work crews hovered over the Portland skyline, building high-end condos and shopping complexes. Victor had approached Burnam & Green about a rebrand, but George had laughed it off. If a company wasn't in the Fortune 500 with a valuation equal to the net worth of a small European country, George wasn't interested. Not worth the effort.

In truth, George was scared of Victor. Most people with any sense were. Victor was rumored in his youth to have killed a man with only a fountain pen—the same pen now affixed to the jacket pocket of his well-cut suit.

George watched as Victor gripped Sheila's bare arm tightly. As she tried to pull away, George saw that her eyes were bright with fear under her thin, arched brows.

"Where is it?" Victor demanded.

Sheila answered, her voice shrill, "Your goons will never find it."

Victor's face darkened. "Maybe they can't find it because it's always on you." Still grasping Sheila's arm, he reached for her purse, but she held it just out of reach.

"Do you really think I'm that stupid?" she hissed.

"Thought I might get lucky."

"Victor. I'm not being unreasonable. I'll hand it over when you agree to my terms," she said.

"You're a power-hungry bitch, Sheila. I've always liked that about you, but you're pushing it too far. Almost four years I've been dealing with your bullshit. My patience has worn thin."

Sheila's eyes glanced toward George. "We have company," she said.

Victor released his grip and turned, seeing George. In an instant, his threatening look was replaced with a warm smile. He held out his hand. George reciprocated in spite of the jolt of unease he felt at Victor's abrupt change of mood.

"George," said Victor heartily. "Great to see you."

"I hope I'm not interrupting anything," George said, pulling his hand away and resisting the urge to wipe it on his jacket. He glanced at Sheila, who was lighting a cigarette. Her hands trembled. "Everything all right here?" he asked.

"Grand, just grand," Victor said. His eyes left George's and scanned the crowd. "I see that son of a bitch the chief of police. She owes me C-note from our last poker game. When you're ready to sell me your building, George, you let me know. It's the perfect spot for a two-hundred-unit condo complex. I'll even throw a penthouse suite into the deal." Without another word, Victor made his exit.

George stepped closer to Sheila. "What was that all about?" he asked.

Sheila rubbed her arm where the pink imprint of Victor's fingertips lingered. "That was nothing."

"Didn't look like nothing. How do you know him anyway? Is he a customer?"

"Victor Smith?" She laughed bitterly. "Never. Listen, George, do me a favor and forget you saw that. It was just a little misunderstanding."

"Consider it forgotten," George said. The last thing he needed was to get caught up in his drug dealer's drama. "You have something for me?"

She smiled. "Always right to the point. That's what I like about you, George. This way." She led him through the crowd, past the pod of food trucks to a vintage Airstream trailer. Unlocking the metal door, she motioned for George to enter, then followed him inside, securing the door behind her. "Wouldn't want anyone barging in on us."

"Speaking of, I'm surprised you're here tonight," said George. "Pretty ballsy to deal coke at the mayor's big event."

"Consider it a fuck you to Mayor Law and Order," Sheila said. She crushed out her cigarette in a clean ashtray, then opened a small cabinet and set out a mirror, a packet of white powder, and a razor blade. "Here, give it a try. It's organic coke from Peru."

"Organic, really? Sue keeps telling me to watch my health."

"Is your lovely wife here tonight?"

"God no, she hates these things. She's been at a silent yoga retreat all week. I expect her back on Sunday."

"So that's why I haven't seen her at the gym lately. Please tell her I said hello."

"Of course," said George, knowing he'd do no such thing. He didn't approve of the friendship between Sheila and his wife, even if Sue was unaware of Sheila's side gig as drug dealer to Portland's elite. He cut a line, took a hundred-dollar bill from his wallet, rolled it up, and held it out to Sheila. "Ladies first."

Sheila shook her head no. "You know I never touch the stuff. Another client assures me this is the best he's had since the eighties. I call it 'Like a Virgin.' High for the very first time."

George laughed and bent to snort a line. He straightened and paused for a moment. "Incredible," he whispered. The rush of the drug was immediate and thrilling. He was ready to give another keynote speech, do a thousand push-ups, fuck a beautiful girl. He took another hit. "I'll take a gram now and send one of your boys over with an eight ball tomorrow."

"Always a pleasure doing business with you, George."

He smiled and handed her a few bills from his wallet. "Likewise, Sheila."

Sheila gave him an appraising look. "Listen George, could you do me a favor? I'll make it worth your while." She pressed the money back into his hand.

"What is it?" he asked. He was suddenly eager to get back to the party.

"Could you hold onto something for me? Just for a day or so." She opened her leather handbag and pulled out a thin, square DVD case.

"You want me to hold on to your copy of *Die Hard*?"

"That's just a case I had handy." She opened his suit jacket and slid the case into the inside breast pocket. "A perfect fit. You won't even know it's there. And George, don't watch it. It's a private video."

George gave her a knowing smile and patted his lapel. An odd request, but it seemed harmless enough. He unlocked the Airstream's door and rejoined the party. Either it had picked up considerably in the brief time he'd been conducting his transaction, or the coke was really doing its job. He felt fantastic.

And then he saw her. She was blond, with a great figure, wearing a tight sequined dress that picked up the last of the evening's light and the unusual golden shade of her eyes.

It was clear to him what she was doing here. Same as Sheila, making a living. Sheila with her drugs, this girl with her body.

A pudgy young man eagerly handed the girl a drink, spilling a few drops in his haste. She smiled at something he said, then discreetly poured the drink out behind her back. George laughed at her artifice. Then, he remembered his empty house and smiled. He may as well enjoy the weekend with someone young, hot, and for sale.

CHAPTER 3

STRAIGHT UP WITH A TWIST

Lisa made the rounds. She flirted shamelessly with bland, overly-confident men. Listened attentively to lame jokes and laughed at punchlines on cue. She feigned interest in tales of economic pursuits and exaggerated successes. Already, a margarita, two cosmopolitans, and a gin and tonic had watered the lawn of the party.

All in a night's work, she thought. Lisa glanced at her phone, checking the time. She was due at the Karaoke tent in ten minutes. "Don't Stop Believin'" was already stuck in her head. Maybe she'd just bite the bullet and sing the damn song.

Then Lisa saw *her*. Mother . . .

Her heart pounding, Lisa quickly excused herself from her third Jeff of the evening, and looked desperately for Jamie, knowing her friend would act as a willing shield. As she searched the crowd, she caught the eye of a man walking toward her from the food truck pod.

He was tall, fit, a bit on the older side, but still the most handsome man at the party. He had a full head of salt and pepper hair and a confident smile that reached his dark gray eyes. His outfit was obviously expensive, perfectly tailored, and slightly ridiculous for a man his age, yet he owned the look with a confidence that allowed him to pull it off, barely. She glanced quickly at his ring finger, and saw it was bare.

"A beautiful woman in distress. How can I be of service?" he asked.

"I could use a cocktail," she said, knowing that if he gave her one, she'd drink it, Nigel be damned. She glanced at the man's shoes.

Sneakers. Good. Easy to replace.

Lisa let the man lead her toward the bar, his hand warm at the small of her back.

Just one drink, she thought, to calm my nerves. Then I'll find Jamie and we'll get out of here. Lisa's eyes swept across the crowd again, but she saw no sign of her friend.

"I'm Lisa," she said as they walked in step together. "And you are?"

"George. George Green." He stopped and held out his hand, and she held out hers in return. Instead of shaking Lisa's hand, he grasped it gently and kissed the inside of her wrist, his lips barely grazing the skin.

Despite the heat, she shivered and pulled away, a bit taken aback. Who does that, she thought. She should just walk away. Though, his name. Green. It couldn't be. She reminded herself that she wasn't at this party to socialize, to mix and mingle, or to network. But she couldn't help herself and the words just spilled out. "George Green, of Burnam & Green?"

"Yes, you've heard of it?" he asked, looking quite pleased with himself.

"I've worked a few of your parties," she said, instantly regretting it. Key to the role of party hostess was to pretend you were actually an attendee. If this got back to Nigel, he might ask for his money back. But it seemed unlikely, and she was curious about George's company. Everyone at art school wanted a job at B&G. It was the big fish in town, and she was already looking forward to bragging to her classmates about meeting the great George Green.

"So you are a working girl," he said, with a smile.

Lisa went cold. Working girl? Seriously? Of course, the one man she actually found attractive at this party assumed she was a hooker. It was rare, but had happened before, and she and Jamie had a deal. Whoever was propositioned had to cover a round the next night at the corner bar. Damn it. In that case, she was definitely going to order a drink. A proper cocktail. And she'd enjoy it.

They'd reached the front of the bar line. "What's your poison?" asked George.

"Vodka martini, very dry, straight up with a twist," said Lisa directly to the bartender, who she recognized from one of her drawing classes.

"And I'll have a bourbon, neat," said George, dropping a twenty in the tip jar. He turned back to Lisa. "The lady likes her cocktails. That's a pretty grown-up order."

"I started early and had lots of practice," she answered.

"I bet," he said.

The bartender handed George and Lisa their drinks. They took a few steps from the bar and clinked glasses.

George looked at her thoughtfully. "I once read that the martini is the most pure of cocktails, with nowhere to hide if badly prepared. And just now, you had nowhere to hide and looked badly prepared. Who are you trying to avoid?" he asked.

Lisa just sipped the astringent drink, knowing the only person at the party more infamous than George Green was her mother Ellen, the mayor of Portland.

CHAPTER 4
CHANCE ENCOUNTER

As Patrick neared the party, he saw no evidence of the drug addicts, vagrants, and runaways who usually roamed this patch. Bouncers guarded every entrance, but fortunately they were his people, and one tattooed giant who was a friend of a friend handed Patrick a bright yellow wristband and let him slip through the velvet rope.

Patrick clumsily secured the band, the adhesive catching on his arm hair, as he took in the crowd. So many unfamiliar faces, except among the waiters and waitresses. He waved down the closest one. "Jarred, dude," he said. They clasped hands by way of hello.

"Whoa, man, what are you doing here?" asked Jarred.

"Meeting someone about a job."

"Thought you were full time at River City Bikes."

"Too many mechanics in this town, man. The pay sucks."

"I hear you." Jarred gestured widely at the crowd with his free hand. "You're in the right place if you're looking for money. This party is flush with the tech elite. Are you pitching an app or a startup?"

Patrick laughed and shook his head. "Neither."

"Good luck, whatever it is. Have some grub on the house." Jarred flourished a silver tray of tiny blintzes dabbed with salmon roe.

"No," said Patrick, looking it over. "I'm not hungry."

"Hey, Lisa's here. Saw her earlier. She's looking hot tonight."

"What do you mean Lisa's here?" asked Patrick. He pulled his phone from his beat-up messenger bag. She hadn't texted anything about her plans tonight and had barely responded to the photo of his tattoo. Not a great sign. He'd gotten a little high after his shift last night and had biked over to Lady Luck Tattoo. Betty and her tattoo gun were more than happy to accommodate his request for a grand, romantic gesture. After he pulled off the bandage this morning, he wasn't so sure it had been a good idea. He glanced at his arm. The red heart peeked out from under the sleeve of his white T-shirt. He tugged on the fabric to hide it, wincing at the still tender skin.

"Saw her over by the bar a few minutes ago. The dudes have been swarming," said Jarred with a smirk. It faded at Patrick's scowl. "But you know Lisa, she loves you, man. This is just a gig for her."

"She's working the party?" asked Patrick. He felt his heart in his throat. He couldn't believe it. She'd lied to him. Said she was done with this shit.

"Yeah." Jarred paused awkwardly. "Well, I better get back to work. I'll see you around, man."

Patrick nodded and headed toward the bar. After walking through the crowded party for a few minutes, he finally caught sight of Lisa. She was wearing the gold dress he recognized from last New Year's Eve. It had been totally inappropriate for the freezing night. He remembered how she'd laughed it off and said it was more important to be pretty than warm.

She looked plenty comfortable tonight as she flirted with some old dude in a suit jacket. What kind of asshole wears a jacket in eighty-degree weather, wondered Patrick.

Suddenly, Lisa turned as though sensing she was being watched. Her eyes met Patrick's, and her coquettish smile instantly disappeared. She said something to the man that made him laugh, then headed toward Patrick, her thin heels sticking in the trampled grass.

"Patrick, what are you doing here?" She stood stiffly and held an empty martini glass in one hand.

He leaned down to kiss her but she quickly turned her head so his lips touched her cheek instead. "Meeting someone," he said, trying to keep his cool.

Lisa raised an eyebrow. "You're meeting someone at the 'Rose City Ripe for Disruption Gala.' Who?"

Patrick shrugged. "No one you know. And what's wrong with my being here? I like galas."

Lisa rolled her eyes. "You are so full of shit." She pushed up the sleeve of his T-shirt and ran her finger lightly across his tattoo. "You really did it."

"Do you like it?" he asked, feeling a little too eager.

"It's sweet," she said, though Patrick thought her voice sounded flat.

"You hate it."

"No, I don't. I just think it's very permanent." She pulled his T-shirt sleeve back down so only the bottom tip of the heart showed.

"Well, that's what I'd like us to be. You know. Permanent."

"Is this tattoo your way of proposing?" She placed her empty glass on a passing waiter's tray.

"No, no. I mean, I just thought maybe we could move in together. I'm over at your apartment all the time anyway. Maybe we should find our own place. A little house with a yard. Just me and you."

Lisa sighed and shook her head. "Patrick, I'm still in school and we don't have the money. I'm barely covering rent as it is."

"I'm working on that," he said.

"What do you mean?" she asked, giving him a wary look.

"I have a new gig. Something Joe set up for me."

"Your roommate Joe? He's a creep."

"He's a good guy."

"He's also a drug dealer," she said. "Don't tell me you're getting mixed up in that."

"Like selling drugs is worse than what you're doing," he said, feeling defensive.

Lisa stared at him. "What do you mean by that?" she asked.

"You know exactly what I mean."

She took a step away and raised her hands in frustration. "Patrick, I really don't need this tonight."

"Lisa, I don't like you working these parties. I mean your job is literally to get men to hit on you." He'd said this all before and she hadn't listened, but he couldn't help himself.

"I have never given you a reason not to trust me."

"What about that guy," he said, glaring at the man in the jacket. "Look at him staring at you like he owns you."

"No one owns me."

"Well, it looks like you're for sale. Your hair, and all that makeup. It's embarrassing."

"Patrick," said Lisa, stunned. She looked on the verge of tears.

He'd gone too far. Sure, he'd been thinking it ever since she and Jamie had started doing this hostess thing, but he wanted desperately to take the words back. He realized he'd heard them before, spoken by their teachers, if you could call them that, at the Academy.

"You know this is an act. You know it's not really me," she said, her voice breaking.

Lisa was right. He did know, and yet he'd gone right to the place that would hurt her most. He grabbed her hand. "Listen, I'm so sorry. I didn't mean it. I need to go meet with someone, then let's just get out of here. Please."

"I'm not going anywhere with you," she said, pulling away. "I'm done trying to be your perfect girlfriend. Figure out your own mess of a life."

"Lisa, please. I'm sorry."

"Just go. And you're right. I hate that tattoo!" She turned abruptly and walked back to the man in the suit jacket.

The man raised his glass to Patrick. In reply, Patrick flipped him the bird and stalked off, Lisa's words still ringing in his ears.

CHAPTER 5
HELLO MOTHER

"Can I have that?" Lisa asked George, pointing at the remains of his drink.

"Of course," he said.

Lisa took his half-empty glass of bourbon and downed it, coughing slightly as the liquid burned her throat. She wiped her mouth with her hand and looked in the direction Patrick had gone. His dark head bobbed above the other partygoers.

"Another?" George asked, taking the empty glass from her hand.

"Yes, please," she said, and watched George walk toward the bar.

The alcohol was doing its job, slowing everything down. She closed her eyes for a moment, the party ebbing away around her.

It's just so depressing, she thought. All of it. These people, this stupid party, my life. Maybe when I open my eyes, Jamie will appear. I'll convince her to bail, and we can go home.

Lisa looked up, but instead of Jamie she saw George approach with a fresh round of drinks.

"Sorry that took so long," he said handing her a martini, this time with olives. "The line was insane."

She immediately drank half the cocktail, wishing the alcohol would drown out the running loop of Patrick's voice in her head: You look like you're for sale. You look like you're for sale. You look like you're for sale. Lisa could see George obviously agreed with Patrick, but he didn't seem embarrassed by her in the least. He kept his arm around her waist, securing her to his side as he addressed a small crowd that had gathered around them. Maybe all these people think it too, she wondered. She looked from face to face, but the men and women alike avoided her gaze. When they did steal a look, their expressions ranged from judgmental to lewd.

Well, she thought, at least I haven't run into my mother.

"George, what a pleasure."

Lisa felt a little faint as she turned in the direction of the voice. Her mother looked exactly as she had that morning in the kitchen when everything changed—the beautifully coiffed hair, a string of lustrous pearls around her neck. She hadn't been the mayor then, she'd just been Lisa's mother.

Lisa stood frozen in place, eyes darting left and right, but her escape was blocked on all sides by party attendees who crowded around George and her mother. Willing herself to become invisible, she prayed Jamie would magically pop out of somewhere and save her.

"Mayor Salder." George's voice sounded forced as he shook her hand.

Lisa noted George didn't dare kiss the inside of her mother's wrist.

"Please, George, we're all friends here. Call me Ellen," she said with a tepid smile.

"Ellen, may I introduce my friend Lisa," George said.

Her mother appeared to barely register Lisa's presence, and gave her a brief dismissive glance. But then she looked again, and Lisa watched as Ellen's pleasant expression soured, and her eyes, hazel like her daughter's, narrowed. "Hello, Lisa." Deep disapproval rang clear in her voice.

Lisa's cheeks flushed, and she held out her hand, praying her mother would just play along. "Mayor Salder, it's so nice to meet you."

On reflex, her mother shook Lisa's hand. A photographer with a heavy camera slung around his neck, his dark green shirt stained with sweat, snapped a few shots. Her mother glared at him, and the man blanched with fear.

"Geoff, get that camera and erase the last several photos," she said to a young man who shadowed her.

Geoff obediently grabbed the photographer's camera still hanging from the man's neck and deftly scrolled through the photos. After a few staccato beeps, the images were gone. Her mother composed herself and turned back to George. With just the slightest edge to her voice, she said, "Let's get a photo of just me and George, please." They stood side by side, both smiling brightly.

As the camera flashed, Lisa thought again about making a run for it, but she stayed put, knowing it would only delay an unavoidable confrontation.

The photographer finished and the smile on her mother's face vanished. "George, would you please excuse me for a moment? I need to visit the ladies' room. Perhaps, your young friend would care to join me?" she asked.

George looked at Lisa with surprise.

Ellen walked off, not looking back, as though certain that her daughter would do as told. Lisa followed.

They reached the Presidential Potty and Ellen stepped behind the trailer to hide from prying eyes. She turned to Lisa and snapped, "What are you doing here, dressed like that?" Ellen looked at the martini glass still clutched in Lisa's hand. "Are you drunk?"

"Hi, Mom."

"Don't 'Hi, Mom' me. Did George put you up to this? Are you trying to ruin me?"

"George? No, I just met him," said Lisa. "No one at the party knows who I am."

"It would take some reporter about five seconds to figure out you're my daughter. And look at you. Didn't that school do anything to clean you up? Six thousand dollars in tuition per month, and you're just the same. Drunk, hanging on to some man, dressed like a prostitute. What would your father think?"

Tears rushed to Lisa's eyes. "How dare you bring up Dad."

"Why shouldn't I bring up your father? He would be so ashamed."

"No, he wouldn't. He believed me when I told him the truth. You only believe what you see." Lisa thought about trying to explain herself, telling her mom about art school, how much she loved it. About the bills she and Jamie had to cover so they could afford to stay in their apartment together. Every day recovering a little bit from the horror of the Academy, leaning on each other, and trying to laugh through the worst of it. Her father would have understood. To her mom, it was all black-and-white. If you wore the right clothes and followed the rules, maybe you were worth her time. But if you looked and acted like Lisa, you were nothing.

"What I see is my daughter dressed like one of George Green's tramps."

"Then maybe that's what I am," Lisa said, turning away. Her mother stood her ground, about to say more, but Lisa had had enough. She'd heard it all before.

George was mid-sentence when she returned to his side. She whispered in his ear, "Can we get out of here?"

"Absolutely. What do you have in mind?"

Lisa forced a smile. "I think you know." She grabbed his hand and tugged him toward the exit.

"I guess this is when I ask how much?"

Lisa took a deep breath. I could walk away, she thought. Find Jamie and go home. Or I could just do it. No one would be surprised. Isn't this where they all expected me to end up? The teachers at the Academy, Patrick, my mom. And anyway, how would anyone ever find out? She thought guiltily of Jamie and how hard it would be to keep this from her best friend. "Don't let me do anything stupid," they'd promised each other in the Presidential Potty. It felt like days had passed since that moment, not hours. Well, it was too late now. She'd made her choice.

She spoke, trying to sound confident. "One thousand."

"All night?" he asked.

"Of course."

George smiled. "Perfect."

CHAPTER 6
CALLED OUT

Ellen watched as Lisa melted into the crowd. The last spark from her daughter's vulgar dress winked out as the party closed in around her.

The girl is infuriating, thought Ellen. She twisted the heavy gold band that she still wore on her ring finger even years after her husband's death. If only Ben were here to see what had become of Lisa. Maybe he'd know what to do. Everything Ellen had tried failed spectacularly. So much animosity persisted between them that a reasonable conversation seemed impossible.

As usual, Ellen was of two minds about Lisa. The dominant, where her ambition and drive reigned, wanted to free herself from all responsibility for Lisa's fate. The girl was an adult now, after all. If she wanted to throw her life away, fine. It would be a relief to just let her go.

Even as Ellen willed it to be so, a small voice buried deep inside urged her to rush after Lisa and beg forgiveness for having thrown her father's memory in her face. Instead, Ellen took a deep breath and pushed away all thoughts of her daughter. Tonight's event was important. The election was only a few months away and she needed to be at her best. Lisa always brought out her worst.

She straightened her shoulders, forced a smile, and stepped forward to return to the party, almost colliding with Victor Smith.

"Ellen. Such a pleasant surprise," Victor exclaimed, his voice full of warmth and affection.

Her smile disappeared. Victor didn't seem to notice nor care. "Victor, always a pleasure," she said coldly.

"You know my friends Commissioner Frank Lindsey and Police Chief Anna Garcia?"

"Of course, I do," Ellen said, unable to hide her irritation at his condescending tone. Victor had been nothing but a thorn in her side since she'd taken office. He took great pleasure in making her job as difficult as possible, from planting false stories in the weeklies, bank-rolling campaigns to sabotage her every initiative, and now apparently ingratiating himself with the rest of the city government. "Victor, you're well aware that I work directly with Anna and Frank in my role as mayor and police commissioner." Ellen smiled at her colleagues. In turn, she shook hands with Anna, who looked incongruous in her officer's dress uniform, and then with Frank, who returned Ellen's handshake but not her smile, choosing instead to maintain the persistent scowl he wore during City Council meetings. Frank was her primary competitor in the mayoral race with a campaign focused solely on the platform that he wasn't Mayor Ellen Salder.

"I thought the police commissioner title was just ceremonial," said Victor. "It has real responsibilities, you say?" He laughed heartily. "You'd never know that considering the number of false drug arrests that have been made since you took office."

Victor was referring to an article on Oregon's historic drug initiative in the latest issue of *The Portland Journal*. Striking a blow against the failed war on drugs, the voters of Oregon had decriminalized possession of small amounts of all illegal substances, including cocaine, heroin, and methamphetamines. Publicly, Ellen had supported the measure. Inwardly, she was apprehensive, her belief in right and wrong was very black-and-white, and the measure verged into serious gray territory. In her dual role as mayor and police commissioner, she directed that the measure's guidelines be enforced to the letter of the law. The press and her critics hadn't been kind. The article had profiled an addict who'd been caught with forty-one pills of oxycodone, a single pill over the legal limit.

"The article you're referring to grossly exaggerated the numbers and was riddled with falsehoods. The man they featured is a known dealer, and he was carrying four-hundred and one pills, not forty-one."

"Is it my fault *The Portland Journal* had to lay off their fact checking team due to budgetary issues?" asked Victor.

"Yes, Victor. You own a majority stake in the paper."

"Touché," he said with a shrug.

"It may be the case for that individual, Ellen," said Frank, crossing his arms, "but not for the dozens of others mentioned in the story who are currently sitting in jail instead of getting the addiction treatment they so desperately need. Your relentless pursuit of drug violations is out of control. I'm disgusted by your lack of faith in the voter's mandate."

"Now, Frank," said Victor, in a soothing yet obviously disingenuous tone. "We all know Mayor Law and Order is all about the letter, not the spirit of the law."

Ellen's eyebrows shot up and she took a moment to collect herself. She turned to face her colleagues and did her best to ignore Victor, who was obviously enjoying seeing her put on the spot. "I agreed with the measure to decriminalize drug possession. However, that doesn't mean we stop our efforts at identifying and destroying the supply chain. Sure, a few people who should be in treatment slipped through the cracks, but of the dozens you're referring to, Frank, most are dealers. The voter's mandate didn't include the rampant sale of illegal substances. If I just had your support to set up a special task force, we could root out the criminals flooding our city with drugs. The DEA is ready to work with us. We only have to ask."

Frank shook his head in disgust. "Please. You want to ask the feds for help? It's a task force today, then SWAT teams patrolling our neighborhoods tomorrow."

Ellen turned to the chief of police. "Anna, you can't possibly agree with him?"

"We've followed your direction, and as a result we've gotten a lot of bad press. I'm sorry to say it, Ellen, but I think we need a big change in November. I'm going to have to throw my support behind Frank. I feel you're making this issue too personal. As mayor, you should leave the policing to me and my team and stick to policy."

Ellen had always liked and trusted the police chief. She'd even been tempted to confide in her about Lisa's problems with drinking and drugs. After hearing the police chief's reply, though, Ellen was relieved she'd had the sense to keep her mouth shut. No one needed to know just how personal the issue was.

"Watching our city government at work makes me thirsty," said Victor. "I'm ready for a drink. Will you join us, Ellen?"

"I prefer dehydration."

"Your loss," Victor said, and headed toward the bar, his cronies following at his heels.

Worthless bureaucrats, thought Ellen. She knew Frank despised her methods, but she had thought Anna supported her. Neither had what it took to lead. Ellen was only comforted by the fact she'd already started taking matters into her own hands.

CHAPTER 7
JAMIE WORRIES

Jamie tried vainly to keep her manufactured smile from becoming a grimace. She'd already told her litany of terrible jokes a few dozen times with varying success. These Googled gems were most effective on shy, anxiety-ridden super-nerds.

"Yesterday I saw a guy spill all his Scrabble letters on the road. I asked him, 'What's the word on the street?'"

"Helvetica and Times New Roman walk into a bar. 'Get out of here,' shouts the bartender. 'We don't serve your type!'"

"What's a pirate's favorite letter? You might think it's *R*, but a pirate's first love is the *C*."

One by one, Jamie built up their confidence and then smoothly pawned them off onto other partygoers.

The unjustifiably confident tech bros however, well, they all seemed to think it was funnier that a girl would even attempt to tell a joke. Their condescension was infuriating, but nothing compared to their microaggressions.

"Where are you from?" they'd ask.

"I'm from Portland," Jamie would reply coldly, knowing what was coming.

They'd give her disbelieving looks. "No, you're not. You're Asian, right? Anyway, your American is so good. Teach me how to swear in Chinese."

She'd smile and say, "Fuck you."

To top it off, her sequined dress was itchy in all the worst places, her feet ached, she didn't dare drink alcohol, enjoy herself, or partake in any real or meaningful conversations. She wove her way past the hordes of guests until she reached the white karaoke tent and peeked in. Disco lights swirled in the empty space, void of humanity except for a lonely DJ who waved hopefully at her. She waved back, then ducked outside and glanced at her watch. It was definitely game time. Standing on her tiptoes, she scanned the grounds, but Lisa was nowhere to be seen. She pulled out her phone but didn't see any messages from her tardy friend. For the millionth time, she was annoyed that Lisa refused to enable location tracking on her phone, citing the right to privacy she was denied during her time at the Academy.

Jamie had just finished texting Lisa, *Dude! Karaoke! Stat!* when she spotted Nigel talking with a stressed-looking food cart owner. She walked over and waited impatiently for him to finish berating the poor man about running out of personal poutine pizzas only a few hours into the party.

Finally, Nigel turned to her.

"Have you seen Lisa?" Jamie asked.

"You, my dear, are the hit of the party," he said, his eyes sweeping the crowd.

"Seriously, have you seen her? I'm a little worried. She's late for karaoke."

"Oh dear, what a tragedy," he said. "I'm sure she's fine. I saw her with one of the city's elite, the great George Green, of Blurb and Green, or Blunt and Green, hmmm . . . Anyway, I just hope George's wife isn't here." He shuddered. "She's terrifying."

"If you see Lisa, please ask her to text me," said Jamie.

"Yes, of course. Now go make some young tech geek's wet dreams come true." He gently pushed her away and she glared back at him.

Jamie stomped past the food carts back toward the karaoke tent, determined to sing with or without Lisa, and almost ran into a tall man very underdressed in a white T-shirt and faded jeans.

"Hey, watch it," she said, but the man ignored her and kept going.

Jamie realized with shock that it was Patrick and called out his name, but her voice was lost in the mix of blaring music and conversation. Curious, she followed, and watched him wander around the food trucks. Even with the slouch to his posture, he towered over most of the guests and was easy to follow in the crowd. He stopped at an Airstream trailer that looked closed—odd, considering the steady business the other carts were doing. He glanced around, as though worried he were being watched. And he was, she realized, by her. She ducked behind Double D Donuts.

Patrick knocked on the Airstream's door. A woman with spiky black hair opened it and brusquely motioned Patrick to join her inside.

Jamie frowned. The woman looked familiar, however Jamie couldn't quite place her. She mentally flipped through the last few weeks. Another of Nigel's parties? No. School? No. Then it hit her. Sheila. She'd been introduced to Sheila a couple years ago by an ex-boyfriend slash wannabe professional cyclist at a house party. He'd whispered to her that Sheila had hooked up his team with performance enhancing drugs in addition to other recreational and illegal pharmaceuticals.

She stared at the Airstream's closed door and wondered what Patrick was up to. Whatever it is, it can't be good, she thought.

CHAPTER 8
THE INTERVIEW

Patrick pushed his way through the crowd.

"Hey, watch out!" yelled an offended female voice.

He ignored it and continued cutting a path through the snaking lines of hungry party attendees sweating in their business casual. He'd reached a cluster of food trucks, all with owners who apparently loved alliteration. The Naughty Noodle, the Cheeky Chimichanga, and the Big Buns Bus were each doing a brisk business. One vintage Airstream, parked behind the Prussian Pierogi, appeared to be locked up tight. He glanced at the text message from Joe: *Airstream behind PP*. Bingo.

Patrick's tattooed arm throbbed painfully, and his thoughts returned to Lisa. They'd fought before. What couple didn't? But this time felt different. Seeing her working the party had made him feel at once angry and helpless. Angry that she was lowering herself to do this job, and helpless because he knew she needed the money and there was no way he could help her, no legal way. Working as a bike mechanic was great—until payday. He'd never make enough to cover all their rent if they moved in together. Why hadn't he gone after her? His heart ached. But he was already late for this meeting—and it was his best chance to make some quick money. He took a deep breath. After, he'd find Lisa and apologize. She'd forgive him. She always had before.

He stepped up to the Airstream and knocked on the door.

Out of the corner of his eye, he caught a blur of green. For a second, it felt like someone was watching him, but he shook it off. After all, he thought, who besides Lisa gave a shit what he was up to?

A woman opened the door and peered down at him.

"Hello ma'am, I'm looking for Sheila. Joe sent me." He politely held out his hand. "My name is Patrick."

Ignoring his outstretched hand, she said, "Never call me ma'am again."

"Sorry ma'am," he said, panicking.

"Just get inside."

He stepped into the Airstream and quickly gave Sheila an appraising look. She was as decked out as any attendee in a black pantsuit with heels. Patrick could see that unlike the rest of the crowd that she was stone-cold sober and was by far the most serious person he'd seen tonight. There was something else. Most of the attendees only wanted to sell themselves. They'd lie, bullshit, and exaggerate to pass themselves off as legitimate. Sheila, on the other hand, was here to make money. Real money.

"Joe tells me you're looking for work," she said.

"Yes, I am."

Sheila motioned toward a small built-in table and bench, indicating that he should sit. His lanky frame barely fit, yet he managed to cram his body onto the seat. She remained standing and stared at him with narrowed, slightly feline eyes.

"Why are we meeting in a food truck?" he asked nervously.

"What's wrong with it?"

"Nothing. You don't seem to be cooking anything."

"Your powers of observation astound me," said Sheila. "So, tell me. Can you use a microwave? Press buttons?"

"Yeah, I think I can handle that."

"Great. You're hired."

Patrick felt very confused, and wasn't sure yet if he wanted to work for Sheila, but he sighed with relief that the interview was over. "What's the job?" he asked.

"Selling drugs."

"Sure, but what does that have to do with microwave ovens?"

"For you, nothing yet. The microwave comes later."

Patrick had a sudden inspiration. "You're dealing out of food trucks."

Sheila looked surprised though not displeased, and he decided it was best to keep it coming.

He thought quickly. "I can imagine it's tough working in a cash business, but with the trucks, it's all small transactions, right?"

"Joe didn't tell me you were smart," she said dryly.

"And the trucks are mobile, of course. You can move around, show up at clubs late at night, everyone's hungry and looking for a fix. And they're easy to dump."

"Something like that."

"Which food truck do I get?" he asked eagerly.

"Oh no, you'll be on deliveries to start. You have to get to know the product and how to deal with customers. I need to figure out which cart to assign you. You're too cute. I can't have lots of ladies— or dudes, for that matter—lining up to get served by a young Keanu Reeves clone. We need to keep a low profile after all. Attention is the enemy." Sheila continued thoughtfully, "It'll have to be something unappetizing and slightly offensive. I'll give it some thought, but in the meantime, take this."

She handed him a small black device. He clicked a button and read on a tiny strip of screen: *No Messages.* "What is this thing?" he asked.

"A beeper."

"Oh man! My dad used to have one of these. Kept it in a dorky case on his belt."

She handed Patrick a dorky case. "Put this on your belt so you don't lose it."

He took the beeper case reluctantly.

"Well, what are you waiting for?" asked Sheila.

"I have to put it on now?"

"Yes. Now."

He popped the beeper into the holder and clipped it to his belt, tugging his T-shirt down to cover it.

"I'll send locations, instructions, and times. Make your deliveries within thirty minutes or you're fired." Sheila unlocked a cabinet and pulled out a paper bag. "You'll start with cocaine deliveries. This is everything you should need. I only deal in pure organic coke. My clientele like to think they're making a positive drug choice, so sell it that way."

He nodded. "Absolutely. What do I do with the cash?"

"I'm giving you five thousand in product. When it's sold, deliver the money to the Prussian Pierogi. Most days Boris parks his cart in the Five Firs lot on Glisan, but follow his social feed and you'll be able to find him. Boris will give you your share. And keep clear of the police. The mayor has everyone on high alert. Even the cops we pay off are giving us grief. You get caught, you talk, and I will kill you. Seriously."

Patrick didn't doubt her sincerity. He stashed the sack in his messenger bag.

She pulled a pack of cigarettes from her purse and lit one. She offered the pack to Patrick, but he shook his head no.

Feeling slightly more relaxed, he looked more closely around the Airstream. "This trailer looks just like the old Clam Shack food truck," he said.

"Oh my god." Sheila stared at him with menace. "Did you seriously have to bring up the Clam Shack?"

He coughed at the second-hand smoke that was quickly filling the small space and rambled on. "Sorry, Sheila. I loved their food. I didn't know clams could be so good. That thing with bacon and the broth. It was transcendent."

"Get out."

"I'm sorry." He got up to leave but got stuck trying to extract his knees from under the small table.

After watching him struggle for a moment, Sheila said, "Oh, just stay there."

She lit another cigarette from her first and took a deep drag.

"What I'm about to tell you doesn't leave this trailer. This gets out, I break your knee caps."

Patrick wished he'd kept his mouth shut. "I'll take it to the grave."

"You got that right," she said forcefully, then her voice softened. "It was the first food truck I managed."

"The Clam Shack was yours?"

"I don't know why I'm telling you." She looked at him closely. "It's your face. It feels so familiar. Like you already know the story. Anyway. Yes, I came up with the concept."

"Holy shit."

"It should have been so simple. Who the hell would be stupid enough to eat a clam from a goddamned food truck? You're just asking for trouble. I'm thinking, load up on frozen boxed clam entrees from Trader Joe's, toss 'em in the microwave, serve them in the least appetizing way possible, you know, in big nasty Styrofoam bowls and single-use plastic utensils. Then sell drugs out the back window and doctor the books. Easy, right?"

"Seems reasonable. What went wrong?"

"I hired a real chef. It was a nightmare. First, he started complaining about all the waste, so he started serving the clams in bowls he picked up at a restaurant supply store, with chopsticks and these big stupid bottles of . . . you know. The spicy red stuff."

"Sriracha?"

"That's it. Then he wanted to try his own recipes with a special broth, local clams, and organic bacon. When he asked for the air fryer for Belgian fries, I knew I had to put a stop to it. But we were in too deep. The Clam Shack was named restaurant of the year by *The Oregonian*. Within hours, the lines were out of control."

She stubbed out her lipstick-stained cigarette in an ashtray. "Even the chief of police tweeted it was her favorite. I almost couldn't sell any product. I had to let it go."

"You sold it?"

"No. I murdered the chef."

"What?"

Sheila laughed. "I'm kidding. No. I just fired him and changed the truck's name to Hells Shells. After a few customers came down with food poisoning, I was back in business. I sell drugs, not clams."

"Sure but . . ."

"Now I only hire people who don't give a shit about food, who understand their real job is to move cash and sell drugs—lots of drugs. Work hard, don't use, and you'll have your own food truck soon enough."

"Yes, ma'am," said Patrick.

CHAPTER 9
THE LAMBO

"I should probably stick around a little longer, but fuck it," said George, as he walked with Lisa toward the exit. They reached the valet line, and he glanced back at the party. "I used to be just like them. Eating up all this shit like it's candy. Can you believe I got a standing ovation? No one even noticed it was the same speech I gave last year."

He fished through his wallet. Mortified, Lisa thought he was going to pay her right then and there for whatever services he thought she'd render. Instead, he pulled out a claim ticket and a twenty-dollar bill and handed both to the waiting valet.

Lisa could feel her buzz starting to fade, and along with it, the temporary insanity that had led to her decision to go home with George. She looked through the crowd hoping to catch sight of Jamie. But the only other familiar face she spotted in the distance was her mother's. For a moment, she felt like she was floating above herself watching the whole awful scene play out. Did this guy really think she was a hooker? Lisa looked down at her gold dress. Earlier it had seemed so fun and pretty. Now, as she compared it to the other attendees' cocktail dresses and suits, it looked unbearably cheap. She noticed that she was stepping on something, and shifted her foot to reveal a headshot of George on a conference brochure. It read in large type, "Closing Night Address: George Green, Creative-at-Large." The photo looked at least a decade old. George's artifice made her feel a little bit better. We all pretend, she thought.

"Have to admit though, I was in top form," George droned on. "And I threw in the Cock-a-Doodle story. They were all dying for it."

He sure does love the sound of his own voice, she thought. Lisa saw a waiter with a tray of champagne glasses and waved him over, handing one to George and taking two for herself.

"The Cock-a-Doodle Triple Meat Sandwich. It's the hottest selling quick-serve fast food product on the market right now, thanks to me," said George with pride. "Well, me and a few dozen junior creatives. Sure, the ad has been banned in some states. All flyovers." He ticked off a few names. "Tennessee, Alabama, Kentucky. But who cares. It's the most watched ad on YouTube ever. The Meat Hut can't keep up with demand." He reached into a pocket and pulled out a pack of cigarettes. He tapped one out of the pack and offered it to her.

Lisa didn't smoke, but figured, hey, at this point, why not pick up another vice.

"Even I admit it's a pretty suggestive ad," he said, pausing to light her cigarette first, then his. Inhaling deeply, he continued, "Maybe the spicy sauce wrestling sequence was taking it too far, but people are eating it up, no pun intended. It's a very sexy sandwich. You've tried it?" asked George.

Lisa nodded yes. She hadn't.

"Brave girl. Its success is really thanks to the aggressive non-stop ad play and product placement. I tell my media team to 'violate the space,'" said George using air quotes.

Lisa finished off her first glass of champagne and started on the second. She was having a hard time remembering why she'd found George attractive.

A bright yellow sports car roared up. It was low to the ground, long and lean, all angles and geometric shapes. The driver's side door lifted up like an insect's wing, and a valet stepped out, obviously thrilled. He reverently handed George the keys. "Here you are Mr. Green. Great car," he gushed.

Lisa had to choke back a laugh. She'd expected something more age appropriate, like a black sedan by some German car maker. But no, George had opted for pure midlife crisis.

George lifted the passenger side door open and held her hand as she awkwardly lowered herself into the deep seat. He closed her door, and the car purred around her like a wild beast.

He stepped around to the driver's side, got in, and turned on the stereo. Classic rock poured out of the speakers. Grabbing a looped handle, he pulled his door closed, sealing them in. He put the car into gear, hit the gas, and the car coughed and stalled. Visibly gritting his teeth, he shifted into first and stepped on the accelerator, more gently this time. Slowly, the Lambo started to move. "She can be a bit temperamental," he muttered.

After a moment, he relaxed. "How do you like the ride?"

She could barely hear him over the blaring stereo.

"I'm sorry, what?" She cupped her hand around her ear to catch his words.

The car jerked to a halt at an intersection, and he turned down the music.

"My Lambo. My Lamborghini. Bought this baby last year." He stroked the steering wheel lovingly. "Cost me six hundred grand. I got a great deal. It's been a dream of mine to own one, and finally I reached a point in my life where it just made sense. You know? And it's quite practical, really. You'd be surprised how useful it is to have in the city. The V twelve engine is incredible. But it swills fuel like a frat bro chugs beer." He laughed. "I read that in *Car and Driver.*"

Cars didn't interest her in the least. Lisa hadn't driven since she was sixteen and borrowed her mom's car without asking. Her mother called the police and had Lisa arrested.

"I can hit three hundred and fifty kilometers per hour—oh, sorry," he said. "When I'm in this baby, I go metric. That's two hundred and seventeen miles per hour. Sometimes I take her to the track and let her fly. Amazing. All that power. I always think of this one line in the marketing materials that really touched me. It said the vehicle is made with a unique material—passion. You can feel that passion, can't you Lisa?"

Lisa found herself in awe of his complete lack of self-awareness. She flipped down the car's sun visor and looked in the small mirror. A familiar face looked back, though not one she'd worn since the Academy. Eyes open a little too wide, a bland, sweet smile on an amiable face. A face that made other people, particularly men, feel important and smart. It was a mask of survival. She was starting to feel nauseated. Digging in her purse, she found her lipstick and touched it up.

"Don't worry babe, you look amazing," said George, glancing at her. "So, I have to ask. What did you and the mayor talk about?"

Lisa chose to ignore the question, and looked out the tinted passenger window as Portland flew by in a blur. Her mother's words droned on and on in her mind. "You're just the same. Didn't that school do anything to clean you up? Your father would be so ashamed."

That school, thought Lisa, where so many terrible things happened. Tears pricked at her eyes. Her mind flew unwillingly back to that day years ago, when her mother betrayed her.

Y

The harsh morning light had cracked through the curtains, revealing objects strewn across the room like a storm had blown through; her dresser hulked in a corner, drawers pulled open, a mess of clothing overflowing in waves onto the floor; discarded school books flipped open to forgotten lessons; mismatched sneakers that peeked between piles of papers, reports, and tests highlighted with C's and D's in aggressive circles of red ink. A thousand items in chaos, the detritus of her teenage existence. Detritus. She'd always liked the word. Little bits of her decomposing erratically, unpredictably.

Her bedroom walls, however, had symmetry. Sketches and watercolors were arranged neatly. Only the earlier works were carefully framed by her once-proud parents. The others, newer and better, were tacked to the walls with pushpins. Lisa knew she had talent. But her parents no longer encouraged her, preferring their daughter to have interests in the medical, the mineral, or the mechanical.

She heard voices. Low male murmurs. Contractors arriving to start another remodel, she guessed. The master bath, or maybe the guest bedroom. Lisa's room had narrowly avoided any improvements or alterations and stood in stark contrast to the rest of her parents' house where every color coordinated and every object had its place. She'd held her ground with screaming fits and slammed doors against her mother's unending campaign to create the mirage of a perfect home despite the cost or inconvenience to those who actually lived there. "Throw money at the problem," her mother liked to say. Yet the custom tilework and parquet floors hadn't translated into a perfect life, marriage, or daughter.

Lisa flung an arm over her eyes to block out the morning light. Or was it afternoon light? She couldn't be sure. It didn't matter. School was out. She'd spend the summer like this. Stay out late. Sneak back in. Hide in her room. Nurse a hangover. Avoid her parents. Summers past had been packed with lessons—swimming, soccer, piano, dance. Then her interests waned, replaced by the demands of teenage rivalries, the horrors of social media, and the temptation of forbidden vices—boys, beer, pot, liquor, drugs. Her grades dropped, and her extracurricular activities were supplanted by summer school. She found that half-empty classrooms filled with like-minded slackers were the best places to meet the kind of boys and girls her mother hated. Oh, the fun they'd had!

This summer was different. There were no activities or classes, only therapy twice a week. At least they weren't forcing her back into rehab. Her mom had cancelled everything else after Lisa borrowed her car. She'd totally overreacted, calling the police and reporting the car stolen. Like Lisa had a choice? She had tickets to a concert in Eugene and would have died to miss it. Of course the cops stopped her when she'd failed to use her signal on a turn. Spent the night in juvie.

Between that and her bad grades, her teachers and parents had apparently decided that talking about her feelings was the only remaining option. She hated her new therapist. He was an idiot. Some indeterminate age between thirty and old man. Plus, he was kind of creepy. She'd bailed on the last few sessions, hiding out at a friend's house till it was safe to go home.

Lisa reached over to her bedside table and grabbed her phone, pulling it with her under the covers. She winced at the brightness of the screen. Dozens of messages flickered by from friends who obviously felt better than she did. She'd had way too much to drink last night, but could only recall the pilfered cans of light beer. She licked her dry lips. Salt and a faint taste of tequila. Her stomach churned. An image of a shot glass wavered unsteadily. Its edge coated with salt, the warm liquid hitting her tongue, a bite of lime and peals of laughter. She couldn't remember what she'd found so funny.

Her bedroom door opened. She pushed the blanket away and looked up. Two figures stood in the doorway, dressed in black. Even their faces were covered, with only slits for their eyes and mouths. Confused, she sat up too fast. Bile rose up in her throat. She held herself steady for a moment and willed it to pass. She couldn't understand why they would dress this way. None of the other contractors had. The men just stood there, one slightly in front of the other. Their eyes scanned the room, then rested on her. One of them spoke. "Get up."

She almost laughed. It was so ridiculous, these men in her room, ordering her around. "No," she said. "Go install some drywall."

"Get up," the man repeated.

"Get out of my room."

He took a step toward her. She started to feel nervous.

"Mom? Dad?" she called out loudly, for once hoping her parents were home. She wasn't sure what day of the week it was.

"I said get up."

Suddenly she understood. Kidnappers. Of course. Her parents were rich. She scooted away from the men and yelled for her parents again. Nothing. No hurried steps, no worried cries, no rescue. A rush of fear and adrenaline momentarily cleared her head. Her bathroom. It also connected to the guest room, and then to the hallway. A way out. Lisa leapt from the bed and almost tripped on her tangled blankets. She reached for the bathroom door, grabbed the knob and pulled it open. The man was faster. He pulled her back and pinned her arms. Terror clouded her mind. Her instincts took over. She kicked and screamed. "Get your hands off me. Let me go." She struggled to pull herself from the man's grip. "You're hurting me!"

The other man walked toward her. He had something in his hands. In a moment, everything went dark. A hood. She almost gagged at the smell. The rough fabric scratched her skin. She screamed again, louder, and her throat ached with the effort. They didn't try to stop her. They didn't care if she was quiet.

My parents, she thought desperately. Are they hurt, or dead? She fought harder. "Please," she said, her voice muffled, her pounding heart almost drowning out her words. "My parents, are they all right? Did you hurt them?" The thought was too terrifying.

The men remained silent as they carried her out of her room and down the stairs. The harder she struggled, the tighter they gripped. Finally, some instinct told her to shut down, be quiet, go limp. Maybe they would think she'd given up and would loosen their hold. They reached the bottom of the stairs; her bare feet dragged across the wood floor. She felt the men relax slightly.

Then she sprang, broke free and ripped the hood from her face. She ran into the kitchen and headed straight for the knife block beside the stove. But there were two people in the way. Her mother. Her father. It could have been any morning. The sun streamed through the windows. White tile and stainless steel gleamed. Her mother, already dressed for work, leaned against the kitchen counter holding her favorite coffee mug. The blue one with the white rim. The one Lisa had dropped only last week, and fixed with Krazy Glue before her mother could notice.

Her dad was still in pajamas and robe, his feet bare. Even in her panic and confusion, it struck Lisa how much older he looked. In contrast, her mother seemed to pulse with youthful energy.

The relief at seeing them alive overwhelmed her. She wanted to feel their arms around her. But as she moved toward them, she was pulled back. The men. They were still here. It didn't make sense. She fought against them. Her parents made no move to help.

"Mom. Dad. Please!" Her parents didn't speak. Didn't move. "Why are you just standing there? What's wrong with you?" she pleaded.

Her mother glared at the men, and Lisa thought she could see her mouthing the word "idiots."

They know, she thought. My parents know these men.

"What is this?" Lisa screamed.

Her parents remained silent.

"Dad," she said urgently. She held his eyes for a moment; she could see his indecision.

"Ellen," he said, "we have to stop this." He put his hand on her mother's arm, but she shrugged him off.

Lisa continued to struggle in vain. "Mom, please."

Hands wrapped around her coffee cup, her mother ignored Lisa. "It's too late. We signed all the papers. They wouldn't let her stay even if we begged. We shouldn't even be home."

"I wasn't going to just let them take her," said her dad. "I needed to be here. To make sure she was okay."

"Take me? Where? And I am definitely not okay."

Her mother's eyes flicked toward Lisa, then away.

"Ben, why are you making this so much harder than it needs to be? You already agreed. We've been trying to fix her for months, years even. I can't do it anymore."

"Ellen, please."

"No more." Her mother's voice was hard. "I've given up enough for her. I'm not losing anything else."

"You're going to win."

Her mother shook her head and glared at Lisa's father. "You know it's not just about the election. She needs professional help. Look at her."

Lisa listened, confused. She wasn't that bad. Sure she partied, but no more than any of the other kids. If she could only explain, they'd let her stay. They'd understand that this was all a horrible mistake.

"Mom, Dad," Lisa begged. "Please. I'll be good. I promise."

"It's going to be okay honey, we're going to get you some help," said her father, his voice breaking.

"I don't need help. I just want to be here with you."

Her mother looked past Lisa at the two men and nodded slightly. The men pulled Lisa toward the front door, then outside.

Cool morning air streamed over her, and goose bumps rose on Lisa's bare arms. She looked back into the house. She saw her mother sipping coffee calmly; her father had disappeared. Suddenly, her fight was gone. "Let me go," she said to the men. "I'll stop."

A white van idled in the driveway. On the side was the insignia of a mountain and the stenciled words "Lost Lake Academy." Next to it, stuck in the grass of the front lawn, was a large sign that read "Make the Right Choice: Ellen Salder for Mayor."

As she finally understood the truth, Lisa grew furious. It was laughably simple. She was just an embarrassment, nothing more than a potential obstacle to her mother's political ambitions.

Lisa broke away from the men and rushed at the sign, kicking it, tearing at it, screaming as loud as she could. She could see the neighbors pulling back curtains and cracking open their front doors to witness yet another meltdown of the great Ellen Salder's misfit daughter. Through her tears, Lisa smiled at her mother's humiliation as the men dragged her into the van.

Y

"Earth to Lisa? You still with me?" asked George, placing his hand over hers.

She pulled her hand away and crossed her arms over her chest. "Sorry. What did you ask again?"

"What were you and the mayor talking about?"

She imagined telling George the truth. Like he'd believe it, she thought. Instead, she kept it simple. "She said she'd call security if I didn't leave."

"I'm not surprised. She's all about the straight and narrow. Law and order. That's what she campaigned on, but we all know it was really the sympathy vote after her husband's death that won her the election."

Lisa stared at George, letting this sink in. She'd never heard this theory before.

He continued, "Ben Salder died just a few weeks before. Mugged and murdered. They found his body in a parking garage. Really terrible. Her daughter was away at some private school. Maybe in Europe? Rumors were that she refused to come home. Left the mayor to handle it alone."

Lisa gasped and started coughing.

"I wonder what happened to the daughter. Bet she's a looker if she's anything like her mother. Are you okay?" He handed Lisa a flask from his jacket pocket. "Here, take a sip."

She opened the flask and took a long drink, not pausing to breathe.

"Hey, slow down," said George.

Lisa tried to steady her breath but couldn't catch it. Her mother had used her father's death to win an election.

And she'd lied about me, she thought.

She lied.

The only thing that really shocked Lisa was that her mother's actions could still surprise her. She took another drink and felt relief as the liquor dulled her senses.

George pulled into a narrow alley behind a row of elegant townhouses, each with its own private garage. He tapped a button and a garage door opened revealing an uncomfortably tight parking spot.

"Do you mind jumping out here?"

She looked at the passenger door, having no idea how to open it. He reached over and lifted what was apparently the handle. The door ascended and she heaved herself out of the Lamborghini. George rolled the car forward, then slowly backed into the spot, a move Lisa had only ever seen men do. Why exactly was it necessary? she asked herself. She couldn't imagine where on earth George Green would need to go so quickly that he had to park facing out. He turned off the ignition and stepped out. He pulled her into the garage, then pressed her back against the car.

"I've always wanted to do it on a Lambo, how about you?" he asked.

She pushed him away and held him at arm's length. "Let's go upstairs. I could use another drink."

"No one will see us," he said, obviously excited that someone might.

The garage door next to George's lifted up, revealing first a pair of tiny yapping dogs followed by an elderly woman. She wore a bedazzled tracksuit and thick pink glasses.

"Georgie Green. Is that you?"

George let go of Lisa like she was on fire and stepped away from her. "Hello, Mrs. Johnson. How are you today?"

Mrs. Johnson took in the scene with bright, calculating eyes. "Doing better already. Georgie, how is your lovely wife?"

George coughed, and behind his back, motioned for to Lisa to leave. But she was feeling unsteady. The alcohol was taking its toll. She stayed where she was, leaning against the car, and concentrated on keeping her balance.

"Sue? She's great," said George nervously.

"Hmmm . . . And who is this lovely young lady? Another niece? Family is so important, Georgie. Remember my son Peter? The one with all the children? His youngest Johnny is so interested in advertising. Maybe you can help him, Georgie."

"Now Mrs. Johnson, we don't have any more open positions . . ."

"Georgie, don't be silly. You'll talk to him." She walked close to George and patted his arm.

"Yes, of course, ma'am."

She turned to leave, a smile on her lips, her dogs pulling on their leashes.

As soon as she was out of ear shot, George swore. "Another damn Johnson on the payroll." He tapped a button to lower the garage door, then unlocked an interior door that led to his townhouse. He motioned for Lisa to follow. "Are you coming?" he asked.

This is it, she thought. She could still turn around and leave. Go back to the party and find Jamie. They could head home, drink that boxed wine they'd swiped from an art opening last week, and laugh about the insanity of the night. But a thousand dollars was a lot of money. She could cover her rent and even replenish her art supplies for the fall semester. Wasn't one night with George Green worth a few worry-free months? And no one would ever know. She'd make sure of that.

"Come on," he said. "Promise I won't bite."

He held the door for her, and, stumbling slightly, she stepped through.

CHAPTER 10

HOME SWEET HOME

Sue was exhausted. One would think that a week at a luxury spa would relax her, but the twenty-something yoga instructors, with their perfectly toned bodies and banal mantras about seeking inner peace and finding the goddess within, only filled her with a simmering rage.

After picking through another meal of baby kale, quinoa, and chia seeds, she packed her bag, dropped off her room key, and vacated the premises. Within twenty minutes she was on the highway, a Meat Hut crispy chicken sandwich and a large order of fries on her lap.

Now, just minutes from home, Sue reached into the greasy paper bag and pulled from its depths a final cold fry. She chewed it fretfully. Maybe selling the business hadn't been the right decision, she wondered for the thousandth time.

Her company, GASS, had been an instant success when she'd started selling directly to yoga studios a decade ago. She'd been inspired during a stay at the Bellagio in Las Vegas. In spite of the chain-smoking crowds, the air inside the casino was cool and smelled of citrus and rose. It filled Sue with such a rare feeling of optimism that she sat down to play blackjack certain she could win. A wizened lady seated next to her saw Sue smile and mentioned that her feeling of euphoria was likely thanks to the oxygen the casino pumped into the air. Sue knew this was an urban myth, yet it triggered a spark of genius. Once home, she spent weeks perfecting a vegan candy shell that could hold a dose of pure oxygen. Each serving gave the user a completely legal rush. When the largest cannabis company on the West Coast approached her with an offer to start a CBD line, she decided to exit, and sold the company for a comfortable profit.

For years she'd coveted the lives of leisure enjoyed by her jobless girlfriends with rich husbands. At long last, Sue was able to join their ranks in afternoons of Pilates and mani-pedis, their evenings of wine and canapés. Still, part of her ached for the hectic tenor of her days at the office. Sue loved the money and the security, but she missed her staff, even knowing most of them had celebrated her departure. She thrived on giving orders and seeing them executed without question. Her body wasn't so obedient. And so, her compulsion to overwork had evolved into a rigid regimen of fitness classes and extreme self-care. She'd never felt so stressed.

Sue maintained standing appointments at hair salons, colorists, and brow studios, and endured bi-weekly waxes. Her days were filled with hot yoga, CrossFit, and cross-training. Her body fat, which now hovered between 21 to 22 percent, was tracked daily along with other crucial measurements, which gave her a fleeting sense of control over the dread of middle age and oncoming menopause. Each waking moment was spent obsessing over the minute details of her appearance, barring the occasional french fry cheat. Nevertheless, being a woman in her forties, she was beginning to realize that it was a losing battle. Gravity was winning.

She drove up to the elegant home that she shared with her husband George. It was in a row of rare and expensive brick townhouses sinking in a rising sea of glossy Pearl District condos. For once the parking spot in front was free, and she deftly maneuvered her black Audi sedan into place. George insisted on parking his midlife crisis-mobile in their single-car garage. She tugged her handbag from the deep red leather passenger seat, irritated by its dragging weight. "Why is my purse always so heavy?" she screamed at no one and everyone, wanting to flip the bag upside down and dump out its contents right then and there. Instead, she took a deep breath, leaned back into the luxurious leather, and closed her eyes. "Control the rage. Control the rage," she whispered.

She stepped out of the car into the warm night air and shook out her glossy hair. Her face was framed with severe bangs cut straight across her brow, emphasizing her angular nose, high cheekbones, and tanned olive skin. There was no grace to her beauty, only harsh lines and unforgiving perfection. She pulled her suitcase from the trunk and walked the few steps to her front door.

Something was wrong. She glanced at the rose gold watch hanging on her thin wrist, a gift from George for her thirty-ninth birthday. Quarter to eleven. She could see the lights were on in the upstairs bedroom window. George was still up. And she could hear music playing. Chet Baker. George only listened to Chet Baker for one reason.

"That son of a bitch."

Sue unlocked the front door roughly and slammed it shut behind her, dropping her heavy handbag and suitcase on the floor. Through the foyer she could see into the gleaming white kitchen and spied a bottle of wine and two glasses, one smeared with a garish pink lipstick. She walked into the room to examine the scene more closely. Next to the wine bottle was a residue of white powder. She licked her finger, tapped it in the powder and tasted. Cocaine. She rolled her eyes. Would her husband ever grow up? Picking up the wine bottle, she cursed when she looked at the label. They'd bought it during a trip to Sonoma last spring, and she recalled the vintner mentioning it was a young wine that would need to breathe for an hour or two if opened in the next year. They'd even purchased a blown glass decanter for that purpose. However, Sue suspected the one being blown now was George.

"Asshole can't keep his pants on long enough to aerate the damn wine," she said aloud. "God, I hate him so much." Sue picked up the bottle, took a swig, and savored the rich, earthy tang. She set it back down, and turned toward the staircase. She took the stairs slowly, her feet sinking into the deep carpet, dreading what awaited her. With each step, she imagined the aftermath of her discovery, the fights, the humiliating marriage counseling, the inevitable divorce. She couldn't understand her trepidation. She'd never been afraid of being alone; in fact, almost preferred it. Perhaps it was the fear of defeat, the realization of having failed at reaching happiness. She paused at the threshold of the bedroom and took a deep breath, channeling her anger. As Chet Baker sang, "The Thrill is Gone," Sue replied, "Ain't that the truth, Chet, ain't that the truth," and braced herself for what was to come.

She flung open the bedroom door slamming it against the wall and screamed, "George!"

George's head popped up from his side of the bed.

A moment later, a girl with tousled blond hair dove out of a mess of blankets and pillows, wearing only panties and a bra. In a blur, the girl scooped up a few belongings and ran for the door.

Sue, unnerved by the girl's speed, let her slip by.

"Sue, it's not what it looks like," pleaded George as he stumbled toward her dressed only in boxers. He clumsily pulled on a pair of jeans. "She wasn't feeling well. We were just going to sleep. I was on the floor, for god's sake."

Glaring at her husband, she yelled, "You are an idiot." She turned away from him and ran back down the stairs. The front door was open, and just outside the girl was trying to slip into her tight cock-tail dress under cover of the bushes that bordered the townhouse, but one arm was tangled in stretchy fabric. She looked up at Sue in horror.

"I am so sorry. So sorry," said the girl as she backed away, finally freeing her arm and pulling her dress into place.

"You're going to be sorry, you goddamn husband-stealing floozy," screamed Sue.

The girl backed up a few steps farther, then turned and ran down the street.

George stumbled to the door as he struggled to pull on a T-shirt.

"Honey, really, she's just some girl I met at a party tonight. It means nothing. I mean, nothing happened," he said.

She stared at him for a long moment, shaking her head, then walked back inside, grabbed her handbag, and rummaged through it for her car keys. Not finding them, she flipped the bag and dumped it, feeling a sense of satisfaction as the contents crashed onto the floor. The Audi's keys dropped heavily on the tile. Snatching them up, she scooped the rest of the scattered contents back into her bag, then grabbed her small suitcase and walked out the front door, slamming it behind her.

A moment later, her much-abused vehicle roared to life. She gunned the engine, whipped around the corner, and drove a few minutes down quiet streets, barely aware she was just circling the block. Her boiling anger had lowered to a simmer, and she felt drained and chilled. She turned off the air conditioner and opened the window, glad for the warm evening breeze.

Proof. She had proof. Gone was the blind hope that she was just being paranoid about the all-nighters at the office, and the last-minute business trips. She should have confronted him earlier and dragged the truth out, but something always held her back. Her mother had always said—Don't ask a question if you don't want the answer.

Sue slowed to let a pedestrian cross. The girl looked miserable, her dress askew, her hair a mess.

Walk of shame, thought Sue.

As the girl's glazed expression met Sue's through the windshield, she stopped abruptly and stared wide-eyed.

Sue's eyes narrowed to slits. It's not just a girl, realized Sue. It's *the* girl. The girl was so young, and looked so skinny in that ridiculous dress, with her messy fuck-me hair and perfect skin. The hate pulsed through Sue like a living thing. The girl suddenly represented everything that was wrong with her life—her marriage, her future, her past, all the mistakes she had ever made, all the regrets she carried with her. Conflicting scenarios rushed through her mind as her eyes locked on her prey.

Let her go.

Run her down.

Give her a ride.

Run her down.

Offer womanly advice about pricks like George.

Run. Her. Down.

Sue shifted the car into gear and hit the gas.

The girl spun and ran. Sue could hear her bare feet slapping against the asphalt as she dashed from the street to the sidewalk and ran into a small city park. Trapped between the oncoming car and a bench, the girl leapt up and over just as the car grazed her side. Sue slammed on the brakes, but the car skidded and hit a concrete trash can head-on, stunning her.

George appeared at her open window. "Thank god I caught up. Are you hurt?"

She gasped, startled by his sudden appearance. He looked truly worried about her, and for a moment, her anger faded.

The girl moaned.

"What was that?" George asked, his voice hushed and afraid. He approached the park bench and looked cautiously behind it, then reached down and helped the girl to her feet. "Are you all right?" he asked.

Sue could see the girl had a few leaves in her hair, her dress was torn and dirty, and she had a lump on her forehead that seemed to grow before Sue's eyes.

The girl hid behind George, her expression wild-eyed. She held out a red stiletto heel like a weapon. "Don't let her hurt me."

George looked at his wife with uncertainty. "You promise you won't try to kill her again?"

"Of course. You, however . . . you should be worried." Sue put the Audi into gear and backed out of the park. She knew she should stay and make sure the girl really was okay, but that was George's problem now. This whole mess was his fault. After all, she would never have tried to murder someone if George hadn't driven her to it.

CHAPTER 11
CALL FOR HELP

"Oh my god. She is terrifying," said Lisa, still clutching her purse and a single red shoe. Tires squealed as the black car whipped away like a wraith.

"You don't know the half of it," George said. He helped Lisa limp to the bench and together they sat down. Awkwardly he patted her shoulder and pulled a few leaves from her hair. "Hey, so are you okay?" he asked.

"I don't know . . . " Lisa put her hand to her forehead. It stung painfully when she touched it.

George looked over his shoulder in the direction Sue had driven. "Listen, I'm really sorry. I have to go after her or she might do something stupid."

"More stupid than trying to kill me?"

He was up and running, heading back toward his house. George yelled over his shoulder, "I'll call you!"

"Please don't—." He was already out of sight. "Leave . . ."

Weakly, Lisa assessed her situation. An hour spent vomiting in George's guest bathroom had sobered her up considerably. It was the glass of wine that pushed her over the edge. A special bottle, very expensive and of a rare vintage, according to George. Lisa took a sip and thought it tasted all right. Then George insisted she smell it. Really smell it. She did as he did. Tipped the glass and put her nose in as far as it would go and sniffed. The odor was a wretched mix of sad pony ride, tire fire, and wet gym sock. She quickly set down her glass, almost spilling it, and covered her mouth with her hands. George stopped talking about himself long enough to recognize her symptoms. He led her to a small bathroom down the hall and discreetly closed the door.

George had actually been kind of decent when Lisa finally emerged, promising to drive her home after she'd slept off the worst of it. She got undressed and settled into his big soft bed, relieved to just close her eyes. But too soon the lights blazed on and there was George's wife, screaming like a banshee.

And now she was alone on a city park bench in the middle of the night. She'd managed to get her dress back on. Good. She had her purse. Very good. But her feet were bare. She looked at the shoe still clutched in her hand. It was red, Prada, in a tiny size six. Definitely not hers. This one shoe probably cost more than a semester's tuition. It must be the woman's shoe. His wife's shoe.

Guess I'll never get that dream job at Burnam & Green, she thought. She would have laughed if her head didn't hurt so badly. Hopefully this whole night would just disappear into the ether. She'd never say a word to anyone. George had no idea who she was, after all. And she was graduating soon. She could just pick up, move to a new city, or country even. Yes. Somewhere far, far away. Preferably an island. Fiji. Malta. Guam.

Her phone rang. She looked in her handbag. Keys. Phone. Pile of cash. She gasped. George had paid her upfront. She still had the money. His money. One thousand dollars in cash. The ringing continued. She grabbed her phone and saw it was Jamie calling. Clumsily she jabbed at the answer icon and pressed the phone to her ear. "Hello?"

"Lisa, where are you?" yelled Jamie, the blaring noise of the party leaking through the phone's speaker. "I've been wandering around this stupid party for hours looking for you."

"I'm in a park."

"A park? Where?"

"I was in an accident. But not really . . . I don't know." She was struck by a wave of dizziness and tried to steady herself.

Maybe I should lie down, she thought.

"Lisa? Lisa, are you there?"

"I'm in a park," she repeated.

"Yes, you said that already. Okay. I'm coming to get you. What street are you on? Can you tell me that?"

"I think it's a park?"

"Lisa, maybe you should call 911. Is there anyone there who can help you?"

Lisa had closed her eyes at some point during the call. She opened them again and looked around. It was deserted. "No. I'll be all right till you get here." She squinted at the street sign. "I'm in the Pearl, at Irving and Tenth, I think. By the pretty brick townhouses."

"Yes, I know it. Just sit there. Do not move."

Lisa lay down on the bench, her head resting against the cool metal. Several minutes later the quiet was broken by the sound of a car pulling up, and Jamie's voice asking the driver to wait. She heard footsteps and opened her eyes to see Patrick and Jamie kneeling next to her.

"Hey, you're here . . . you're both here. Why are you both here?" Lisa asked, feeling very disoriented.

"I ran into Patrick at the party. We grabbed a Lyft and came right over. Lisa, are you okay? What happened?" asked Jamie.

"Nothing," said Lisa, her head still resting on the park bench. "I'm fine," she mumbled.

"Lisa, where does it hurt?" asked Patrick. He ran his hands over her arms and legs looking for injuries. "Doesn't look like anything's broken, and I don't see any bleeding."

Lisa sat up slowly, feeling dizzy and pointed at her forehead. Patrick gently brushed her messy hair out of the way.

"Oh, shit. That looks serious. We need to get her out of here," Patrick said to Jamie. Together they gently helped Lisa to her feet.

"Thanks for picking me up. I just want to go home."

Jamie shook her head. "We are not going home, young lady. You need medical attention ASAP."

"No. No. I'm fine. Totally fine," she said, thinking only about lying on her own bed, safe from George's wife.

"Holy shit," said Patrick, bending down to pick something up off the ground. "Jamie, look at this. I think she got hit by a car."

Lisa tried to focus her eyes on what Patrick held in his hand. To her horror, she realized it was a bent Oregon license plate that read "SUE ME."

"That's amazing," said Jamie. "We can take it to the police. Look, there's even a little piece of her dress on it." Jamie pointed at a scrap of sparkling gold fabric stuck to the corner of the metal plate. "Lisa, you're so lucky."

"No, no," said Lisa, panicking. She tried to swipe it out of Patrick's hand and swayed dangerously. "That's not anything. That was already laying here."

"Patrick, help me," said Jamie, struggling to keep Lisa upright.

Patrick took Lisa's other arm, and together he and Jamie walked Lisa to the waiting car and helped her in. Jamie started to buckle Lisa's seat belt for her.

"I am not a child," said Lisa in protest.

"Fine," said Jamie.

Lisa took the belt and tried to insert it with shaking hands. After several tries, Jamie grabbed the seat belt back and buckled it with an exasperated sigh, then got into the seat next to her.

Patrick settled into the front seat next to the driver.

"Can you take us to Good Samaritan?" Jamie asked the driver. "And hurry, please."

The driver nodded, stepped on the gas, and barreled down the street right past George's house. Lisa glanced up to see all the lights ablaze and Sue tossing a pair of burning jeans out the open bedroom window.

"Lisa, what happened? Who hit you?" Patrick asked, looking over his shoulder at her.

She couldn't bear to meet his eyes. He looked so worried. "It doesn't matter," said Lisa, shuddering.

"Of course it does," said Jamie. "We're taking you to the hospital, and then I'm calling the police. Whoever did this is going to pay."

"No," said Lisa, shaking her aching head. "You can't. You can't tell anyone."

"We're trying to help. Just tell us what happened," said Jamie.

"You really don't want to know," Lisa said.

Jamie put her arm around Lisa, "Just spill. You'll feel better."

"I don't think I will actually," she said. "I had too much to drink. That pretty much sums it up."

"What? We weren't supposed to drink anything. You heard Nigel," said Jamie, her voice full of righteous indignation. "I didn't drink. I wanted to. All these stupid waiters, wandering around with their delicious beverages."

"Jamie, it was after I saw my mom," said Lisa. "She was at the party."

"You didn't tell me she was there," said Patrick.

"Well, you were being such a jerk, I never got a chance to."

"I'm sorry. If I'd known, I would have stayed with you. You should have told me," he said quietly.

"It's fine," said Lisa.

"So, who hit you? And what were you doing in this part of town anyway?" asked Jamie.

"It was just some crazy woman." Tears welled up in Lisa's eyes as she relived the moment. "I really think she wanted to kill me. Sorry. I don't know why I'm crying."

"Because you're in shock. Let me get you a tissue." Jamie looked in her purse and, not finding any, snapped open Lisa's.

Lisa tried to stop her but was too slow. "Please don't."

Along with a packet of tissues, Jamie pulled out the small roll of hundred-dollar bills George had given her. "What's this? Did Nigel pay you extra? No fair."

"It's nothing," said Lisa.

"That is not nothing. Where did you get that money?" asked Patrick suspiciously.

Lisa glanced at him and could see him putting the pieces together.

"You left with that guy, didn't you." It wasn't a question. Patrick reached over the seat and grabbed the bills from Jamie's hand then dropped them back into Lisa's purse like he'd been burned. "You took his money."

"You stole it?" asked Jamie.

"No, Jamie. She didn't steal it," said Patrick. "He paid her."

"For what?" asked Jamie, still not getting it.

Lisa loved her friend for not immediately thinking the worst of her. Not like everyone else did.

"You know what," scoffed Patrick.

Jamie gasped. "Lisa would never."

"Lisa, just tell us the truth," demanded Patrick.

Lisa sat silent. What options did she have? She could keep lying, but they'd figure it out. Or they'd go to the police with the license plate. And if her mother found out . . . "I'm sorry, Jamie," said Lisa. "I was drunk. I wasn't thinking. Nothing actually happened. I got sick and was just going to sleep it off. Then his wife walked in on us.

She's the one who came after me in the car. That's why you can't tell anyone. You can't go to the police."

"How much did you get?" asked Jamie.

"Seriously?" asked Lisa.

"Yes. I want to know."

"One thousand," said Lisa. "But I'm going to give it back."

"American dollars?"

"No. Canadian," said Lisa, exasperated.

"Wow. That is both disturbing and impressive," said Jamie.

"Jamie, do you think this is a joke?" asked Patrick, incredulous.

"Well, no, I mean, of course not. But technically she didn't do anything," said Jamie. "You heard her, she got sick. You know how Lisa always throws up when she drinks too much. That would definitely kill the mood. If the wife hadn't come home, this whole thing would be a nonissue."

"I can't believe this." He handed Jamie the license plate. "Hey," he said to the driver. "I need to get out of the car, now. Can you pull over?"

"Patrick, what are you doing?" asked Jamie.

"I'm leaving."

The driver stopped at the next intersection and Patrick got out, and slammed the door shut.

Jamie rolled down her window. "Come on, don't go," she called.

"She's your problem now," Patrick said as he walked away.

"Maybe you thinking that she's a problem *is* the problem!" yelled Jamie after him, but he didn't turn back.

Lisa and Jamie sat quietly for a moment in the vacuum Patrick had left behind.

"Are you mad at me? You can go too if you want," said Lisa. "I wouldn't blame you. I don't want to be around me right now either."

"No. I'm not mad. You know I've always prided myself on my moral ambiguity," said Jamie. She motioned to the driver to keep going. The car pulled slowly away from the curb. "So who was he?" Jamie asked.

Lisa shook her head, then immediately regretted it as a fresh wave of pain overwhelmed her. She leaned back in her seat and closed her eyes. "You won't believe me."

"Sure I will. Come on. Spill."

Lisa looked at her friend, expecting signs of disappointment and judgment. So far, Jamie just looked curious. "You know that huge ad agency downtown? Burnam & Green."

"Yeah?"

"He's the Green."

"You mean *the* Green."

"Yep."

"Damn. Was he at least attractive?"

"Eh . . . He was until he opened his mouth."

"Can I tell my mom? She'll be super disappointed in you of course, but kind of impressed too. The Green paid you a thousand bucks. Is that seriously the going rate?"

Lisa felt herself smile, something she thought she'd never do again. "Jamie, you are the worst," she said, squeezing her friend's hand.

CHAPTER 12
THE TATTOO PARLOR

Patrick shoved his hands in his pockets and walked away from the car, each step taking him farther away from the former love of his life. The vehicle idled briefly on the corner, and he listened as the driver slowly moved down the street as though hopeful Patrick would turn back.

He didn't. He could never forgive her. This was it. They were over for good.

Breathing in the night air, he felt his resolve slip. He glanced over his shoulder, but the car was gone. Patrick had never felt so alone.

🍸

The first time Patrick saw Lisa, she had just stepped off the Lost Lake Academy bus straight from a month of wilderness therapy, which was, in reality, just camping in the mountains. No running water. No facilities. Had to melt snow to drink. Dig holes to shit. Fun for anyone who'd grown up with it. Pure agony for spoiled brats pulled from wealthy suburbs, which covered most of them. Patrick included. Except for a few real delinquents sent by the state, the kids at the Academy were all rich. At least their parents were.

Patrick sat outside the school lodge sharing a smoke with a few buddies from his assigned peer group. Watching the newbies arrive was one of the few forms of entertainment available at the Academy. The new inmates emerged one by one, boys and girls, some in their late teens, others barely ten years old, each more scared than the last. But Lisa just looked pissed. She carried a heavy backpack, probably packed in secret by her parents, full of supplies for weathering rain showers, snowstorms, and cold nights sleeping on hard, frozen ground. She wore khakis torn at the knees, a dusty-looking black sweater, and combat boots. An inch of blond roots showed underneath the faded blue dye she'd used on her hair. She had a black eye, and her face was set in a scowl. She was the angriest and most beautiful girl he'd ever seen.

Patrick acted like a typical boy for the first few days: hazing the new kids, giving them a hard time about anything and everything. He pretended to completely ignore Lisa. But he watched and waited for an opening.

They had a regular schedule of classes, most of them poorly taught by teachers not much older than the students. The behavior modification sessions were the worst. The school had files on all of them, including detailed questionnaires filled out by parents— sometimes even friends—and records that detailed run-ins with principals, teachers, and police. Dossiers on their brief sex lives were cobbled together, most of them grossly exaggerated by parents with overactive imaginations. No secret was safe, no embarrassment too mortifying—the therapists used it all.

About twenty students sat on folding chairs in a circle in the gym and one victim was chosen. Dr. Bob, or Bob the Nob as the students called him, picked Lisa during her first session. Her black eye had faded to an ugly yellow, and she wore the same clothes as when she'd stepped off the school bus. Dr. Bob called her name, and she stood. He read aloud from Lisa's file, listing her infractions one by one as she stood humiliated in front of her fellow students. Her crimes included all the usual stuff. Drugs, alcohol, crashing cars, starting a fire in the girl's bathroom at school, and worst of all, sex with boys too old for her age. He explained the prescribed cure for Lisa's rampant promiscuity. She was to role-play with students and teachers. Her shame would prevent Lisa from ever straying from the proper norms of society again.

Dr. Bob held up a skimpy black outfit adorned with white lace. He pointed Lisa toward the girls locker room. She stood, her face wearing that what-the-hell look all the new students had at this point. She mouthed *no*, but before she could speak, two female teacher's aides grabbed her arms and dragged her to the locker room, the costume swinging from Dr. Bob's hand as he followed.

Patrick and the other students sat silently as they heard Lisa hurl expletives through the closed locker room door. He thought he heard a few punches being thrown and smiled, knowing it was probably Lisa doing the hitting.

Several minutes later she stomped out of the locker room, slamming the door open ahead of the teacher's aides and Dr. Bob. She wore the ridiculous, ill-fitting costume though her feet were still clad in her untied combat boots. She refused to speak, and just did as she was told in hopes that it would end more quickly. It didn't. Lisa was ordered to mime a lap dance with another embarrassed student as the rest of the kids screamed at Lisa that she was a whore, a prostitute, a slut, and worse. It was Bob the Nob's special brand of aversion therapy.

Patrick couldn't stand it, but he didn't speak up. He knew what would happen if he were to protest. The teacher's aides would grab him, and he'd get thrown in the hole again. But he needed to do something, so he figured if he was going to be punished, he might as well make an impression. He raised his hand and asked to use the bathroom. Dr. Bob absently waved him out of the room.

Patrick walked across the gym, then entered the boys locker room. He rushed by lockers and sinks toward an exit that led outside. He reentered through the girls' side, ran past a few startled half-dressed students, and headed to a closet where he knew they stored the costumes. He dug around for a moment and pulled out a garment in just the right size for a huskier girl. He slipped out of his jeans and T-shirt, then pulled the costume over his head.

He snuck back into the gym. Dr. Bob and the aides had their backs to him, and the students who saw him kept quiet for once. A small cabinet held the gym's sound system, and he sprinted up the few steps to it and sat down. He was familiar with the equipment, having helped with the annual talent show, and rifled through a pile of CDs until he found something appropriate. Tapping a button, the CD player tray opened and he dropped in a disc, forwarded to the right track, and hit play. Moments later Beyoncé's "Single Ladies" roared out of the speaker system.

Stunned students and teachers turned toward the music, only to see Patrick dance down the steps doing his best Beyoncé impression, wearing a French maid's costume identical to Lisa's. Dr. Bob and the teacher's aides jumped to their feet and chased him around the gym, stumbling over students, folding chairs, and exercise equipment, until they finally caught him. As they pulled him down from where he hung grasping the basketball hoop after a Michael Jordan-esque leap, Patrick caught sight of Lisa doubled over with laughter.

Impression made, he thought with a smile.

$$\Upsilon$$

Patrick heard a chirp. Then another. He fished his phone out of his back pocket and tapped the screen. He expected to see an angry text from Jamie and hoped for an apology from Lisa. But there was nothing. No new messages. The chirping continued, insistent.

Finally, he remembered the old-school beeper Sheila had given him earlier at the party. He pulled it out of the small case clipped to his belt. The screen lit up with a message, and his stomach sank. It was his first gig. Patrick read the address and looked up at the street signs. Only a few blocks away. He paused at a trash can on the corner and for a moment considered dumping the drugs and the beeper. What was the point? Lisa wouldn't be moving in with him. He didn't need the extra money. And selling drugs was a line he never thought he'd have to cross. He pulled the paper sack out of his messenger bag. It was nondescript, generic; it could be holding the remains of today's lunch, a fifth of gin, or five thousand dollars' worth of cocaine.

A police car rolled past. Spooked, Patrick stuffed the drugs back into his bag and walked with purpose, willing the car not to stop. Sheila had promised to murder him if anything went wrong, and he had no reason not to believe her. Anyway, if he dumped the drugs, he'd have no way of pulling together the cash to pay her back. He'd made his bed.

A flash of pink neon caught his eye: "Your Mother's Tattoo" with "Open 24 Hours" in yellow underneath. He double-checked the address on his phone. It was a match.

He pushed open the barred glass door. The place was brightly lit with fluorescent lights. Drawings of tattoos meant to inspire the uncertain papered the walls. An ancient air conditioner worked overtime in a window and emitted an irritating buzz. "Dust in the Wind" played quietly on the stereo. In spite of the lights and signage, the place looked deserted. No customers, no staff.

"Hello? Anyone here?" asked Patrick.

A red barber's chair swung around to reveal a man with a likable face sporting a dark mustache of ample proportions. The sleeves of his embroidered western-wear shirt were rolled up past his elbows, exposing muscular arms covered in tattoos. An image of Elvis as Jesus on his left forearm was of particular artistic significance. The man spoke. "As my mother used to say: 'When it comes to tattoos, those who hesitate are lost.'" His smile was a medley of white enamel and silver caps. "How may I assist you?"

Patrick stood for a moment on the threshold half in, half out. The message from Sheila had just indicated the address, no name. What if this wasn't the right guy? A wave of hot, muggy air wafted in, and he could feel the room's temperature rise with each passing moment. The air conditioner rattled impatiently.

"Now, just come on in. I won't bite. Though my needle might," said the tattoo artist with a grin.

"Sorry," said Patrick, as he crossed the threshold and firmly shut the door. "Still pretty hot out."

"Then how about a cold beer?" The tattoo artist stood and walked to a dented mini fridge in the corner. He pulled out two bottles, opened them both, and handed one to Patrick.

Patrick looked at the label with approval and drank deeply. "Thanks," he said, wiping his mouth with his hand. "I needed that."

"What can I do for you?"

"I'm here to make a delivery," said Patrick.

"That was quick."

"I was in the neighborhood."

"And you are?"

"Patrick," he said as he held out his hand, realizing too late he probably shouldn't have used his real name.

The tattoo artist gripped his hand briefly, then stepped to the front door and locked it. He flipped a switch to extinguish the neon signs and pulled down a pair of blinds. "Wouldn't want anyone to disturb us."

"Good call." Patrick set his messenger bag on the counter next to the cash register and pulled out the paper bag Sheila had given him. He set out several packets.

The tattoo artist looked the stash over. "Interesting packaging..." The packets were made of a waxy brown paper with a clear plastic window that revealed the white powder within. An artfully printed sticker in a serif font labeled each.

"Yeah," said Patrick, embarrassed. "The coke is organic. Is that all right?"

"No, no. It's all good. I've been meaning to start a healthier drug habit." He selected an assortment.

Smart ass, thought Patrick. "What are you doing with all this?" he asked, waving at the pile of drugs. "Definitely over the legal limit for possession."

The tattoo artist opened the register, counted out some cash, and held it out to Patrick. "Just doing my best to keep it off the streets."

"Seriously?" Patrick suddenly felt nervous. What if this guy was a narc? Just his luck, having his first deal go south.

The man chuckled. "No. I resell it. A place like this has a clientele that's always interested in a little pick-me-up. I heard Sheila's operation carried the best coke in town, so figured I'd stock up."

Patrick relaxed a bit knowing this guy was on a first-name basis with Sheila. He took the money, burying the bills in his back pocket, and stored the remaining drugs in his messenger bag. He took another long drink of beer. Well, that was easy enough, he thought as he set down his empty bottle and turned to go. "Nice doing business with you."

"Hey, want me to cut that off?" asked the tattoo artist, pointing to the yellow wristband from the party.

"Sure."

The tattoo artist grabbed a pair of scissors from his work bench. He carefully snipped off the wristband and gave it a look. "'Rose City Ripe for Disruption Gala,'" he read. "I'm sorry, but you don't look like the gala type."

Patrick snorted a laugh. "No, I was just there to conduct some business."

"You were dealing at this party? That's ballsy," said the tattoo artist.

"No, it was just a pickup," he said. "I met Sheila there. She has this sweet trailer. An Airstream. Just sits there with all the other food trucks."

"Interesting . . ." The tattoo artist gave Patrick an appraising look. "Is that fresh ink?" he asked.

Patrick glanced down at his arm. "Yeah." He'd have to start wearing long-sleeved shirts till he could afford to have it fixed. "Got it yesterday."

"May I?"

Patrick pushed up the sleeve of his T-shirt, and the tattoo artist peered at it closely. "Nice work. Let's see . . . 'Lisa Forever.' Very optimistic." He straightened. "I knew a Lisa once. She broke my heart."

"Ditto."

"You don't say?"

"Yep. We ended it tonight."

"That's terrible. Well, how about I take care of this little inaccuracy on your arm," he offered.

"Really?" asked Patrick. "How much will this set me back?"

"No worries. Let's just consider it a favor from one broken heart to another."

Patrick dropped his messenger bag on the floor and sat down in the leather chair.

The artist reached for his tattoo gun and selected one of several bottles of ink that sat ready. "Before I start, are you sure? You may feel different in the morning."

Patrick shook his head. "Not likely. Just cover it up, fill it in, whatever it takes."

"You got it." Soon the sound of a buzzing tattoo gun filled the room. The needle worked its way across Patrick's skin, back and forth. "Tell me about Lisa," prompted the tattoo artist.

"Not really in the mood," said Patrick.

"She must have been pretty important to you if you went through the trouble of getting this tattoo."

"She was worth it, once."

"Come on, tell me."

He knew he shouldn't share any of this, but it was rare someone gave a shit enough to ask. He spent most of his free time with Lisa and Jamie, and since they'd all experienced the same nightmare at the Academy, it wasn't a topic they talked about very often. Mostly they just wanted to forget and move on.

"I met her at a boarding school for disturbed youth," said Patrick. "The great Lost Lake Academy."

The tattoo artist whistled. "I remember reading about that place. Your parents must have been rolling in dough."

"I guess so. My dad runs a construction company. Mom used to work with him, but she stopped when I was a kid."

"How did you end up there?"

"Got into some trouble."

"What kind?"

"The petty theft and drug possession kind. My counselors at the Academy told me I was just acting out, that I wanted my father to acknowledge me. And maybe that's true. Anyway, he noticed. He tricked me. Told me we were going on a family ski trip. What a joke. He drove me to the school and dropped me off with a couple of thugs dressed up as counselors. I remember him saying it was all my mom's fault. That never made any sense to me. She was a good mom, really," said Patrick. "I think he was tired of having me around and hoped I'd just disappear."

"I'm sorry," said the tattoo artist.

"Don't be. I'm better off without him. He's into some sketchy shit. Saw in the paper a few years ago that the feds were after him. He dodged it of course. Anyway, he doesn't give a shit about me. Haven't seen him in years." Patrick stretched his arms as the tattoo artist switched inks. "My parents never even visited. Kept paying the bills though."

"Didn't they shut that school down?" the tattoo artist asked.

"Yeah, a bunch of students sued," said Patrick.

"Well, I hope they won big," he said as he carefully moved the needle across Patrick's skin. "So, tell me, why did you and Lisa break up?"

Patrick didn't know why, but he found himself telling the tattoo artist almost everything. Yet he held back the truth about how Lisa had taken money from that asshole at the party.

When Patrick finished his story, the tattoo artist shook his head sympathetically and said, "That's terrible. Where is Lisa now?"

"She's probably still at the hospital."

"I bet. Sounds like her injuries were pretty serious."

Oh god, thought Patrick. Lisa had looked fine except for the lump on her head, but what if she'd suffered a concussion? What if she went into a coma? His heart in his throat, he quickly pulled his phone from his back pocket, and read a text from Jamie. *Lisa is fine. Dr is w her. U r a dick.* Well, that's that, he thought.

"Her roommate is with her at Good Samaritan. Says she's fine."

"That's a relief." The tattoo artist set down the needle and surveyed his work. "I think we're done here. Want to take a look?" he asked.

"Naw, dude, just as long as Lisa is gone."

"Her name has been obscured." He cleaned up Patrick's arm and wrapped it in a few layers of sterile gauze, then tied the ends in a knot and advised Patrick to keep the bandage in place overnight.

As Patrick turned to go, the tattoo artist spoke. "Can I give you a word of advice?"

Patrick shrugged.

"Your life reads like a white trash shit show, and I can see you're smarter than that. Dump the drugs, dump the girl, and move on."

Patrick just nodded glumly. "You're right." He unlocked the door and pushed it open to leave, then paused and turned back. "You want to hear something really crazy?"

"Absolutely."

"Lisa's mom. She's the mayor of Portland. How messed up is that?"

𝖸

Theo locked the door behind Patrick, then stood for a moment at the large, plate glass window that fronted the tattoo parlor. He pinched open a slot in the blinds and watched as Patrick walked slowly down the street. Poor kid, he thought. Theo had known a few too many young men like Patrick over the years. He'd almost been one himself.

Stepping to the counter, he opened a drawer and pulled out a laptop. He searched and clicked, and in moments images from the party Patrick had attended popped up onscreen. Sure enough, he spotted Sheila mixing and mingling with party attendees. The woman had balls, he thought. He checked a few other sites and found a selfie of a twenty-something taking a bite of a soggy pierogi. In the background, just as Patrick had described, a silver Airstream was parked discreetly amid the busy food trucks.

He picked up a battered-looking cellphone and speed-dialed a number. One ring, two, three.

"Yes? What is it, Theo?" The voice sounded impatient.

"We got a lucky break tonight. My fishing expedition has finally paid off. I know how Sheila's distributing."

"Tell me everything."

"I will, but first you need to get to Good Samaritan. Your daughter's been in an accident."

CHAPTER 13
THE WAITING ROOM

A police drama played on the TV in the hospital's waiting room. The sound was off, as were the subtitles, yet Jamie was still mesmerized. Gorgeous detectives caught in a love triangle anguished over the fate of a traumatized victim. (Such amazing hair. I bet that guy uses hot curlers). At a crucial moment, the scene ended, followed by five minutes of ads hyping erectile dysfunction pills (Those old dudes have really satisfied-looking wives), knife sets (That serrated blade cuts tomatoes like nobody's business), and countertop sausage grills (Wonder how it would handle a bratwurst).

Jamie's stomach grumbled. Her emergency candy bar was long gone, as were her twenty-two remaining mints and all her loose change. Only the stack of bills remained, and she was too embarrassed to ask the receptionist at the front desk to break a hundred. She slipped off her shoes, slouched in her seat, and rested her head on the back of her chair. Should she ask about Lisa again? The doctor had stopped by to give her an update, but that was at least an hour ago.

Waiting rooms inevitably reminded Jamie of the Academy and sitting for hours in the student center for the five-minute call home that she was allowed every few weeks. She was always nervous that her parents might not pick up. Maybe they'd be busy with something more important than their delinquent daughter.

Y

It was a gray and snowy day, like most at the Academy. Jamie watched snowflakes drift past the dingy windows of the student center. She grasped the dated MP3 player her brother had slipped to her on his last visit. Smart-phones, or even stupid ones, were absolutely prohibited on campus, as the school administrators controlled all communications with the outside world. She tapped the buttons to flip through songs—indie rock, classic rock, riot grrrl. All of his favorites. The music was her constant companion. She hated to admit it, but her big brother had great taste. She loved him, even though he was the reason she was stuck here. Well, it was mostly his fault.

Sitting and waiting, she felt a little sick. Lunch that day had been a bowl of yellowish tomato soup and a bologna-and-cheese sandwich on white bread. The food at the school was terrible, but meals were a distraction and she never missed one. One of her roommates had stolen a promotional pamphlet from Bob the Nob's office, and they'd tacked it on their wall like a poster. A whole section was dedicated to the healthy meals that were supposed to be served to students. It featured a veritable cornucopia of tasty delights. Lies. All lies. Fresh vegetables rarely appeared on their trays, and Jamie hadn't seen a piece of fruit since she'd left home.

Jamie shifted in her seat. She needed to use the bathroom, but she couldn't risk it. The staff would use any excuse to deny the students privileges. It had been weeks since she'd talked to her family.

Finally, a voice came over the intercom. "Jamie Kim, please come to Dr. Donna's office."

Jamie stood, quickly headed down a dim hallway, and opened a door.

A middle-aged woman sat at a desk in the middle of a windowless room. A pair of glasses on a beaded lanyard hung around her neck. She wore a white coat with a tag labeled "Dr. Donna" crookedly pinned to her lapel. A stack of files and a notepad sat on the desk's scratched surface next to a cup of coffee. Dr. Donna gestured at Jamie to sit in one of the chairs opposite her desk. The wooden chair creaked uneasily as Jamie sat down.

"Jamie, it's good to see you," said Dr. Donna. She put her glasses on and slowly turned the pages of Jamie's file. She wore a headset plugged into an office phone. "It's been a week since we met?"

"Three."

"Three weeks, really? How are you feeling today?"

"Fine."

"Just 'fine.'" Dr. Donna made a note in Jamie's file, then looked at Jamie above her glasses. "I was hoping you'd made some progress since we last spoke."

Jamie regretted her response. She needed to do better. "I have, absolutely. I'm in a really good place and am ready to have an appropriate conversation with my parents."

Dr. Donna settled back in her chair. "Now, I just want to go over a few things with you. I need you to understand how much stress your parents are under. When you were living at home, you brought them nothing but trouble, Jamie. They are finally in a good place. Do you remember that incident at the mall? They are just now getting over it."

Jamie remembered. Dr. Donna and the other counselors would never let her forget the day she'd raced after her brother down the concourse of the Lloyd Center mall and skidded across the open-air ice rink carrying a backpack stuffed full of stolen Xbox and PlayStation games. She remembered her brother glancing back at her, the excitement in his eyes turning to dismay as he realized they were being chased by a mall cop. He made it out the door to the parking lot and disappeared into a maze of cars and SUVs. Jamie didn't.

"We talk to your parents regularly, and they confide in us," continued Dr. Donna. "It's been a long period of recovery for them and for your brother. They don't need to hear anything negative that you might want to say about your experience here." Dr. Donna sighed deeply and took off her glasses. She leaned forward and stared intently at Jamie. "Do you want to cause them more heartache, Jamie? Or do you want to tell them how happy you are, how much the school is helping you, and how glad and grateful you are that they sent you here instead of juvenile detention?"

"I only want to share with them how well I'm doing, and how wonderful the Academy is," said Jamie, doing her best to smile. She wondered how much more of this crap she'd have to stomach before Dr. Donna got on with it. "I'm so lucky to be here."

It had been months since her court-ordered sentence had come and gone. Jamie had started to suspect it was the school, not the judge or her parents, who plotted to keep her trapped here.

Dr. Donna smiled and closed the file. "Well, then I think we're ready to get started. Shall we make the call?"

This wouldn't be a private conversation between Jamie and her parents. As usual, Dr. Donna would listen in and monitor every word, and if she didn't like what was said on either side, the conversation would end, and this thin thread to Jamie's life back home would be severed.

Dr. Donna slowly dialed her parent's number, and Jamie couldn't help but watch hungrily as the familiar sequence of numbers was typed into the phone.

"Remember, Jamie, the call will only last five minutes, so make it count." She held the receiver out to Jamie.

"Hello," answered her mother.

"Hello?" said Jamie, "Hello?" then realized her mother couldn't hear her yet.

Dr. Donna spoke through her headset. "Mrs. Kim?"

"Yes."

"This is Dr. Donna from the Lost Lake Academy."

Jamie suspected Dr. Donna had nothing close to a doctorate, a detail she was dying to share with her parents yet couldn't because it would immediately end the call. Jamie was convinced the entire school was a scam. She doubted any of the teachers had legitimate degrees. She'd learned from the other kids that most of the instructors and therapists were locals with barely more than high school diplomas.

"Of course. We've been waiting for your call for two hours," said Jamie's mom. Jamie loved how irritated her mother sounded.

"So sorry for the delay. You know how it is dealing with troubled teens."

"Well, no, I don't . . ."

"I have Jamie here now, and she's so excited to talk to you. I'll remind you, according to your signed agreement with the school, if I feel the conversation is taking an unhealthy turn, I will terminate the call. Do you understand?"

"Yes, Dr. Donna," said Jamie's mother. "One moment while I find Jamie's father and brother."

Jamie sat impatiently as the seconds ticked by. Mom must be in the kitchen, she thought, and pictured the room in her mind—the black-and-white tiled floor, the old-fashioned, refurbished stove and oak kitchen table, and the big window that looked over the backyard.

Finally, she heard voices.

"Mom?"

"How are you?"

"Good. Is Dad there too?"

"Yes, and Roderick. He's home for spring break," she explained.

Spring break already, thought Jamie. Her concept of time was perpetually off-kilter. With the endless snowfall in winter and gray rainy days in summer, it had all started to blur. The idea of getting a break from the Academy's daily routine felt unimaginable to her. "That's great, Mom, but I only have five minutes."

Dr. Donna held up four fingers.

"Can you all get on the speaker-phone?"

"Yes, of course," her mom said. Jamie heard a click, and their voices echoed around her.

"Jamie, how are you?" Her dad's warm voice filled her ears. They usually spoke Korean when they were together as a family, but Dr. Donna wouldn't allow that. She needed to hear every word Jamie said to her parents.

"Hey, sis. How're things at that spa you call a school?" asked her brother, sounding as cocky and confident as ever.

"Yeah, it's great. How's Stanford? Are you staying out of trouble?"

Roderick laughed. "Of course, you know me. I've decided on a major."

"What is it?" she asked.

"Journalism."

"Jamie," said her mother, "tell your brother he should go pre-med or pre-law. No one makes money writing."

"But Mom," said Roderick in a dramatic voice. "I need to tell the story of Jamie's life of crime and her path to redemption."

Jamie laughed, losing herself for a moment in her family's cheerful banter. "When can you visit?" she asked.

Dr. Donna gave her a warning look. She scribbled a note and held it up. "Don't act needy," it read.

"We'll be there next month," said her mom. "For your birthday. Do you need anything?"

Dr. Donna shook her head at Jamie, her finger perched above the End Call button.

"No, Mom, I don't need anything. The school provides everything. Everything is good."

"Are they feeding you?"

"Absolutely, just like in the pamphlets. You wouldn't believe how healthy the environment is here, lots of fresh air, the classes are really challenging, and I'm receiving the very best tutoring. I feel like I'm really getting better. Great, really great."

Jamie could hear whispers and then a moment of silence on the other end.

She heard her brother's voice again, all joking gone from it. "Jamie, how about the counseling?" he asked.

She blinked back tears, loath to let Dr. Donna witness her cry. She swallowed and cleared her throat. "No worries, Roderick. I'm getting the best care," she said, her voice choking. Suddenly she couldn't help herself. She switched to Korean and rushed out the words. "The school is a prison. Get me out of here. Please. Mom and Dad, let me come home."

Before her parents or brother could say another word, the phone went dead, Dr. Donna's finger pressed firmly on the End Call button.

It took her parents a few weeks to get her out, but she was almost eighteen by then, and after that, the school couldn't hold her any longer. They let her go without too much of a fight. It was the state funding they wanted—thousands every month.

Y

The hospital's lobby doors slid open with a whoosh followed by the staccato click of high heels.

"Hello? Is anyone here? I'm looking for my daughter."

Jamie turned, glad for the distraction. It was a well-dressed woman with white hair. Maybe I could ask her for some money, thought Jamie. Mothers always have cash. Jamie had fully inventoried the vending machine. Her first choice was a Snickers—very filling. Then a bag of sour cream and onion chips. Or maybe the peanut butter pretzels. Crunchy and creamy.

"Does no one work here?" asked the woman loudly to the empty reception area. "Or has everyone taken the night off? With all the public funding this facility receives, one would think at least the front desk could be properly staffed."

A door labeled Patients and Staff Only opened, and the receptionist hurried back to her desk. "Sorry to keep you waiting. How can I help you?"

"It's about time," said the woman. "I've been waiting here for an eternity. What if I were bleeding out? I could be dead by now."

Jamie was thoroughly enjoying her tirade. Only a big bowl of buttered popcorn could improve the show.

"My daughter Lisa was in an accident. Lisa Salder. I'm Ellen Salder."

Jamie's mouth dropped open, all thoughts of salty snacks gone.

"Let me call the doctor."

"Can't you check on your computer? My daughter is here, and I demand to know exactly where she is and what condition she's in. You must be able to tell me something. You can't imagine how worried I am."

"Please take a seat. I just need a moment." The receptionist pointed accusingly at Jamie. "She brought the young woman in."

As the receptionist made her escape, Ellen directed her scowl at Jamie and didn't look pleased by what she saw. Jamie was still wearing her party dress, and in that moment, she would have given almost anything for a change of clothes. Or to disappear in a puff of smoke.

Jamie sat up, jammed her feet back into her sandals and stood. Should she commandeer a wheelchair, force her way through the staff door, and roll Lisa to safety? Or just abandon all hope and make a run for it? Jamie tried to compose herself as Lisa's mother walked over. "Hello," she said, and held out her hand.

Ellen ignored it. "How do you know my daughter?" she demanded.

"I'm Jamie. Lisa's roommate," she said, and let her hand drop limply back to her side. "I talked to the doctor about an hour ago. She said Lisa would be fine."

"Don't tell me she's going to be fine. What do you know?" snapped Ellen.

I know that I really dislike you, thought Jamie.

A doctor swept down the hall toward them.

"Mayor Salder. My goodness, it's such a pleasure to see you again. I'm Dr. Adair." The doctor held out her hand, her voice and manner the perfect antidote to the mayor's animosity. "We met last year at an OHSU benefit."

Ellen's expression instantly changed from utter irritation into a warm smile, and she grasped the doctor's hand firmly. "Yes, of course. Dr. Adair. Jennifer, isn't it? It's so good to see you."

Jamie was unnerved by Ellen's transformation. Disturbed, she stepped away from the pair as they continued to exchange pleasantries. She sat down a safe distance away and resumed staring at the television. The gorgeous detectives were gone, and the screen had been taken over by an infomercial for a countertop deep fryer. Homemade donuts bubbled in steaming oil. Jamie's stomach rumbled.

I'm not going to ask her for vending machine money, no matter how hungry I get, she thought sullenly. She couldn't imagine Lisa's mother had anything so pedestrian and utterly useful as crumpled bills and change at the bottom of her purse.

"How is Lisa?" Ellen asked.

Jamie shifted her attention back to the doctor, eager for any information about her friend.

"Lisa, yes. I examined her when she first came in." The doctor's eyes quickly scanned the tablet computer she held. "The results of her MRI are already back," said the doctor. Her finger swiped across the tablet as she read Lisa's chart. She smiled. "Nothing to worry about. Lisa is doing very well."

"When can I see her?"

"In a few minutes. She suffered a nasty bump on the head, but everything else looks completely normal. We've had her under close observation, and there are no signs of a concussion. I feel comfortable sending her home at this point. Two Tylenol every six hours should help with any pain. Just give us a few minutes and the nurse will bring her out." Dr. Adair shook Ellen's hand again and walked away briskly.

Ellen stood motionless for a long moment after the doctor had left, as though unsure what to do next. She sat down a few seats away from Jamie.

The hospital's sliding lobby doors whooshed open again. A severe-looking woman with long black hair led in a barefoot man in a T-shirt and jeans. His clothing and face were covered in soot and his left hand was wrapped loosely in white gauze. The woman pulled him toward the receptionist's desk. "Will you please help my idiot husband?"

Must be a good story there, thought Jamie.

The receptionist handed the woman a clipboard with a few sheets of paper and said to fill out the form.

"Please tell the doctor to take his time," said the woman. "I want my husband to suffer as much as possible."

The man sat down, closed his eyes, and gently cradled his swaddled hand. The woman grabbed a stack of magazines, sat down next to him, and started aggressively flipping through them, page by page.

"I'm sorry about earlier. I didn't mean to be so harsh."

Jamie looked away from the couple and realized Ellen was speaking to her.

"I just felt so helpless, and that makes me lash out. My therapist is always telling me to pause and breathe and then speak. There's not always time for that when I need people to do their damn jobs." She shifted a few seats closer and held out her hand. "Let's start again. I'm Ellen Salder."

Jamie wondered if it was a trap. Hesitantly, she held out hers and they shook hands. "Nice to meet you," she said. "I'm Jamie Kim." Ellen's grip felt firm and professional. She probably shook hands a thousand times a day.

"How do you know my daughter, again?" Ellen asked. "You're her roommate?"

"Yes," said Jamie. She felt incredibly uncomfortable, as though she were betraying her best friend just having this conversation. She could fake an attack of some kind. She could faint. Or play dead. This was a hospital, after all. Some nice nurse would swing by, put her on a gurney, and sweep her away.

"And how did you meet?"

Maybe I should lie, thought Jamie. Make up a story and say we met volunteering with sad orphans, or tagging a public building with profanity. Of course, life was always much worse than fiction. "We met at the Lost Lake Academy. She may have mentioned my parents, the Kims? Lisa lived with us for a while after she was released."

Ellen's face suddenly looked pinched, like she'd tasted something sour. "The Kims. Of course. Your parents are such generous people."

"Yes. They are." Jamie imagined what her mother would say if she were here. Mrs. Kim had wanted to give Lisa's mother a piece of her mind for quite some time.

The Patients and Staff Only door opened, and an aide wheeled Lisa into the waiting room. Lisa looked pale, but the knot on her forehead had subsided to a more reasonable size, more grape than chicken egg. She was dressed in scrubs and resting on her lap was a clear plastic bag containing her belongings. Jamie rushed to Lisa's side and gave her a quick hug.

"Thanks for sticking around," said Lisa. "That took forever. Can we please go home now? I just need to check out. Don't think I need a prescrip—"

Jamie cut her off, and blurted out, "Lisa, I'm so sorry. I swear I didn't call her."

"What are you talking about, crazy lady?" asked Lisa. "Call who?"

"Hello darling," said Ellen, as she walked toward Lisa.

Jamie blurted out. "I have no idea how she found out you were here."

"How I found out isn't relevant right now," said Ellen.

Jamie watched as Lisa's mother looked over her daughter carefully. Jamie wished she'd called her own mom. By now, Mrs. Kim would have smothered Lisa with hugs and would be outlining a full regimen of soups, teas and herbal remedies to get Lisa on the mend. Not this cold, clinical inspection.

"I just want to make sure that you're being well taken care of," said Ellen crisply.

"Now you worry?" asked Lisa.

"Your health and safety are all I've ever cared about."

They both crossed their arms and glared at each other in silence.

Oh my god, they're going to kill each other, thought Jamie. At least we're in a hospital.

A hissed argument could be heard from the couple who sat across the waiting room. Jamie looked over and saw that the woman with black hair was glaring viciously at Lisa.

"Lisa, that woman is staring at you," whispered Jamie.

Lisa broke off her gaze and followed Jamie's line of sight. She blinked a few times and said stiffly, "It's nothing. Can we go?"

Jamie looked back at the couple, trying to understand what they could possibly want. They were probably just interested in what the mayor was doing in a hospital at this late hour.

Ellen looked too. "What is George Green doing here?" She sighed irritably. "I better say hello."

"George Green? You mean *the* Green?" asked Jamie.

"Yes," Ellen said. "He runs that awful ad agency in the Pearl District."

"Son of a bitch." Jamie stood. Her adrenaline kicked in, her cheeks flushed, and her fists raised themselves in a fighting pose.

"Jamie, what's wrong?" asked Ellen.

"And the woman with him, that's George Green's wife?"

"It is," Ellen said, with a nod. "She is terrifying."

"Well, that woman hit Lisa with her car." Jamie picked up the license plate from where she'd left it under her seat. "And I have proof."

CHAPTER 14
BURN UNIT

Sue flipped through the pages of a year-old *Marie Claire*. As long as you're rich and anorexic, you can get away with wearing anything, she thought. Why do the eighties insist on coming back every five years? Fluorescent pink is simply not flattering. Ooh. I've been looking for a new red heel and in such a lovely suede.

The glossy ad reminded her of a pair the Burnam & Green CFO had worn to the agency holiday party. She ripped out the page and tucked it in her purse for future reference. She pulled out a small bottle of antibacterial gel and rubbed a dab on her hands to shield herself from the germs of the sick and maimed who may have handled the magazine. She considered offering the bottle to George, but he was covered in soot. It would just make him more of a mess.

Sue had only meant to burn a few of his favorite things. She started with the ADDY Award he kept on his bedside table and his smartphone, but she only succeeded in charring them, creating a small cloud of toxic gas in the process. Instead she tossed them out the window, where each met the sidewalk with a satisfying crunch. His clothing burned with ease. Flaming French-cuff dress shirts, vintage T-shirts, and raw denim jeans all floated down to the street, each filling her heart with the warm glow of revenge. The fool tried to save them.

George shifted in his seat, and she glared at him, another insult on the tip of her tongue. Then she noticed that his eyes were no longer downcast with the self-loathing and regret she so enjoyed. He was alert and staring across the room. Suddenly, he cursed under his breath.

"What now?" she asked loudly, annoyed.

"Sue. Be quiet. We need to get out of here," he whispered back.

"What? No. You're burned and in pain, and as much as that fills me with joy, you need medical attention." She flipped her hair over her shoulder and shrugged. "We aren't going anywhere."

"Shush. Look over there," George said urgently.

Sue glanced over at three people across the waiting room. "Oh! Is that the mayor? You should go say hi," she said.

He looked at his wife, aghast.

"Look again," he hissed.

She looked again. Mayor Salder appeared as perfect and photo-op-ready as ever, and the other two young women: one in a tight green cocktail dress (Very inappropriate attire for a hospital) and the second in a wheelchair. Despite the scrubs, the girl looked familiar. She turned back to George. "You idiot. It's your little tramp. Why did you tell me to take you to this hospital?"

"We need to get out of here," he repeated.

She looked at the girl. She looked at the mayor. Their eyes were the same, and there was a certain similarity in the angle at which they held their heads as they both turned to look at George and Sue.

"I think they're related," she said, very quietly.

"She must be the mayor's daughter, Lisa," said George. "I would have paid a lot more than a grand if I'd known that."

"What do you mean, 'paid'?"

"She's a prostitute."

"No," said Sue.

"Yeah. But she got sick. When it comes right down to it, I really just paid her to vomit in the guest bathroom for an hour."

"George, that is disgusting."

"I know," he agreed, then understood her meaning. "It wasn't like that. No one is into that. Are they?"

Suddenly, the girl in the tight cocktail dress rushed at them in an angry flash of sparkles. "Mr. and Mrs. Green, I found something of yours." She brandished a bent license plate that read SUE ME, and pointed to a tiny piece of gold fabric hanging on the corner. "It was lying right next to my best friend. Who you left alone on a park bench. In the middle of the night. With a head injury. After you hit her with your car! What is wrong with you?"

Sue's heart raced. Oh my god, she thought. Why did I tempt fate with that stupid vanity plate? Now I'm going to jail, and it's my nit-wit husband's fault.

Mayor Salder approached them, her heels tapping across the floor. She stopped and stared at Sue. The mayor's eyes seemed to drill right into Sue's soul. "Jamie," she said to the girl, "why don't you let me handle this?"

Sue tried to stand but suddenly felt too weak. So much for the fifty thousand squats she'd done over the last year. She blurted out, "Your daughter is a prostitute. George paid her for sex."

"No, she's not," said Jamie. "And what difference does it make anyway? She's a human being. You don't leave injured people alone, you morons."

"And I didn't run her over. Technically, she hit her head running away from me," said Sue, panicking. "So really, it was her own fault. Plus, George said that she looked fine. If we'd known she was in such bad shape, we wouldn't have left her there. Right, George?" She elbowed her husband.

George added quickly, "I did call an ambulance, but they told me she was gone by the time they arrived."

"What upstanding citizens you both are," said Mayor Salder in a biting voice.

Sue's anger flared. How dare this woman judge her. "Well, I caught your little spawn turning tricks in my own house," exclaimed Sue, pointing at Lisa. "If that got out, it would ruin you." Sue's voice gained strength. "You'd be impeached. Like Nixon. Ellen Salder—the once-great ex-mayor of Portland with a prostitute for a daughter."

"Mayors aren't impeached. They resign. And my career has survived worse."

"I doubt that," said Sue.

"Let's call the cops," said Jamie eagerly.

"Can you all stop yelling, please?" said Lisa. She stood up from her wheelchair and slowly walked toward them, grabbing the backs of chairs for support.

The little tramp wasn't looking so great now, thought Sue. Her hair was limp against her head, and the sickly blue color of the scrubs wasn't doing her any favors.

Lisa pulled a few items from a plastic bag she carried, then dropped it on a nearby chair. She held out a crumpled wad of cash to George and offered Sue a red shoe. Suddenly the room was silent except for the hum of a vending machine in the corner.

Sue took the shoe in her hand. The upper was deep red, crafted from a supple suede leather, with a tiny silver Prada insignia pressed into the sole. It was small, pointy, and aggressive, with a four-inch stiletto heel, and it was a size six. Sue wore a size nine. "This isn't my shoe," Sue said.

"It's not mine, either," said Lisa. "I picked it up by accident with my dress."

They both looked at George, whose face had assumed a look of barely feigned innocence.

"Honey," he said to Sue. "It's not what it looks like."

Sue stood, gripped the shoe tightly in her hand, and walked toward the exit just as George's name was finally called. She turned back and said to the nurse, "Can you please tell the doctor that my husband is allergic to painkillers?"

"Of course," answered the nurse. "Which ones?"

"All of them." And with that, the doors whooshed open, and Sue walked out.

CHAPTER 15
MOTHER & DAUGHTER

Lisa still held the crumpled wad of bills in her hand. "I'd like you to take the money back," she said to George.

"You can use it to pay your divorce lawyer," added Jamie in a cheery voice.

Lisa shot her a you're-not-helping look.

George ignored them both and stumbled over to the large window that faced the emergency room's small parking lot. He pressed his hands against the glass as his wife sped off with a squeal of tires. "She'll be back," he said. "She always comes back."

"Dude, I wouldn't hold your breath," said Jamie.

The nurse stood waiting. "Mr. Green, the doctor will see you now."

He turned and looked at her as though puzzled by who she was or what she wanted.

"Mr. Green, do you have your completed form?" she asked.

He looked toward the exit with longing, and then back at the nurse. He walked slowly to his wife's vacant chair and picked up the clipboard with his good hand. "Yes, here it is. My wife filled it out for me." He looked at the sheet sadly, then handed it to the nurse.

The nurse looked it over and ticked a box with the attached ball point pen. "I'll just mark you as allergic to painkillers, and we're all ready to go. This way, please."

Weakly, George started to protest, but the nurse had already disappeared through the double doors. He followed, his bare feet leaving a trail of smudged, ashy footprints in his wake.

"I'd almost feel bad for the guy if he weren't such a creep," said Jamie.

"Indeed," said Ellen. "George Green has quite the reputation. I guess I shouldn't be too surprised my daughter is mixed up with him."

Zero to sixty in two seconds, thought Lisa. That's how fast my mother fills me with rage. She forced herself to not talk back and spoke to Jamie instead. "So what should I do with the money?" Despite her sad financial situation, deep down she wanted to burn it.

"I'll take care of it," said Ellen, picking the bills out of Lisa's hand.

"Fine." Lisa wiped her hands on her scrubs, relieved to have it gone. If anyone knew how to make embarrassing evidence disappear, it was her mother.

"And the license plate," Ellen added to Jamie.

"No way," said Jamie. "I'm holding on to this baby. I'm hanging it above the front door as warning for young ladies to stay on the straight and narrow."

"Hilarious," said Lisa.

"Jamie, please," continued her mother, holding out her hand.

Reluctantly, Jamie handed over the license plate. "Are you going to take it to the police? You should take Lisa's clothes too." She picked up the plastic bag with Lisa's torn cocktail dress. "You can have the CSI team analyze it, the license plate, and Sue's car. Oh god, what if Sue goes to a car wash or a twenty-four-hour emergency auto mechanic? Or she might flee the country. She's probably halfway to Canada by now."

Ellen took the bag and tucked the license plate and money into it, then turned to Lisa. "Dear, I think you'll agree that involving the police will only complicate matters further."

"For once, I do agree with you, Mother," said Lisa.

"Are you kidding?" asked Jamie looking from one to the other. "No, no, no. We want revenge, retribution, reprisals."

"Jamie, I just want this all to go away. I want to forget it ever happened," said Lisa.

"Lisa, that woman tried to murder you."

"It was just a stupid accident. I'm fine now. Can we go home?"

"Yes," said Ellen. "I think a few days at home would be good for you. Your room is just as you left it. Well, except that it's clean of course."

Lisa glared at her. "Not your home, Mother. Mine." Lisa felt a wave of dizziness. She grasped the back of a chair until her head cleared, and with as much dignity as she could muster—dressed as she was in scrubs and hospital slippers—she straightened her back and walked determinedly past her mother toward the hospital's exit. "Jamie, let's go."

"Young lady, the best place for you right now is with me. You need to be properly taken care of."

Lisa turned and faced Ellen. "You don't get to tell me what to do anymore. I'm not a child."

"It doesn't appear that way to me."

"How dare . . ." The rush of anger she felt at her mother's insult knocked her off-balance again. Her knees felt like they were about to give out.

Jamie rushed to Lisa's side and grasped her around the waist to help steady her. Lisa put her arm over Jamie's shoulders.

"Stop it, both of you," said Jamie. "This is ridiculous. Mayor Salder, do you have a car?"

"Of course. It's just outside."

"Can you give us a ride?" Jamie asked. "Lisa will be fine at our apartment. Please. Don't make this any worse."

For a moment, Ellen looked on the verge of lashing out at Jamie, and Lisa could feel her friend bracing for an onslaught. To Lisa's astonishment, her mother held back her words. She twisted her wedding ring around her finger a few times, and her anger seemed to subside. Lisa saw a look she'd never imagined would appear on her mother's face: shame.

"Yes, of course I can give you a ride," Ellen said, her voice quiet and more in control. "Give me a moment to take care of Lisa's paperwork, and then we can go." She turned to the reception desk.

"What was that?" whispered Lisa. "Did my mother actually back down?"

"I think so. She told me she's in therapy for anger management."

"Seriously?"

"Yeah. Lisa, you should have seen her when she first walked in. She gave the poor receptionist hell." Jamie helped Lisa settle back into a chair, then sat down next to her. "I think your mom was really worried about you."

Lisa shook her head. "No. She's just protecting herself. Can't have her wayward daughter making her look bad. Hiding me from the public has been her mission in life since I was thirteen."

"Maybe," said Jamie thoughtfully. She turned to Lisa and looked at her closely. "Listen, are you sure you don't want to report this to the police? You obviously don't have to do anything your mom says."

Lisa nodded. "I'm sure."

"All right, you nut bar," said Jamie. "But if I ever see George and Sue again, they are going to suffer some seriously righteous indignation courtesy of *moi*."

"Fortunately, the chances we'll run into them again are slim to none," said Lisa as she rested her head on Jamie's shoulder and closed her eyes.

A few minutes later, they followed Ellen out to the emergency room parking lot toward a black sedan. Jamie opened the door for Lisa, and they both settled into the back seat. As Lisa closed her eyes, she heard Jamie give her mother directions to their apartment.

She must have dozed off because in what felt like seconds, Jamie tapped her on the shoulder, and Lisa saw that the car had pulled up in front of their building. Shaking off her drowsiness, she stepped out of the car, took Jamie's arm, and headed up the concrete stairs.

Uninvited, Ellen followed them inside. Together they walked in silence up the three flights, and with each creak of the old floorboards, Lisa saw her home through her mother's eyes. The apartment door with its unconvincing display of deadbolts. The cramped kitchen and tiny bathroom with barely enough space to turn around. And down the dimly lit hall, a pair of bedrooms. The first was Jamie's, a room smaller than her mother's walk-in closet. The second was Lisa's. It had once been a small living room, complete with a dormant fireplace and built-in cabinets. Lisa walked directly there without a word and closed her door firmly. She sat on her neatly made bed and smoothed the blanket with her hand, glad to be home, surrounded by things she loved. She lay back and sunk into her pillow. Her head ached, and she longed for more painkillers but couldn't bear the thought of getting up to fetch them. She could hear Jamie and her mother talking quietly in the kitchen and mercifully couldn't make out their words.

Lisa heard a knock at her door, and it opened immediately, the intruder not waiting for permission. Ellen entered with two cups of tea and a bottle of Tylenol tucked under her arm. Lisa sat up stiffly and wrapped her arms around her chest. She thought about calling for Jamie, though she knew her friend was probably listening from her room next door, ready to bust in if Lisa needed her.

"I just wanted to make sure you were settled in for the night," said her mother stiffly. She set down both cups on Lisa's bedside table, then opened the bottle of painkillers, handing Lisa two pills.

"Thanks," said Lisa. She gazed at the tablets in her hand for a moment before swallowing them with a sip of tea. They dissolved slightly on her tongue when they made contact with the hot liquid, leaving a bitter taste in her mouth.

"So, this is your room," said Ellen. "It's so . . . clean."

Lisa's tidy habits were an unexpected relic from the Academy, where the staff enforced strict rules about cleanliness and organization for the simple reason that it made inspections easier. It was tough to hide contraband like cigarettes, ramen noodles, and cell phones in a spare and spotless room. She'd kept her space at the Kims' house just as neat. After moving into the apartment with Jamie, Lisa had toyed with returning to her slovenly ways, but she found that a messy bed and unfolded clothes were no longer tolerable.

Yet disorder reigned at her work desk and easel. Colored pencils, charcoals, watercolors, oil paints, sketchbooks, and canvases littered the space. A piece of white newsprint was tacked on her easel, and her favorite subject, Mount Hood, was just coming into focus. Strokes of thick charcoal pencil were hinting at deep crevices and tall craggy peaks. She was obsessed with the view of the mountain from Lost Lake and even now, years later, couldn't let it go.

"Yeah. Nothing like my old room," said Lisa. "What have you done with it? Filled it with interns and turned into your reelection headquarters?"

"No. As I said at the hospital, it's still yours. Everything is just the same." Ellen walked around the small space. A family photo on Lisa's dresser caught her attention. "We all look so young. Even your father," she said. She touched the frame lightly, then continued her examination, looking at the crowded walls, taking a closer look at one or two of the paintings. "Just like your bedroom, every inch of wall covered with artwork." Her mother smiled wistfully and cleared off a small chair next to the fireplace. She sat, wiping a tear from her eye. "I kept every picture in place, just as you left it."

Lisa thought for a moment about showing mercy. She could let her mother have her moment of nostalgia, let her cry a little bit over her daughter and the room she kept like a memorial to her lost motherhood, but why?

"You should throw it all in the trash like you did with Dad's stuff."

Her mother looked up, shocked. "That's not fair."

"You erased him," said Lisa, her eyes filling with tears. She'd only been home once since returning from the Academy. She'd arrived to her mother's lukewarm welcome and wandered around the rooms. Something felt very wrong, then she realized what it was. All of her father's belongings were gone. His office had been emptied out. Even gifts Lisa had given him had disappeared. She'd asked why. Her mother offered no explanation. Disgusted, she walked out of that house without another word, silently vowing to never return.

"He wasn't the man you thought he was."

"Mom, what is that supposed to mean?"

Her mother sighed. "Just that sometimes you don't really know the people closest to you."

Lisa wasn't falling for it. "Or how far they're willing to go to protect themselves."

"What do you mean by that?" asked Ellen sharply.

"I learned a fun fact tonight from George Green. He said you used me for the sympathy vote after Dad died. You told the press I was off at some boarding school in Europe and couldn't be bothered to come home for my own father's funeral."

"I did no such thing."

"Then where the hell did he get that idea?"

"Language, young lady. When the press asked, I was simply vague. I said you were away at school and let them assume the rest. It was for your own good. I didn't want you exposed to that media circus."

"So you just left me there."

"Of course I wanted you at home. But you were doing so much better. You were safe at the boarding school. They had therapists and a support system in place."

"The 'boarding school,'" said Lisa sarcastically. "I hate when you call it that. The only support I got was a pamphlet on surviving my grief. If it weren't for Patrick and Jamie, I would have been completely alone."

"Dr. Nobile said that if you left, it could harm your recovery. I wasn't going to put you at risk."

"You do realize the Lost Lake Academy was a complete scam, right? How did you even hear about it?"

Her mother closed her eyes and rubbed her forehead. "I saw an ad in a magazine. A colleague of your father's recommended it too. He said that he'd had great luck sending his son there. He'd visited and thought the facilities adequate, the staff competent and their methods sound. I took him at his word."

"Sound methods?" Lisa's voice rose along with her anger. "You had them send masked men to pull me from my bed. I thought I was going to be murdered."

Ellen shrugged helplessly. "I was afraid if your father and I told you about the school, you'd run away again. It seemed like the only option."

"I never ran away. I just borrowed your car. And you called the cops on me."

"And thank god I did. Who knows what that hitchhiker you picked up would have done to you."

The bedroom door swung open. Jamie stood in the doorway dressed in pink pajamas and wearing a thick, green mud mask on her face. "Everything all right?" she asked brightly. "It's getting a little loud in here."

Ellen looked at Jamie for a long moment. "I should go." She paused at the door. "I'll pick you up in the morning. We'll have brunch."

Before Lisa could protest, her mother had swept out of the room, down the hall, and closed the front door solidly behind her. Lisa listened as her mother's heels echoed aggressively down all three flights.

"How did you do that?" asked Lisa.

"What?"

"That thing with my mom. You show up and she starts acting human. It's amazing. I am never spending a minute alone with her again."

"As long as every future encounter includes her buying us a meal, I'm cool with it."

Jamie sat down next to Lisa on the bed. "Are you okay?"

"As I'll ever be," said Lisa.

"Let's get some sleep then. I'll see you in the morning. Love you." Jamie got up, flipped off the light, and closed the door quietly behind her.

"Love you too," said Lisa, and closed her eyes.

CHAPTER 16
WAKE UP

Lisa dreamt of coffee. She could smell it, almost taste it. In her dream, she was wrapped in a blanket, lying on a lumpy sofa in a cafe. A woman with a wicked grin and hair sharp as needles turned toward her. It was Sue Green, and she held a cup of coffee topped with a small foam mountain. Storm clouds swirled above it in turmoil and flashed tiny bolts of lightning. "Lisa! Watch out!" called Patrick from where he stood at the bar pouring martinis. Lisa turned back to Sue. The woman floated toward her and Lisa struggled to free herself, but the blanket held her down, its warmth and weight trapping her. She couldn't move, could barely breathe. Sue tossed the coffee at Lisa's face, the black liquid slowly drifting in space.

"Lisa, wake up."

Lisa woke with a gasp and untangled herself from her thin blanket.

Jamie sat perched on the edge of her bed. "Good morning, sunshine. How are you feeling?"

An image of a shirtless George popped into her head. Lisa groaned and covered her face with a pillow.

"I brought you coffee. Drink up."

"Will you smother me?" asked Lisa, her voice muffled by the pillow.

"No." Jamie pulled the pillow off Lisa's face and tossed it aside.

"Jamie, what is wrong with me?" she asked.

"The usual things. Impulse control issues. Possible substance abuse problems. Generalized anxiety. And most recently—sexual deviance. Just your average twenty-something with an over-controlling mother."

"Can I blame her for everything?"

"Absolutely," said Jamie. "And, speaking of your mother, she texted that she's on her way here. She was not kidding about breakfast."

"No . . ." groaned Lisa as she pulled the pillow back over her face.

"So you best get up and get ready. Also, I'm really hungry, so I'll be joining your special mother-daughter brunch because I assume your mother will pay the bill."

"Just five more minutes."

"Right on. Take your time. I'm sure your mother won't mind waiting downstairs. She seems like such a patient and reasonable woman," said Jamie, leaving the room.

Lisa pushed the pillow aside, sat up, and took a sip of coffee. She felt achy and grimy and she needed a shower.

She lay back down and closed her eyes, feeling a vague sense of déjà vu. Another place, another time, another fateful meeting with her mother.

Ⓨ

The day had started well enough with an invitation from Patrick to sit by the lake after fourth period. A light breeze churned the water, causing the dock to sway gently beneath her. She felt the rough, weathered boards through the threadbare bath towel she lay on. Sleepily, she wondered how many students the cloth had dried during its life at the Academy, and she imagined particles of those lives seeping into her body.

She opened her eyes and leaned back on her elbows. The sky was a startling blue, for once devoid of clouds. Dragonflies danced along the lake's surface, darting into reeds that bordered the shoreline, hunting tiny prey. The mountain rose before her, dominating the view, its mirror image visible on the lake's surface. She pressed her index finger to her leg, testing. Its pink surface tingled with pinpricks of pain that would lead to the inevitable sunburn and peeling skin. She should have put on sunscreen, but it would have taken so much effort.

Turning over onto her stomach, she lowered her head onto her crossed arms and glanced over at Patrick, who lay on his back beside her.

He held up a tattered paperback of *On the Road* with both hands like a shield against the sun's rays. "Let's steal Bob the Nob's car. We'll hit the road and drive to San Francisco like Kerouac."

"Bob drives a Nissan Sentra," said Lisa.

"I know. Sweet ride."

"There is nothing sweet about that sad, rusty excuse for a car. We wouldn't make it past Eugene."

"Listen to this," said Patrick, squinting at the well-thumbed page. He read aloud: "'I was surprised, as always, how easy the act of leaving was, and how good it felt. The world was suddenly rich with possibility.'" He turned onto his side and smiled at her.

The breeze drifted Patrick's dark hair over his eyes, and she brushed it gently away. On most days, the Academy felt like a prison, but in this moment Lisa felt almost like an ordinary girl enjoying a sunny afternoon with her crush. She'd resisted Patrick at first. He was such a dork, she kept telling herself, always going on about sci-fi movies she'd never heard of and pulling crazy stunts like the one in the gym to get her attention. And she had a boyfriend back home, Garrett, a tattooed twenty-two-year-old with a dented Harley motorcycle that he called vintage but was really just junk. As the weeks turned to months and her letters to Garrett went unanswered, she started hanging with Patrick. They hadn't even kissed yet. It wasn't as if the school discouraged it. The counselors turned a blind eye to sex between students.

If only her mother knew what really happened here.

With a sudden rush of air, a clump of mud sailed overhead and splashed down between them.

"What the hell," protested Patrick. He jumped to his feet and narrowly dodged a second projectile.

Lisa sat up and wiped the mud from her legs. Looking back toward the shore, she saw a pack of kids preparing another onslaught.

"This is our dock," yelled a short, stocky kid named Willy. His pudgy fists rested on his hips in righteous indignation. Five cohorts stood behind their ringleader, their faces cocksure and confident.

"The hell it is, you little shits," yelled Patrick.

"You have to leave. We have seniority, you pathetic worm," said Willy.

Encouraged by Willy's bold words, his counterparts hurled more mud, this time hitting Patrick's book. Patrick threw it down angrily and charged at them, but the boys held their ground.

"Patrick, stop," begged Lisa, knowing they had no choice but to leave the dock to the kids. Some of these boys had been at the school since they were ten years old. Now thirteen or fourteen, the school's twisted system of hierarchy meant they had seniority over older students like Lisa and Patrick. The longer you were stuck at the Academy, the more levels you passed, the more "in agreement" you were with the staff. Each level attained equaled more privileges and more power over your peers.

They're a bunch of chubby sociopaths, thought Lisa. She wondered when the school's sadistic practices would finally drive her to their level of madness. She picked up the paperback from where Patrick had flung it on the dock and tried to wipe off the mud with her towel. It was pointless. The book was ruined.

She looked up and saw with dread two of the school's security staff rushing toward them from the main campus. Lisa had a hard time remembering the staff's names as turnover at the school was so high, but she thought the pair were called Dwayne and Stanley. The little pack of monsters had probably given them a heads up.

"Patrick, stop it. We have to get out of here." She pointed at the men stumbling down a stone pathway toward the lake. Patrick was too angry to hear. He was twisting Willy's arm as the boy yelped in pain.

Dwayne reached them first, breathing heavily from exertion. He doubled over, trying to catch his breath, his chest heaving up and down painfully. He was dressed in a bright blue polo shirt with Lost Lake Academy stitched on the left breast and a pair of khaki cargo shorts sporting massive pockets stuffed with gear. "Let Willy go," he said to Patrick between desperate gulps of air.

"They threw mud at me and my girlfriend," said Patrick angrily, still holding Willy roughly.

"Let him go, and we'll talk about this."

"He's hurting me!" screamed Willy. "We didn't do anything wrong."

"The little shit is lying," said Patrick, tightening his grip.

"We don't tolerate that kind of language," said Dwayne.

Stanley, dressed in a green polo and faded jeans, finally caught up, his thin, flushed face covered in a sheen of sweat. "What's going on?" he asked Dwayne angrily.

"Dude, take it easy, I just got here too," he said.

"Get this situation under control now," said Stanley, obviously thinking he was in charge.

Dwayne looked at Patrick uncertainly. Patrick was several inches taller and in much better shape. Slowly, the man reached into a pocket and pulled out a Taser. He pressed the trigger, and it made a menacing crackling sound. The kids circled around them, taunting Patrick and cheering on Dwayne.

"Patrick, please, let Willy go," pleaded Lisa. "It was just a little mud."

Patrick looked at her, then back toward the men. "Fine, I surrender." He released Willy and held both hands up. The pair tackled him to the ground.

"Just you wait, you little motherless fuckwits," yelled Patrick at the boys. "You'll regret this."

Lisa clutched the muddy book tightly to her chest, and watched the men drag Patrick away. She guessed they'd drop him in the hole for "self-study." It would be his third time. He didn't speak to anyone for a week after the first. She noticed suddenly that the little cretins had crept up and surrounded her.

Willy spoke. "What's wrong, hottie?"

Another kid named Martin said, "You don't have to leave. Stay with us."

They were all at least a foot shorter than she was, but there were too many of them. Unloved creatures, abandoned by family, allowed to roam this hideous place with impunity, as long as they followed the ridiculous rules set out by the school administrators. One, John, was even from her peer group, and she tried to catch his eye, but he wouldn't meet her gaze. She'd make him pay later. He'd confessed to her during their "truth counseling" session that he regularly stole jars of mayo from the cafeteria and ate it like ice cream. She'd report him to the staff, and he'd get his. Her eyes darted around, looking for a way out.

"We'll cheer you up," said Willy, his hand roughly grabbing her arm. She slapped him away and started up the hill back toward the main school grounds.

Someone still out of sight was calling her name.

"I'm telling Dr. Bob that you're out of agreement," said a boy behind her.

"Go to hell," she said, not looking back. She kept along the path, leaving the lost boys behind her. She looked for whoever had called her name and saw with relief it was Jamie. Having Jamie in her peer group was the only thing, besides Patrick, that made the Academy remotely tolerable.

"Why aren't you ready?" Jamie asked as she reached Lisa.

"Ready for what?" asked Lisa, feeling confused. She looked behind her to make sure the boys hadn't followed.

"It's visiting day," said Jamie urgently.

"So?" Lisa just wanted to head back to the girls' dorm, lie down on her twin bed, drift off, and forget everything for a few precious hours.

"Well, your mom is here. Why are you covered in mud? Anyway, I was talking with my parents and my brother Roderick, and I saw this woman. She was so pissed, yelling at the staff, asking why her daughter wasn't waiting for her. She was seriously giving them hell, and then she said your name, and I took a closer look at her and could totally see the resemblance." Jamie rattled on, not noticing that Lisa had slumped down and was sitting on the ground. "What are you doing down there?" she asked.

Lisa looked up at Jamie, not quite able to breathe. She whispered, "Who?"

"Your mother."

Lisa felt nauseous. "My mom can't see me like this. She'll never let me come home if I look like this." Lisa brushed at her mud-spattered tank top and shorts, vainly trying to wipe away the stains. She pulled a clump of dirt from her short, messy hair. It was hopeless. She felt naked, raw, and powerless. Tears spilled down her face as she cried for her lost life, for her father who was too scared to stand up for her, for all the stupid shit she'd pulled to make her mom believe this horrible school was the only way to deal with her sad excuse for a daughter.

Jamie knelt next to her. "You don't have to see her, you know." She gently patted Lisa's back as a few more helpless sobs escaped. "You have a choice."

Lisa lifted her eyes to Jamie's. "I wish I did, Jamie. I really wish I did."

Y

And now, her mother was back. For a moment Lisa felt as helpless as ever. Angrily, she wiped away her tears and got out of bed. Hell if her mother was going to have that kind of power over her again. This time would be different.

Pulling on her old flannel robe, she headed to the bathroom. She turned on the water in the shower to let it heat up and examined her face in the bathroom mirror. The bump on her forehead had turned a sickly shade of purple. Lovely. At least she hadn't needed stitches. She'd only have emotional scars.

Boohoo, she thought as she stepped into the shower, it's all my own damn fault.

Minutes later she was clean and dressed in a T-shirt, shorts, and flip flops. She pulled her wet hair into a pony tail and gently dotted some cover-up on her forehead and around her eye.

"Nice shiner," said Jamie, squeezing into the bathroom next to her.

"Thanks, friend."

"My phone is about to explode from the twenty texts your mother sent in the last minute." Jamie's phone buzzed again. "She is seriously going to lose her mind if we don't get downstairs now."

They headed down the creaky wooden steps to the lobby where a fake ficus tree sat dusty and forlorn in a corner. A row of mailboxes full of flyers and junk mail was fitted in one wall, and a faded mural of Mount Hood adorned the wall opposite. Over the years, tenants of varying artistic skill had embellished the wall with flourishes of their own, some philosophical, some political, some making commentary on the landlord's lack of prowess as a lover. Oddly, said landlord had never made an effort to alter or fix the painting. As Lisa and Jamie passed the mural, they smacked the mountain with their palms for luck.

"Are you ready?" asked Jamie.

"As I'll ever be," said Lisa.

CHAPTER 17
MEMORY LANE

Ellen sent another impatient text just as the two girls spilled out of the front door of their apartment building, chatting and laughing. They looked like they'd just stepped out of a tampon commercial. Fun, active, adventurous young women without a care in the world. Both fell silent when they spotted her BMW.

Youth is wasted on the young, she thought. An overused adage, yet so true.

The girls piled into the car, Jamie in front, Lisa in back, as though they'd already discussed seating arrangements.

"Good morning, Mayor Salder," said Jamie brightly.

Such a polite young woman, thought Ellen. A little rough around the edges, but at least she had manners. "Good morning, girls," she said, as she put the vehicle into drive. "How does Screen Door sound?"

Lisa snorted from the back seat. "Great, but we'll never get a table."

"Don't worry, dear, it won't be a problem." She turned the radio to a classical station, setting the volume just loud enough to discourage conversation. There'd be time enough for talk at the restaurant. As she drove, her mind wandered to another drive, on a winding mountain road far from the congested streets of Portland.

Υ

The boarding school was located just three hours east of the city, though it felt a world away. The last leg of the journey required navigating hairpin turns through miles of state forest roads. Dizzying glimpses of Mount Hood loomed unexpectedly around sharp corners, and Ellen's stomach twisted nervously with each curve. She couldn't deny that part of the upset was anxiety at seeing her daughter for the first time in months. Her campaign for mayor was going well, and with her polling numbers looking solid, she'd finally had time for the trip. Ben had asked to join her. Ellen refused, feeling it best that she visit alone. She had a decision to make. His presence wouldn't help matters. And, she no longer trusted Ben after how he'd betrayed her.

The GPS announced her arrival, and she pulled up to a security gate and gave her name. The guard directed her to the guest lot. She parked and inspected the scene.

The lot was situated slightly above the small valley where the school sat, and it offered a panorama of the entire campus. She recalled the basic layout from the materials she'd received after first inquiring about the school. She'd spotted the ad in *Sunset Magazine* on a flight to Los Angeles. "Lost Lake Academy for Troubled Youth," it had read above a color photo of smiling boys and girls being guided by responsible-looking adults. She remembered the moment clearly. She'd ripped the page out and leaned back in her seat, fantasizing about handing over the responsibility of Lisa to competent professionals.

Deep in her heart of hearts, where she rarely went, she hid a truth she'd never admitted to anyone. Not her husband, not even her therapist. Ellen had never really wanted children. The mere thought of having a child made her feel trapped. She remembered babysitting as a teenager and being so infinitely bored by the repetitive games, the constant necessity of care. But her husband had wanted children so badly and he finally convinced her. Ben even promised he'd dedicate himself to raising them. After all, it was what everyone expected. It wasn't normal to not have children. She'd never succeed at her political ambitions if she weren't a mother. The pundits would call her mannish, selfish, and unwomanly.

Throughout her pregnancy, she worked just as hard, was just as driven, and she made partner at her law firm the day before her water broke. Despite her misgivings, when she finally held Lisa in her arms after nine months of nausea, bizarre cravings, an aching back, and twenty hours of labor, she'd immediately felt a fierce protective instinct, knowing she'd give up her own life for her daughter's.

Good to his word, Ben took an extended leave from his law firm to raise Lisa, only going back to work after she was in grade school. And what a mess he'd made of it. No discipline, no repercussions for any mischief or misdeeds. He always took Lisa's side, defending every broken rule as an expression of creativity, saying that she was simply pushing boundaries.

Sometimes Ellen woke late at night and knew she'd made the wrong decision. Maybe her husband was right. Maybe Lisa should come home. Then she'd get up in the morning, and during her day, something would remind her why she'd made her choice. A motorcycle roaring by on the freeway would trigger a memory— Lisa driving away on the back of her boyfriend's bike the day she'd returned home from rehab. Ellen had been so angry. She'd screamed at Lisa that she was ruining her life, throwing it all away on boys, drinking, and drugs. She'd felt the eyes of the entire neighborhood watching their family drama play out. Ben didn't help. He kept on repeating that it was just a phase, that it would pass, and Lisa was a good girl, capable of great things. Lisa just needed to know that they both believed in her. Ellen didn't agree.

Then Lisa stole Ellen's car. The girl wouldn't answer her cell phone, and Ellen had no choice but to call the police. Lisa, her boyfriend, and a hitchhiker they'd picked up were finally arrested just outside Eugene. Her daughter spent a night in juvenile hall. What really took years off Ellen's life was that the hitchhiker was a known felon, wanted for assault. She called the Academy the next day and put down a deposit.

Ellen looked over the valley. The massive hulk of Mount Hood was reflected in the crystal blue lake at the far end of campus. She could see a group of teenagers playing on a sliver of golden beach and a wooden dock that extended out into the lake. She wondered if Lisa could be among them, enjoying the beautiful sunny day.

Situated on either side of the lake were the co-ed dorms, with beds for fifty girls and fifty boys. She wondered how Lisa was doing sharing a room. Ellen thought of the easy, privileged life she'd given her daughter. She hoped the girl had finally learned to appreciate it, now that it was out of reach.

Closer in sat a cluster of classrooms, the gymnasium, a baseball diamond, and tennis courts. Finally, her eyes rested appreciatively on the massive lodge described in the literature as "the heart of the school, where students gather to share their dreams and hopes for the future." It reminded her of a set of Lincoln Logs that Lisa had played with during happier times. Ellen imagined pushing the building aside, and seeing the logs spill out over the brilliant green carpet of the old-growth forest that bordered the grounds.

Ellen opened the car door. When she'd left the city, the temperature had been in the mid-eighties, so she was surprised to find the air outside was crisp and smelled of pine with whispers of wood smoke. She grabbed a cardigan from the passenger seat and pulled it on as she walked across the lot toward the lodge.

Something caught her eye. Ellen followed the line of a high fence that she'd passed through when entering the parking lot, and saw it extended all around the property. It was topped with razor wire and had video cameras positioned at key vantage points. She felt a sense of déjà vu. She shrugged it off and continued on her way. Suddenly she realized the source of the feeling. She'd taken a tour of a state-of-the-art minimum-security penitentiary a few months ago. The facility had a similar fence and the same type of camera. The school was nothing like that, she told herself. Surely, the fence was as much to keep people out as to keep the children in. She felt a small twinge of nausea but convinced herself it was simply from the drive.

Ellen walked from the parking lot down a wide gravel path toward the lodge entrance. She pulled open the heavy wooden door and stepped into a great room with soaring beams and leaded windows. An entire wall was given over to a massive fireplace of rough-hewn stone. Throughout the room, leather sofas and armchairs were grouped companionably around craftsman coffee tables.

On the surface, it was every bit as impressive as the school's literature described. Yet Ellen was surprised by how quiet and chilly the room felt. She'd expected a roaring blaze in the hearth, a room full of excited children meeting with parents, teachers, and counselors. Instead, the yawning grate was empty and cold, and there were only unsmiling children grasping their parent's hands or sitting silently.

The only moment of levity came from a girl and boy, both with jet-black hair, who sat talking animatedly with their parents. The quartet suddenly erupted with laughter, their guffaws echoing around the otherwise hushed room.

Ellen glared at them and then looked around, but saw no sign of her daughter. Lisa should be here, waiting for her. She stepped toward a reception area to the left of the entrance. Behind it was a door marked Staff Only. A young woman with mousey brown hair sat at a desk tapping furiously at a computer keyboard. She was wearing a gray polo with the Lost Lake insignia and a name tag that read Tammy. Tammy paused her typing and kept her fingers poised on the keyboard as she looked up at Ellen with a bright smile.

"Good morning and welcome to the Lost Lake Academy, where your child's future grows brighter each day. How may I help you?" Tammy stated her greeting carefully, as though she'd rehearsed it.

"I'm looking for my daughter, Lisa Salder."

"Is she a student here?"

Ellen decided she didn't like Tammy. "Yes. She's a student here. Her name is Lisa Salder," she repeated impatiently. "Why isn't she waiting for me?"

"One of our counselors can go find her."

Ellen paused, feeling her irritation grow. "What do you mean, find her? This is a school for troubled teens. Are you telling me you don't know where the students are at all times?" Ellen paused. The already quiet hall had grown completely silent, and she realized the entire room was listening to her tirade.

Well, let them, she thought. It felt good to vent.

A door behind Tammy's desk opened, and a man appeared. He held out his hand and shook Ellen's vigorously. "Mrs. Salder, it's such an honor to finally meet you. I'm Dr. Robert Nobile."

Dr. Nobile wore a comfortably worn-in tweed jacket with leather patches at the elbows. His hair was dark and speckled with gray, and his tanned skin spoke of days taking his young wards on vigorous hikes through the surrounding wilderness.

Finally, thought Ellen, someone who lived up to her impression of the school.

Ellen followed him through the door, down a hallway, and entered a large wood-paneled office, lined with bookshelves filled with leather-bound volumes. Official documents hung in frames behind a large desk, lauding Dr. Nobile with educational certifications from prestigious-looking universities. Ellen glanced at them but didn't recognize any of the institutions.

"Please excuse Tammy, it's only her second day," he continued.

"It should be her last," said Ellen. She would never put up with that level of incompetence from her staff.

Dr. Nobile nodded, and said, "Perhaps. Now, about your daughter, why don't we get caught up on her progress."

Ellen smiled at him gratefully. "Yes, let's."

"Have a seat," he said, pointing to a pair of brown leather armchairs opposite his desk. "Can I have Tammy fetch you some coffee or tea?"

"Thank you, Dr. Nobile, but I'm fine," said Ellen as she settled into a chair.

"Please call me Dr. Bob. That's what all the young people call me, and it just makes everyone feel a little more comfortable and at home." He stepped to a cabinet and pulled out a thick file with Lisa's name. He sat down at his desk, put on a pair of reading glasses, and began scanning the pages within. He looked up and met her eyes. "This is your first visit?"

"Yes," she said, feeling her shoulders rise defensively.

The doctor simply smiled and nodded, obviously not disturbed that Ellen hadn't been to visit her only child before today. He set the file aside, took off his glasses, and tucked them into his jacket's breast pocket. "Lisa has been doing fairly well. She's the kind of young person who really blossoms in the environment that the Academy provides."

"That's a relief to hear. She's always been so rebellious. I hope she hasn't been too much trouble."

"We've made a lot of progress dealing with her promiscuity. But, like most of our students who also have problems with drug and alcohol addiction, Lisa had a challenging first month. Her withdrawal symptoms were severe, though we offset that with wilderness therapy. We find that living off the land is an effective distraction from the more acute symptoms. Since you weren't able to submit a blood sample for us, we can only guess what drugs Lisa had been taking while she was living at home. Almost certainly MDMA and bath salts, and we can't rule out methamphetamines, LSD, cocaine, fentanyl, even heroin."

Ellen couldn't believe what she was hearing from Dr. Bob. "I'm aware that Lisa has experimented with drugs. Still, I have a hard time believing that she was on heroin or LSD while living under my roof."

Dr. Bob shook his head sadly. "It's easy for young people to get their hands on almost anything, particularly in a crime-filled city like Portland." He gave her a sympathetic look. "For the good of Lisa, we have to assume the worst, to guide her to her best self."

Ellen sat back in her chair, feeling suddenly exhausted by the drive and now Dr. Bob's evaluation. "I suppose that makes sense. Surely, she's doing better? It's been months."

"Yes, of course. However, there is still a lot of work to be done. Our challenge now is dealing with post-acute withdrawal."

"I'm not familiar with that term."

"These symptoms can be triggered by situations involving people, places, or things that remind Lisa of when she was doing drugs. That's why, Mrs. Salder, I would advise keeping Lisa enrolled at the Academy for a full year. Maybe longer."

"A year? She'll be eighteen next May. I'd imagined she'd leave by then and, god willing, head to college in the fall."

"We have a wonderful college-prep curriculum that will prepare her for university life. Though, honestly, I'm not confident she will be ready for that."

Ellen felt deflated. Lisa's tuition had already been such an expense. But if the school was making progress with her daughter where she'd only experienced failure, how could she say no?

Dr. Bob's phone rang. "I need to take this," he said.

"Of course."

He held the receiver to his ear and listened for a moment. "Excellent. Yes, please send her in." He hung up and smiled at Ellen. "You'll be happy to hear your daughter just made it to the lodge. It turns out she'd been in her dorm room getting ready for your visit this whole time. Girls just love getting dressed up, don't they?"

Ellen stood up from her chair, her heart in her throat. The moment had come. She took a deep breath. She shouldn't have come, she realized. This was a mistake. She should have let her husband handle these visits.

Dr. Bob's office door opened and a counselor stepped in followed by a teenage girl with sun-kissed skin and neatly combed short blonde hair.

"Hi Mom."

Ellen looked at this version of Lisa, who was so obviously her daughter, and yet so changed. The heavy makeup and that awful blue hair dye were gone, along with the ragged used clothes her daughter had insisted on wearing. This Lisa was everything Ellen had always hoped she'd be. Her daughter had put on some weight, and it made her look healthy and rosy-cheeked. Her skin was clear and tan. She wore a pair of cargo pants, white tennis shoes, and a clean blue T-shirt that read Lost Lake Academy in bold black letters. She looked preppy and adorable.

Ellen smiled. "Hello, darling."

Together, they walked down a path through a small copse of fir trees near the lodge. Dr. Bob had tried to insist that the counselor join them, but Ellen was so disarmed by this new Lisa that she wanted to have her daughter all to herself. Together they walked for several minutes down the trail. The only sounds were of birds and a light breeze rustling the branches above them.

Lisa looked back at the lodge nervously.

"What's wrong, dear?" She wondered if Lisa was afraid to be alone with her. "Should we ask the counselor to join us? Would that make you feel better?"

Lisa grabbed Ellen's arm. "Mom, this place is insane. You have to get me out of here. You wouldn't believe the kinds of things they've made me do. It's torture."

Lisa's words came out in a whispered jumble, and Ellen could barely follow what her daughter was saying.

"They do it to all of us. Like my friend Jamie, they caught her smoking one time. Just one time. And they locked her in a room and wouldn't let her out till she'd smoked ten packs of cigarettes. She caught bronchitis and was sick for weeks. And my friend Patrick. We were just down by the lake and these horrible kids attacked us. He was just trying to stop them. Then the guards showed up and threatened him with Tasers and they literally dragged him away. Can you believe it? They'll probably throw him in the hole."

"The hole?"

"Yes, the hole is a nightmare. It's, like, pitch black and they play this horrible music and then flash the lights so you can't sleep.

Patrick was in there for three days last time. He was a mess after. He could barely speak. They watch us all the time. And all the other kids spy." Lisa looked around nervously, as though afraid someone would jump out at them from behind a tree. She lowered her voice even more. "You get rewarded when you lie and punished for telling the truth. The more you rat on your classmates, the better they treat you. It's unbelievable. And the teachers. They don't know anything. I don't think most of them are even real teachers. Our schoolbooks are all old and falling apart. The computers we work on are ancient, of course there's no internet, and the library is a joke. Mom, you have to get me out of here."

Lisa paused to catch her breath. Her hand was wrapped around Ellen's arm so tight, it started to hurt. Ellen pulled away from her daughter's grasp.

"Absolutely not. I wouldn't hear of it."

The blood drained from Lisa's face. "Aren't you listening to me?"

Ellen shook her head sadly. "Lisa, we both know what an excellent liar you are. How can you expect me to believe anything you say?"

Her daughter looked stunned. "Because it's true."

"I've already decided," said Ellen, as she continued down the trail. "You're staying. Dr. Bob and I discussed it. He thinks it's for the best."

"Please, Mom. No. You can't trust him. If you knew what he's done to me . . ."

Ellen softened her tone. "He says you're making excellent progress. And look at you. You finally look like a normal girl."

Lisa's eyes narrowed and Ellen knew immediately she'd made a mistake.

"What do you mean, a normal girl?" asked Lisa, her voice rising with each word. "Like someone who doesn't embarrass you. Someone who doesn't look like a juvenile delinquent? Or a slut?"

"You are putting words in my mouth."

"I'm just saying out loud what you're thinking."

"Enough," Ellen said. She'd feared it would go this way. "Dr. Bob is afraid you'll suffer a relapse if you come home too soon. You'll start using again."

"Using what exactly?" asked Lisa. She sounded confused.

"You know. Drugs. MDMA, opioids, methamphetamines." She stopped when she saw the thunderous look on Lisa's face.

"That's what Dr. Bob's been telling you? That I'm a meth addict?" She shook her head with disgust. "You know you can't keep me here after I turn eighteen. After that, I can walk out."

"And walking is what you'll be doing, young lady."

"I'll talk to Dad about it. He'll let me come home," said Lisa.

"Your father will do exactly what I tell him to."

Lisa angrily wiped tears from her eyes. "Dad told me everything. He said you threatened to leave him if he didn't agree to send me here."

Ellen gasped. "How could you know that? All your calls are monitored, and students aren't allowed cell phones."

"I snuck into one of the offices and I called him at work."

Ben. How dare he. Another betrayal. That man was doing everything he could to ruin what little bond remained between her and Lisa. She steeled her resolve. "You will stay at this school, or you'll lose all financial support."

"I don't need your money," said Lisa defiantly.

"You'll feel differently when you realize what life is like without it. You don't know what I've sacrificed for you."

"Sacrificed? Are you kidding me? You hide me away in the mountains from your rich political friends so I can't embarrass you. You can't be bothered to talk to me for a few minutes every couple of weeks when these assholes let me call home. I've been here for months, and you couldn't get away until now to see me? You don't care about me at all."

Ellen turned away from her daughter and started heading back toward the lodge.

"Don't you have anything to say to me?" demanded Lisa.

"I'm sorry. Motherhood never came easily to me."

"You've never been my mother. You've always just been some stranger in the background. I wish it were just me and Dad."

"Your father has no say in this. He left the decision up to me."

Her daughter's face was stricken with disbelief. Ellen realized that if she didn't take Lisa home with her today, whatever bond remained between them might be permanently broken. A sacrifice she was willing to make, for the good of her daughter.

Ellen reached Screen Door and parked in the yellow zone in front of the restaurant, a perk of her office that always filled her with deep satisfaction. She adjusted the rearview mirror to catch her daughter's reflection in the back seat, expecting to see her sulking. To her surprise, Lisa was in a deep sleep. For once, she appeared peaceful and serene. Considering the demand Ellen was about to make of her daughter, she felt sure that serenity wouldn't last long.

CHAPTER 18
BRUNCH NATION

Jamie looked skeptically at the haphazard line in front of Screen Door that stretched down the street and out of sight around the corner. People held cups of coffee in white-knuckled hands. Parents shielded their children's sweaty faces from the bright hot sun with newspapers scavenged from nearby dispensers. Hipsters feigned relaxed postures, all the while nervously shooting glances at the front of the line, willing it to move faster.

"Are you sure about this, Mayor Salder?" asked Jamie, opening her car door to the warm summer air. "You must have better things to do than wait in line for fried chicken and waffles."

"Don't worry, dear," said Ellen as she stepped out of the car, cool and collected as ever.

Jamie wondered if the mayor ever perspired.

"Would you mind waking Lisa? She fell asleep on the drive over."

"Oh, yes," said Jamie. "Of course." She peeked through Lisa's window and saw her friend had dozed off. Not realizing Lisa was leaning against the car door, she opened it. Lisa woke and almost fell out and onto the curb.

"What the . . ." said Lisa, trying to steady herself.

"Whoa, sorry about that, sleeping beauty," said Jamie, as she helped Lisa to her feet. "Wakey wakey, eggs and bakey. Oh, but first," Jamie made a circular motion around her face. "Drool. So much drool."

Lisa glared at Jamie and wiped her mouth. She yawned widely, blinked at the bright sunlight, and slipped on her sunglasses. "Holy shit. Look at that line."

"Language, dear," said Ellen, with a raised eyebrow.

"Yes, mother," said Lisa. She gave Jamie a dramatic you-see-what-I-mean expression.

Jamie ignored her and watched, amazed, as Ellen headed straight for the hostess. The crowd cleared a path for her as if she were Moses parting the Red Sea.

"Are we supposed to follow?" asked Jamie.

Lisa just shrugged. "Do we have a choice?"

Lisa and Jamie jostled their way inside, suffering glares and muttered curses. Jamie rubbed a spot on her arm where she'd been elbowed by an angry mother of two. She caught sight of Ellen at the hostess station.

"Mayor Salder, it's such a pleasure to have you with us again." The hostess appeared to glow in the presence of this minor celebrity.

"How long is the wait for a table?" Ellen asked.

"Don't be silly," said the hostess. "We always have a table ready for you. How many in your party?"

"Three."

"Excellent." She gathered a stack of menus, and said brightly, "Right this way."

Jamie stood next to Lisa awkwardly, embarrassed by this preferential treatment.

Ellen summoned them both with a sharp look and a commanding wave of her hand. "Power has its privileges, girls," she murmured quietly.

As they made their way through the busy restaurant, Ellen smiled as a few patrons recognized her. She stopped to shake a hand here and there, always with a kind word or a remembered detail about when they'd last met. Jamie could see the rush of pleasure it gave them.

The hostess sat the trio at a table in a corner and handed them each a menu. Jamie wondered if this wasn't a regular spot for Ellen. From her seat, Jamie could see they had an excellent view of the other diners and would instantly notice if anyone approached, and the restaurant was so loud and busy that no overly curious parties would have a chance of eavesdropping on their conversation.

"Remember the kitchen at the Academy?" Lisa asked Jamie. "The slop Chef used to churn out?"

"How could I forget? I swear I gained fifteen pounds in my first three months." Jamie didn't want to stray too far into uncomfortable territory and focused on the food at hand instead. "Speaking of gaining weight, this seems like a great opportunity to pack on a few pounds. I think I'll have chicken and waffles with a side of scrambled eggs. Maybe biscuits and sausage gravy. And grits. I have to order grits."

A smiling waitress approached the table and filled their mugs with hot coffee. She outlined the specials, which Jamie thoughtfully appraised but silently rejected for the old standbys.

"Jamie, why don't you order for all of us," suggested Ellen, then added. "And let's definitely get hush puppies."

Feeling flattered by the responsibility, Jamie gave the waitress a long list of items, much more than the three of them would be able to consume in one sitting, and requested extra plates so they could share. She was comforted by the prospect of leftovers filling her and Lisa's creaky old fridge.

The waitress left and Ellen took a sip of coffee. She looked at the two of them thoughtfully, then set down her cup and leaned toward them. "Girls, I need your help."

Jamie had expected a lecture from Ellen, a dressing down, an airing of grievances all directed at Lisa, and by virtue of association, herself. She never expected a plea for aid.

"What I'm about to tell you has to stay in the strictest confidence. Can I trust you to keep it to yourselves?" asked Ellen.

She looked first at Jamie, who nodded, comfortable being bribed with a delicious meal.

Lisa, however, was not going to be so easy. "What is this all about?" she asked suspiciously.

"Lisa, let's just listen," said Jamie. "How much worse can it be than everything else that's happened in the last eighteen hours?"

"Good point," said Lisa. "Mother, fine. I'll keep my mouth shut. However, until I know what this is all about, I'm not agreeing to help you."

Jamie didn't like the look Ellen gave her daughter. The single raised eyebrow and a slight pursing of the lips all signaled that Lisa probably wouldn't have a choice.

"We'll see. Regardless, I'm sure that first and foremost on your minds are the unfortunate events that took place last night. However, something even more pressing has come up."

"More pressing?" asked Jamie, pointing at Lisa. "Mayor Salder, I thought we were here to talk about, well, you know."

"Just say it," said Lisa.

"Fine." Jamie turned back to Ellen. "I know we don't want Lisa's spotless reputation marred forever by one bad choice, but I still think we should go after the Greens."

Lisa looked at Jamie with raised brows. "Pretty sure my reputation hasn't been spotless since the third grade." Turning to Ellen, she said, "I shouldn't have taken the money from George, I know that. But you need to understand how worthless you made me feel last night. You've always thought the worst of me, so I figured, hell, why not go home with George? At least I'd be able to cover the rent for a couple of months. And for the record, we didn't, you know, do anything."

Jamie looked from Lisa to Ellen, whose face had taken on a bright red color.

"You know you can always come to me for money," Ellen said quietly.

Lisa snorted. "Sure, with strings attached."

"Lisa, I'm sorry you feel that way."

Ellen's reply had an edge to it that Jamie didn't like, and she tried to steer the conversation back to the Greens. "We have Sue Green's license plate. That's a pretty awesome smoking gun. Couldn't Lisa press charges for the hit-and-run?" asked Jamie.

Ellen shook her head no. "Lisa could press charges, but she would have to divulge the circumstances of the attack. I think doing nothing at this point is best."

Lisa stirred her coffee absently. "I could create a new identity and move to a different country, always on the run from my dark past."

Jamie elbowed Lisa. "Dude, you are not taking this seriously enough. That crazy woman tried to murder you."

"And the point, Lisa," said Ellen sternly, "is to do something with your life. I will not have this weighing on you, pushing you down some bad path. Of course, if this all came to light, it would affect me as well. I'm sure you're aware I'm running for reelection."

"Ah, finally, the heart of the matter," said Lisa. "Mother, you are the most narcissistic, self-obsessed, self-centered . . ."

Jamie realized she'd better intervene, and fast. Videos of a screaming match between Lisa and her mother were not going to end up on social media, not on her watch. As Lisa raged on, Jamie's mind raced to think of a distraction. She could knock her glass of orange juice into Lisa's lap. Ellen was more deserving, but also a lot scarier. Hell, her best option may be to just flip over the entire table. That would end it.

Jamie moved to rise, then mercifully saw her saviors—three waiters were headed their way, balancing a ridiculous number of plates piled high with food. "Oh, thank god," Jamie muttered under her breath.

Lisa paused mid-diatribe as fried chicken, waffles, eggs, hush-puppies, grits, strips of bacon, sliced fruit, and biscuits and gravy were carefully placed in the center of the table.

"Damn," said Lisa. "That's a lot of food."

Jamie smiled widely. "I should have worn my eating pants." She started piling items on her plate and Ellen followed.

"How can either of you possibly eat at a time like this?" Lisa asked.

Ellen and Jamie both looked up at Lisa, each with a forkful.

"Oh, yes." Ellen set her fork down on her plate and wiped her hands on her napkin.

Jamie took a large bite of chicken. "I can always eat," she said, her mouth full.

Lisa glared. "So, if the point of this delightful brunch isn't to talk about me, George Green, and his unhinged wife, then why are we here? Jamie and I can't possibly be of any use to you in your political schemes."

"You'd be surprised," said Ellen. "As you may know from recent election press coverage, my opponent in the mayoral race has accused me of being too tough on drug users, if you can believe that. Yes, a few people were jailed who should have been sent to treatment centers, but I've remedied that, clearing their records and getting them the help they need. Really, the whole thing has been blown out of proportion by overzealous journalists. The more important issue that my opponent is ignoring is the massive influx of drugs into the city. Heroin, meth, cocaine—they're all easier to get than ever. I want to get to the bottom of it so I can focus on other issues—increasing critical funding for schools, improving our earthquake preparedness, fulfilling my pledge to make Portland the greenest city in the nation with more bike lanes, more electric car charging stations, and putting a stop to illegal dumping of industrial waste in the Willamette—"

"Enough with the stump speech," Lisa interrupted. "You already know I would never vote for you."

"I voted for you, Mayor Salder," said Jamie as she poured maple syrup on a waffle.

"You are such a kiss ass," said Lisa.

"Thank you, Jamie. Every vote counts," said Ellen.

"And the other candidate was so awful. Like we had a choice," said Jamie, with a sheepish grin.

"So, what do you want from us?" asked Lisa.

"I have confidential informants all over the city, digging for information on the dealers and suppliers, and I finally have an in with the architect of this crime syndicate." Ellen pointed at Lisa. "You."

Lisa sat back in her chair, her eyebrows raised.

Jamie could see the storm cloud brewing in her friend's eyes. She placed a piece of perfectly cooked bacon onto Lisa's plate in a desperate attempt to distract her.

"You have got to be kidding me," said Lisa. "I've been clean since the Academy. How dare you accuse me of being mixed up in dealing drugs."

"Not you exactly." Ellen took a sip of coffee. "Your boyfriend, Patrick."

Lisa narrowed her eyes. "How do you know about Patrick? Leave him out of this. And you can't use me to get at him because Patrick isn't my boyfriend, at least not anymore. We broke up last night," said Lisa, her voice rising.

"Please calm down and let me explain," said Ellen.

"I saw Patrick talking with Sheila last night," blurted out Jamie before Ellen could continue.

"Who?" asked Lisa.

"You know. Sheila. Remember from a few years ago, at that party in Ladd's Addition?"

Lisa looked shocked. "No. No. No. There is no way." She crossed her arms defensively. "He's not that stupid."

"Didn't he tell you about some new job?" asked Jamie.

"Yeah, that was with Joe, which is bad enough. You don't think he'd deal for Sheila, do you? That's insane," said Lisa, her eyes widening.

"I kind of do. Whatever he was up to last night with Sheila, it was sketchy," said Jamie.

"And why did it take you so long to tell me about this?" asked Lisa.

"We've been a little busy," said Jamie.

"This is all just great," muttered Lisa, listlessly pushing food around her plate. "Mom, how could you possibly know about any of this?"

"It was, for lack of a better phrase, a lucky break," said Ellen, slicing into a waffle. "Jamie, were you referring to Sheila Elkins?"

"Yes. She sold steroids and drugs to some cyclists I know."

"Lisa, it's true," said Ellen as she cut her waffle into precise squares. "Patrick is working for Sheila. Patrick's activities last night have helped me and an informant put the pieces together. We suspect Sheila's been running a fairly large operation through food cart pods scattered throughout the city. You can't imagine how angry this makes me, after all the work I've done, helping hundreds of small businesses get started. Food trucks draw national press, bring in tourism dollars, and have generated dozens of brick-and-mortar restaurants in the city, and thousands of jobs."

"Still not voting for you," said Lisa.

"The fact that Sheila had the gall to deal at last night's event, an event planned by the Mayor's Office, my office. To put it frankly, it pissed me off." Ellen took a sip of water and composed herself. "I want to shut her down. With a little assistance from Patrick, perhaps we can."

"Why would he help you? Why would any of us?" asked Lisa.

"Because Lisa, he'll be facing some serious charges if not. We know where he is and we're fairly confident he has a large supply of drugs in his possession. Either he helps me, or he goes to jail." Ellen glanced at her watch. "His shift at the bike shop started an hour ago. I have officers watching the building."

Jamie looked down at her plate of congealing biscuits and gravy. She wasn't feeling very hungry anymore.

CHAPTER 19
RIVER CITY

Lisa sat silent and seething during the short drive from Screen Door to River City Bikes. Ellen's words echoed in her head. 'Either Patrick helps me, or he goes to jail.' As soon as the car rolled to a stop in the parking lot, Lisa leapt out and slammed her door shut. Determined to reach Patrick before Ellen did, she sped ahead, not waiting for her mother or Jamie.

Maybe he could still make a run for it, Lisa thought. Or toss the drugs. As she turned toward the entrance, she saw a cop car. Two officers sat waiting and watching. She gave them the finger and made a beeline for the door.

She stepped into the cavernous store, momentarily distracted by the bright lights and loud music. A shopper wearing a garish jersey and bike shorts walked past, his cycling shoes making his gait unnatural and birdlike.

Lisa glanced back and saw Jamie holding the door open for Ellen. The friends exchanged sympathetic looks. Lisa turned to head further into the shop but was momentarily stopped by a traffic jam of customers.

A sales clerk wearing a River City T-shirt was espousing the merits of bike lights to a customer, but paused mid-sentence as he caught sight of Lisa. He called out to her and held up his palm for a high five. Lisa accommodated, smacking his large hand.

"Woah, you've been working out, girl? Damn," he said, shaking his hand as though it stung.

Lisa smiled and said, "Hi Damon. Have you seen Patrick?" Damon was one of Patrick's three roommates, definitely the best of the bunch, in Lisa's opinion. His tidy room was a standout among the others, including Patrick's.

"Sure, he's upstairs in the shop. Be warned, he looks like shit. What's he gotten into?"

"You really don't want to know," she said.

"Anytime you're done with him, you have my number," Damon said with a wink.

She just smiled. Walking past, she couldn't stop herself from glancing over her shoulder to see if he was still smiling at her. The customer raised his hand in a feeble attempt to regain Damon's attention, but his focus had already turned to Jamie, who had followed close at Lisa's heels.

"Jamie! How've you been, woman? Why don't you call me?" Damon wrapped Jamie in a bear hug.

"Shameless," Lisa muttered.

Ellen caught up with Lisa and looked nervously around the sales floor. Compulsively, she brushed invisible dirt from her pale linen jacket and looked suspiciously at the sales staff who sported an assortment of tattoos, creative facial hair, mohawks, and shaved heads. Her mother was, for once, completely out of her element, and it gave Lisa a feeling of intense satisfaction.

"Maybe you should wait in the car. You don't want to get bike grease on that two-thousand-dollar pantsuit," said Lisa.

"This is not a pantsuit, young lady. It's just a suit. And it was very reasonably priced from Anne Taylor. Oh god, never mind. Where is Patrick?"

"He's upstairs in the mechanic's shop, and I'm going to talk to him first. Alone."

"How do I know you won't destroy the evidence?" she hissed, just as Jamie joined them.

"Lisa," said Jamie, "please tell your mother you won't destroy the evidence."

"No," said Lisa, defiantly.

"Then take me to Patrick, now," Ellen demanded, narrowly dodging a mechanic who rushed by with a well-oiled bike chain hanging from his fingers.

"Mother, no," said Lisa firmly. "I would like a moment to explain to Patrick just how much you're going to F-up his life if he doesn't play along. Maybe he'll actually listen to me because there is no way he'll listen to you."

"Fine. But hurry. I don't have all day."

Lisa nodded, then turned and ran up a set of rubber-coated stairs to the second floor. She reached the top of the landing and paused briefly where she had to cross the indoor track to reach the mechanic's shop. A customer test driving a bike swept by. The track had been constructed along the perimeter of the store's second-level balcony, which overlooked the main shopping floor and gave customers a place to evaluate the merits of road bikes rain or shine. It also served as a treacherous pathway to the employee's only area. She double-checked the way was clear and quickly stepped into the mechanic's shop. She was relieved to see Patrick was the only person in the room.

Patrick didn't notice her enter. She watched for a moment as he stood at his workbench, absorbed in gently threading a bike chain. His long thin fingers nimbly maneuvered the metal links, fitting them perfectly into place. He gave the back wheel a spin and it produced a satisfying purr. He wiped his grease-covered hands with a rag. Finally sensing another presence, he looked toward the door. Lisa stood leaning against the frame and felt the periodic swish of a bike coasting by, stirring her ponytail. Patrick threw the rag on his workbench and turned away.

"Why are you here?" he asked, his back to her. He restlessly cleaned his tools and straightened his already organized workbench.

"We have to talk."

"I have nothing to say to you," he said.

"Fine, then let's play show and tell. Where's your messenger bag?" she asked.

He kicked at it under his workstation where it sat, a sad lump of canvas.

She walked over, grabbed the shoulder strap, and dragged it out.

"What are you doing?" asked Patrick.

Ignoring him, she flipped the bag open and dug around, finding a crumpled paper sack in amongst a motley collection of paperbacks, tattered notebooks, and bike tools. She pulled the sack out and dumped its contents onto his bench. A pile of small brown paper packets filled with white powder spilled over the wrenches and tubes of grease and oil.

"What the hell, Lisa?"

"What the hell indeed, Patrick." She held up a packet and read, "'Like a Virgin'? What is this crap?"

He grabbed the packet from her hand, and frantically pushed it and the rest of the drugs back into the paper bag. "It's coke. Jesus, Lisa. Someone could see. Are you trying to get me fired?"

"What do you care? Looks like you have a new job selling this shit," she said. "Why did you even bother coming to work? Shouldn't you be standing on some corner in Old Town with the other dealers?"

He looked stricken at her words, and she immediately regretted saying them.

"Fine," he responded gruffly. "And why aren't you out turning tricks?"

Just as quickly, she wished she'd been harsher. "You're such a jerk."

"Yeah, well, you broke my heart." He sat down on a stool and looked at the paper bag in his hand. Neither spoke for a long moment. He had a smear of grease across one cheek. His hair was a snarled mess, and his eyes looked almost bruised with dark circles of exhaustion. She realized with a pang of guilt how much she'd hurt him.

"Listen, that guy and I . . . It was all a terrible, stupid mistake," she said. "Nothing happened between us."

"You took his money."

"I was drunk, and I was angry with you and with my mom. I was just doing what you both expected of me."

"Let's be honest. You took the cash because you need it. Don't you see? That's why I'm dealing. I'm trying to help you."

She touched his arm gently. "Selling drugs is not what I'd call helping. You have no idea how much trouble you're in." Her eyes held his, and for a moment everything was quiet and still between them. Then his gaze shifted to something behind her.

Lisa turned and saw her very impatient mother and a sheepish-looking Jamie behind her.

"Sorry. She insisted on coming up," said Jamie. "I couldn't stop her."

"Does he have the drugs with him?" Ellen asked Lisa.

Lisa glared at her mother, then turned to Patrick. With an exaggerated sweep of her hand, she said, "Patrick, I'd like you to meet my mother, Ellen Salder, the great mayor of Portland."

Ellen ignored the introduction and held out her hand. "Give me the bag, please."

Lisa took the paper bag from Patrick, who gave it up without a fight, and handed it to her mother.

Ellen took a look inside. Satisfied, she tucked it into her purse. "That's everything?" she asked.

Lisa looked at Patrick.

"Yeah. That's all of it," he said, sounding more mystified than concerned.

"I take it Lisa has explained things," said Ellen.

"Not even a little bit," he said.

"I'll give you a few more minutes. Don't make me wait too long." She turned to leave, then leapt back with a gasp as another bike rolled by at top speed. "What was that? This place is a nightmare."

"Let me help, Mayor Salder," said Jamie, who checked the bike path and waved her forward when it was clear.

Lisa and Patrick stood for a moment in silence.

"What was that all about?" asked Patrick.

"My mom knows about the drugs, that you're dealing for Sheila, and everything else that happened last night."

Patrick just shook his head helplessly. "You told her? How did you even know?"

"I didn't tell her shit. She picked me and Jamie up this morning and told us this crazy story about Sheila selling drugs out of food carts, and that you were in the middle of it. She said if you didn't cooperate, she'd have you thrown in jail."

"Listen, I don't want to have anything to do with this."

"Patrick, we have to go with her. She wants to bring down Sheila, and she wants you to help her do it. If you don't, she'll mess with your life in ways you can't imagine. Trust me, I know. She already has cops waiting out front."

"Sheila said she'd kill me," he said, looking pale.

Lisa just shrugged. "My mother will do worse. Get your stuff. We need to go." She motioned for him to go ahead of her.

He looked at her helplessly. "What? Do you think I'll make a run for it?" he asked.

She shrugged. "I would."

Together they headed down the stairs, toward the unexpected sounds of cheers and applause. A crowd had gathered around Ellen, and the horrifying truth dawned on Lisa—her mother was giving a speech. She grabbed Patrick's hand and pulled him behind a rack of bike shorts with padded crotches that bulged pornographically.

"This city needs strong leadership. Let me continue to work for you, the people of Portland," said Ellen, emphasizing each phrase with a gesture. "With your support, I can stop the flow of drugs that continue to pour into our city. I will strive to improve Portland's infrastructure and emergency preparedness as we face challenges ranging from the specter of a long-predicted earthquake to forest fires and climate change."

A man standing next to Lisa and Patrick yelled out, "I bet you don't even recycle!"

Impressed that anyone would dare insult her mother, Lisa whispered to him, "She doesn't, and she flat-out refuses to compost." Her gaze returned to her mother, and she saw that Jamie was now standing at Ellen's side with a stony expression vaguely matching that of a secret service agent. Her friend appeared to scan the room, looking for potential attackers. Flanking Ellen's right stood the store's manager, smiling widely and nodding enthusiastically at everything she had to say. Lisa had once heard him call Ellen a right-wing-blowhard-hack. Apparently, her mother's charisma had won him over.

Lisa rolled her eyes. "What a nightmare," she whispered to Patrick.

In her most sonorous voice, Ellen concluded with, "Last, and certainly not least, I want to further underline my commitment to Portland's bike culture. I will not rest until there are five bikes to every car in this city."

The crowd erupted in cheers, chanting, "Share the road! Share the road! Share the road!"

Ellen caught Lisa's eye through the mass of shoppers and staff. The tiniest twitch of her eyebrow indicated that it was time to leave. Jamie cleared a path through the crowd toward the entrance, and Lisa followed, pulling Patrick along behind her.

The manager escorted Ellen outside and shook her hand enthusiastically. Her face was frozen in a look of canned pleasure that nearly betrayed her irritation.

To Lisa's surprise, Jamie stepped between the two of them and spoke. "It has been such a thrill for the mayor to visit the shop and speak to your staff and customers, but she has to get back to City Hall."

"Of course. Official business. It was so great to meet you, Mayor Salder, thank you."

Ellen waved goodbye and briskly headed toward her parked car.

"Thanks, and don't forget to vote," called Jamie, as she, Lisa, and Patrick followed quickly behind.

"I actually liked that job," said Patrick, glumly.

"You're not fired. Mayor Salder took care of it. That's what started the whole speech thing. She met the manager and said that she needed you to assist with," Jamie held up her fingers in air quotes, "'official City Hall business.' He was so starstruck. It was kind of hilarious. That was a great speech, Mayor Salder. Really inspiring."

They'd reached the car. Lisa got in the back seat with Jamie and whispered in her ear, "What is wrong with you? Have you forgotten my mother is a monster?"

Jamie just shook her head. "I don't know, Lisa. Something came over me. Your mom was giving her speech, and a dude started heckling her. I just sensed a void that needed to be filled. Being a public figure must be stressful."

Lisa choked back a sarcastic retort and said instead, "For a minute there, you looked like you were ready to tackle half the crowd."

Jamie laughed, "Oh my god, I think I might have."

"Yeah, well, watch out. Help her too much, and she might just offer you a job."

CHAPTER 20
THEO WAITS

The mayor was late.

Rather unlike Ellen, Theo thought as he rolled a toothpick inside his mouth. His foot tapped nervously, the heel of his alligator skin cowboy boot drumming a steady rhythm on the floor. Ellen's secretary sighed with irritation. Theo mumbled an apology and stilled his leg.

It seemed unlikely that Lisa would recognize him. He'd worn a ski mask that morning, but even so, Theo felt anxious. He was still ashamed of how badly the transport had gone. Months later, after he read that Ellen's husband had died, he got in touch to offer his sympathy and to apologize. Ellen accepted both gravely, then surprised Theo by asking about his plans. He shared his aspirations to earn his private investigator license. It was slow going though, as he was having trouble accruing the required hours of experience. Ellen said she might be able to help and offered him a part time job—special investigator to the mayor's office. She needed someone who could work around the edges, where law enforcement couldn't go. Theo was happy to oblige.

He yawned widely and shook his head. He'd had only a few hours of sleep. After his brief call to Ellen last night about Sheila's drug operation and Lisa's accident, he'd headed straight to the gala, which, by that time, was winding down. He found Sheila in the karaoke tent singing a baleful version of "Patience" by Guns N' Roses, then discretely trailed her as she hauled her Airstream to the Five Firs food cart pod. After she'd driven off, he'd picked the Airstream's lock and methodically searched and inventoried the contents. Months of fishing for leads had finally paid off. He called Ellen to report even though it was almost dawn. She'd grilled him on every last detail about the drugs he'd found. None of the intel he'd gathered would help their case against Sheila, of course. He'd broken in without cause or a warrant, but as Ellen always said, information was power. The mayor had also been particularly interested in Patrick, asking for precise details of Theo's conversation with him.

Theo stood, stretched his back, and walked over to the secretary's desk. He cleared his throat. No response. The young man wore earbuds and was completely absorbed in a game on his phone, tapping small jewels as they bounced on the screen. Theo could hear the tinny music that accompanied each play. A can of energy drink and a crumpled wrapper from the Meat Hut littered his desk.

"Excuse me, young man? Could I trouble you for a cup of coffee?" Theo asked.

The secretary looked up from his phone, brown eyes dulled with boredom. He pulled out a single earbud with an impatient gesture. "I'm sorry, what was that?" he asked.

"Could I trouble you for a cup of coffee?" Theo repeated, slower this time.

The secretary looked at him coldly. "I don't do coffee. I'm an assistant, not a secretary," he said with a clipped voice, then sighed as though just speaking was exhausting. "There's a Starbucks down the street." He pushed the earbud back in and returned to his game.

With some effort, Theo resisted the urge to grab the young man and toss him out the window. He stepped back, returned to the sofa, and sat back down. Finally, he heard the pitch of women's voices through the tempered glass lobby door, recognizing Ellen's piercing and authoritative tone in the midst of a verbal melee.

He noticed a flurry of activity at the assistant's desk. The energy drink, burger wrapper, and phone had disappeared, replaced with an open laptop and official-looking documents neatly arrayed in a false display of efficiency.

The door flung open, and a rush of bodies pushed through. The first was a young woman with a long blond ponytail, dark sunglasses still perched on her nose. Her head was tilted in that imperious and defiant way Theo immediately recognized as a characteristic pose of the mayor.

This must be the daughter, Lisa, he thought. The girl removed her sunglasses and looked at him with her hazel eyes, just like Ellen's.

Theo waited for some flicker of recognition.

Lisa scowled at him briefly, then turned her attention back to her mother.

Nothing. He sighed with relief.

"I can't believe you're bringing that up now," said Lisa. "For the last time, I did not set fire to the girl's bathroom at that cross-country match. It was Sarah Baker."

Ellen looked slightly flushed, her brow creased. "Sarah was a lovely girl, a cheerleader, always went to church with her family. I remember once, at mass, she sang the loveliest version of 'Ave Maria.'"

Lisa turned, hands on hips. "She was lip-syncing to a Celine Dion recording."

Ellen paused for a moment, then said quietly, "I thought it sounded familiar . . ."

The third member of the group held several paper takeout bags close to her chest, as though afraid someone would snatch them away. She gently placed them on the coffee table, then sat down next to Theo on the sofa. She pulled out a brown paper carton, opened it, and offered it to him. He saw that it was filled with hushpuppies, but he shook his head no and returned his attention to the doorway.

Finally, a young man carrying a heavy messenger bag stepped in. It was the boy, Patrick, looking wan and dejected. He barely registered his surroundings and just slouched over to an over-stuffed armchair and sat down.

Selfishly, Theo was glad the boy hadn't taken his advice to dump the girl and the drugs, but still he felt a little guilty. With any luck, Patrick would bring him closer to Sheila, but at what cost, he wondered. He'd always been a good judge of character and sensed Patrick was probably an all right kid. With a little help and guidance, he might even turn out to be a decent man. For now, Theo needed Patrick to be bad just a little bit longer.

"That skank was screwing the entire audio-visual club," continued Lisa. "They helped her set it up in the church as a big joke. She told me at school the next day that she thought it was quote, 'hilarious,' unquote."

"That's beside the point," Ellen said. "It still marked the beginning of the end for you."

"Because that's what you believed. You thought I was lying. You stopped trusting me or even listening to me. You always assumed the worst."

"And that's what you gave me."

"Exactly."

The mother and daughter stared each other down.

The girl had some cojones, thought Theo. He smirked as the assistant took this unfortunate moment to step from behind his desk and approach Ellen, clearing his throat loudly.

"What is it, Geoff?" asked Ellen. Theo could see she was just barely keeping her temper in check.

"You're looking radiant today, Mayor Salder," Geoff said.

Ellen glared at him and his ingratiating compliment.

She was looking anything but. Theo had never seen the mayor in such a state. The daughter was really doing a number on her, he thought.

"Thank you, Geoff," she said, handing him her sunglasses and purse. "And I appreciate your coming in on a Saturday. Did Levine's drop off the dry cleaning?"

"Of course. Everything is waiting in your office. I organized each outfit according to your schedule, as you instructed."

"Excellent. I would love a cup of coffee. Run down the street to Starbucks and get me a double espresso."

"Of course. It would be my great pleasure."

Great pleasure, my ass, thought Theo.

"Would anyone else like a coffee?" asked Ellen.

"I'll take an espresso too, and make it a triple shot," called out Theo. The others shook their heads no. Geoff carefully placed the mayor's purse and sunglasses on the edge of his desk, then slipped from the room, closing the glass door behind him.

"All right, that should keep Geoff busy for a while," said Ellen. "Everyone, I'd like to introduce an associate of mine. This gentleman is Theo Alvarez."

"You!"

The boy had finally recognized him.

Patrick rose from his seat and walked toward him, pointing his finger accusingly. "You did this. You set me up."

Theo stood and stepped away from the sofa, toward the middle of the room. "Now, let's just take it easy," he said calmly.

Patrick lunged.

CHAPTER 21
THE BEEPER

Before Patrick realized what had happened, he found himself face down on the floor, his arms roughly pinned back by Theo. He twisted and thrashed, but no amount of resistance would loosen the tattoo artist's iron grip.

Man, this dude is strong, thought Patrick. He turned his head and gazed helplessly at the faces staring down at him. Lisa looked mortified, Ellen shook her head in disbelief, and Jamie just laughed.

"Are you ready to calm down?" asked Theo.

"Hell no!"

"Patrick," said Lisa. "Please."

The stress in her voice quickly smothered his outburst. He went limp. "Okay, okay. I'm fine. You can let me go," said Patrick.

Theo unceremoniously hauled Patrick up by his T-shirt collar and dragged him over to the sofa. Patrick sat, and Theo stood over him as though daring Patrick to make another move.

Lisa leaned closer and lightly touched the gauze that was wrapped around his arm. "Patrick, what happened to you? Did you hurt yourself?"

Patrick had completely forgotten about his tattoo. He pushed Lisa's hand away and pulled off the gauze. He gasped, then glared at Theo. "You fucking asshole." He pushed up the sleeve of his T-shirt, revealing a tattoo that now read USA FOREVER, the heart as flaming red as Patrick's enraged face.

Jamie choked back a laugh. "Wow, Patrick, that is some do over. I didn't realize you were so patriotic."

"You already changed your LISA FOREVER tattoo?" asked Lisa, her voice petulant.

An insistent chirp came from Patrick's waist.

"What is that horrible sound?" asked Ellen.

"Is that a phone?" asked Jamie.

Theo reached down and pulled the beeper from where it was clipped to Patrick's belt.

"Hey, watch it," said Patrick, irked by this further invasion of his personal space.

Theo palmed the small device.

Jamie leaned in to look. "What is it?"

"Looks like a beeper," said Ellen.

"What's a beeper?" asked Lisa.

Theo read the message on the beeper's tiny screen aloud: "Fifteen hundred Northwest Tenth at three."

"What does that mean?" asked Ellen.

"It doesn't mean anything," said Patrick. "It's just an old piece of junk."

"I've never seen you with that thing Patrick, and I'm your ex-girl-friend. Which you've made absolutely clear by the mess you made of your tattoo," said Lisa. "Jerk."

"You hated that tattoo," said Patrick.

"Did not."

Patrick couldn't believe what Lisa was saying. "You literally spoke the words 'I hate that tattoo' only last night."

"Well, sure, but I also said it was kind of sweet."

"Enough, you two," said Jamie. "Patrick, just tell us. What's the beeper for?"

Patrick looked around wildly for an escape route and struggled to his feet. Theo firmly pressed him back down. Patrick racked his brain for an excuse. "It's the bike shop," he said. "They must need me back at work."

"River City Bikes gave you a beeper? Sounds pretty fishy," said Jamie, sounding like a beat cop confronting a perp. "You have a perfectly fine smartphone. Why don't they just text you on that?"

"The shop is getting us ready for the big one. Mayor Salder, you know all about this. Earthquakes. Subduction zones. Tectonic plates. Pagers are super reliable and less susceptible in the event of a natural disaster, right? The bike shop has to be able to reach me no matter what." He looked hopefully at Ellen, then Lisa and Jamie, and finally Theo. They did not look convinced. "Okay, fine. Sheila gave it to me."

Theo looked thoughtfully at the beeper. "The numbers are an address. I assume for a delivery. The number three likely refers to the time." Theo pulled his phone from his back pocket and typed the address into a map application. In seconds, a Portland neighborhood loaded on screen.

"The address is about a five-minute drive from here. Appears to be on a residential street in the Pearl. Fifteen hundred Northwest Tenth Avenue. Nearest cross street is Irving."

Jamie moved closer to Theo and glanced over his shoulder at the phone.

"Tenth and Irving?" asked Jamie. "Hey, that's near where we found Lisa last night."

"I don't remember," Lisa said, suddenly looking pale under her tan. "Head injury and all that."

"Yes, I'm almost positive. You were in that little park near the row of gorgeous brick townhouses. Patrick, am I right?"

Patrick nodded, remembering the frantic drive with Jamie, feeling terrified that Lisa might be really hurt.

"Here's the street view," said Theo, passing his phone around so they could all see the screen. It showed a clear image of a three-story brick townhouse, steps leading from the street to an opaque glass door.

Theo tapped for a few more moments. "The property is owned by a George and Susan Green," he said.

Lisa let out a gasp and slumped down on the sofa next to Patrick. "No, no, no . . ." She covered her face with her hands.

"George Green, you say. That is unfortunate," said Jamie as she squeezed in between Lisa and Patrick, putting her arm over Lisa's shoulders supportively.

"What's the big deal?" asked Patrick. "Who's George Green?"

"Patrick, sometimes you can be so dense," said Jamie. "He's the dude Lisa hooked up with last night."

"Nothing happened!" wailed Lisa.

Patrick felt reenergized. Finally, things were looking up. He spoke eagerly to Ellen. "I'll tell you anything you want to know. I met Sheila at the gala last night. She gave me that beeper and the cocaine and said to keep both on me at all times in case I needed to deliver." Patrick smiled. Confronting the prick who had tried to sleep with the love of his life was well worth the humiliation he'd just endured. "Let me do this. Let's nail this asshole."

"You can't be serious. You are not going over there," said Lisa.

"Oh, I am," said Patrick. "I've never been more serious. I'd love to meet your new boyfriend, or should I say John?"

"He's too close to it," said Theo. "I can handle it."

"All of Sheila's crew are my age," said Patrick firmly, even though he had no idea if it were true. "George would think it was weird if some old dude showed up at his house."

"Old dude?" protested Theo. "I'm twenty-nine."

"Exactly," said Patrick.

"Patrick makes a good point," said Ellen. "We need Sheila and George to think it's business as usual."

"So, what's the plan?" asked Patrick. He imagined pinning George to the floor, just as Theo had done to him, and beating George senseless till he spilled his guts.

"Recording the conversation is a must. Ideally, we need George actually saying he's exchanging money for drugs," said Ellen.

Lisa leaned across Jamie and grabbed Patrick's hand. "Just text back or do whatever you do on that beeper thing. Tell Sheila that you got stuck at work and can't make the delivery. She'll send someone else."

"Lisa," said Ellen. "I'm sorry, but we need information. If Sheila is sending deliveries directly to George's home, he must trust her. If we have enough leverage, maybe he'll have additional details that will help build a case against her."

"The recording won't be admissible," said Theo.

"George won't know that," said Ellen with a smile.

Patrick pulled away from Lisa's grasp and stood. He didn't like siding with Ellen over Lisa, but his desire for revenge won out. "So, we're on?"

Ellen and Theo nodded.

"All right then," said Patrick eagerly. "We don't have a lot of time. As soon as I get a message, I'm supposed to deliver within thirty minutes. You know. Like pizza."

CHAPTER 22
SPECIAL DELIVERY

Patrick cupped his hand around a cigarette and flicked his lighter until the tobacco burned red. Verbal instructions poured through his earbuds. They'd gone through the details back in the mayor's office, and he knew his part. Theo had given him a small device that snapped in place between the earbuds' wire and his smartphone. That, along with a newly installed app, would capture every word George spoke. Patrick just needed to stay within a few feet of George, as painful as that might be.

Jamie's voice piped through, doing her best impression of an FBI agent. "Patrick, do you copy?" He pictured Jamie, Lisa, and Ellen perched in Theo's cramped Volkswagen Vanagon around the corner. In addition to listening in, they apparently planned to coach his every move. He sighed.

"Patrick, if you need to, we can go over the logistics again," said Ellen, her deep condescension seeping through the earbuds.

He spoke quietly, knowing they could hear him clearly through Theo's speaker. "I'm fine, Mayor Salder. I got this."

Patrick tried to block out their voices and focus his attention on the townhouse that faced him. The sidewalk in front was littered with debris. Torn wedding photos with broken frames and shattered glass lay like rubble after an errant missile strike. Charred jeans and men's shirts were strewn over the artfully trimmed hedges that lined the front of the house.

Taking one last drag on his cigarette, Patrick dropped it on the cracked concrete, crushing the ember with the toe of his scuffed black sneaker. Squaring his shoulders, he walked up the steps to the front door and knocked loudly. A long moment passed. Finally, a shadow appeared against the opaque glass door. It swung open, and in the dim light of the hallway, he saw George. The suave businessman from yesterday was almost unrecognizable. He'd been replaced by a hungover mess in gray sweatpants and a baggy T-shirt, his eyes bleary and bloodshot. White gauze was wrapped around his left hand. In his right was a rocks glass filled with a dark liquor and ice.

Patrick formed his hand into a fist and imagined starting the conversation with a sucker punch to George's face. Resisting the impulse, he took a deep breath, smiled, and said brightly, "Special delivery."

"Who are you?" asked George, his voice scratchy and suspicious. He took a long drink from the glass, ice cubes tinkling.

Patrick shrugged. "You ordered some product last night. I'm the delivery boy."

George looked warily at Patrick. "Sheila sent you?"

"She sure did. Said to treat you right. That you're one of her best customers," Patrick continued, a shit-eating grin frozen on his face.

George brushed past him and peered outside to check the street. Apparently satisfied there was nothing fishy, he motioned Patrick in and closed the door.

"Follow me and keep it quiet. My wife is upstairs and I don't want to disturb her."

Patrick followed George through a dim hallway into a brightly-lit chef's kitchen. Shiny white cabinets lined the walls, and a full set of stainless-steel appliances gleamed. All was spotless and artfully arranged except for the marble countertop of the kitchen island. It was stained with drops of red wine. Two stemmed glasses sat side by side, with dregs the color of dried blood at the bottom of each. One was stained with lipstick in a tell-tale rose shade. As George turned to top off his drink from a well-stocked bar cabinet, Patrick discreetly erased the smear of color with his thumb.

"You're looking a little rough. Late night?" asked Patrick.

Still pouring, George looked back at him sharply. "Just give me what I ordered and let's get this over with."

Patrick set his heavy messenger bag on the kitchen island next to the glasses. "This is a nice place. I bet the ladies love it." He selected an orange from a large bowl of fruit and wandered leisurely around the kitchen. Patrick tossed the orange from hand to hand.

George followed him closely, his drink balanced on his gauze wrapped palm. "My wife certainly does."

"Your wife, huh?" Patrick chucked the orange at George who barely caught it with his uninjured hand.

"We've been married for almost fifteen years," said George, carefully placing the orange back in the bowl.

"Wow, that's commitment. Any kids?"

"No."

"Dude, think about it. Seriously, my buddies say it's life affirming. But I totally understand. Your wife must be, what, in her forties, right? Maybe it's time to upgrade. Find a nice young twenty-something."

Lisa's voice erupted though his earbuds. "Patrick, what are you doing?"

Patrick ignored his ex and paused at the knife block, tempted to pull one out and throw it at George like he'd done the orange. Maybe he'd catch it. Probably not. Patrick moved on.

"Wolf Range. Nice shit, dude." Patrick turned on a burner, and listened to it tick tick tick for a few uncomfortable moments until a spark finally flared to life, leaving a strong scent of natural gas in the air. Patrick pulled a cigarette out of the pack in his back pocket and bent, lighting it on the open flame.

"You can't smoke in here," George said, rushing over to turn off the burner.

Patrick took a deep drag then tapped out some ash on the floor. "Fine, dude." He went to the white enamel sink, doused the butt, and dropped it down the drain.

Patrick continued his self-guided tour, opening the Sub-Zero fridge. He pulled out a beer. It was some European pilsner, tasteless and pale.

What a dick, thought Patrick. Two-hundred-plus microbreweries in Oregon, and he buys this skunky shit. He added it to the growing list of reasons to hate George Green. He rummaged through a few kitchen drawers till he found a bottle opener, then popped the top off and took a deep drink. "You want one?" he asked.

George shook his head no.

Motioning around the room with the open bottle, Patrick asked, "How do you pay for all this stuff? You rich?"

"None of your business," said George.

Jamie's voice hissed in Patrick's ear. "Get him to talk about the drugs."

"Speaking of business, let's get down to it." Patrick returned to his bag and set his beer on the marble countertop next to the wineglasses. The damp bottle picked up the residue of powder otherwise hidden by the warm white of the marble. He tapped the powder with the tip of his finger and tasted. Patrick took in a sharp breath. On top of everything else, this asshole had given Lisa coke. He wiped his palms on his jeans, then cracked his knuckles.

"Had a little party last night?"

"Yeah, something like that," said George, running his fingers nervously through his hair. "So, what do I owe you?"

"For what?" asked Patrick lamely.

"For, you know, the goods," said George.

"I have an excellent selection of high-quality, organic coke. Consider me your personal recreational-pharmaceutical minimart." Patrick dug through his messenger bag and dropped several small packets of cocaine onto the counter.

"Put that back. That's way more than I ordered," said George, clearly panicked. "I told you my wife is upstairs. She'd kill me if she saw this."

"Oh, I bet she's already seen plenty."

"What does that mean?" asked George.

"Just that our ladies know all. No use hiding anything from the old ball and chain, right?" Patrick finished laying out his wares on the counter. He read the label on each. "We have 'Like a Virgin.' I think we can guess what that's for. 'Hooked on a Feeling.' And finally, 'Super Freak.'"

"Seriously, put that away. I already told Sheila what I wanted." George looked slightly green.

Patrick realized he may have pushed George a little too far. He dug in his bag and pulled out a plastic bag full of weed and a packet of rolling papers. "This isn't on the menu, but I think it's what the doctor ordered. It's my own personal supply of totally legal marijuana, so your old lady can't give you a hard time about it. Let me roll you one." He removed a pinch of dried bud and, in a moment, an impeccable joint was rolled and lit. Patrick took a puff, then held it out to George as he exhaled a cloud of smoke. "Trust me. This will make you feel better," he said.

George looked warily at Patrick then reached for the joint anyway. He took a deep drag, held the smoke for what felt like just a moment too long, and blew it out with a practiced air. He stood motionless, then took another hit. "That's good stuff," he said, smoke pouring out of his mouth.

"Glad you like it."

George looked from the joint to Patrick. "Maybe I should text Sheila. I don't like that she didn't give you any specifics."

"Dude, seriously? Don't get me in trouble. Here's my pager. She sent me your digits and nothing else."

George took the pager and looked it over carefully. "Fine," he said, handing it back. He sorted through the packets on the counter. "I'll take the Super Freak and that coke I had last night. What was it . . ."

"Don't know dude, she gives it to me and I sell it. How about one of each? May as well stock up."

George nodded.

Patrick left three packets on the counter and packed the rest back into his messenger bag. "Time to pony up."

"What do I owe you?"

Patrick pretended to do a mental calculation, but he was really thinking about the ten crumpled hundred dollar bills he'd seen in Lisa's purse last night. Payment for services rendered. It was more than George owed, but, he figured, why not ask for the same. "One thousand," he said.

Unfazed, George just took another puff on the joint. He was definitely looking more relaxed. "Back in a minute."

Patrick rolled another joint as a voice came through the earbuds.

"Patrick you're doing great," said Jamie. "Just get George to say he's paying for the drugs so we can get it recorded, take the money, and you can get out of there. Mayor Salder will take care of the rest."

"Yeah, I got it," he said just as George returned with the navy suit jacket he'd been wearing last night.

He looked at Patrick suspiciously. "Were you talking to someone?" he asked.

Patrick calmly lit the second joint. "No dude. You're getting paranoid. I read that's an effect of prolonged drug use."

George dug in the suit's inside jacket pocket and pulled out a wallet and a DVD case, dropping the case on the kitchen island.

He flipped open his wallet counting out bills. He handed the cash to Patrick.

Patrick just shook his head. "What's the money for?"

"The drugs."

"The pot?"

"No, the cocaine," said George with a look of wonder at Patrick's stupidity.

"Oh yeah, the coke." He took the money from George, and with the joint hanging from the side of his mouth, he counted the bills out loud and shoved them into a back pocket of his jeans. "I think we got it." Patrick could hear Jamie cheering.

The smoke from the joint burned his eyes, and he took it out of his mouth. He looked at it and considered his next move. He could leave, sure. That's what Lisa's mom, and that asshole tattoo artist wanted him to do. It was "the plan." But why not stay a while, get to know the monster who'd abandoned an injured Lisa on a park bench? His morbid curiosity was getting the better of him.

"My work here is done, but dude, I'm in no rush. Cool if I chill for a few?"

"Actually, no. I have a lot going on today. I need to you leave."

He ignored George's protests and rummaged through a few kitchen cupboards until he found a bag of chips to go with his beer.

"Patrick, what are you doing? Get out of there now," said Lisa.

Patrick ignored her and glanced at the DVD George had left on the counter. The plastic cover sported a stressed-looking Bruce Willis and a burning skyscraper.

"George, my man. *Die Hard* is literally my favorite movie of all time. You still have a DVD player? That's so retro."

George squinted at the DVD. He pulled a pair of reading glasses from a front pocket of his sweatpants, put them on and looked again. "Sheila gave that to me last night. Said she'd send someone over to pick it up today." He picked up the thin case and handed it to Patrick. "Guess that's you."

Patrick took it from George's hand. With an enthusiasm only partially faked, he said, "Let's watch it."

George shook his head. "I don't think it's really *Die Hard.*"

"Looks real enough to me. Where's the living room in this place?" He pushed past a scowling George and stepped further into the house. A wide hallway led to a spacious living room, its polished wood floor layered with white shag rugs. A Nelson bubble lamp at least four feet wide floated above a white-leather, semi-circular sofa large enough to seat twelve. A massive flat-screen television flanked by high-end speakers dominated an entire wall. An array of components, gaming systems, and VR headsets were stored beneath it in a shiny, white media center.

"Holy shit, George. This room is amazing."

"You can't go in there," said George. The sound of a heavy crash came from upstairs.

"Too late," said Patrick as he slouched toward the sofa.

"At least take off your shoes."

"Right on." Patrick glibly kicked off his sneakers and lined them up carefully at the room's threshold. He moved to the sofa and settled himself with his stockinged feet up on the coffee table, one toe poking through a hole in his sock. Patrick saw that George was eyeing his feet with disgust.

"My wife doesn't like it when people are in here," George said.

"Why not?" Patrick ripped open the bag of chips, careful to spill a few.

"The sofa alone cost twenty-five thousand. She doesn't want anyone to ruin it."

"She doesn't let anyone sit on it?"

"Not usually."

"Are you kidding me? This room is made for getting high and watching action films. If not, what's the point? Speaking of which, that is an incredible television. Those babies cost, what, ten grand?"

"Fifteen. Worth every penny," George said, looking proudly at the TV. "Mounted it on the wall myself. No visible wires." Footsteps could be heard upstairs, and another heavy thump. George glanced up with a worried look and said to Patrick, "Listen, you really should go."

Jamie's voice came through the headset. "He's right, Patrick. You need to get out of there now. Mayor Salder and Theo are about to head over."

"Chill. It's all good," said Patrick—half to Jamie, half to George—and stubbed out his joint in a crystal bowl on the coffee table. "Come on, George. What else did you have planned for today?"

Patrick opened a large, white-lacquered box and found a collection of remotes. He picked one at random and clicked the power button. The giant television hummed to life. "Awesome." Sitting back on the sofa, Patrick could see George was torn between wanting to toss him out on his ass and a deep desire to just chill with an action film and get high.

George gave into his baser instincts. "I'm in so much trouble already, why not get in a little more." He sat down next to Patrick. "Forget the movie. Let's play *Call of Duty*." George pressed a few buttons on another remote and pulled two controllers from the white box, handing one to Patrick.

"Right on, dude." Patrick settled into the sofa, the controller resting easy in his hands. He was determined to ignore any further pestering from the Scooby Gang back in the van. He was in a sweet pad, on a comfy sofa, eating chips, and getting high on some excellent weed. As bad as the day had started, right now, life was good.

CHAPTER 23
LISA LISTENS IN

"Patrick? Are you there, Patrick? Please respond," said Jamie, her voice stern. "Get out of there now."

"Maybe his phone went dead?" asked Lisa.

"Nope. We can still hear everything." The sound of Patrick munching chips erupted from the small speaker Theo had set up on the van's fold-out table. "He's completely ignoring us," said Jamie. "Patrick has gone rogue, Mayor Salder. He's gone rogue."

Jamie and Theo had swung the van's driver and passenger seats around to face Lisa and her mother, who sat on the bench seat, transforming the interior of the van into a cramped conference room.

Lisa covered her face with her hands. Her boyfriend was smoking pot and playing video games with George Green. "This is so mortifying. What are they even talking about?" She pointed desperately at the speakerphone. "Jamie, try again. Tell him to leave. He'll listen to you."

Jamie shrugged and ran her hands through her hair in frustration. "I just did. He's totally high and completely ignoring me."

"Remind me again why the voters approved legalizing marijuana and decriminalizing possession of controlled substances?" asked Ellen.

Lisa knew her mother wasn't looking for an answer, but Jamie rattled off a succinct response. "Voters approved the measure to reduce the number of possession arrests and release thousands of prison inmates from what was seen as excessive sentences. The racist and misguided war on drugs has been a complete failure and has been a tool to target Black and Brown Americans, destroying lives and families. The measure changes the focus to treatment, prevention, and support."

"Well said, Jamie," said Ellen, genuinely impressed.

"Jamie, can I vote for you?" asked Lisa.

"Yes, Lisa. Yes, you can."

The speaker erupted with a flurry of gunfire.

"What was that?" asked Lisa with concern.

They listened carefully to rounds of ammunition firing and cheesy dialogue.

"*Call of Duty*," Jamie cried with a note of triumph. "He's never going to leave. Patrick loves that game."

"We should make our move now," said Theo to Ellen. "We have the recording, and the drugs are in George's possession." He took off a faded jean jacket that he'd been wearing over a black T-shirt, revealing muscular forearms covered in tattoos. "I say we go in."

"Is that Elvis as Jesus?" asked Jamie. "So badass."

"Thank you, miss," he said with a smile. He stood, crouching slightly in the small space, pulled a plastic bin from a narrow closet, and set it down on the floor at his feet. Pulling off the lid, he dug through an assortment of folded uniforms, jackets, and hats.

"Jamie," said Lisa. "Can you please focus?" She'd noticed Jamie paying a little too much attention to Theo for her liking. Totally age-inappropriate, thought Lisa. Then the image of a shirtless George flashed into her mind again. She shuddered and silently rebuked herself for her hypocrisy.

"Will this do?" said Theo to Ellen. He held up a wind breaker with DEA stenciled across the back and front.

Ellen smiled. "Perfect."

Patrick's voice snuck through the sounds of gunfire. "This place kind of reminds me of my parents' house."

"Really? Our interior designer said her work was one of a kind," said George peevishly, his voice a little more distant. Still, Lisa could make out every grating syllable that came out of George's mouth.

"Except it was about ten times as big and had a pool and a pool house and a little movie theater and a putting range."

Lisa leaned in. She rarely heard Patrick talk about his life before the Academy.

"Now you're just trying to make me feel bad," said George.

"No, it was nice, you know. Nice, like this place," said Patrick between the sounds of crunching, military orders, and more gunfire. "My dad was in construction—or real estate, maybe? I think he owns a lot of parking lots, but I don't really know. I was always too busy being a pain in the ass to pay much attention. Whatever it was, he made a lot of money. How do you pay for all this, really? The house, the television, the art. Isn't that a Kusama?"

"You recognize that?"

"Sure. My girlfriend—I mean my ex-girlfriend—is into art."

Lisa flinched. She didn't want to hear anymore. "Please. Can we get him out of there? Preferably by force."

"My wife has very expensive tastes," said George. "Though money's less of an issue since she sold her company. Which is a hell of a good thing. Burnam & Green isn't the cash cow it used to be."

"Living off your wife's money and cheating on her with a girl half your age. You are quite a class act, George. Lisa sure knows how to pick 'em."

"Who's Lisa?"

"Seriously? George. She's the chick you hooked up with last night."

Jamie and Lisa stared at each other, their eyes wide with shock, and Jamie spoke urgently into the speaker, "Patrick, shut up."

"You shut up," Patrick said back.

"Why are you telling me to shut up?" asked George. "And how do you know about Lisa?"

"Oh yeah, you're still catching up. Lisa, that girl you took home last night? She's my girlfriend. Well, I mean *ex-girlfriend.*"

Lisa shook her head wearily. "I'm going to strangle him."

"Ok. Time to go," said Theo to Ellen. He pulled open the sliding door of the van and jumped out.

Lisa waited as Theo helped her mother out of the van, then she slid the door closed behind them. She moved to the driver's seat next to Jamie and together they watched as Ellen and Theo, now wearing the black DEA windbreaker, headed toward George's house. "I feel like I should be going with them."

"No way. You don't ever need to see George Green again. Your mom and Theo can handle it." Jamie turned up the volume on the speaker. "We can hear everything and still talk to Patrick from here."

"You know how to use all the stuff?"

"Sure, easy peasy. I was watching Theo."

"Yeah, you were. You like him," said Lisa with a grin.

"I admire his particular set of skills," said Jamie, her mouth curling uncontrollably into a smile.

"What did you say about his tattoo? 'So badass'?"

"Shut up. He's a thousand years old. You're the one who likes older men."

Lisa stuck her tongue out at Jamie. "Anyway, what's his deal? He's definitely not a cop, or a DEA agent."

Jamie riffled through the plastic bin Theo had left on the floor of the van, guessing at the array of acronyms on jackets, uniforms, and hats. She pulled out a black ski mask and grimaced. "I don't want to know what this one's for."

Lisa felt her stomach drop. "Me neither." She gave Jamie a meaningful look.

"Sorry," said Jamie, who stuffed it back into the bin. She kept searching through the disguises and laughed as she dug out a baseball cap, holding it up for Lisa to see.

"NASA!" Lisa exclaimed.

"Who does this guy think he's kidding?" asked Jamie.

"Well, he's kind of handsome in a rugged, mature way. And you've always had a thing for men with moustaches," said Lisa.

"I hate moustaches. And if you don't shut it, I will not hesitate to try out those crazy karate moves he used on Patrick."

"I bet you'd like him to try some moves on you," said Lisa as she waggled her eyebrows up and down.

"You're a nightmare." Jamie leaned toward the speaker, punched the volume button a few more times, and listened closely. "Patrick and George are still talking. Oh, I just heard the doorbell."

"Jamie and Theo sitting in a tree . . . K-I-S-S-I-N-G."

"Seriously, I will punch you. Now shush."

CHAPTER 24
GEORGE GETS NERVOUS

George realized he'd made a critical error. He wasn't quite sure when or how or why, but something was definitely off. His head felt thick and fuzzy, and a severe bout of paranoia had kicked in. He should have laid off the pot and stuck to bourbon. Now he was playing video games with his drug dealer. His drug dealer who knew Lisa and everything that had happened last night.

George heard footsteps coming down the stairs. Sue.

Oh god, he thought. He stood up quickly—hoping to usher Patrick out the backdoor before she found them—but in his haste, he knocked over his glass of bourbon. Startled, he dropped his lit joint. Smoke rose from where the joint's embers ignited the alcohol and started a tiny fire on the white rug. Frantically he snatched the joint up and stomped the flames out.

Sue walked into the room holding her phone and scanning messages. George stood back up awkwardly, hiding the stained carpet with his stockinged feet. He glanced around. With a couple strategic shoves, he could reposition the furniture and hide the evidence. He sighed with relief.

"George, how many times do I need to tell you, no food in here. And could you please use coasters? You are such a child."

She was dressed in her yoga gear again. A thousand pieces of designer clothing in her walk-in closet, and all she ever wore were stretchy black pants and ridiculous exercise tops. Not that he wasn't proud of how well his wife took care of herself. Couldn't she just once wear something soft and loose, something that left a little to the imagination? George glanced over at Patrick and noticed that he didn't seem to mind Sue's apparel.

"Hey," said Patrick. He remained seated on the sofa, a joint in one hand, his other wrapped around a beer, looking very much at home. "How're you doing." It wasn't a question so much as a way of expressing his obvious appreciation for her shapely form.

George didn't like how Patrick was ogling his wife.

"Who are you?" Sue asked Patrick, looking both irritated by the defilement of her pristine living room and pleased at the young man's attention.

"I'm your husband's drug dealer," Patrick said with a smile.

"Lovely," she said, her eyes leaving Patrick's and scanning the room as though looking for damage.

George spoke impulsively, "Sue, there's something up with this kid."

Sue walked to her husband, plucked the joint from George's hand, and sniffed it.

"He knows about last night," continued George.

"You get so paranoid when you smoke pot." She took a hit. "Good stuff."

"No, Sue, really, I can hear him talking to . . . someone. And it's not me."

"He's probably just talking to the voices coming from his drug-addled brain. You know how kids are these days. Anyway, I'm going to yoga. What are you two idiots going to do all day? Play video games?"

Patrick smiled. "Video games are just the warmup." He waved the *Die Hard* DVD case at her. "Next up is the greatest action film of all time. Blow off your yoga class and join us."

"*Die Hard* in August? It's a Christmas movie," she said with disgust. She handed the joint back to George and looked pointedly at him. "You better have moved into the guest bedroom by the time I get back. I will burn anything you leave behind."

George collapsed in on himself a little bit and mumbled, "Yes, dear."

Sue shook her head. "I can't believe I'm letting you stay. And I'm taking your car. At least I know how to drive the damn thing." She turned and walked out of the room, and moments later Patrick heard a door slam shut.

"Your old lady is hot."

George glared at Patrick. Who was this kid, anyway? Sitting on his sofa. Eating his chips. Drinking his beer.

The front door bell rang. Then rang again. Now what? "Stay here, and don't touch anything," he said.

"Sure, whatever."

George smashed the remnants of his joint out in the crystal bowl and walked down the hall and through the kitchen. He noticed the packets of cocaine still sitting on the counter and shrugged. He'd simply turn away whomever was at the door. Two forms were visible through the glass, obviously a man and a woman.

Probably missionaries, he thought, come to haggle for his soul. He opened the door narrowly, prepared to slam it shut.

"Hello, George," said Ellen.

CHAPTER 25
DIE HARDER

The dulcet tones of Ellen and Theo berating George drifted in from the kitchen and Patrick smiled. He'd done his part, and for the moment he opted to enjoy this sweet pad and a few minutes of action film perfection. Spotting a DVD player among the many components neatly stored in the media center, he stood and opened the *Die Hard* case. The silver disc wasn't labeled and appeared to be a bootleg, but he just shrugged and slid it into the tray. Returning to his spot on the sofa, he picked up the remote, switched the inputs, and hit play.

The massive television was dark for a few seconds, then displayed a grainy, low-res image. Patrick scowled. Definitely not the greatest action film of all time. The black and white footage appeared to be from a parking garage security camera, though he could only see one parked car from its vantage point. The rest of the parking spots were empty. Patrick was about to hit stop when a person stepped into frame. The camera landed squarely on a man he'd recognize anywhere. He was tall, wore dark-rimmed glasses on a thin, lined face, and had thick hair swept back from his forehead. His hands were tucked deep into the pockets of his long overcoat, and he stared intently at something off screen.

Patrick paused the video and stared at the man's face for a long moment, feeling suddenly chilled. Although the footage was crude, he felt like the man was right there, standing next to him in George's living room.

Voices seeped in from the kitchen. He didn't have much time. Every instinct told him he should leave George with whatever this recording contained, but something compelled him to see it through. He hit play.

The man turned his back to the camera as another figure entered the frame, a man Patrick didn't recognize. This second player was shorter and smaller, dressed in a dark suit and carrying a briefcase. The pair exchanged words, their body language becoming more aggressive with each moment. In vain, Patrick turned up the volume, but there was no audio.

As though giving up the fight, the newcomer started to walk off, then paused and turned back in response to something the taller man said. In a rage, he dropped his briefcase and lunged, but it was a futile gesture. In a moment, he'd been roughly pushed to the ground. His face contorted with anger, which quickly changed to fear when he saw the gun. Patrick gasped as the gun silently fired twice in rapid succession. The taller man stood towering over his victim as a pool of blood began to spread darkly. After a long moment, he checked for a pulse, then pulled off the dead man's watch and removed his wallet from an inside jacket pocket. Picking up the briefcase, he opened it and scattered its contents over the body, then dropped it. The footage ended and the screen went dark.

Patrick jumped to his feet, his heart racing. Frantically he pressed buttons on the DVD player until the tray slid open. His hands shaking, he carefully lifted the silver disc out and placed it back in its case. He suspected George had no idea what was on the DVD. If he had, he never would have agreed to hold onto it for Sheila. This video was a death sentence to anyone who saw it.

He dropped the case on the coffee table and turned to leave, then hesitated. George told him to return it to Sheila. If he could get home first, he still had the ancient laptop he'd swiped when he left the Academy. He might be able to make a copy. No one would ever know he'd seen the footage and he'd have a backup if he ever needed it.

Picking up the case, he slid it into the back pocket of his jeans. He took a deep breath and walked from the room, grabbing his sneakers on the way out.

CHAPTER 26
SINK DEEPER

"I was in the neighborhood, George," said Ellen pleasantly. "I thought I'd stop by and check in. Your wife seemed so angry with you at the hospital last night. I wanted to make sure that you'd received the medical attention you deserved."

George felt blood rush to his face and stammered out a reply. "That is so considerate." He held up his burned hand, which was wrapped in gauze. "On the mend."

"That's wonderful." She stood there calmly, waiting.

"I appreciate the visit, but I'm really busy today."

"Hmm . . . well, before you get back to whatever that is, I'd like to introduce you to my associate."

She stepped back, revealing her companion. George saw that the man was wearing a black zip-up jacket adorned with the letters DEA. The acronym slowly cohered in George's muddled brain. DEA agent. Drug Enforcement Agency.

Oh my god, he thought. George stepped back into the house and tried to slam the door shut, but it was pointless. The agent pushed the door firmly open for Ellen, who crossed the threshold serenely.

"George, I'm surprised at you. There's no reason to turn us away. This is a friendly visit."

George spun around and ran for the kitchen, its Italian marble countertop currently littered with several grams over the legal limit of cocaine. He heard the agent following close behind, but George was faster. He scooped up the drugs, skirted around the kitchen island, and dumped them in the sink, pushing them down the food disposal. He turned on the faucet and flipped the disposal switch with glee. Nothing happened. He flipped the switch again, realizing it was just turning the light above the sink on and off. Panicking, he searched the wall, flipping switches at random. He felt a firm hand on his shoulder.

The agent turned off the faucet and asked, "Are you looking for this?" He pointed to a switch placed conveniently at waist level.

If only I'd helped Sue with the dishes more often, George thought, feeling distraught.

"Sir, please step away from the sink."

George sullenly backed away.

"What do we have here?" asked the agent. He reached into the disposal and pulled out the packets of coke, setting them carefully on the kitchen counter. The packets were dripping wet, but otherwise intact.

"I have no idea," said George. "I don't know anything about this stuff. I don't know how it got here."

"I brought it, and you bought it," said Patrick, who'd stepped into the room. "And it's about time you all showed up. Hey, Mayor Salder. I got you what you wanted—one bird, two stoned dudes. Or is it two birds, one stoned dude?" He hiccupped.

"Patrick, are you high?" Ellen whispered the last word, then shook her head with disapproval.

"What?" Patrick said. "It's my cover." He slipped on a pair of worn black sneakers, then opened a beat-up messenger bag that sat on the kitchen island. He removed the paper bag containing the rest of the drugs Sheila had given him and handed it to Ellen.

George was completely bewildered. He turned to Ellen. "How do you know this kid? Are you behind all this?" He stared at her for a moment, putting the pieces together in his head. "I knew Sheila had to be working with someone powerful, but I would never have guessed it was you."

He saw Ellen and the agent exchange a glance and felt a flush of triumph. "All your talk about wanting to get drugs off the streets. All lies. You're a mere mortal like the rest of us."

Ellen didn't crumple like he'd hoped. "We have very little in common, George. I'm not behind Portland's recent influx of drugs, though I'd certainly like to know who is. And you're going to help me."

He scrambled for some other defense. "What about your daughter? She's a hooker and dates a drug dealer," he said, pointing accusingly at Patrick. "I'll leak it to the press. Your career will be over."

"Wouldn't that be terrible?" Her voice dripped with sarcasm. "I wouldn't have to deal with all the idiots on the city council." She gingerly picked up a packet and weighed it in her hand. "But you, George, well, you're looking at a misdemeanor for this level of drug possession, giving you a criminal record easily searchable by the public. Just think about how your more conservative clients will feel when they learn about your cocaine habit."

George's heart started racing. "I'll say the kid broke in, that it was a home invasion."

"He broke in and left cocaine behind?"

"He planted the coke. To set me up."

"George, Patrick's wearing a microphone. We recorded every word you said." Ellen turned to Patrick. "Please go back to the van. The agent and I need to have a talk with George, alone."

"Bye, George, it was nice doing business with you. Anytime you want to hang, you know how to reach me." Patrick flashed his beeper at George and left through the front door.

That little prick, thought George. Once I'm out of this mess, I'm going to bury him.

CHAPTER 27
CITY HALL

Theo pulled the Vanagon into a vacant parking spot in front of City Hall. As soon as the vehicle came to a stop, Lisa slid the Volkswagen's side door open and jumped out, Patrick following right on her heels.

"Lisa, you should have seen it. George tried to shove the drugs down the garbage disposal," said Patrick, doubling over with laughter.

Lisa just rolled her eyes. Patrick was enjoying George Green's humiliation all too much. She'd seen her boyfriend high plenty of times and usually it just made him mellow and quiet. This version of Patrick was almost frantic, like he was acting. At this point he'd told the story about half a dozen times. "I'll take your word for it," she said. She passed the rose-colored granite columns that supported the building's portico and paused, waiting for the others.

Theo pushed open one of the heavy glass doors leading into the lobby and held it as they all entered the building. Lisa noticed that he'd left the DEA jacket in the van and wondered again who this guy was. Ellen waved the group past a pair of security guards and headed to the elevator. She pressed the call button, the door immediately opened, and the five of them stepped in together.

Patrick continued retelling the story. "And then George couldn't find the disposal switch in his own kitchen. What an asshole."

"Yes, Patrick. It was so funny you could have died," said Lisa.

"Too bad George will never see the inside of a jail cell, but it was still awesome," said Patrick. "Mayor Salder, you scared the shit out of him. And tattoo guy—or is it DEA guy—what's your name again?"

"I'm not a DEA agent. And it's Theo."

"Where'd you get the jacket?" asked Jamie.

"Just a souvenir I picked up along the way," he said with a wink.

The elevator door opened, and they walked down the hall to Ellen's office suite. Lisa charged ahead and pushed open the lobby door.

Patrick started retelling the story again, but Ellen cut him off. "Lisa, can you please get your boyfriend under control."

"He's not my boyfriend anymore, and there is literally nothing I can do. He is totally high." Lisa flopped down on the sofa.

"Yes, we can all see that."

"He needs some junk food and a nap," said Jamie, who took a seat next to Lisa.

"Fine," said Ellen. "He can sleep it off on the sofa in my office." She dug through her purse, found a granola bar, and handed it to Patrick.

"Mayor, you're the best. I don't know why Lisa always says you're the worst mother ever," said Patrick.

An uncomfortable pause followed, and Lisa glared at him.

"Did I say that out loud?" whispered Patrick loudly.

"Patrick, please try to remember to use your inner monologue," said Lisa.

Ellen scowled at them both, then unlocked her office door and pointed Patrick toward a brown leather sofa. She closed the door behind him, kicked off her heels, and sat down on one of the upholstered armchairs. "Lisa dear, I know I'm the worst mother ever, but could you pour me a drink? I could murder a gin and tonic." Ellen nodded toward a large cabinet in the corner.

Lisa stood, silently cursing Patrick as she walked to the cabinet. She opened the doors to reveal a dozen liquor bottles, a mini fridge full of mixers, and even a small bowl filled with fresh lemons and limes. "Mother!" she said, aghast. "You have a bar in your office?"

Jamie joined her and looked through the bottles. "Badass."

"I'm the mayor, Lisa. Of course I have a bar. How else do you expect me to survive this job?" said Ellen. "On second thought, dear, can you make that a vodka martini? Twist, please."

"Yes, mother," she said curtly. Lisa couldn't help but wonder if her mother's choice of drink was intentional, thinking of the two or maybe three martinis she'd downed with George last night. She vowed to never drink that particular cocktail again.

CHAPTER 28
PATRICK PRETENDS

Patrick lay quietly on the sofa in Ellen's office for a few moments in case someone checked up on him, but it appeared even Lisa had fallen for his "I'm so high" routine. In reality, he'd never felt so sober. He sat up and rubbed his forehead, racking his brain for an excuse to leave. Food poisoning? Toothache? Sick goldfish? He was coming up empty. And anyway, Lisa and Jamie would call him on his bullshit.

Desperate for inspiration, Patrick stood and paced around the room. In addition to the leather sofa, Ellen's office featured an armchair, a wall of bookshelves filled with legal journals, a tropical potted plant, and several landscapes of Portland and Mount Hood. He paused and looked closer, recognizing Lisa's signature style in a framed watercolor.

The painting appeared to depict an idyllic scene of children playing by a beautiful mountain lake. Patrick knew what Lisa had actually captured, though. It was that afternoon at the Academy when a pack of children had hurled mud at Lisa and Patrick as they tried to hold their ground on the wooden dock. Even the pair of security guards could be seen stumbling toward the figures in the painting. Mount Hood stood towering in the background, its reflection a mirror image on the still water. He shuddered at the memory and wondered if Lisa knew her artwork was hanging in Ellen's office.

Right now, though, Patrick had bigger problems. He turned toward Ellen's desk. It was large, built of some dark wood and covered with a leather blotter, a tray of files, three framed photographs, and a very out-of-date desktop computer. Taking a closer look, he saw it had a built-in drive, and Patrick thanked the gods of budget shortfalls. He moved the vintage PC's mouse and the screen lit up, showing a password prompt.

Damn, he thought, I guess I couldn't be that lucky. He looked over the desk and opened a few drawers, but there were no clues as to what the password could be. Then, with a rush of inspiration, he flipped over the mouse pad. There it was—a yellow post-it note with *"Littlelisa1"* written on it. Perfect. He typed it in, and the computer unlocked.

Patrick stepped back to the sofa where he'd left his messenger bag. He carried it to Ellen's desk and pulled out the DVD from George's house. He slotted it into the computer's drive, silently praying the computer would read the disc, and breathed a sigh of relief when it did. Once loaded, he located a movie player utility and ripped a video file, watching in agony as the progress bar slowly crawled from zero to one hundred percent. His eyes kept flipping back to the office door, willing it to stay closed. Finally, the file was ready, and he emailed a copy of it to himself. He almost deleted the video from Ellen's computer, then stopped. What better place to hide a smoking gun? He buried the file in a folder titled an uninspiringly "Quarterly tax audit archive do not delete."

He ejected the DVD, returned it to its case, and tucked it safely in his bag. Logging out of the computer, he set it back to sleep mode. With a sigh, he sat back in Ellen's chair and enjoyed a moment of relief at having a backup. The feeling was short lived.

His eyes rested on the three framed photographs on Ellen's desk. One was a portrait of Lisa as a toddler with blond pigtails and a mischievous smile. Another featured Ellen posing with a group of men and women in suits. The third was a family photo. Slowly, Patrick picked up the frame. The picture must have been taken shortly before Lisa was sent to the Academy. He saw Lisa as a sullen teenager dressed all in black, her hair dyed a vibrant blue. Ellen stood next to her wearing a grim expression. The only person smiling was a man. Though they'd never met, Patrick recognized him instantly. He was the shorter of the two men in the video. The one who'd been murdered in the parking garage. This was Lisa's father.

"Shit," he whispered. His hands trembling, Patrick returned the photo to its place on Ellen's desk. He flipped over the mousepad and frantically started retyping in the password so he could delete the backup video. He was too late.

"Patrick? What are you doing on my mother's computer?"

Lisa stood at the open door, flanked by a very angry Ellen holding a martini glass and a dangerous-looking Theo.

Patrick stared back, completely at a loss. Part of him was tempted to just tell the truth and show them the video. But he wasn't ready for that yet, or for what it meant for him and Lisa. He needed more time and decided that the right thing to do was nothing at all. And so, he lied. "I thought I'd do some research and look up more intel about Sheila." He tried to control the tremor in his voice.

"My computer is password-protected," said Ellen.

"Yeah, about that." Patrick held up the post-it note and shrugged. "Found this under your mouse pad. You might want to do something about your security."

"Mother," said Lisa reproachfully.

"Yes, well, I have more important things to worry about than passwords," said Ellen, looking flustered.

"And your computer should be in a museum. Maybe it's time for an upgrade?" he asked hopefully, thinking it would be one way to wipe the evidence.

Ellen quickly shifted from embarrassed to irritated. "I'll take it under advisement."

"Hey, I found her police record," Jamie called out from the lobby.

Patrick grabbed his messenger bag and followed Lisa, Ellen and Theo out of the office. They clustered around Jamie where she sat at Geoff's desk using his laptop.

"Sheila Elkins has a pretty impressive rap sheet, but she was last arrested about four years ago. After serving a short sentence, there's nothing else. She's been on the straight and narrow as far as the police are concerned. Not even a parking ticket. Either she's being very careful, or someone is protecting her," said Jamie.

"Can you do a web search on her name?" asked Ellen. "Let's see what else she's been up to."

Jamie typed and clicked on the first promising search result, opening a site titled "All Star Property Management." She clicked on "About Us" and scrolled to a headshot of a respectable-looking Sheila, her spiky hair neatly arranged. She wore a navy blue business suit with a bright yellow scarf wrapped stylishly around her neck.

"Are you sure that's Sheila?" asked Ellen. "She doesn't look like a drug dealer."

"You always were fooled by appearances, Mother," said Lisa, obviously pleased to get in a dig.

"It's absolutely Sheila," said Jamie. "I recognize her from a party Lisa and I went to at this gorgeous house in Ladd's Addition. Best jello shots I've ever had. Anyway, she looked different then, more meth head than middle management, if you know what I mean. But that's her."

"Patrick, is this the woman you're working for?" asked Ellen.

"Yep," he answered, nodding mournfully.

"This property management thing must be her front," said Jamie. She pointed at the laptop's screen which now displayed a map of All Star's properties across Portland. "Look at the locations she manages—parking lots scattered all over town. It even mentions she works directly with the city to establish new food cart pods in All Star lots and follows all licensing guidelines and requirements."

"Delightful," said Ellen, her voice conveying no joy.

"Based on Patrick's loose lips, I followed Sheila last night and searched her Airstream," said Theo. "At the very least, she's using her own cart to distribute."

"No. Not just her own," said Patrick with conviction. "She's selling through carts all over the place. Remember the Clam Shack?"

"Oh! I loved that place," said Jamie. "My favorite was the clams with all that garlic and a side of fried plantains cooked to crispy perfection. I still dream about that dish."

"Sheila's invention."

"You have got to be kidding," said Jamie.

Patrick shook his head. "Sheila said she fired the chef and shut down the cart because it was too popular and drawing unwanted attention."

Jamie's mouth dropped open. "That bitch. We need to destroy her."

Ellen turned to Lisa and Jamie. "Did you notice the names of any other carts at the party last night? I have to assume that since Sheila was there, the other carts were also hers."

"Yeah, Double D Donuts and the Prussian Pierogi were there," said Jamie.

"You're sure it was the Prussian Pierogi?" asked Patrick.

"What is it, Patrick?" asked Ellen.

"Last night, Sheila said when I ran out of product to drop off the cash at the Prussian Pierogi cart."

"Not to her?"

"Nope."

"Of course," said Ellen. "The cart owners claim they earned the cash as legitimate revenue. They're using the carts not just to sell drugs, but to launder money." Ellen tapped Jamie's shoulder. "May I?" she asked.

"Of course, Mayor Salder," said Jamie, leaving her spot at Geoff's desk.

Ellen sat down and opened the city tax site, logging into a detailed view of records. "Here are the tax filings for the Prussian Pierogi. That single food truck earned over two-hundred thousand dollars in gross revenue last year."

"That's a lot of dumplings," said Lisa.

"Actually, that amount is just over average revenue for most carts in Portland," said Ellen.

"How about Double D?" asked Jamie.

"Let's see," said Ellen, tapping on the keyboard. "Similar. Makes sense. She would want earnings to stay under the radar."

"If she's running carts in lots all over the city, that adds up to millions," said Theo.

Ellen nodded. "And if her operation is as big as Patrick says, I find it hard to believe just one person is running it." She returned to the All Star website and scrolled through the rest of the page, scanning the other headshots and bios. "George told us he thought Sheila worked for someone powerful, someone who everyone else considers legitimate. No one else on this site is of any interest."

"Mayor Salder, could you scroll to the bottom?" asked Jamie. She pointed at the website's footer. "It says All Star's parent company is something called VSC."

Ellen clicked and opened to a property developer's web site, featuring a render of the company's latest project in downtown Portland, a massive high rise with three hundred condo units and twenty thousand feet of retail space. She continued to scroll through the webpage and paused on a photo of a respectable-looking man with dark gray hair and thick-rimmed glasses. The photo's caption read, "Victor Smith, CEO of Victor Smith Construction."

"Maybe he's the 'big bad' George mentioned," said Jamie.

"Looks like the type," said Lisa.

"Definitely evil," said Jamie. "Do you know him, Mayor Salder?" she asked.

"Unfortunately, I do," said Ellen. "Over the last twenty years, Victor Smith has been under investigation for everything from money laundering to racketeering, even bribery of election officials. Nothing sticks. Lately he's painted himself as a legitimate business-man and philanthropist. Everyone's fallen for it. And he's doing everything he can to derail my campaign for reelection."

"George mentioned he saw Victor and Sheila arguing at the party last night," said Theo. "Since she's an employee, maybe it was just a work issue."

"Or she's running the food cart drug cartel for him," suggested Jamie eagerly.

Patrick barely heard their words. He couldn't tear his eyes away from the photo, again feeling as though the man was here, standing next to him. The man who'd murdered Lisa's father in the parking garage.

"Patrick, what's wrong?" asked Lisa.

"Dude, you are looking even more pale than usual," said Jamie.

"I'm fine," said Patrick. He stepped away from Geoff's desk. Apparently, things could get worse. The truth wanted out, but Patrick wasn't about to help it along.

"I'm starting to worry about your mood swings," said Jamie.

"I said I'm fine, just leave it." A chirping sound erupted from where the beeper was still attached to his belt. He felt like ripping it off and throwing it across the room.

"Patrick, it's your beeper. Are you going to get that?" asked Jamie.

"Yeah." He pulled the beeper out of its case.

"What does it say?" asked Ellen.

"Nineteen Glisan now," he read.

"Patrick, do you know what it means?"

Patrick just shrugged and turned to Lisa. "Can I talk to you, alone?"

Theo plucked the beeper from Patrick's hand and studied it. "Nineteenth and Glisan. That's the Five Firs pod."

"No shit, Sherlock," said Patrick.

"Best vegan corn dogs in town," said Jamie.

Patrick looked at Ellen. "Listen, I need to talk to Lisa. Just a for a minute. Can we use your office?"

Ellen looked hesitant but nodded her assent. Patrick pulled Lisa by the hand into the room and closed the door.

"Patrick, what is it? You're scaring me," said Lisa.

He looked at her beautiful face, her black eye reminding him of the one she'd sported the first time he saw her at the Academy. He knew things were bad between them at the moment. Now, with Victor Smith involved, it would only get worse.

"Lisa, let's just take off. We can make a run for it and get out of here. I have a few grand saved up. It'll keep us going on the road until we can find work."

"What are you talking about? We can't go."

"Why not? I love you. I know you love me. Let's leave all this shit behind us and start over."

Lisa looked at him sadly and took his hand. "If we take off, my mom will come after us. The only reason you're in the clear is because we're doing what she's asked. The last time I ran away, I ended up locked up at the Academy. And for you it could be worse. You could end up in prison."

"Please, Lisa."

"I can't. We need to see this through. And then we can go on with our lives and leave this all behind."

Patrick pulled his hand away and shook his head. "I hope you're right." He looked longingly at Ellen's computer and imagined throwing it out the window and onto the sidewalk four floors below. Instead he opened the office door and stepped back into the lobby.

"I think we should send him in," said Theo.

"I don't like it," said Ellen.

"Patrick can ask about Victor Smith and see how Sheila reacts," said Theo.

"No," protested Lisa. "What if George talked to Sheila? Patrick could be walking into a trap."

"We made it perfectly clear to George what would happen if he took any action," said Ellen. "Let's not get melodramatic."

"Are you kidding me? Sheila is a drug dealer who apparently works for the biggest crook in town, and you're telling me to not get melodramatic?"

"It's fine. I'll do it," said Patrick. The universe was offering him the perfect opportunity to return the DVD to Sheila. He'd forget he ever saw the video and find another way to delete the copy from Ellen's computer. Maybe Lisa was right. If they just saw this through, they'd be done with the mayor, George Green, Sheila, Victor Smith, and the whole mess. They could go back to their lives and pretend none of this had ever happened.

But deep down, he knew that was impossible. Nothing would ever be the same.

CHAPTER 29
PERFORMANCE REVIEW

Patrick walked through a maze of carts, including personal favorites Sorry Hips! Hamburgers and You'll Love Our Yule Logs. The food cart pod oozed with a quaint Portland charm; the casual observer would never have guessed its darker purpose. The five towering Douglas firs that lent the pod its name gave the space a lush, forested feel despite the urban location. Hipster families sat at picnic tables and around a large firepit with their designer doodles, pugs, and labs. As he walked by, a leggy Great Dane started barking urgently, pulling at his lead. Several other dogs followed suit, struggling against their leashes and ignoring commands from their embarrassed owners to quiet down.

Patrick slunk by them. He assumed the dogs were barking at him, aware with some ancient animal instinct of his guilt at lying to those he held most dear.

He spotted Sheila's vintage Airstream at the far end of the pod nearest the fir trees. It was tucked just behind the Prussian Pierogi cart. A large heavily tattooed man looked out the cart's window. His face lit up when Patrick glanced up at the menu and sniffed. This must be Boris, thought Patrick.

Boris rushed out his pitch. "How about a pierogi? I use my grand-mother's recipe. God bless her dear departed soul, she died making them for me. She set down the plate then dropped dead." He paused. "It was unexpected."

Patrick wasn't sure how to respond. "I'm sorry to hear that, man."

"No. It's all good. I hope I'm that lucky when my time comes. I don't want to linger, you know what I'm saying? Now I make pierogis fresh every day in her memory," said Boris solemnly.

"That's really sweet, but I can't order anything right now. I'll definitely come back though. Smells delicious." Patrick stepped past the cart and headed toward Sheila's trailer.

"Hey, where do you think you're going?" Boris suddenly looked ready to leap over the counter.

"Nowhere dude, just checking things out."

"That cart is off limits."

Jamie's voice came through the earbuds. "Everything all right?" she asked.

Patrick whispered back, "Sure, if the three-hundred-pound gorilla in the pierogi cart doesn't tackle me."

Suddenly the door of the Airstream popped open, and Sheila appeared. "It's all good, Boris. He's expected," she called out.

Boris looked placated, but concern still wrinkled his massive brow.

"All right, Sheila. If you need anything, you just give a holler." He glared at Patrick and pointed two fingers at his eyes in an "I'm watching you" gesture.

Patrick stepped through the open door of the trailer, squeezing past Sheila. Her elegant black pantsuit from last night had been replaced by skin-tight yoga clothes. Similar to Sue's outfit this afternoon, thought Patrick.

Sheila leaned back out the door. "Boris, see if you can do anything about the dogs. What the hell are they barking at?"

Patrick heard him yell back, "On it, ma'am."

Sheila closed the door, which muffled most of the noise. "Don't mind Boris. He's loyal, but dumb as a stump. He brings by a few pierogis every day. Would you like one?" she asked, pointing to a soggy paper plate of pale brown doughy lumps.

"Any good?" Patrick asked.

"No, they're terrible. Just terrible. I don't have the heart to tell him to stop." She dropped the paper plate into a small garbage can. "It's tough finding good help in this town."

"He works for you?"

"They all do, the whole pod."

"Even the chicks in Double D?"

"Even those two tons of fun."

Jamie's voice came through Patrick's ear pods, "That's great, Patrick. Now ask her about Victor Smith."

"Cool, yeah. Sheila, I wanted to ask you about something. Or actually about someone that George mentioned when I made my delivery earlier. He said that he saw you and Victor Smith talking at the party. How do you know him?"

Sheila scowled. "What do you care about Victor Smith?"

Patrick swallowed. His mind had gone blank.

Jamie's voice whispered through the ear pods. "Tell her you rent one of his apartments."

"He's my landlord," he said with a shrug he hoped looked nonchalant.

"Yeah? Well, he's my boss, and our conversation at the party is none of your business."

"I just wondered if he wasn't part of this whole thing. You know. The food cart drug cartel."

Sheila raised a plucked brow. "Food cart drug cartel? A bit of an exaggeration, but it has a nice ring to it. And aren't you the curious cat asking about Victor."

"I guess."

"Mind if I smoke?"

"No, that's cool." He figured that covered his instructions from Ellen and Theo. He'd asked about Victor, now it was time to hand over the DVD so he could get out of there.

While Sheila was busy pulling a pack of cigarettes from her purse, Patrick quickly tapped his phone to end the call and the recording. He knew Lisa would freak out, but he didn't have a choice. Patrick pulled the *Die Hard* DVD out of his messenger bag and held it out to Sheila. "George said to give you this."

"Did he?"

Patrick gasped.

Sheila held a small silver pistol in her hand, pointed at Patrick's chest. "I talked to George's wife after my yoga class this afternoon. Sue mentioned George and his new drug dealer were getting cozy and watching *Die Hard*. How sweet."

His heart pounding, Patrick took a step back and reached for the Airstream's door. He wondered at the karmic retribution of George Green's wife ratting him out to Sheila.

"Where do you think you're going?" Sheila asked.

"I didn't watch it, I swear."

Her face darkened. "I don't think I've ever met a worse liar."

"I'm serious. I'm just doing what George told me."

"I'll have Boris take care of you. He's a pro. You won't feel a thing. George though, he might need to suffer a bit more," she said, shaking her head in disgust. "I gave the DVD to that idiot last night for safekeeping. I told him not to watch it, and of course he does the first chance he gets. God, that man. I feel bad for Sue. For some reason she still loves him, but she'll be better off once he's dead."

As much as Patrick hated George, he didn't want the man killed. "Fine. I watched it," Patrick confessed, "but George wasn't even in the room. I don't think he has any idea what's on it."

"Sorry, kid. I can't take that chance." Keeping the gun level with his chest, her eyes never leaving his, Sheila picked up her phone.

"Please, stop."

"Why should I?" she asked.

Patrick's heart beat faster. "Because I'm Victor Smith's son."

She laughed. "Bullshit."

"I'm not lying."

She rolled her eyes. "Prove it."

"I grew up at nine five one Westshore Drive in Lake Oswego. My mom's name is Anne. My dad's yacht is named Dorothy. There are three elk heads mounted in his home office named Don, Vito, and Corleone. He's never eaten soup. He hates live music and I used to have to sneak out of the house to see bands. He gave me this for going to a Weezer concert when I was fourteen." Patrick pointed to a cigarette burn on his left arm. "And he's afraid of rabbits. Should I keep going?"

Sheila glared at him and lowered the gun. "I thought you looked familiar. Victor's son," she said, shaking her head. "Well that complicates things. You close?"

"No," he said. "I haven't talked to him in years."

She nodded.

Patrick held the DVD out to her. "I promise I'll just forget the whole thing. No one ever needs to know I saw the video. Just tell me what happened that day."

"You're making demands now? Like father like son." Sheila lit a cigarette, took a drag and exhaled, filling the small space with smoke. "Oh, what the hell. I was working at one of Victor's parking lots downtown and got caught stealing credit card numbers. Victor said he'd do me a solid and not call the cops if I did him a favor. He asked me to block off one of the floors and kill all the security camera feeds. Only, I left one on by accident and caught that little gem," she said, nodding at the DVD still in Patrick's hand. "I've been using it as a bargaining chip, to get a bigger piece of the—what did you call it again? 'Food cart drug cartel.'" She paused and gave him an appraising look. "Maybe I should give you a more prominent role. Interested in a promotion? Me and you versus big daddy?"

"No," said Patrick, shaking his head. "I'm not interested in any of that. I just want to know why my dad shot the mayor's husband."

"Oh, that's all," said Sheila sarcastically.

"He must have had a good reason, right?" Patrick was surprised by how desperately he hoped it were true. He knew his father wasn't a great guy. Patrick had more scars than that one cigarette burn to prove it. Victor could be cruel, yet there had also been moments when he'd shown Patrick real affection. Despite everything, Patrick loved his father. He loved Lisa too, and he knew that she and Ellen deserved to know the truth. Right now, though, his loyalty was to a father who likely didn't deserve it. He knew his hope and fear were all plainly written on his face for Sheila to see, and she looked back at him with pity. As he waited anxiously for her answer, Patrick noticed the barking dogs outside had gone quiet and absently wondered what Boris had done to silence them.

Someone knocked sharply at the door. "DEA, open up," said a gruff voice that Patrick recognized as Theo's.

"What the hell! Are you a narc?" shrieked Sheila.

Dammit, thought Patrick. He'd never get an answer from Sheila now. He shoved the DVD back in his messenger bag.

Theo knocked on the door again. "Open up. This is your last warning."

Sheila swung the gun away from Patrick and toward the door. She yelled, "Back off. I have a gun and a hostage."

Patrick saw his chance. He knocked the gun out of Sheila's hand, and it clattered to the floor. Sheila shoved him out of the way, scrambling for the weapon. Quickly, he stepped toward the door to open it for Theo, but before he could reach it, the Airstream suddenly heaved back and forth violently, and Patrick dropped to his knees.

"Hey!" he yelled at Sheila, thinking she must have tripped him, but then he saw that she'd fallen as well. The Airstream continued to shake, causing cabinet doors to fly open and the few dishes and utensils contained inside clattered around the small space.

What on earth is Theo doing? thought Patrick.

Just as suddenly as it had begun, the shaking ceased and the trailer righted itself.

"Did we just get hit by a truck?" asked Sheila. She'd managed to retrieve the gun, but Patrick saw that her hand was trembling.

Another tremor violently shook the Airstream. Patrick's left shoulder struck the prep counter. He screamed in pain as he fell, landing heavily on his back. Finally, everything was still. Relieved, he assessed his situation. Though his left arm and shoulder ached horribly, he otherwise seemed to be in one piece.

Outside, alarms and sirens wailed. The dogs had restarted their frantic chorus, and people screamed for help. Suddenly, he heard a deafening crack, a sound both primeval and ancient. Fear seized Patrick as he remembered the five colossal Douglas firs that towered over Sheila's Airstream. He looked at Sheila and she stared back, her eyes wide with terror. They both desperately clawed their way toward the Airstream's door.

An unearthly screech of ripping metal rent the air, and for a moment Patrick could see the sky. Then a dark rush of falling branches engulfed him.

CHAPTER 30
CRITICAL CONDITION

"Sorry about the bumpy ride. How are Patrick and Sheila doing?" asked Theo over his shoulder. The van swayed roughly as it hit another patch of cracked asphalt. Lisa caught hold of the sliding door's grab handle to steady herself with her free hand. Her other was in Patrick's vise-like grip. He lay on the van's carpeted floor, grimacing in pain with each jolt. A makeshift sling held his dislocated shoulder in place across his chest. He still had his messenger bag tucked by his side and had refused to let it go, so Lisa decided to leave it be.

Lisa glanced back at Sheila, who lay across the van's back bench, a seat belt holding her in place. The drug dealer was breathing, though unconscious. The aluminum trailer had been almost cleaved in two when the uprooted Douglas fir crashed onto it. Miraculously the Airstream's door had remained somewhat functional. Theo was able to pry it open with a crowbar and drag Sheila and Patrick from the wreckage. Sheila had been knocked out cold, and Lisa resented the drug dealer's oblivious state. They'd found Patrick awake and gasping for air under a blanket of fir needles and branches. Other than his injured shoulder and some bloody scratches, he seemed okay, but there was no way to know what internal injuries he may have suffered.

"No change," said Lisa, trying to hide the panic from her voice. She didn't need to cause Patrick anymore distress. She blinked back tears. "How much farther?"

"Just another couple of blocks."

In the chaos following the earthquake, Ellen had instructed Theo to drive Patrick and Sheila to the hospital. The Five Firs food cart pod was just a half mile from Good Samaritan. If they waited for an ambulance, it might be too late.

Ellen had called for a police car to take her to City Hall, but before she left, Ellen wrapped Lisa in a hug and kissed her forehead. "Lisa, please be careful and stay close to Jamie." She turned to Jamie and hugged her too, then looked at them both sternly. "The aftershocks could go on for hours. Don't try to cross the river to your apartment. When you're done here, head straight to City Hall. My aides texted that the building is safe." As though hesitant to leave them, she paused before closing the police car's passenger door, "I'll meet you there as soon as I can."

Now in the painfully slow van, Lisa looked at Patrick's pale face. His eyes were tightly closed and his forehead was covered in a sheen of perspiration.

It might be too late already, she thought.

She craned her neck and looked out the front windshield. Jamie walked in front of the van guiding Theo, pointing out obstacles, and dragging fallen branches, street signs, and other debris out of the way. Their biggest concern had been downed power lines, but so far none had blocked their path. The streets were clogged with people, some injured or just disoriented, while others begged for help and even more offered it, assisting with first aid and rescues as best they could. The constant wail of sirens and car alarms added to the pandemonium.

"Should I help Jamie?" asked Lisa.

"No, just stay put and keep an eye on Patrick and Sheila. We're almost there."

In her head, Lisa mentally screamed in frustration at the snail's pace they were moving, yet on the outside, she stayed calm, kissed Patrick's clammy forehead, and spoke soothing words. "You're going to be all right. We're almost to the hospital. I love you so much, Patrick. Just hang in there a little longer." She kissed him gently on the lips and squeezed his hand.

Lisa felt the van pull to a stop and looked up, wondering what new obstacle had halted their progress, but she was relieved to see they'd pulled up to the emergency room entrance. The van's door slid open to reveal Jamie directing a pair of EMTs, who quickly wheeled over stretchers. In moments, Patrick, clutching his messenger bag, and Sheila, still unconscious, were removed from the van and rolled toward the glass doors.

Theo drove off to allow a stream of newly arrived ambulances to take his place. Trotting after the EMTs, Lisa and Jamie stepped into the lobby. The crush of people and motion amazed Lisa. She was stunned that this was the same hospital where she'd been treated just last night. Ceiling panels had broken loose, light fixtures hung precariously from wires, computers lay smashed and useless on the floor, and cracks stood out ominously on the sliding glass doors and windows.

Without warning, Lisa felt the earth sway under her feet, and she grabbed at Patrick's stretcher. Lights flickered and patients gasped, but the team of doctors, nurses, and aides never stopped moving. Their seemingly erratic motions resolved into a symmetry of treating patients and placing them in levels of triage—critical, emergency, acute. Patrick and Sheila were evaluated in turn by a nurse, and Lisa and Jamie quickly filled him in on what they knew about each of their conditions. In tandem, Patrick and Sheila were wheeled away for treatment.

Lisa and Jamie stood silent and stunned for a moment, a quiet duo in the midst of madness.

"If you don't require medical attention, I'll need you to move out of the way," said a nurse, not unkindly.

Jamie mumbled an apology and said to Lisa, "I think there's a little flower garden on the side of the building. Let's wait there."

Quickly, they stepped outside, and Lisa followed Jamie down a path that led behind the hospital to a small courtyard filled with trees and plants. Some of the paving stones had heaved up and a few planters were cracked, but the roses still bloomed.

They found a bench that was intact and sat down. The cacophony of disaster was muted amidst the greenery, and Lisa noticed that despite the chaos, it was a beautiful evening. The sky was clear and tinted with a golden twilight. A jet plane soared lazily overhead, leaving a white line of vapor in its wake.

"He'll be okay, Lisa," said Jamie. "Try not to worry."

Lisa looked at her best friend and her eyes filled with tears. "What if we didn't get here soon enough? What if the doctors can't treat him in time?"

"I'll go check on him. Will you be okay here by yourself for a little while?"

Lisa nodded.

"If I can find a vending machine, I'll get us some chocolate. I think we both deserve an emergency candy bar."

Lisa smiled. "Be careful," she said. "And I'll have a Snickers."

"You got it. I'll be right back," said Jamie.

Lisa closed her eyes and tried to block out the noise and concentrate on breathing in and out to calm her rapidly beating heart. Just last night at the party she'd doubted her feelings for Patrick, but seeing him in danger somehow snapped everything into focus. She loved him and she'd do whatever it took to make it up to him. Her mind fled to another moment when, although she'd been hurt and upset, Patrick had known just what to do and say to make everything better.

Y

Lisa remembered that night so clearly. She lay awake on her dorm room bed, still reeling from her mother's visit to the Academy. Desperate for sleep, Lisa just wanted to drift into nothingness, but she'd never gotten used to sharing a room. The sound of her two roommates' breathing grew more and more deafening. In and out, in and out, the two girls were just slightly out of sync. It was loud enough to keep her awake, but not enough to drown out the sound of her mother's voice in her head.

If she'd had time to prepare, maybe she could have gotten through to her mom. Lisa ran through their conversation again and again. For a second, Lisa had thought her mom was actually listening to her. Then things had gone south as they always did. It was all so unfair. And now Lisa was sentenced to a year away from her friends, her school, and her family. No one wanted her. No one would help her. She was trapped. She was alone.

One of the girls started to snore. Lisa sighed and rolled over, impatiently wiping her tears away. This was her life now, she thought. This place. These people.

Lisa wished she could share a room with Jamie. She felt a little in awe of her friend and totally jealous. Well, as much as she could be of anyone else stuck at the Academy. The way Jamie talked about her parents wasn't something Lisa could relate to at all. Jamie was only here because her parents didn't want her sent to juvie. Her parents actually missed her.

Lisa got up and pushed open the small window next to her bed, breathing in the cool air. Most of the lights were out on the school grounds, and in the sky she could just see the glow of a full moon.

"Lisa," a voice whispered from outside. She almost jumped out of her skin, then looked into the darkness and saw a shadowy form.

"Lisa, it's Patrick," he whispered. "Come outside. I want to show you something."

"Patrick, what the hell," she whispered back. "Aren't you in enough trouble?" She realized with guilt that she'd completely forgotten about him after her encounter with her mother.

"It's all good," he said. "Come on. Meet me out front."

Lisa thought for a minute about saying no, but getting in trouble for breaking curfew was the least of her problems. She could use someone to talk to right now. And she knew she could talk to Patrick. It's all they'd been doing, she thought ruefully.

"Sure, give me a sec," she whispered.

Lisa changed out of her pajamas and into a baggy sweatshirt and khaki shorts. She remembered a time when she would never have met a boy without rethinking every article of clothing a dozen times. Here, none of that mattered.

Hastily, she arranged her bed to look like someone was still in it. Carrying a pair of sneakers in one hand, she slipped out of the bedroom, trying not to wake the other girls. She closed her dorm room door and slipped out the side entrance where Patrick waited.

Patrick motioned for her to follow him. She slipped on her sneakers quickly, placing her hand on his shoulder for balance. He felt surprisingly warm in the chill air. Side by side, they made their way down a path toward the lake, Lisa keeping her eyes on the ground so she wouldn't trip in the darkness. After a few minutes, they were far enough away from the dorms to talk.

"What did you want to show me?" she asked, shivering.

Patrick took her hand. He'd never held it before. She looked at him, expecting him to kiss her. Instead, he was looking at the sky.

"Look up," he said.

She followed his gaze and gasped. A huge golden moon was rising just over the mountain. The sky was a deep, dark blue, and the mountain was so illuminated by moonlight that its snowy peak glowed.

For a moment, the chill was gone, and she forgot all about her mother. Right now, a cute boy was holding her hand under a glorious sky.

"The mountain is so beautiful," she whispered.

"Want to sit? I brought a blanket," Patrick said. He let go of her hand, and it felt suddenly empty and cold. He spread the blanket on the grass and sat, motioning for her to join him. She sat down, the wool of the blanket tickling her bare legs.

"Jamie told me about your mom's visit. I'm sorry," he said.

"Thanks."

They sat silent for a moment.

"You know what I miss most about home? Not my family or any of my friends. I miss my stuff, and my room," said Patrick. "I mean, it was a mess and my mom was always on my ass to clean it up, but it was mine. Here, I don't have anything."

Lisa thought about her bedroom at home and the last time she'd seen it. She realized she hadn't given much thought to it, so overwhelming was her experience at the Academy. She blushed, feeling a sudden rush of heat at the thought of all the secret things she had hidden away under her bed and in the back of her closet where she thought they were safe. Her diary, dirty books, half-empty packs of cigarettes, that bong she'd picked up in San Francisco, and photos of her and her friends doing stupid things. She wasn't there to protect them, and the thought of her mother looking through them all filled her with a helpless rage.

She wrapped her arms around her chest.

"What's wrong?" asked Patrick. "Are you cold?"

"A little. I was just thinking about my mom going through my stuff."

"Did you keep a diary?" he asked.

"Yep," she answered, feeling suddenly very worried.

"Ouch. I'm sorry."

"Why?"

"It's pretty likely the school has it."

"Are you kidding me?" Lisa said, astonished.

"How else do you think they know so much about you?"

"She wouldn't dare," Lisa said, knowing as the words came out of her mouth that Patrick was likely speaking the truth. At least now she knew where the school's intel came from.

"Well, maybe they don't," he said. "Maybe you got lucky and your parents just threw out all your stuff and turned your room into a gym."

She couldn't help laughing. "You're not helping," she said.

"Sorry. What do you miss most?"

Lisa thought for a moment. "I keep thinking about this jewelry box my dad gave me for my seventh birthday. It had a little ballerina in a yellow tutu that twirled around when you opened the top, and it played a song."

"What song?"

"'Love Me Tender,'" she said. "I used to listen to it every night before bed." She felt herself starting to relax. It felt good to talk. "I miss my friends too. They probably think I'm a complete loser."

"It's more likely they've forgotten you."

"Again, not helping." Lisa leaned against Patrick, her eyes on the moonlit mountain. His hand found hers again, and for the first time since her kidnapping, she felt safe. She almost didn't recognize the feeling. Before the Academy, she'd never felt fear. She used to think of her parents as solid, invincible beings who would never let her down, no matter what she did or said. Ever since those men had dragged her from her bed while her parents stood by and did nothing, she was always afraid. In her time at the Academy, she'd learned again and again not to trust anyone. It felt different with Patrick. He understood because his parents had betrayed him too.

"Does it really matter?" he asked.

"Does what matter?"

"That they've all forgotten us. Abandoned us." Patrick paused, then turned to look at Lisa, his eyes glittering with emotion. "I don't think my friends or even my parents would recognize me anymore. I mean, I guess I look the same, but on the inside, I'm different. You and me, we're stuck here, we're frozen, while the rest of the world keeps moving on. I say we forget them. We don't need them. From now on, I choose my own family."

She leaned in and kissed him. "Me too," she said, then kissed him again.

Hearing footsteps approaching, Lisa snapped out of her reverie. She was a little sad to see that Jamie had returned empty-handed. "No chocolate?" she asked.

Her friend's face looked oddly frozen, her eyes wide. Jamie sat down heavily beside her on the bench. She opened a clenched fist to reveal a folded piece of paper, which she handed to Lisa.

"Jamie, what is it? What's wrong?" Fear seized her heart. "Is it Patrick?"

"Lisa. He's gone."

CHAPTER 31
NOTED

Ellen opened her office door and sighed with relief. A beam of light from the lobby illuminated the dark room enough to reveal two sleeping figures. The first, Jamie, was curled up in an armchair, snoring quietly. The second, Lisa, lay on the sofa, legs stretched out and one arm hanging off the edge. A piece of folded paper lay on the floor next to her as though she'd dropped it in her sleep. Curious, Ellen stepped closer and picked it up. The note was written on a sheet from a doctor's prescription pad. In an untidy scrawl, it read: "Lisa, I can't see you again. It's over. I'm so sorry. Patrick."

"Good riddance," said Ellen under her breath, then immediately regretted it, surprised by the depth of her guilt. Patrick could have died today, and it would have been her fault. She couldn't possibly have anticipated an earthquake would strike, but he had been in the wrong place at the worst time because of her.

Still, Patrick had been a means to an end. Even in the chaos surrounding the earthquake, Ellen had managed to lock down the Five Firs pod with an officer on guard. Within days, the remains of Sheila's Airstream and those of her associates would be dragged to a city lot where they would be carefully examined by all the legitimate DEA agents Ellen desired. Arrest warrants would follow. The theory that Victor was the real kingpin behind Sheila's operation was a tantalizing puzzle, though it was nothing Ellen wouldn't work out soon.

First though, Ellen knew she had to apologize to Lisa. She looked at her sleeping daughter and was reminded of the fierce love she'd had for her when Lisa was a child. Over the past several hours spent coordinating rescue efforts, her thoughts kept returning to Lisa. What if she and Jamie hadn't heeded Ellen's warning and had attempted to cross the river and return to their apartment in the southeast? Another bridge could collapse, there could be more aftershocks, and what about the downed power lines all over town? So many hazards and obstacles barred their way. But for once Lisa had listened to Ellen—or more likely Jamie—and here the girls were, safe and sound.

"Mom?" Lisa yawned and sat up, rubbing the sleep from her eyes.

"I didn't mean to wake you, darling." Ellen joined Lisa on the sofa, then handed her the note. "I'm so sorry, dear," she said, surprised to realize that she was being honest. She put an arm around Lisa and squeezed her shoulders gently.

"Thanks," said Lisa, with a rueful smile, as though unsure how to read her mother's affections. Carefully Lisa folded the note and then crushed the paper in her fist. She glanced at Ellen. "I know you didn't like him."

"My opinion isn't important. You obviously cared for Patrick very much."

"He's a jerk," said Jamie, who had uncurled from her chair. She yawned widely and stretched. "He's also going to survive."

"Patrick is going to be okay?" asked Ellen.

"Got away with a dislocated shoulder, which I hope really hurts. Lisa was worried, so I went to check up on him. He was signing some paperwork when I finally tracked him down. The hospital was in absolute chaos. Anyway, he told me he was fine and that he needed to take off. He gave me that note for Lisa and just walked out. It was so bizarre. Why would he leave like that?"

Lisa sighed. "Maybe almost dying made him realize that he and I shouldn't be together. My life is a big mess. I can't really blame him."

"Bullshit," said Jamie. "There's something else going on. He was acting so strange earlier."

"Really, it's okay, Jamie," said Lisa, her voice tense. "Can we talk about something else?"

"Yeah, of course. I'm sorry," said Jamie quietly.

"My office is looking much better than when I stopped in earlier," said Ellen.

Jamie nodded. "Everything was on the floor, so we picked up what wasn't entirely broken and put it back. We even managed to rehang your artwork, though some of the glass is cracked."

"That's so considerate of you both. Thank you."

"No problem, Mayor Salder. How bad is the damage from the quake? We haven't been able to get online. I did get through to my parents on their landline, and they said their neighborhood wasn't hit too hard."

"I'm glad to hear they're safe, Jamie." Ellen looked at their worried faces and decided for tonight to spare them the worst. Lisa and Jamie had already been through so much today. Soon enough they'd hear of the search and rescue teams who were pulling victims from the wreckage, and about the bridges that had collapsed, leaving untold numbers of bodies floating in the Willamette River.

Keeping her voice confident and upbeat, she said, "Our first responders are working around the clock to keep everyone safe. The governor has issued a state of emergency and the National Guard is on their way. It's going to be tough going, but we'll get through it." They looked reassured by her words, and Ellen was glad she'd stretched the truth. "It almost seems trivial now, but before I forget, did you happen to check on Sheila before you left the hospital?"

Jamie nodded. "She was still unconscious. I saw an officer guarding her door in case she wakes up and tries to make a run for it. Theo said he'd stick around too." She yawned again. "I'm hungry. I wonder if our leftovers are still in the fridge."

"Why don't you go check, dear. And, I really shouldn't, but could you make me a . . ."

"Martini? You got it."

After Jamie left the room, Ellen turned to her daughter. "Lisa, I want to apologize."

"Really? Mom, you never apologize."

Ellen grimaced. "It's something about myself that I'm trying to change."

"Okay," said Lisa, clearly not convinced.

"You never make anything easy, do you honey?"

Lisa shrugged. "Sorry."

"No, you have nothing to be sorry about. I'm sorry for what I said to you last night at the party." Ellen took Lisa's hand. "I should never have brought up your father. He loved you so much. The thought that my words pushed you to leave with George Green kills me. I've been thinking about what you said at brunch too, how my help always comes with strings attached. You're right. I want you to know that I can change. Anything you need, just ask. I never want you to be in a position where you feel helpless or worthless. You're neither of those things. You're my daughter." She paused and waited for Lisa to respond, certain that she would be impressed by this rare display of humility. The bright tinkle of a cocktail shaker sounded through the open door.

Lisa didn't look ready to forgive. She pulled her hand away, narrowed her eyes and said coldly, "All day you've been using me and Patrick to get what you wanted. And you expect me to believe that you've suddenly changed?"

Ellen nodded. "I absolutely deserve that. It's true." She paused as she searched for the right words. "I'm responsible for what happened to Patrick. I was so focused on my goal that I was willing to sacrifice him to get it."

"Was it worth it?"

Ellen sat back and wondered if she could ever convince her daughter she was being honest. Her guilt was real, but so was her satisfaction that she'd brought down Sheila's operation. "Today I realized that all my plans and ambitions mean nothing if I don't have you in my life. You're my family, Lisa. All I ask is a chance to be your mom again. Let me try to do better."

Lisa stood up from the sofa and stepped toward a group of paintings that hung opposite Ellen's desk. She pointed at one, a watercolor of children playing near a mountain lake. "Where did you get this?"

Thrown off by the sudden change of topic, Ellen stammered out, "Oh, that. The school sent me that painting along with a few other belongings you'd left behind."

"Why is it here?" Lisa demanded.

Ellen stood and looked more closely at the image. "It reminds me of that beautiful day I came to visit you at the Academy."

Lisa just stared at Ellen for a moment, then turned back to the painting. Her next words were tinged with bitterness. "You're right. It was that day. But it wasn't beautiful. It was terrible." She looked at Ellen, her eyes pleading. "Mom, if you really want me back in your life, you're going to hear the truth behind this painting and every other awful thing that happened to me at that school. And this time, I need you to believe me."

Ellen swallowed and blinked back tears. She'd never seen Lisa look so vulnerable. "Yes, honey," she said, nodding. "I will listen and I'll try—"

Lisa placed her hand on Ellen's arm to stop her from saying more. "No, Mom." Lisa paused and took a deep breath. "Trying isn't good enough. I need to know that you'll believe me. Please."

Ellen nodded and said softly, "I will, honey. I will."

Jamie appeared at the door, looking nervously from mother to daughter. "Just checking in. Doing okay in here?"

Ellen brushed an errant tear away and composed herself. "Yes, Jamie. I believe we're doing better. Lisa?"

Lisa looked at Ellen carefully, then turned to Jamie with a quiet smile. "We'll get there."

"Then how about some tasty leftovers," said Jamie. With a grand gesture, she motioned Ellen and Lisa toward the lobby. The coffee table was strewn with to-go containers from their brunch at Screen Door earlier that day, along with paper plates and napkins. A martini glass filled to the brim sat waiting for Ellen, and two bottles of mineral water for Lisa and Jamie. They gathered round, opening the white boxes and filling their plates.

As Ellen sipped her cocktail and watched the girls argue over who deserved the last hushpuppy, she wondered at how much could change in a single day. The party last night; that awful George Green and his wife, Sue; Patrick and Sheila; the specter of Victor Smith; and finally a devastating earthquake that would have her city in chaos for months, possibly for years to come. Yet all of it led here, to this moment. A trio enjoying the simple pleasures of a midnight picnic.

Ellen reached across the coffee table, plucked the final hushpuppy from its white box, and popped it in her mouth. Lisa and Jamie looked at her, astonished, and they all burst out laughing.

🍸

Patrick reached the stone wall that curved around the property and rolled his bicycle to a stop. Trying to catch his breath, he dismounted and walked the last hundred feet.

His shoulder was feeling better, but he knew it would ache badly tomorrow after the long ride from Portland. Considering how he'd treated Lisa, he deserved the pain. He couldn't stop thinking about her tearstained face, how it had turned from terror to pure joy after Theo had pulled him from Sheila's smashed Airstream trailer. All the way to the hospital Lisa had held his hand, saying over and over that she loved him. When they finally reached the emergency room and he was wheeled away, Patrick knew he could never see her again. If he did, he'd confess the truth—how her father had died and that Patrick was the son of a murderer.

Before he could lose his nerve, he stepped to a small keypad set in the stone wall and tapped in a sequence of numbers. A pair of heavy wooden gates opened and he walked through. He continued down a short path to the front door and rang the bell. After a few moments, the door opened.

"Hi Dad," he said.

CHAPTER 32
SIX MONTHS LATER

Lisa took a sip of coffee from her travel mug, then glanced at her phone. Six months had passed, but her heart still skipped a beat every time she looked at her screen, hoping for a message from Patrick. Nothing. Just the time, making it very clear that she was going to be late.

She sighed. Another day, another temp job. At this rate, she'd just make it to her assignment with no chance to pick up breakfast on the way. Gridlock had seized Portland, and the city bus was inching along at a painfully slow rate. Her stomach growled. Opening her backpack, she pulled out a granola bar from the emergency supplies Jamie insisted she carry at all times. She'd have to remember to replace it before her friend's next surprise spot check.

When the bus finally rolled across the Burnside Bridge, one of the few that had survived the quake intact, Lisa wiped a smear of condensation from the window beside her seat to reveal Portland's battered skyline. The city had always been modest compared to other West Coast cities like Seattle or San Francisco. Now, many of its prominent buildings stood jagged and broken, stark reminders of the earthquake that had jolted the city. It wasn't the long-predicted collapse of the Cascadia subduction zone that had triggered the quake. Instead, snaking across the city from the West Hills through downtown, the modestly named Portland Hills Fault had produced the 6.2-magnitude tremor that shook the city for twenty terrifying seconds, followed by a dozen aftershocks in the days that followed.

A man sitting in the seat across from Lisa refolded his *Oregonian.* The front-page banner headline read "The Big One? Experts Say No." She rolled her eyes and crumpled the empty granola bar wrapper, tucking it into the front pocket of her backpack. Experts. What a bunch of jackasses. Like they had any idea what was going to happen next. No warning had come on that hot day in August, and there would be none the next time the earth chose to tear their city and their lives apart.

The only mercy was that the earthquake had hit on a Saturday. Schools and office buildings were mostly empty, and the streets, highways, and bridges were less jammed with traffic than they would have been in a midweek rush hour. Even so, several bridges had collapsed, taking cars, pedestrians and bicyclists with them into the river. Even with brave citizens diving into the water to save their fellow Portlanders, not everyone made it out alive. Downtown residents had fared even worse. Search and rescue operations had gone on for days around damaged buildings. Later, rescuers had shifted to the somber task of clearing rubble, never knowing when a piece of concrete or twisted metal might reveal someone's desperate end. The buildings hit hardest were from an era well before Oregon was considered a highly seismic region. New homes and high-rises built to recent codes had withstood the worst of it. In the end, the quake was responsible for fifty-three deaths and hundreds of injuries, a terrible toll the city wouldn't soon forget.

The near constant noise of construction had everyone on edge. Dump trucks and cranes seemed to block every major street. At any loud crash or boom, people dove for doorjambs, hid under desks and tables, or fled outside. Lisa was no different. She jumped at every ambulance siren, car alarm, or freight train. Post-traumatic stress had gripped the entire population of Portland.

Everyone except, of course, Lisa's mother Ellen. From the moment the shaking stopped, the mayor of Portland had leapt into action. She worked tirelessly next to firefighters, police officers, and volunteers to pull people from the wreckage. Footage of her on national television captured a compassionate and vulnerable leader. Her steely persona was forgotten as she helped to rescue grateful survivors and comforted the friends and families of those less fortunate. Ellen became the symbol of Portland's recovery—white hair held back with a red bandana, sensible mom jeans, and an emergency responder jacket. The city loved her for it, and she won the November election in a landslide. Now there was talk of a run for governor and whispers of a presidential future. For the first time in Ellen's long career, she could do no wrong. She pledged from the outset to rebuild the city for a sustainable future. Every damaged street would be rebuilt with bike lanes, every building would be repaired with green roofs and solar panels. Conserving water and harnessing wind were key, with a city- and county-wide focus on zero waste. Portland would become the model city of a green future.

The quake had also been a massive boom for Victor Smith's construction company. Tower cranes swayed above the city, most emblazoned with the VSC logo. Ellen tried to keep her distance, but as long as Victor followed her edict to rebuild sustainably, the city continued approving more and more of his company's contracts. Lisa's mother knew Victor was hiding something, but with Sheila still in a coma, Ellen couldn't find the connection between Victor and the drug dealer.

Lisa knew way more than she cared to about her mother's drama. She heard regular updates about the rebuilding plans and Victor Smith from Jamie, who'd replaced Ellen's old assistant Geoff after he had fled to a more seismically stable Iowa. And from Ellen, who'd become Lisa's new housemate.

After the quake, Lisa and Jamie's apartment building had taken on a troubling slant that forewarned of full collapse. The girls had been given an hour to remove what they could carry out. After stuffing what they could into boxes and bags, they hauled their luggage to the street, where their respective parents waited for them. Lisa loaded her belongings into the trunk of her mother's BMW, Jamie into her parents' Subaru. Before leaving, the friends walked back into the lobby for a moment to slap the cracked mural of Mount Hood one last time.

Jamie had lived with her parents for a few months, and had since found a studio apartment near City Hall. With Ellen's demanding schedule, it was just easier that way, she'd explained to Lisa. Lisa had moved back home to the colonial-style house in Eastmoreland where she'd grown up, into her old room with the robin's-egg blue walls, the white, shabby-chic furniture, the walls covered in old drawings and paintings, and a dresser still full of her old clothes. Really, it wasn't so bad living with her mother, thought Lisa. Three square meals a day, and no rent to pay.

Lisa's phone dinged with a reminder that dinner with Ellen was scheduled for tonight. No matter how busy she was rebuilding the city, shoring up the economy, and giving stump speeches, Ellen and Lisa met once a week, and Lisa would always share a story about the Academy. True to her word, Ellen had made it a priority to hear Lisa's side of things. She was a surprisingly good listener, asked thoughtful questions and gave Lisa space when she needed a moment to collect her thoughts.

Lisa clicked open the reminder and smiled. Tonight they were to meet at Jake's Famous Crawfish, luckily just a few blocks from her temp job. A Portland institution for over a century, the landmark restaurant had suffered considerable damage and had only just reopened.

Lisa remembered as a kid begging her parents to take her there during crawfish season, when a giant inflatable version of the crustacean was installed on top of the restaurant. Finally, for her eighth birthday, her mother relented. Lisa would never forget sitting between her parents as the waiter presented her with a heaping platter of the tiny red creatures. She'd burst into tears at the sight. Her mother scoffed and shook her head in disappointment. Her father, anticipating her reaction, had ordered wisely. In a moment, the dish was whisked away and replaced by a kid's-size cheeseburger and crinkle-cut fries. Tonight, just to be safe, she'd stick with a burger.

The bus jerked to a halt, and passengers gasped and grabbed seats and handrails as though for dear life.

"Sorry, everyone," said the bus driver sheepishly. "Broadway and Davis. Careful exiting. The street's still pretty broken up. Have a good morning."

Lisa shouldered her backpack and stepped off the bus into a steady drizzle that pattered softly on the cracked sidewalk. She clicked her phone again and rechecked the address for her temp job. Eleventh and Flanders. Just a few blocks. Pulling up the hood on her black raincoat, she stepped carefully over the buckled concrete. She crossed the street and made her way into the Pearl District.

The Pearl had suffered less than most areas of the city. Having been so built up in the last decade, most buildings were modern or heavily renovated according to the latest seismic standards. Still, the crumbled streets lent an air of chaos to the trendy neighborhood.

Lisa glanced at a street sign that stood upright but slightly askew and found herself in front of a modern six-story concrete-and-glass building that took up the entire block. This couldn't be right, she thought with a frown. She'd made it very clear to the temp agency that this was the one company that she would never work for. She glanced at the email with her day's assignment again, reading it more carefully, and her stomach dropped. She quickly called the temp agency's number.

A woman with a chirpy voice answered. "Temporary Heroes. How can I help?"

"Angelica? This is Lisa."

"Hi honey. How's it going over at Burnam & Green this morning?"

"It's not. I told you, any office in town but Burnam & Green."

"They loved you last time," said Angelica. "Said you were a real lifesaver."

"I've never had an assignment there," said Lisa.

"Oh, shoot. I guess I mixed you and Nisha up. Sorry, hon. Well, don't worry. Those creative types might be a little intimidating, but I'm sure you'll do fine."

"Angelica. I can't. You don't understand. It's impossible."

"Now Lisa, you can and you will," said Angelica, her voice shifting to an uncharacteristically stern tone. "You know we're shorthanded what with all the scared young people hightailing it out of town. Half of them are moving down to California. Can you imagine? Like it's any safer there."

"Angelica . . ." Lisa pleaded.

"I just don't have anyone else who can cover the partner's office. George Green has fired everyone else we've sent over."

Lisa attempted to interrupt, but Angelica talked over her. "We'll find a replacement for you tomorrow. Just get through today. With any luck, he'll fire you too."

CHAPTER 33
FAMILY COURT

Jamie felt the smooth cold metal of the chair's arms under her fingertips. She shifted her chair a little just to hear the sound, that awful scrape of its legs on the granite floor. She imagined traveling back in time to the moment, so many years ago, when she'd sat in this very chair outside the judge's office. She'd stop that horrible lawyer from talking her parents into sending her to the Academy. Eyes closed, she concentrated and took a few deep breaths, visualizing that day. After several moments, she popped her eyes open. It hadn't worked. She was still sitting alone in the hallway of the county courthouse. It was still today. It would always be today.

A different judge presided behind that closed door now. Judge Reinhardt had retired, probably to a charmed life spent fishing in the mountains and bunking in a rustic yet comfortable cabin. Who knew, thought Jamie, he could be living somewhere near the school.

School. What a joke. Jamie had left the Academy without a high school diploma and was still mortified that she'd had to get a GED after her release. But her SAT scores had been high, and her parents determined. Jamie had managed to get into Portland State University. She'd been just two semesters away from earning her degree in political science when the quake hit.

Over the years, Jamie had spent an inordinate amount of time imagining what type of criminal mastermind she could have become if her parents had opted for juvenile detention instead of the Academy. Nothing pedestrian like robbing liquor stores or local bank branches. Being a cat-burglar sounded appealing. Or high-tech crime. She didn't want to think what the kids would have been like in juvie though. Her classmates at the Academy had been tough enough.

Regardless, here she sat, years later. Her life could be worse. It also could have been better. Her brother, Roderick, had gone to Stanford.

Y

Roderick had sat next to her in this very spot on the day Jamie's fate was sealed. Elbows on knees, head in his hands, black hair standing up in thatches between his fingers. She could almost believe he felt guilty, but she knew that all he really felt was relief at having dodged a bullet.

"Roderick," she whispered to get his attention. He ignored her. She sighed audibly. "Roderick," she repeated, louder this time.

He looked up, his eyes appeared black in the fluorescent lights. He looked strange, unfamiliar. She knew his eyes to be warm, full of mischief and fun. Everything was off here. It was all too bright. Her stomach started to hurt.

"What?" he hissed back.

Jamie nodded toward the closed door. "What do you think they're talking about?"

"I don't know."

She groaned. "Come on, you must have some idea." Her right leg had started to bounce up and down. She tried to steady it. Parents with babies and toddlers on laps, children with legs dangling, teenagers slumped in boredom, and grandparents all sat scattered in bunches up and down the long hallway of the courthouse, waiting to learn the fate of loved ones. "Go check."

"I'm not going in there," he said, sitting up and crossing his arms over his chest defensively.

Roderick was dressed in the white shirt and black tie he'd worn to Aunt Evelyn's funeral the month before. Jamie's cousins, Maddie and Matilda, had gotten super weird around him. They asked her stupid questions, like, if he had a girlfriend or what types of music he liked, so they could pretend to like the same bands. She'd overheard them whispering and giggling about how cute he was. Gross, she thought.

"Come on," Jamie said again. "You're eighteen. That makes you a grown up." She emphasized the last phrase with air quotes. "Go check."

"Mom and Dad won't like it. I'm supposed to stay out here with you. Make sure you don't make a run for it. You are a criminal after all."

"Oh, really. Just me?" Jamie asked, a warning in her voice.

That day at the Lloyd Center Mall, she and Roderick had stolen over a thousand dollars' worth of games. It was enough to get into real trouble. When the mall cop handed her over to the police, Jamie didn't give up her brother to them, or to her parents. She took the blame for everything. Roderick was eighteen, after all. Eighteen-year-olds went to prison.

"Please, Roderick. I'm freaking out."

Roderick held her gaze as though hoping she'd relent. Jamie didn't. He grimaced as he looked at the judge's closed door, then stood.

The door opened. Jamie's parents and their lawyer walked briskly into the hall. Her father wore his best suit and tie. Her mother wore her lucky blue dress with the yellow stripes. She'd worn it to every family wedding over the last ten years and was convinced it was what kept the extended family's divorce rate so low.

"Where do you think you're going?" asked Jamie's mother to Roderick in Korean, her voice sharp. Roderick sat back down and resumed his previous hunched over position.

Jamie turned her attention to her parents and their lawyer, a stout woman with hair dyed henna red. Gray had started to appear at the roots. After the rush of their exit, her parents stood awkwardly, as though confused where to go now that they'd left the confines of the judge's chambers.

"Why don't we take a seat?" The lawyer's voice was unnaturally bright. She dragged two extra chairs toward Jamie and Roderick, the harsh scraping sound echoed through the courthouse hallway.

Her parents sat—her mother visibly irritated, her father scowling.

The lawyer turned toward Jamie. "I think we've worked toward a solution with Judge Reinhardt that will be acceptable to both you and your parents." She smiled brightly.

Jamie felt like she might throw up. "Am I going to jail?" she whispered.

"No, dear. No." She patted Jamie's hand. "You aren't going to jail or juvenile detention. Nothing like that, as long as your parents accept Judge Reinhardt's proposal." She paused and smiled again.

Jamie wanted to scream; the anticipation was almost too much. She didn't think it was her place to speak directly to the lawyer, but her parents stayed silent. She couldn't help herself. "What did the judge say?" Her leg had started to shake again.

"There's a boarding school called the Lost Lake Academy. Considering your excellent academic record, and the letters of support from your teachers and pastor, the judge felt this was an acceptable option."

"So, I shoplifted, and now I get to go to a boarding school?"

"Well, it's not that simple, but in a way, yes."

"In the mountains?" asked Jamie.

"Yes, it's about three hours away on Mount Hood," said the lawyer.

Jamie had lived on the Eastside of Portland her whole life and had only been to Mount Hood once. The gaping voids between the deep, snow-blanketed valleys and the dizzying mountain peaks had made her nauseous. She'd spent most of the trip with her head between her knees, breathing into a paper bag.

The lawyer continued. "You have to understand that you'll need to be on your best behavior. If you break any rules at the school, you'll go right back into the system."

"How long do I need to stay there?"

"The judge is suggesting one year. The alternative is six months in juvenile detention."

A whole year. She couldn't quite grasp it. A year away from home, her parents, her room. What about Mr. Whiskers, her cat? Who would take care of him? She felt a pang of homesickness. Maybe she should take the six months in juvie. She'd be okay. She was tough. Tough enough to take the fall for her stupid brother, anyway.

"Jamie, can you help explain the judge's proposal to your parents? I want to be sure they understand all the details." The lawyer handed Jamie a pamphlet. "Here's some information."

Jamie looked it over. A photo of adults with caring expressions led a group of multi-cultural teens on a hike in the mountains, and another showed a tidy classroom of students, arms raised, eager to learn.

Jamie turned to her mother and said in Korean, "Mom, the lawyer has some questions."

"Why are you speaking in Korean?" her mother asked in the same language, annoyed.

Jamie nodded toward the lawyer. "She wants me to translate. She thought it might be better."

"My English is fine. Better than hers. I understood everything," Jamie's mother said.

Jamie ignored her mother's comment and handed her the pamphlet. "She says I can either spend six months in juvenile detention, or a year at this boarding school."

Roderick leaned over to glance at the photos. "Looks nice."

"Looks expensive," said Jamie's mother.

Jamie turned to the lawyer. "She says it looks expensive."

The lawyer nodded. "It can be, but the state has an agreement with the school. The cost will be subsidized and will be quite affordable for your family. I reached out to an administrator there yesterday, and as luck would have it, they have a spot open for you."

Her mother rattled off more questions, which Jamie translated back and forth.

"What kind of school?"

"It's specifically for boys and girls who need extra help and supervision."

"Hmmm ... bad children. How are the teachers?"

"The Lost Lake Academy has a quality staff of counselors and educators."

Her mother sat silent for a moment, considering the lawyer's words. "I hate this woman. She's stupid. How did we end up with such a stupid lawyer? You should be allowed to stay at home with us."

Jamie was grateful for the language barrier.

"Mom, the lawyer's just trying to help," said Roderick.

Her mother shook her head. "My daughter, a criminal. How will I ever face our family or friends? I'm so ashamed."

Jamie looked at her father, "Dad, what do you think?"

Her father sat silent, brooding. Finally, he spoke in English. "No prisons."

"Juvenile detention isn't technically a prison," said the lawyer.

"It is a prison. This country has too many." He turned to Jamie. "You're going to the school."

"But it's a whole year," said Jamie. "Juvenile detention is only six months."

"The school. That's final," said her father. Her mother nodded in agreement.

The lawyer smiled. "Wonderful. I'll get in touch tomorrow with the details."

Jamie and Roderick followed their parents as they made their way out of the courthouse past bored police officers, rumpled lawyers, and disoriented jurors.

"Jamie, I'm really sorry," said Roderick. He kept his voice low so only she could hear.

"It's fine," she said glumly.

"No, it's not," he said. "I should have stepped up."

"I'm the idiot who tried to outrun a mall cop. Anyway, you're too soft. You'd never survive prison."

"I owe you, little sister. I owe you big time," Roderick said. "I'm glad you're going to the school."

"I'm going to have to give up forensics, band, and yearbook."

"Oh yeah, I forgot your life already sucks," he joked.

"Shut up." She punched his arm. Already the world was starting to look a little more normal. "Will you visit me?"

"Sure."

"And you promise to stay out of trouble?" she asked. "I won't be around to save you next time."

"Promise," he said, with a smile.

Y

A door opened further down the hall and out swept Ellen, begging forgiveness for her early departure to those remaining behind. She said something vague about the number of items still on her agenda. For a moment she looked confused, staring at an empty chair outside the office she'd just left. She looked around, growing irritated until she finally spotted Jamie. "Jamie, why are you sitting over there? Let's go."

Ellen looked as imperious as ever. Gone was the casual rescue wear that followed the immediate aftermath of the earthquake. It had been replaced with an elegant gray suit and a red blouse open at the neck, revealing a string of lustrous pearls. She had kept her white hair short, but it was swept elegantly away from her face. In the months Jamie had worked for her, she'd never once seen it move, even under the stormiest conditions.

Jamie stood. The rush of anxiety she always felt when in the presence of the mayor succeeded in pushing back any lingering memories of the past. She never knew what Ellen would ask for, it might be a breath mint or a demand to move a mountain. Out of habit, Jamie pulled a small bottle of antibacterial gel from her well-stocked bag and handed it to Ellen, who took it automatically.

"You're supposed to keep me on schedule, not the other way around." Ellen rubbed a small dab of gel on her hands and then handed the bottle back to Jamie. "What's on today's agenda?" she asked, walking rapidly down the hall. Jamie pulled her cellphone out of her coat pocket and skimmed the calendar, feeling Ellen's impatience.

"You're meeting with concerned parents who want their kids back in school."

"We're not ready. Most of the buildings are still being repaired. Postpone the meeting until next month. I'll issue a statement that online classes will continue for now and that we're working around the clock to reopen schools. I, of all people, know what a nightmare it is having a child underfoot." Ellen paused and looked at Jamie. "Please don't tell Lisa I said that."

Jamie nodded.

"Thank you," said Ellen. "What's next?"

"Representatives from the Gluten-Free Portland Project are protesting outside the fourth street entrance to City Hall."

"What do they want now?

"No gluten."

"Obviously. Why are they bothering me today?" As Ellen walked, she smiled and nodded at passersby who recognized her, looking friendly enough not to offend yet too busy to be bothered.

"In addition to your green policies in rebuilding the city, they want gluten free options in all restaurants who receive city funds to reopen," said Jamie.

"Order twenty pies from Apizza Scholls. We'll see how long they last."

"Really?" Jamie asked, already planning to order a spare for herself from Portland's best pizzeria.

"No, though it is tempting."

Jamie found Ellen's sense of humor inscrutable and had learned the hard way when to follow her instructions to the letter, and when not.

Ellen continued with her rant. "With everything else I have to deal with, gluten is very last on my list. Tell them gluten is outside my jurisdiction and they need to reach out to the county."

"Consider it done."

"Have you heard from the hospital today?" asked Ellen eagerly. "Has Sheila regained consciousness?"

"Nothing yet," said Jamie, checking for messages. The hospital was under strict instructions to alert Ellen if Sheila woke from her coma.

"Please call, just in case."

"Mayor Salder, it's been months. Sheila might never wake up, and even if she does, who knows what she'll remember." Jamie was still disturbed by the last time they'd gone to the hospital to see the coma-tose drug dealer. Ellen was convinced Sheila was faking her coma to avoid prison. She insisted the hospital keep Sheila handcuffed to her bed. The police and hospital staff had vetoed that idea, saying having an officer stationed outside Sheila's room around the clock was sufficient to prevent her escape, and more importantly, to pre-vent anyone else from attempting to silence her permanently. Ellen's success in breaking up Sheila's drug trafficking operation would be an empty victory if she couldn't link Sheila to anyone other than a few dozen low-level dealers. She needed the woman alive and awake.

"Well, that's the question isn't it. What Sheila will remember?" snapped Ellen. She stopped mid-stride and put her hand gently on Jamie's arm. "I'm sorry. I don't mean to take it out on you. I know you understand what's at stake. Anything else on today's docket?"

"The reporter from the *Times*," said Jamie. "She emailed ques-tions this morning."

"Yes, excellent. May I see them?"

Jamie pulled the printed list out of her bag and handed it to Ellen, who skimmed it quickly.

"All softballs about the six-month anniversary of the earthquake," Ellen said. They'd reached a bank of elevators and Ellen pressed the call button. "I wonder what's really up her sleeve. You'll sit in. I'd like you to record it and take notes."

"Yes, Mayor Salder. And finally, you have dinner at Jake's Famous Crawfish with Lisa tonight."

Ellen's smile disappeared. "You'll join us."

"I wasn't planning on it."

"That wasn't a question. Just don't order the actual crawfish. They make Lisa cry." Ellen jabbed the call button again. "What is taking so long? These damn elevators are the slowest in the city."

Jamie paused for a moment. "Don't you think you need some more alone time with her? I feel like I'm always getting in the middle. I thought you were getting along better."

The elevator doors slid open and Jamie repressed a shudder as she stepped in. The local news and social media had been full of horror stories of people stuck in elevators for days after the quake. Jamie glanced at Ellen who looked as cool and comfortable as ever. Nothing ruffled the mayor, thought Jamie, except Lisa.

"Yes, it's been fine. More of a truce than a reconciliation," said Ellen with a shrug. "She's been sharing a lot about her experiences at the Academy. But I thought tonight we could take a break and just have a nice dinner. And your presence always helps keep us civil. You know how Lisa is." She pressed the button for the ground floor.

"And I know how you are," said Jamie, not afraid to be honest with Ellen on this subject.

"Yes," Ellen said, conceding the point. "My daughter doesn't always bring out the best in me. I would still prefer you join. And Lisa will want you there."

Jamie wasn't so sure. Her best friend and former roommate hadn't been too keen on Jamie taking this job with her mother. Every time she brought up her all-consuming work, Lisa immediately changed the subject. It had started to hurt Jamie's feelings.

"Okay, I'll go. I've always wanted to try their seafood appetizer tower. It's like three feet tall," said Jamie hopefully.

"You can order whatever you'd like. On me of course," said Ellen in a rare light tone.

The doors opened. Relieved to be out of the cramped space, Jamie took a deep breath of courthouse lobby air. Her phone chimed. She glanced at it, hoping for a message from the hospital with good news about Sheila. Instead, the text read, "In town. Can I crash at your place tonight?" The message was from her brother Roderick.

CHAPTER 34
MAN UP

Lisa had been stationed outside George Green's office for over an hour, yet there'd been no sign of the notorious ad man. In fact, there'd been no sign of anyone, and she was beginning to hope that George was away on vacation, or out of town on business, or trapped under something heavy. Then she remembered the earthquake victims and cringed. Not even George deserved that. She settled for stuck at the dentist, getting a root canal.

A year ago, she would have been thrilled to get inside the hallowed halls of Burnam & Green, or B&G, as everyone in the know referred to it. However, this morning she'd been so mortified by being in the same building as George that she'd barely noticed the architectural marvel. She only dimly recalled the atrium held aloft by massive, reclaimed Douglas fir beams, and the graceful skylights that flooded the space with a warm glow.

She'd once aspired to join this moneyed, hipster cult. Now that she was here, all Lisa wanted to do was run away. Temporary Heroes had been good to her, and assured her they'd help her find a full-time job once she'd finished her degree, if that ever happened. Her art school had been closed for months. She'd heard nothing from them but vague assurances they'd reopen as soon as repairs were complete.

A man stepped out of the elevator. Lisa peeked from behind her computer monitor and to her immense relief, saw that it wasn't George. Leaning back in her chair, she eased her shoulders down and looked cautiously at the first visitor to the sixth floor she'd seen all day.

Typical ad agency creative, thought Lisa. She'd seen plenty in her months as a temp, and they were all starting to blur together in their banal faux-eccentricity. He was another white male thirty-something pretending to be twenty-something in raw denim jeans and a See See Motorcycle hoody. The man wore a precisely trimmed mustache and looked overly caffeinated and utterly full of himself. Walking directly toward her, he kept his eyes locked on his phone the entire distance. He stopped and glanced up just before colliding with her desk.

"Where's the other girl?" he demanded.

Lisa flushed with irritation at his tone. Why were all agency types such assholes, she thought. She took another deep breath, willing herself to not be intimidated, and answered with a shrug. "I don't know."

He sighed loudly. "Seriously? The girl from yesterday? How can she not be here?"

"I'm sorry, I really have no idea. I'm a temp."

"A temp," he repeated, his voice dripping with disdain. "Well, that's just great. She almost seemed capable of getting shit done." He went back to staring at his phone, tapping quickly. "How is George today?" he asked, gritting his teeth.

"No idea. I don't think he's in his office."

"Oh, he's in there. Rumor has it, George hasn't left the building in weeks," he said with raised eyebrows. "We think he's living here."

"Really?" Lisa asked. She had been too nervous to take in much of her surroundings. Now as she glanced around the lobby, she saw there were only two offices, a small kitchenette, and a door marked WC. Looking toward George's office, she realized if she leaned far enough in her chair, she could just see through his clear glass door.

Lisa cringed and her heart started pounding. She could see George. He'd been in his office this whole time. She looked more closely and realized the creative genius behind Burnam & Green sat at his desk with his head buried in his arms, crying.

She turned back to the man. "I can confirm Mr. Green is in his office, and he appears to be weeping."

The creative rolled his eyes. "Will this company ever get real leadership?" He dropped a folder on Lisa's desk. "George needs to review this presentation. We're meeting with the client at eleven."

"You're welcome to check in with him directly. Just head on in. I'm not going to stop you," said Lisa with a sweep of her hand.

He looked deeply uncomfortable with this suggestion. "Why can't you give it to him?"

"No. I don't do that," said Lisa, the panic rising in her voice. "That's not in my job description."

The man leaned over, looked in the office and watched as George's shoulders heaved with sobs. "You're a temp. Everything is in your job description. I'll be back soon. Make sure George is ready to go. The client asked for him personally."

Lisa watched helplessly as the creative walked back to the elevator and stabbed at the down button with his index finger.

"Can I at least get your name?" she called out to him.

"Steve." In a moment, the elevator dinged its arrival, and the creative disappeared.

Lisa rubbed her temples. Why does this keep happening to me, she thought. She picked up her phone and tapped Jamie's number. At least she could laugh about this with her best friend. The phone rang once, twice, and then went to voicemail. Disappointed, she hung up without leaving a message.

She tried to remind herself that she'd been through so much worse. Today she'd face whatever chaos the universe decided to throw at her. If that meant seeing George again, bring it on. He probably wouldn't even recognize her. Her hair was shorter now, and she was dressed in understated business casual, the polar opposite of the sparkly gold cocktail dress she'd worn on that fateful night last summer.

Feeling the tiniest bit more confident, Lisa picked up the presentation and stood. She'd hand the folder to George, along with a big cup of coffee. Then, she'd head right back to her desk and hide behind the giant monitor. He wouldn't even have time to remember her, Lisa assured herself.

She walked to the kitchenette and assessed the upscale equipment. Fortunately, it featured the same upmarket coffee machine that her mother had at home. It ate small metal pods filled with coffee grounds and spit out espresso. Lisa fed the machine three until she had a full cup. Presentation tucked under her arm and coffee cup in hand, she steadied her nerves and walked to George's door.

With a jolt, she saw that his desk was empty. He couldn't have snuck by her. How could he have escaped? Frantically, she craned her neck and scanned the vast corner office. Finally, she spotted him. George had moved to a large sofa along the far wall and was lying down with his back to her, his knees tucked up.

Knocking lightly on the door, she waited. Nothing. No movement, no sound. What if he's passed out, she thought. She noted a fifth of bourbon and a collection of prescription bottles sitting on the coffee table next to the sofa. Suicide attempt? No. The George she'd met last summer was far too much of a narcissist to kill himself.

She pushed the door open a crack. "Mr. Green?"

He didn't respond.

She spoke more loudly, "Mr. Green, are you awake?"

"Yes? Who's there?" George sat up. His expression was hopeful. "Has Sue called?" Lisa could see he held a framed photo clasped to his chest. It was of George and Sue on their wedding day.

"No, Mr. Green, I'm sorry. Your wife hasn't called." Lisa cleared a small space on the cluttered coffee table and set down the cup. "I brought you some coffee."

He looked at it suspiciously and grabbed the liquor bottle instead. He pulled the top off and took a swig.

Lisa counted to three before he finally stopped drinking and set down the now empty bottle. She looked George over. The man was a mess. His button-down shirt and jeans were rumpled and had obviously been slept in. His hair was peppered with more gray than she remembered, and his five o'clock shadow was a few days old. She couldn't imagine that a cup of coffee was going to be enough to prop him up for a client meeting. What he needed was a shot of adrenaline to the heart.

"The team needs you to review this for a meeting at eleven. It's offsite so you should be ready to leave soon," said Lisa. She handed him the presentation.

He gently set down the wedding photo, then took the folder from her. He flipped through the pages. "We've been trying to get face time with these pricks for weeks," said George, rubbing his eyes. "With the earthquake keeping us offline for so long, most of our big clients have jumped ship, so we had to go local. Never thought I'd be begging them for work. Then out of the blue, boom, we get the call. I should be celebrating. But I . . ." He paused for a long moment. "I don't think I'll ever celebrate again." George stood and turned to face the floor to ceiling glass windows of his office. They overlooked the city, currently obscured by rain and fog. "I don't care about anything anymore. It's all so meaningless without Sue. She was my angel. My rock." George looked back at Lisa, his eyes bright, his face yearning for her to understand. "She won't even talk to me. It's been months."

"How about that coffee?" Lisa suggested. "It's chock full of stimulating caffeine."

"I love Sue more than anything. I have to win her back. I started a list." He pointed at one of his glass walls, covered in scribbles of erasable ink.

Lisa knew she shouldn't linger. She'd delivered the presentation and told him about the meeting. But she couldn't help herself. Morbid curiosity got the better of her. And in this state, George seemed so harmless. She walked to the wall and saw in the middle of some other illegible scrawls a neatly written list titled "How to Save My Marriage."

Holy shit, she thought. Did he make one of the other temps draft this?

The list stated in bold letters, "Buy flowers. Do the dishes. Take out the garbage. Happy wife = happy life. Compromise. Compromise. Compromise. Be better at communicating my needs."

Lisa picked up a black Sharpie from a pile of pens on a large conference table. She glanced back at George to make sure he wasn't watching her. She needn't have worried. He was gazing intently at his wedding photo again, tears streaming down his face.

She quickly added to the list: "Stop cheating. Leaving the scene of a hit-and-run is a crime. Organic coke is not a health food."

Satisfied, Lisa returned the permanent marker to the pile and headed toward the door. "Okay, well, I better get back to my desk. Good luck with the meeting," she said.

"Wait," said George. He wiped the tears from his eyes with his shirt sleeve, then sat up and looked at her more closely. "Do I know you?" he asked.

She stepped quickly toward the door and said over her shoulder, "No. I'm just a temp. We've never met. Ever."

George jumped up from the sofa. "You!" He pointed his finger at her. "You're the mayor's daughter, Lisa."

"I should really go. I need to be at my desk in case the phone rings. Sue might call," she added hopefully.

"Did Sue put you up to this? Is this some kind of a test?" George asked. "She still cares. I knew it." He beamed with joy.

Lisa almost didn't have the heart to crush his hopes. Almost. "No, Sue didn't send me. My temp agency randomly assigned me this job."

"There is nothing random about this," said George, his shoulders slumping. "It's the universe punishing me."

Lisa shrugged. "Probably."

George's face fell. He collapsed back down on the sofa, overwhelmed with sobs.

Wonderful, thought Lisa. She looked around the office for some way to drag George out of his funk. She walked to his desk. One side of it was heaped with self-help books. He must have emptied out Powell Books' entire relationships section. She glanced at a few of the titles: *A Manual for the Unfaithful, Idiots Guide to Surviving Separation,* and *Out of the Doghouse: The Step-by-Step Guide for Men Caught Cheating.* Several were bookmarked with post-it notes and a few lay open with passages highlighted in neon pink and yellow. At least he's doing his homework, she thought. She pulled her phone from her back pocket and snapped a photo, thinking how much Jamie would enjoy seeing the wreckage of George's marriage.

Then, behind the pile, she saw it. A framed photo of Sue was partially obscured by the clutter on George's desk. Lisa picked up the picture for a closer look. Sue was posed on Cannon Beach with the iconic Haystack Rock hulking in the background. Hands on hips, all severe lines and low body fat, she looked at the camera—and presumably at George behind it—with a look that said George, this beach, the state of Oregon, the Pacific Ocean, and the world could all go to hell.

Over the last few months, Lisa had peeked at Sue's social media. Okay, maybe more than a peek, she admitted grimly. It was amazing what one could learn from a few hundred selfies. Lisa visualized starving herself every day in a house full of food, going to yoga, then Pilates, then suffering through painful beauty treatments, all to look perfect for a cheating husband. Sue would be hungry, angry, and wouldn't tolerate George's pity party for a second. Be mad like Sue, she thought.

"George. Get up," Lisa said, in what she hoped was a stern, no-nonsense voice.

George kept crying.

"George. Get up now."

"Why should I?" he wailed.

"George. Your team will be here in fifteen, no," she glanced at her phone, "Ten minutes. Ten minutes, George. They are expecting you be prepared to present to the client. The client who asked for you personally."

George looked up. "Present what?"

"Are you kidding me?" she said, keeping her tone stern. She walked over and picked up the folder from the coffee table. "This." She handed it to him.

He took it and started leafing through the pages again.

"You are totally unprepared," she continued. "You're going to humiliate yourself. Is that what you want, George? To be humiliated in front of your staff? And in front of a potential client? A client that you desperately need to save this sad excuse of an ad agency?" She was kind of enjoying herself. Then she saw his terrified expression and realized she'd probably gone far enough.

"What time is the meeting?" he asked.

"In an hour."

"Shit." He sat up straight. "Shit. Shit. Shit. Those idiots. I can't believe they're trying to pass off these crap logos again. It's the third time they've tried to fit them into a pitch."

George set down the folder. He knelt down and pulled a suitcase out from under the sofa, and started rifling through it.

Wow. Steve with the mustache was right. George has been living out of his office. That's so sad, she thought, looking forward to sharing this juicy tidbit with Jamie.

George pulled a toiletry bag from the suitcase, then stood and stepped behind the sofa, opening a hidden closet door in the corner. Hanging neatly inside were sports jackets, distressed jeans and a collection of bright sneakers—George's standard uniform. He pulled out a few items, then opened another door into a full bathroom.

Lisa watched in fascination. His office was huge.

"Get the team up here now," he said.

"Who should I call?" she asked, grabbing his desk phone.

"Everyone," he called from the bathroom. She could hear water running.

With the help of the very competent Sharon at the front desk, Lisa managed to track down Steve with the mustache and the rest of the team. After several frantic minutes of calls and texts, Steve, two Mikes, and a Chris had assembled around the conference table in George's office.

She knocked on the bathroom door. "George, the team's here."

The door opened and George stepped out. He was clean shaven, and his salt and pepper hair was neatly combed. He wore a pale blue shirt with French cuffs and silver cuff-links, a gray sports jacket, and jeans. His neon yellow sneakers would have been an abomination on anyone else, but somehow, he managed to pull the look off.

He stormed into the room and started yelling. "Why isn't the presentation on screen? What is this, the aughts? Why are you idiots still printing this shit?"

The flock of creatives scurried to find the right connections and dongles. In moments, the presentation was up on a massive flat screen monitor.

"We need to drive faster acceleration, not boil the ocean," yelled George. "Trash the logos and move the social strategy to section one. It's the strongest piece we have."

He continued. Lisa recognized only a fraction of the jargon and acronyms he tossed out, but after thirty minutes of proclaiming loudly that he was still unhappy, that the work was shit, and that he should fire the lot of them, he acceded that it would do for now.

"Sharon called the car service," Lisa told George as he followed the rest of team towards the elevator. "The drivers should be downstairs waiting. Good luck."

"You're coming to the meeting," he said.

She shook her head and said firmly, "No, I'm not."

"That wasn't a question. I need the moral support."

"What about them?" she said, pointing to the creatives.

"They're a bunch of assholes. You, Lisa," George said, as he stepped uncomfortably close to her. "You, I can trust."

Lisa took a step back. She thought she'd had it under control, but now she saw she'd gone too far. She should have left George a sad and pathetic puddle of a man.

George spoke, his voice low. "We know too much about each other. You're going to help me pull my life back together. You're going to help me win back Sue. In return, I'll keep your secrets safe."

His swagger back, George walked past her and stabbed at the elevator call button. "Drinks on me after. Vodka martini, up with olives, right?"

"Nope," she said glumly. "I'm off martinis."

CHAPTER 35
THE PITCH

For a brief, jarring moment Lisa was thrown airborne, only to be slammed back down a fraction of a second later. She rode in the front passenger seat of a town car that sped down Portland's broken patchwork of streets. The driver, in a rumpled suit and tie, murmured a quiet apology and Lisa responded with a weak smile. Her stomach felt stuck in her throat, and she grasped the door handle and braced for the next blow. She was grateful to not be stuck in the back seat. She peeked over her left shoulder at the three creatives who shared her car—the two Mikes and Steve. They seemed unfazed by the bumpy ride, their eyes glued to their phones, laps weighed down with messenger bags, each holding a travel coffee mug. Chris, who apparently had seniority, rode in the other vehicle with George.

Before leaving Burnam & Green, Lisa only had time to grab her raincoat and backpack. She hoped George wasn't expecting her to take notes, or actually say or do anything at this meeting. Her role as a temp was supposed to be limited to sitting at a desk, answering phones, maybe doing some light data entry. Attending a pitch to a major client was not in the Temporary Heroes handbook.

Lisa opened her backpack and took a quick inventory. With a sinking feeling she realized it contained absolutely nothing useful for a situation like this, not even pens or paper. Thanks to Jamie's new-found obsession with earthquake preparedness, it did hold—a two-liter bottle of water, a box of granola bars minus the one she'd had for breakfast, a flashlight, a whistle, a packet of turkey jerky, a basic first aid kit, travel toilet tissue, and a backup battery for her phone.

Jamie told Lisa proudly that with these supplies, she could survive for approximately three days if she also collected her own urine and drank it. Lisa was not terribly comforted by that thought. Urine was just not happening. She'd have to be content with two days.

The car finally slowed and pulled up to the curb. Lisa thought about just waiting with the driver, then her door opened and there stood George with a smile, holding out his hand for her to take. She ignored him and stepped out, hefting her backpack over her shoulder.

She looked straight up at the skyscraper, nicknamed the Big Pink for its sleek rose gold exterior. Momentarily dizzied by its height, she shook off the vertigo and dashed through the drizzling rain, following the creatives through the lobby door to a bank of elevators.

"That bloodsucker Smith bought this building for a song after the quake and put his entire crew on repairs day and night while the rest of the city was still pulling its collective head out of its ass, including your mother," said George to Lisa as he called the elevator.

Lisa's heart skipped a beat at the name Smith. "Who is Smith?" she asked, trying to keep her voice steady. The elevator arrived and they all stepped in, George last.

"Seriously?" he said turning to Lisa. "Victor Smith of VSC. Victor Smith Construction. He owns half the property in Portland and is working on buying the other half. Now that everyone's scared shitless, they're offloading properties as fast as Victor can buy them."

"But he's a crook," Lisa blurted out.

"And that's a problem why?" asked George.

"He should be in jail," said Lisa.

The creatives all laughed, like she'd said the punch line to a joke.

"Probably, but let's hope he stays out of prison. If this pitch goes right, we can drink from the ample VSC teat to the tune of two million a quarter."

The creatives exchanged premature high fives, faces plastered with smug grins. Lisa just glared. The elevator dinged to mark their arrival on the thirtieth floor and the creatives filed out. George followed then turned back when he noticed Lisa hadn't moved. He caught the door before it could close.

"The meeting is this way," he said, gesturing toward a cavernous lobby.

Lisa tapped the button for the ground floor. "I think I should leave," she said in a low voice. "My mother wouldn't like that I'm at Victor's office."

"Your mother? She also wouldn't like me sharing the details of how you and I met with those politicos she's been cozying up to," said George with a smirk. "But maybe I will. That would throw a wrench in her gubernatorial ambitions."

Lisa glared at him. "Remember, George, I have a lot to share as well." She didn't like how the Mikes were hovering nearby, attempting to eavesdrop on every word of their hissed conversation. "Fine, I'll stay," she snapped and stepped out of the elevator.

Steve and Chris had already checked in at the reception desk and were being led across the lobby by a young woman wearing a suit and heels.

Lisa started toward them, then felt George's hand on her shoulder. She shrugged him off and shot him a warning look.

"Sorry," he said, his hands raised apologetically.

Lisa waited for him to step ahead, then followed. She took a quick glance around the lobby. It felt more Las Vegas casino than a place of business. Gold leaf adorned the walls and trim, and the floor was paved with a dozen shades of marble. The space was arranged with white leather sofas and side tables holding ornate vases filled with fresh flowers. A cut-glass chandelier was circled by a fresco of naked nymphs dancing at the foot of Mount Hood.

For a moment, she felt eyes on her. Lisa swung around and scanned the sofas, the reception desk, and each floral monstrosity, but she couldn't see that anyone was watching. She felt a flash of terror that she'd run into her mother. Ellen could easily be here coordinating with VSC on one of a dozen rebuilding projects. Thankfully, her mother was nowhere in sight.

Lisa shook off her uneasiness and followed George into a large conference room. The space was startlingly sparse and modern compared to the repellent splendor of the lobby. An oblong table flanked by black leather executive chairs dominated the room, and a flat-screen monitor pulsed on an otherwise unadorned wall. She turned around and gasped. The opposite wall was entirely glass and featured a stunning view. The rain had stopped, and the sky had cleared enough to reveal the peak of Mount Hood floating in the distance above a thick cloud bank. Below, Portland was spread before them in all its ragged beauty. Cranes embellished with the VSC logo towered over countless buildings.

"Victor is like a virus," her mother had said last week at dinner. "He keeps spreading and building his influence."

Lisa hadn't understood how true that was until this moment.

George waved at her, indicating she should sit next to him. Reluctantly, she did. Everyone seemed to have something to do but her. Remotes, dongles, and laptops were hooked up, turned on and tested. She watched as George flipped rapidly through the slides, his mouth moving silently as he ran through each frame, practicing the words that could bring his firm millions.

Suddenly, everyone looked up, and Lisa followed their gaze to the door. Victor Smith entered, wearing a beautifully tailored pinstripe suit, a blinding white shirt, and a tie with a pattern that was discordant in just the right way. He was tall with full head of dark gray hair. He wore a pair of black-framed glasses that gave him the appearance of a college professor, yet did nothing to diminish the aura of power and confidence he exuded. They all stood, not knowing what else to do.

"George, you son of a bitch." Victor walked around the table and shook George's hand briskly. "I'm so glad we could finally make this meeting happen."

"As am I. Should we get start—"

Victor interrupted him. "My son Patrick will be joining us. He's learning the ropes from his old man." He looked back at the door. "Where is that kid?"

Lisa's heart skipped a beat. Patrick?

George leaned toward Lisa and whispered, "If his son is half the man Victor is, he'll be three feet tall."

In spite of herself, Lisa laughed at George's terrible joke.

Reaching the door, Victor spoke to someone waiting in the hallway. "Patrick, get in here."

CHAPTER 36
MAN AT WORK

Patrick lurked just outside the conference room and silently prayed for another earthquake, an aftershock, or a lightning strike. Any act of God would do as long as it saved him from having to step into that room with Lisa and George.

The last time he'd seen Lisa was the day of the quake. As he lost sight of her in the chaos of the emergency room, Patrick knew that if he ever saw Lisa again, he would confess everything. So, like the coward he was, he'd snuck out of the hospital with his arm in a sling and his old-beat up messenger bag over his good shoulder. The DVD had survived the quake without a scratch. Patrick thought about destroying it, but something stopped him. Fate had placed it into his hands. He just needed to figure out what to do about it.

And so, Patrick went straight to the source, his parent's big house on Lake Oswego. Years had passed since Patrick had stepped over the threshold and he'd forgotten how imposing the house was. After sharing a tiny dorm room at the Academy, and his dumpy apartment off Hawthorne, he felt awed by the sprawling mansion.

Victor's welcome was subdued, but Patrick's mother, Anne, cried and held him close. Patrick asked to speak to his father alone and together they went into Victor's study. His father took off his black-rimmed glasses and wiped the lenses with a handkerchief as Patrick explained how he'd been injured the day of the quake, and that it made him realize how fragile life is. He asked if he could once again be part of the family.

Most of all, Patrick avoided talking about his real intentions. He wasn't ready to give up his own father to the mayor and the police. If he could get close to Victor, maybe he'd eventually learn the truth.

Victor said he'd like nothing more than to have his only son back in his life, and then he surprised Patrick by offering him a job.

Working for his father had its perks. Victor set him up with wheels, a place to crash, and more money than he'd ever need. He moved out of the shitty apartment he'd shared with his three buddies and into a high rise downtown. Two bedrooms, a chef's kitchen, and million-dollar views; it was more than he'd ever dreamed of, yet the space always felt empty and cold. He couldn't help but wonder how different it would feel if he were sharing it with Lisa.

Patrick's first stop on his way to becoming an employee of VSC was his father's barber. With each snip of the sharp scissors, clumps of his long unkempt hair fell to the ground. He barely recognized himself in the mirror as the barber finished styling the short haircut with a touch of product. The second stop was to an ancient tailor who barely spoke except to call out measurements to an assistant. The third was a trip to the firing range. A few days later, he'd returned home to find a dozen black suits of varying weights in his bedroom closet, complete with shirts, ties, shoes, striped socks, and boxer briefs. On his unmade bed lay the model of handgun he'd liked most, a lightweight Glock, and a low-profile holster.

Patrick wasn't surprised his dad, or more likely one of his henchmen, felt free to enter his apartment without permission. Still, it made Patrick deeply uncomfortable. He made a deal with his buddy Joe to keep a few things back at his old apartment for safe keeping. Special things—photos of him and Lisa, his favorite books, a beat-up guitar he loved, and his old laptop. Stuff he'd grab if there were a fire.

That morning, one of his father's lackeys had summoned Patrick to the office, offering no explanation other than he'd better get his ass dressed and down to VSC pronto. Patrick showered and dressed, then clipped on his holster and slid his Glock into place. He'd been strictly ordered to keep the weapon on him at all times. The gun had felt foreign for the first couple of weeks, a heavy weight pressing against his body like the guilt he carried. After a while, both the guilt and the gun just blended into the rest of his new life.

Arriving at VSC fifteen minutes early, Patrick parked his shiny new Triumph motorcycle in his reserved spot in the underground lot. He rode the express elevator to the thirtieth floor and checked in with reception. Learning that his father was otherwise occupied, he waited in the lobby on a white leather chair with his back to the far wall so he could keep an eye on any comings and goings. He glanced at his phone for the time. Whomever they were supposed to meet was late. His father wouldn't like that.

Patrick had been pulled into a lot of meetings over the last several weeks—earthquake repair and seismic retrofitting, permit issues, and bitchy tenants. But he knew that there was much more to his father's company. The real business that all this other bullshit hid. He wondered what he'd have to do to gain entry into that world.

The elevator dinged and a few hipsters in jeans and hoodies exited and headed toward the reception desk. An older man followed. Patrick couldn't believe his eyes. It was that asshole George Green. Patrick stood, ready to charge.

Then a girl stepped out of the elevator behind George. Her hair was different, cut short in a bob, but her face held a look that Patrick recognized from all those years ago when she had first stepped off the bus at the Academy—like she wanted to punch someone in the face.

His head spun. What was Lisa doing at his father's office, and with George Green? He ducked behind a giant vase of flowers and watched.

George leaned in close to Lisa as they spoke at the elevator door. When Green placed his hand on her shoulder, Patrick could just barely contain his rage. Only six months after Lisa had said she loved him, only six months, and here she was with George.

Why hadn't Jamie told him? He couldn't believe that his oldest friend would keep something like this from him. Not that Jamie was the biggest fan of Patrick these days. Guess he couldn't blame her, considering how he'd treated both her and Lisa since the quake.

He pulled his phone out of his jacket pocket and sent Jamie a text demanding an explanation for her lapse in intel. He glanced up as Lisa, George and the others made their way to the conference room.

Now he was standing outside that same room. And Lisa was sitting inside it. And his whole world was about to implode. Again.

"Patrick, get in here," commanded his father. As he'd done for the last six months, Patrick followed orders.

CHAPTER 37
FATHER SON MOMENT

Patrick was back at his perch in the VSC lobby weighing his options. He pulled the DVD out of his inside jacket pocket and flipped the silver disc over in his hands, his blurred reflection flicking by with each turn. All he saw was Lisa. Lisa with George's hand on her shoulder. Lisa sitting next to George in that conference room. Lisa being introduced by George as the mayor's daughter and an integral part of the Burnam & Green team. Lisa laughing at something George said, then having the gall to look sympathetic when Victor called George on his bullshit.

Even though he'd broken up with her, Patrick thought Lisa would wait for him forever. He was wrong. She'd obviously moved on to her dream job at Burnam & Green working for that prick George. Maybe it was time he moved on too. Seeing Lisa today had shattered an illusion that he'd been holding close—that he would do the right thing and eventually hand over the evidence to the police. It was a lie. Deep in his heart, Patrick knew he could never betray his father. Victor was family. Lisa, he realized sadly, was just an ex-girlfriend.

He'd give the DVD to his dad and let him explain what happened that day in the parking garage. Maybe Lisa's father was threatening him, his family, or his business? Nothing excused murder, but Patrick needed answers.

He thought about Victor's words to Lisa after the meeting. Standing a few steps away, he'd pretended to check his phone while his father took Lisa aside. It came as a jolt to see Victor speaking directly to her.

"I knew your father," Victor said. "He was a good and loyal friend once. I'll always regret we couldn't reconcile our differences. Please give your mother my best." His father had spoken with such sincerity. Only a sociopath could do that. Patrick had known a few teenage psychos in his time at the Academy. He hoped he could recognize the same in his own father, but so far Victor had seemed genuine.

Patrick slid the DVD back into his jacket pocket and walked across the lobby, then down a hall with offices on either side. His father's door was ajar, which Patrick knew meant he was free for visitors. He knocked lightly and peered into his father's vast office.

Victor sat at a large mahogany desk reviewing some documents. He looked up and, seeing Patrick, smiled warmly. "Son, come in. And close the door, would you? I don't want anyone to disturb us." He stood and waved Patrick toward a pair of brown leather armchairs that flanked a gas fireplace lit with a cheerful flame. Patrick took the seat closest to the fire.

"Join me in a glass of scotch?" asked Victor.

"Sure," said Patrick from his seat. Patrick hated his father's liquor of choice. It all tasted like ashes to him, but by this point Patrick knew better than to refuse, or to ask for something else.

Victor stepped away from his desk and walked to a built-in cabinet to the left of the fireplace which held a well-stocked bar. He poured them both a drink and dropped a chip of ice into each crystal tumbler. He turned back to Patrick and handed him a glass.

"You really gave George Green what was coming to him," said Patrick.

Victor stood over Patrick and sipped his drink. "Why should you care what happens to Green?" he asked, in his usual direct way.

Patrick froze, forcing himself not to blink or shift his gaze from Victor's while he thought of a way out of his blunder. He'd kept so many secrets over the last six months that telling the truth now felt unnatural. "I don't. It's just, the guy seems like a real jerk. Totally had it coming."

Victor held Patrick's eyes a moment too long. The once charming fire suddenly made the room feel sweltering, and Patrick felt prickles of sweat start to run down his back. Son or not, Victor didn't trust anyone.

"I'm really only interested in George's building," said Victor as he took a seat. "It's valued at one hundred million dollars, but if I can bankrupt Burnam & Green, I think I can talk the owners down to seventy-five easy."

"Bankrupt? How will you do that?" asked Patrick, trying to keep his voice indifferent.

"Shouldn't be tough. I'll hire him."

Patrick blinked. "You're going to hire George? After you threw him out of the building?"

"That was just icing on the cake. Felt good to knock that prick down a few pegs. A few years ago, he wouldn't give me the time of day. And technically, I'm not going to hire him. My offshore company PSC will, but George won't even notice." Victor took another sip and leaned back in his chair, his legs wide. "Burnam was the real brains behind B&G. Since he retired, George has lost half his clients. The earthquake pushed him deep in the red, and I'll finish him off. I'm the nail in George Green's coffin," said Victor with a smile. "We'll keep his staff working round the clock for months on some bullshit campaign. Then PSC will conveniently go belly up, and no pay day for George."

"That's great," said Patrick not meaning it. He thought of the hundreds of Burnam & Green employees who'd lose their jobs.

Leaning forward, Victor set his glass down on the coffee table and clasped his hands together. "Now what can I do for you, son? I'm sure you're not here to talk about George Green."

Patrick paused, then asked, "Did you mean what you said to Lisa Salder about her father? Was he your friend?"

"The mayor's daughter? Do you know her?"

"We met at the Lost Lake Academy."

"Of course. I remember recommending the school to her parents. You were close?"

"No, not really. She was just around."

"Why your interest in the mayor's dead husband?" asked Victor.

Patrick kept his voice measured and careful. "I met the mayor once, at work. She came to the bike shop to give a speech." He shrugged in what he hoped was a nonchalant way. "I'm just curious."

"Right, right," Victor said, not sounding entirely convinced. "Ben Salder was one of my lawyers." He picked up his glass again and finished his drink. "Ben's murder was a real tragedy. Should never have happened, but things get out of hand sometimes."

Patrick looked closely at his dad as he spoke. Victor's eyes glittered, like he was on the verge of tears, and his words sounded heartfelt.

"What's all this really about, son?" asked Victor.

Patrick rolled his glass between his palms. This was it. He'd finally reached the point of no return. He spoke. "Dad, I need to show you something."

CHAPTER 38
CROSSING TOWN

Lisa rushed past midday shoppers and tourists toward Powell's City of Books. Other than a few broken windows and an avalanche of hardcovers and paperbacks, the Portland institution had survived the quake intact. It was a detour she liked to take because it gave her an excuse to stop and browse through art books, magazines, and tchotchkes. In a hurry, it also provided a quick diagonal path out of the Pearl District. The store flew by in a blur of words and pictures.

She'd texted Jamie immediately following the meeting at VSC. Luckily, her friend was free to meet up. Jamie suggested the Daily Feast, an old-school diner that Jamie said had smoothies to die for and the best tuna melt in town. It was also one of the only Jamie-approved restaurants that had reopened near City Hall. Lisa really didn't care where they met. Her mind was spinning, and she needed to unload the insanity of her morning. Mental exfoliation was definitely in order. A tuna melt and fries wouldn't hurt either.

After the meeting at VSC, the Burnam & Green team had ridden the elevator down the thirty flights in silence. Once out the door, Steve, the Mikes, and Chris crowded into the first town car, leaving Lisa alone with George. He cried all the way back to Burnam & Green and had gone through the driver's box of tissues and had even started on the compact toilet roll from Lisa's emergency supplies.

Lisa hadn't bothered to follow George back up to his office. She figured he would be busy drinking himself into a stupor for the rest of the day. As much as she disliked him, seeing his ego shredded by Victor Smith had been brutal. All that swagger bulldozed in minutes.

Not all of Victor's criticisms were fair, but most hit the mark. She'd watched George's eyes as they desperately darted to the members of his team, hoping one of them would save him from drowning. Steve, the Mikes, and Chris had all kept their heads down and remained silent. Lisa sensed they were enjoying it. Schadenfreude for an abusive boss who was finally getting his just rewards.

Only Patrick, wearing a smug look, made direct eye contact with George. Lisa was at least grateful George didn't recognize her ex. It was easy to see why. Somehow in the last six months, Patrick had been transformed from her hipster ex-boyfriend into a stranger wearing a suit and tie. She just couldn't grasp that the one-time love of her life was the bad guy's son. Throughout the meeting, she'd tried to catch his eye, but Patrick avoided her gaze.

It didn't make sense. None of it. Well, the bit about Patrick enjoying George's humiliation did, yet other than that she couldn't reconcile the person who'd sat across from her today with the boy she'd fallen for at the Academy.

A horn blared as Lisa attempted to dart through traffic. Get it together, she thought. Her mind was in too many places. She thought again of their first kiss at the lake all those years ago. Patrick said they could choose their own family. All that had been turned on its head since the quake. She was living at home with her mom. He was working for his dad. They'd never been so far apart. Lisa just needed to get to Jamie to talk it all through.

Lisa waited obediently for the little man to indicate it was safe to cross the street. Even with her distracted state of mind, Lisa's heart hurt at the sight of downtown Portland. For every "Open for Business" sign, there were a half dozen more that read "Property Condemned by Order of the Mayor," "For Lease," or "For Sale." Broken windows were boarded up with plywood, layered with missing person signs, and covered in garish graffiti with mixed messages of remembrance for those lost, hope for a better tomorrow, and a heavy dose of criticism for the mayor, the police, and the city government.

After speed walking the remaining few blocks, she reached the Daily Feast. The entrance was jammed with groups waiting for booths. She slipped in past them and grabbed a swivel chair at the U-shaped counter, setting her backpack on an empty seat beside her so no one else would claim it. She scanned the restaurant but saw no sign of Jamie.

Lisa looked through the lunch options, though she didn't dare order before Jamie arrived. Weighing the pros and cons of each item was part of their dining out ritual. Finally, she saw Jamie push her way through the waiting patrons. Relieved, Lisa waved her over. They exchanged hellos and a quick hug. Lisa moved her bag from the stool next to hers, and Jamie sat down.

Grabbing the menu from Lisa's place, Jamie asked, "Ordered already?"

"Nope, I waited for you."

"Sweet. Let's share some stuff. First this," said Jamie. She held out her phone.

Lisa squinted at the screen, then yelped. It was a text message from Patrick. *Why is Lisa with that asshole Green?!*

"Since when are you texting with Patrick?" she demanded.

"Since . . . I don't know." Jamie looked uncomfortable, and placed her phone on the counter. "We just check in on things, our lives, people we both know."

"Like me?" asked Lisa indignantly.

"You may have come up on occasion," said Jamie.

"And you didn't think to tell me?"

Jamie shrugged. "I know, I know. I should have. Patrick told me not to. I didn't want to scare him off. I felt at least some communication after his disappearing act was a good thing."

Lisa nodded. "Okay, fine. Now show me every text you've ever gotten from him," she said, grabbing for Jamie's phone, but Jamie picked it up and held it at arm's length.

"Don't try to change the subject, missy. Why are you hanging out with George Green?"

"I'm not hanging out with him," said Lisa, not appreciating Jamie's tone. "My temp agency randomly assigned me to Burnam & Green today, even though I specifically told them not to. To top it off, I got stuck at the desk right outside George's office. It was horrible. And that's just the beginning." She stopped to take a breath. "I have so much more to tell you."

"You know, you could have just walked out. George is a bad dude. Anyway, where did Patrick see you two together?"

"I can't just bail on my job. As much as I'd love to, my mom would give me a hard time. Enough about me and my terrible career choices. I guess Patrick hasn't been keeping you entirely up to date on his," said Lisa, crossing her arms. "Has he told you where he's working?"

"No."

"At VSC."

"What? Is he doing construction now?"

"No, he's working with his father, Victor Smith."

Jamie stared at Lisa, her eyes wide. "I'm sorry, what?"

"Victor Smith. The big bad. My mother's greatest frenemy."

Jamie just gawked at Lisa. Speaking slowly, she said, "Patrick, our Patrick, is Victor Smith's son. How is that possible?"

"I don't know. I dated him for years, and I had no idea," said Lisa.

Jamie looked utterly mystified. "He told me a little about his mom, but he never talked about his dad. That topic was totally taboo. All he ever said was that his dad had dumped him off at the Academy. Patrick thought they were going on a ski trip. Asshole." Jamie shook her head in disgust.

"Asshole is right," agreed Lisa. "I knew they were rich and lived in Lake Oswego, but I never pushed him for any other details. I always figured Patrick would talk about his family when he was ready."

"Lisa, this is all so crazy. Are you sure?" asked Jamie.

"Jamie, I'm not making it up. I got dragged into a meeting at VSC by George, and Victor Smith introduced Patrick as his son. He said he was showing Patrick the ropes. The weirdest thing is that Patrick just sat through the entire meeting and completely ignored me."

"Maybe he doesn't want Victor to know about the two of you." Jamie sat quietly for a moment, her brow furrowed. "What do you think Patrick's told him?"

"Nothing. Patrick wouldn't say anything."

"Can we be sure? He could have shared everything that happened the day of the earthquake to prove his loyalty." Jamie tapped at her phone. "I need to get back to City Hall and talk to your mom."

"No wait. I almost forgot the weirdest part. George introduced me at the meeting as the mayor's daughter. It was so embarrassing. He totally lied and said I was an integral part of the team offering insights into VSC's collaboration with the city on reconstruction. Total bullshit. After the meeting, we were all leaving the room, and Victor stopped to talk to me in the lobby." Lisa shuddered, still unsettled by the memory of his hand on her arm. "He told me that he knew my dad. Apparently, they were really good friends once. And he said to give my mom his best."

"Whoa. What did you do?" asked Jamie.

"I just said thanks and got the hell out of there."

"What's he like?"

Lisa paused for a moment to think. "He's taller than Patrick, and in his sixties, I'd guess? I don't know anything about suits, but his looked really expensive. His hair is gray and swooshed back. Wears these kind of old-school dark-framed glasses. And he sounded sincere."

"Did you believe him?" asked Jamie.

Lisa gave her a look of dismay. "No. I didn't like how he looked at me. Something is off about that guy." She shuddered at the memory. "What should I do now?"

"About what?"

"Patrick."

"Nothing," said Jamie with a dismissive shrug. "You can't do anything. Patrick is Victor's son. That makes Patrick the enemy."

"Though like you said, Patrick was probably pretending to not recognize me. He was just acting. Maybe he's doing the same with Victor. Maybe he's spying on him," said Lisa, feeling excited by the prospect that Patrick was still on their side.

"We can't take that chance. You dating Victor Smith's son? The trolls would have a field day."

Lisa was honestly bewildered. "Why?"

"Your mom, obviously. You are the first daughter after all."

Lisa laughed. "The first daughter? Please. Who cares about that?"

"A lot of people. For one, I do."

"You're serious?" Lisa couldn't believe what she was hearing.

Jamie continued, getting more passionate with each word. "I am serious. Your mom is doing a lot to bring Portland back from the dead. And it looks like a gubernatorial run is actually going to happen."

"But it's my life. Patrick means a lot to me. I have to do something."

Jamie scowled. "You'll do exactly what you want, just like you always do, with no thought as to how it might hurt the rest of us."

"That's not fair," exclaimed Lisa. "You sound just like my mom."

"Whatever. I need to go."

As Jamie stood, the waitress materialized in front of them, ready to jot down their order.

"What about lunch? You love lunch," said Lisa plaintively.

"I have a sandwich back at work."

Lisa swiveled her chair and watched Jamie stomp out the door. Glumly, she turned back to the waitress.

"What can I get you? We have a kale salad lunch special."

"I hate kale," said Lisa.

The waitress shrugged. "Everybody hates kale. How about a tuna melt and fries?"

"Yes, please." Lisa felt slightly better at the prospect of drowning her sorrows in carbs.

CHAPTER 39

THE CONFESSION

Patrick reached into his jacket pocket and pulled out the DVD. He held it out to his father.

Victor took the disc from Patrick. As Patrick had done earlier, Victor turned it over in his hands. After a long moment, he looked up and asked, "Where did you get this?" His voice was flat, and all warmth had left his eyes.

Patrick could tell that his father knew exactly what he held. He started to feel nervous. "It's a long story."

Victor gestured widely. "I'll clear my schedule. We'll have all day." His father pulled a phone from his jacket pocket and typed in a message. "There. I let the girls at the front desk know not to bother us. Now start talking."

Patrick took another sip of scotch and almost coughed as it burned a path down his throat. He set the glass down on the coffee table and wiped his damp palms on his suit pants. He'd thought so long and hard about whether or not to give his dad the DVD that he'd never thought about what to actually tell Victor once he'd handed it over. Patrick cleared his throat, willing his voice to stay confident and steady. "I found it at George Green's house."

Victor looked at him in disbelief. "You found this at Green's house?" he said, holding up the silver disc. At Patrick's nod, he asked, "When?"

"The day of the earthquake."

"Interesting." Victor gave Patrick an appraising look. "And how did you and George Green become friends?"

Patrick shook his head. "We aren't friends. I was his drug dealer."

"Why didn't he recognize you today? You could have caught up on old times," said Victor with a mocking tone.

"I don't know why. I mean, I guess I look a lot different now. With the suit and all." This wasn't going as Patrick planned. "You know what's on it?" he asked, pointing at the disc.

Victor gave him a dark look. "We'll get to that." He set the disc down on the coffee table. "Who were you dealing for? Choose your words carefully because I already know the answer."

Patrick swallowed. "Sheila Elkins. I'd just started working for her. I met her at a party the night before. She started me on deliveries. I dropped off some coke at George's house the next day. I stuck around a while. We were just shooting the shit and smoking pot." If he kept close to the truth, maybe he could get through this without mentioning Lisa or the mayor.

"You and Green, the owner of the city's foremost ad agency, were sitting around his house getting high. That's really something, son." He said the final word with venom. "So, you stop by George's house to deliver drugs, and this is just sitting there out in the open. Did he show it to you?"

"No. Like I said, we were getting high, and I saw the DVD. It was in a case, just sitting on his kitchen counter. I thought it was an action film."

"You watched it together?"

"No. George wasn't in the room when I watched it. I don't think George had any idea what was on the DVD."

"Maybe," said Victor thoughtfully. "So why do you have it? Did George give it to you?"

"He said Sheila asked him to hold onto it for her, and that she'd send someone to pick it up. He assumed that was me, and anyway, I couldn't just leave it there," said Patrick.

"Why not?"

"Well, because."

"Say it."

"Because it shows you shooting the mayor's husband. Why would you do that? He was your friend. You just said so."

Victor ignored Patrick's question and continued. "Why wait till now to give me the video?"

"I don't know. I mean, I wanted to get to you know you first, and I wanted to hear your side of the story."

Victor smiled and finished his drink. "I assume so you could blackmail me. What do you want?"

"I don't want anything."

"Bullshit."

"No, really. I thought you could explain what happened, and that maybe you had a good reason for it. Like Mr. Salder was threatening you. If I just knew the truth, we could forget it and move on. I just wanted to be in your life again." Patrick's voice faded to a whisper as he said these last words, realizing how desperately he wanted his family back, but knowing now that his dream would never come true.

Victor nodded, as though absorbing everything Patrick had told him. He set his empty glass down and stood. Stepping away from his seat, he walked behind Patrick's chair.

Suddenly, Patrick felt his father's hands heavy on his shoulders.

Victor spoke slowly, his voice like gravel in Patrick's ear. "Let me tell you what else I already know. A couple days after the earthquake, the pierogi cart guy asks to see me in lockup. He had quite a story to tell about some kid visiting Sheila the day of the quake. How a DEA agent showed up just as all hell broke loose and a tree almost killed this kid and Sheila both. Wonder of wonders, he says, the mayor of Portland, of all people, showed up and helped pull Sheila and this kid to safety. I showed him a photo of you. He couldn't believe it. You were the kid. A couple of days later, my only son shows up at my front door, his arm in a sling. The prodigal son returned." With each word, his father's hands seemed to press down a little harder and tighten a little more around Patrick's neck. "Did you really think I haven't been keeping tabs on my only child?"

Patrick shook his head no.

"Remember your buddy Joe, the one you shared that shithole apartment with? Well, he was also my buddy Joe. He was very informative, but maybe a little too curious. He stopped by a couple weeks ago and dropped off a duffle bag of your stuff. He showed me a couple special items. Photos of you and the mayor's daughter looking very cozy. Then he played me a copy of the video on your laptop. Turns out Joe was a bit of a snoop. Poor kid. You might not see Joe around again. I sent him on an errand to one of my construction sites. Dangerous places."

Patrick couldn't believe it. Victor had been playing him this whole time. Welcoming him home and pretending to be a real father. Setting him up with the apartment, the motorcycle, the job. All lies to get at the truth Patrick was desperate to hide. And he'd put his friend in mortal danger. He was suddenly terrified of who his dad might hurt next.

"Tell me the rest, son," said Victor, his voice gentler. "There's no point in keeping anything from me. If I don't know it already, I will find out. Either from you, or from your little girlfriend. And you might not like how."

Patrick nodded, relieved when Victor finally removed his hands from around his neck.

Victor walked back to the bar and refilled his glass. He returned to his seat and Patrick started talking.

An hour later, Victor opened another cabinet on his wall. This one held a flat screen television and various components. He tapped a button on a DVD player and inserted the disc. In silence, they watched.

"This is the only other copy?" Victor asked.

"Yes." Patrick choked out the word.

"You didn't make more? You didn't send it to anyone else?"

Patrick shook his head no, holding Victor's gaze.

"If you did, and I find out, son . . . Well, you and I are going to have a big problem." Victor pressed another button and the DVD slid out.

Patrick watched as his father broke the silver disc into pieces with his hands.

Victor tossed the shards into a wastebasket next to his desk, then smiled widely. "I feel like celebrating."

Patrick sat, unable to speak, feeling utterly defeated. He'd betrayed Lisa, the mayor, Jamie, even that dick tattoo artist.

"Don't look so glum, son. You can still clean up this mess. You have your gun on you?" asked Victor.

Patrick nodded.

"Give it to me."

Patrick stood and removed the Glock from its holster. He handed it to his father.

Victor walked to the opposite end of the office and slid aside a painting to reveal a large safe. He tapped in a complicated code, then held his thumb against a scanner. The safe opened. Patrick gawked at stacks of gold bars and an assortment of weapons. Victor placed Patrick's gun in the safe and removed a Beretta and a silencer. He checked the magazine, then held out the pistol and silencer to Patrick.

"It's time you made use of your time at the firing range. George needs to go to greener pastures. You understand me?"

Patrick took a step back and looked wildly at his father. "You want me to kill George?" he whispered.

"Yes. And probably his wife too. George could have shown her the video. Make it quick."

"I can't kill anyone, not even George Green," said Patrick. He felt like he was going to be sick.

Victor grabbed Patrick's shirt collar, almost lifting him off the ground. "Listen, you little shit. If you'd come to me right away, I would have had mercy on you. But you've been holding out on me for months. This is your problem now. You did this to yourself."

Patrick nodded. Victor released him and held out the gun and silencer again.

Reluctantly, Patrick took the weapons from him. "Okay," he said. "I'll take care of it." He dropped the silencer into his jacket pocket and holstered the gun.

Patrick turned to leave, then stopped. He knew he was pushing it, yet he had to know. "Before I do this, can you please tell me the truth? Why did you kill Mr. Salder?"

"Mr. Salder," said Victor bitterly as his true face revealed itself. His pale eyes appeared colorless, flat and full of hate. Deep lines etched a grimace around his jaw that Patrick guessed came far more naturally than the easy smile of the father figure Victor had been playing these last few months. "Why did I murder the great Ben Salder? Dead husband of our bitch mayor. Portland's favorite son. I killed him because that piece of human garbage was sleeping with my wife." Victor pointed accusingly at Patrick. "Your mother."

CHAPTER 40

GEORGE CONTEMPLATES HIS LIFE

George lay on his sofa in stocking feet, his back supported by a pile of tasteful throw pillows, and scowled at the rain-heavy clouds that spoiled his view. The year his office was remodeled, George had been all about radical transparency. "Let the smart mob in," he'd said. "We have nothing to hide. Burnam & Green is about openness and communication. Secrecy is dead." His architect had taken George's buzzwords literally and designed his new office as a glass cube that jutted out of the hundred-year-old brick warehouse.

In concept, George loved it. In practice, he soon realized his error. The office was a fishbowl. Instead of looking out on the world, he felt everyone looking in. Eyes watched him from all sides. A rival agency even opened a satellite office in an adjacent building with a telescope pointed directly at George's cube. George could see someone now, a man, peering at him, probably wondering what transformational campaign George was conjuring. George sat up and gave him the finger. The man jumped back into the shadows, knocking over the telescope in the process. "Serves him right," mumbled George as he settled back on the sofa cushions.

George tried in vain to spot Mount Hood through the gloom, thinking of the spectacular view from Victor's conference room. Giving up, he pressed his fingertips to his temples, trying to drive away the pressure building in his head. It was the biggest pitch he'd had since the quake, and he'd messed it up royally.

No one had ever dared ask George to explain his stock phrases before. Rapid progressive regression. Purposeful redundant navigation. Inferring consumer transference. George had a vague sense what they meant, yet clients generally had the decency to nod appreciatively and not ask questions.

And those assholes, his team of so-called creatives, they'd all just sat silent like a herd of mute sheep. George shook his head in disgust.

Victor's voice—so condescending, so combative. It still rang in George's ears.

"I'm not challenging, I'm just asking," Victor had said. "How exactly will this campaign be the . . . what did you call it? The North Star of VSC's digital revolution. Do I need to remind you that VSC is a construction company? Brick and mortar. I don't see how 'purposeful redundant navigation' or 'progressive regression' are relevant. Sounds like bullshit to me." With that, Victor had called the meeting to an end and ordered them to get the hell out of his office.

George had never seen his creatives move so fast.

And Victor's kid. What an asshole. Like father like son, he thought. He saw the resemblance, but something else about the little prick seemed so familiar. George just couldn't place him.

George sighed. None of it mattered now. He needed a drink. George looked over at his side table, usually stocked with a few choice bottles, but they were all empty. He should send the girl out to buy more. Then he remembered who the girl was.

He glanced through his glass office door and could see Lisa sitting at her desk. Maybe she's a stalker, he thought. It had been a while since George had one. Though it seemed doubtful. Even he could see that Lisa loathed him. He shouldn't be surprised that Lisa was here, now, sitting outside of his office. Karma was a bitch.

He thought back to the weekend of the party. It had been a while since he'd slipped up. But he and Sue had been fighting. She wanted marriage counseling. He'd refused, terrified it meant their relationship was over. Sue had driven off in a huff to another yoga retreat, and as usual he overcorrected. He spent Sue's first night away from home with Burnam & Green's CFO, a gorgeous, petite redhead who'd nicknamed George her CFB, or chief fuck buddy.

Then, at the party, he'd met Lisa. She'd seemed so simple, so uncomplicated. What an idiot he'd been, taking home the mayor's toxic daughter.

And so, he'd failed at his marriage, and now at his job. He stood up from the sofa and crossed the room to the back wall, where a tall bookcase buckled under the weight of various awards. ADDYs, Clios, Caddys, Cannes Lions, and Effies. He'd won Gran Prix, Palme d'Ors, Advertiser of the Year, and been inducted into more societies, halls, and academies than he could remember. He'd nominated himself for every one of them, paying top fees for the right to be judged by his peers. Each were phallic symbols of his powers as an ad man, a marketing genius, a creator of digital worlds. Behind the gold, silver, bronze, and crystal accolades, sitting back in the dust where the cleaning staff never bothered to reach, sat a tiny piece of tin on a ribbon of red, white, and blue.

He reached for it, knowing exactly where it would be, almost wishing he wouldn't find it. But it lay there, waiting for him. He pulled it out, the ribbon almost catching on the spiked wings of an Emmy.

He wiped the dust off the medal with his thumb. It felt like nothing. A trifle. Yet its weight was immense. "Participant," it read. He hated this non-award with all his being, yet he was loath to toss it away. The shame of that day, when the teacher had placed the medal around his skinny ten-year-old neck, still burned. Every other student in his class had received lauds for their skills—Math Whiz, Handwriting Hero, Chore Champ. Everyone stood out in some special way, but not George. He had built his life and career on that moment. On that failure. His first. Though sadly, no longer his last.

There was a light knock on his door. It was Lisa. He dropped the medal into the breast pocket of his jacket. "What do you want?" he said.

The door opened. "Sorry to disturb you. It's just, I have something that might interest you."

He couldn't imagine what Lisa could possibly have that would interest him other than a big bottle of bourbon. "I'm really busy right now."

"It's about Sue."

His heart skipped a beat. "Did she call? I didn't hear the phone. Is she okay? What's wrong? Does she need me?"

Lisa stepped back a few steps, obviously alarmed by his outburst. "No, I mean in a way she does. Today is her birthday. A reminder popped up on my computer from your shared calendar. You also have a colonoscopy scheduled for next week. Just FYI."

The blood drained from George's face. "Sue's birthday. Oh my god. I forgot."

"You could take her flowers." Lisa pointed to a tasteful bouquet on his desk.

"You mean today?" George looked at Lisa in horror. "Go see her today?"

Lisa nodded, obviously confused by his hesitancy. "Her birthday is just once a year. You can't really put it off."

"I'm not ready. I still have so much more work to do on myself," he said, his voice reaching an octave not heard since puberty. "What if she rejects me?"

Lisa shrugged. "There's a high probability of that, considering you've been cheating on her for years."

George gasped in fright. He couldn't. He just couldn't face Sue yet.

"At least you'll know," said Lisa.

"I don't know how to find her."

"I do." Lisa held out her phone to display Sue's social media stream. "Your wife is quote 'On my way to the Relentless Rejuvenation Clinic. Hashtag embrace-perfection,' unquote. She posted this about two minutes ago. If you leave now, you might be able to catch her before she checks in."

George looked at Lisa with terrified eyes. "Okay. I'll go."

"Let me wrap up the flowers for you." Lisa picked up the bouquet from his desk, left the office, and disappeared behind the kitchenette partition. Moments later, she reappeared with the flowers carefully wrapped in newspaper and held them out to George. "Just do it."

Taking the bouquet from her hands, he said, "Thank you," and sprinted out of the office.

CHAPTER 41
THE UNIVERSITY CLUB

Ellen sipped her martini. The vodka was still cold, but the shimmer of ice crystals left from the bartender's perfect shake had long since melted. She picked up the bamboo toothpick that garnished her drink and examined the olive speared at its tip. Its slightly oily residue had left a sheen across the vodka's surface.

Other than the bartender, Ellen was currently the only person in the University Club's bar. She used to think drinking alone was in bad taste. However, since the death of her husband, she'd learned to appreciate the contemplative aspects of a solitary cocktail.

On entering the members-only club, she'd set her phone to silent as policy dictated and kept it sitting face up on the bar next to her. Tapping the screen, she saw a string of messages from colleagues and staff, but none from Victor Smith explaining his tardiness. She tapped on a message from Theo reporting in that he'd checked on Sheila this morning and there was no change in her condition. Though disappointed by the news, Ellen was comforted that at least one man in her life was reliable.

Looking idly at her watch, Ellen wondered where Victor was. It was well after noon and she hadn't had lunch. She pulled the olive from the toothpick with her teeth and chewed. The briny flavor was unappealing.

The bartender saw Victor before Ellen did. She noticed him quietly shift to attention, checking that the tools of his trade were in order.

"Good afternoon, sir," he said as Victor slid onto the barstool next to Ellen's.

"Yes, good afternoon, Victor. Only a half hour late," she said with a hint of acid in her voice. She turned to the bartender. "Please give Mr. Smith anything he'd like, and put it on my tab."

"What's your most expensive single malt?" Victor asked him.

"We're proud to serve Macallan Twenty-Five."

Ellen almost choked as she took a sip of her tepid martini and glared at the bartender. She made a mental note to talk to him later about keeping his recommendations on the more economical end.

"Perfect. I'll have a double," said Victor. "I feel like celebrating."

"How do you take it?" asked the bartender.

Victor smiled. "Neat. I want to savor every sip of Mayor Salder's money."

"Excellent, sir."

Victor turned to Ellen with a magnanimous smile. "And I see the mayor was enjoying a cocktail. She'll have another, also on her tab."

The bartender looked to Ellen for approval. She pushed her now empty glass forward and shrugged. "Why not?"

Ellen turned to Victor. "I'm always a little worried when you have something to celebrate."

Victor laughed. "Let's just say I've had quite a successful day, and I have a feeling it's about to get even better."

"Now I'm genuinely afraid," Ellen said wryly. "What did you want to meet about? I have a very busy schedule."

"Right to business, as usual."

The bartender placed their drinks on the bar in front of them. They raised their glasses in a toast.

"To the University Club," said Ellen.

"Fuck the University Club," said Victor. "I've always hated this place."

"Still upset about your failed membership bid?"

He shrugged and sipped his drink in lieu of a response.

"I'm just glad to know there are still some places you can't buy your way into," said Ellen, knowing full well she was to blame for blocking Victor's chances of joining.

Victor glared at her. "Let's not ruin my good mood. I might get mean."

Ellen swung down from her barstool and picked up her phone, purse, and martini. "Why don't we move to the library," she said. "It's more comfortable. And private."

They stepped into a vacant, book-lined room next door to the bar. A fire crackled in the hearth, the shelves were filled with a mix of leather-bound volumes and best sellers, and racks held an assortment of international newspapers and magazines. They settled into a pair of leather armchairs near the fireplace.

Ellen didn't like how comfortable Victor appeared. Usually when they met to cover rebuilding contracts, he was on guard. Today, Victor looked like he owned the place.

"I hear you're running for governor," he said.

She wasn't surprised he knew. The party hadn't exactly kept it a secret. "Nothing's official yet," said Ellen with a demure smile. The mere thought of a gubernatorial run gave her a thrill of pleasure. "Why, would you like to make a contribution to my campaign?"

Victor laughed. "My money is going to the other guy."

"Governor McCullough is finishing his second term. There is no other guy."

"Not yet. Whoever he eventually is, he'll have my full backing."

Ellen paused and shook her head in disgust. "As always, thanks for your support, Victor. I knew I could count on you," she said.

"So, you have decided?" he asked.

"I've been approached by the party, and I'm seriously considering."

"Well, you're going to want to reconsider."

Ellen laughed. "And why is that?" she asked, not at all comfortable with the smug, self-satisfied smile he gave her.

"My son came to work for me recently," said Victor. "He just turned up out of the blue about six months ago. I had some problems with him as a kid, but I took care of it."

"What does your son have to do with me?" she asked with growing irritation.

"I sent him to that Lost Lake Academy. Cost a pretty penny. Didn't you send your daughter there? Lisa, right? I wonder if they knew each other. My son's name is Patrick. Maybe she's mentioned him?"

CHAPTER 42

LATE LUNCH

Jamie unwrapped her backup sandwich from its envelope of wax paper. She'd assembled it last night with leftover roast chicken from Sunday's weekly family dinner. Now that she had a job, she could afford extravagances like real mayonnaise, dill pickles, avocado, hothouse tomatoes with little vines still sticking out of them, and sliced cheese. She'd piled the toppings high on a seemingly healthy multigrain bread that, she justified, offset a bag of potato chips. She'd been looking forward to it all morning, even feeling a tinge of regret when Lisa had called about meeting for lunch. And now, after their argument, the sandwich was still here, faithfully waiting in Jamie's insulated lunch bag.

Jamie took her first bite just as her cellphone rang. She glanced at the screen expecting one of the Salder women, but to her surprise it was Patrick.

She answered immediately and managed to spit out, "Dudeyouareinsomuchtrouble."

"Jamie?" asked Patrick. "Is that you?"

"Onesec." She chewed furiously and swallowed. Once again capable of speech, she said clearly, "Dude. You are in so much trouble."

After a beat Patrick answered. "Yeah. I really am."

Jamie was taken aback by how profoundly depressed he sounded. She'd expected him to demand details on Lisa and George Green, yet obviously something else was on his mind. Regardless, she wasn't about to back down now. She blurted out, "You're Victor Smith's son? How is that possible? I've known you for years and you never talked about your parents, but that kind of detail is pretty important, particularly considering . . ."

"Jamie. Please, can you just listen for a minute?"

"I guess," she said.

"I'm an idiot."

"Agreed."

"I need your help."

"I don't know if I should help my enemy. You do understand that Victor Smith is the bad guy, right?"

"I know that now. But, Jamie. He's my dad. I thought maybe . . . Oh, forget it. You're right."

Jamie paused. She'd never heard Patrick sound so defeated. Angry or frustrated, sure. The Patrick she knew always had a tireless optimism that had helped get him through even the worst times at the Academy. "I'm sorry, Patrick. Are you okay? Is he threatening you?"

"It's not me I'm worried about. I made a really bad call, and there's only one way I might be able to make up for it. Can you help?"

"Sure. Yeah, I can help. Do you want me to talk to Lisa?"

"No, it's not about Lisa. I mean, it is sort of. Anyway, I need you to find something for me on the mayor's computer."

"What? Are you kidding me? You want me to steal information from the mayor?" Jamie couldn't believe it. Patrick was just manipulating her. She shook her head in disgust. Patrick really had gone to the dark side.

"Please, just listen to me," said Patrick quickly. "I need you to find a file that I saved to the mayor's computer on the day of the quake. Remember how embarrassed she was that I'd found her password? I left something really important on it for safekeeping. It's a video."

"Okay, but she's out of the office right now. I can't just log on to her computer and start snooping around. I could get fired."

"Jamie, it's important. Trust me, she won't fire you. I need you to do this for me now. I might not have another chance for a long time."

"What do you mean by that?"

"Nothing. Just help me. Please," Patrick said, the tension rising in his voice.

"Okay, okay, calm down. I'll do it." Jamie stood up from her desk and walked to Ellen's office, hoping the mayor had left the door unlocked. Luckily she had. Jamie looked over her shoulder just in case Ellen was about to walk into the lobby, but saw no one. Quickly she entered, sat down at Ellen's desk, and flipped over the mouse pad. "Ha! She still keeps her password in the same spot."

Patrick chuckled. "Nice to know some things never change."

As she typed in Ellen's password, she said, "You know that Lisa wasn't with George Green voluntarily, right? Her temp agency stuck her at Burnam & Green today."

Patrick didn't respond.

Fine. They'd argued about him and Lisa a dozen times over the last few months, and she wasn't about to start again now. "Anyway, what am I looking for?"

"Search for something about taxes, or maybe audits."

"Dude, there are hundreds of files and folders."

"Then look for a folder that was updated the day of the earthquake."

"Okay." She sorted by date and scrolled through the list. "How about 'Quarterly tax audit archive do not delete'?"

"That could be it," said Patrick eagerly.

She clicked the folder open. "I see a single movie file called *Die Hard*?"

"Holy shit. That's so great," he said.

"Do you want me to watch it?"

"No," he said emphatically. "Do not watch it. No matter what. Only the mayor should see it."

She paused, then asked, "It's not anything kinky, is it?"

"Seriously, Jamie?"

"Just adding some levity."

"Not the time," said Patrick. "Just make sure she watches it as soon as she's back. Tell her I hope this can help make up for my mistakes. And Jamie?"

"Yeah?"

"Thanks for letting me know about Lisa. I lost my shit when I saw her with George."

"Lisa misses you, you know. She was upset that you didn't even say hello."

"I had my reasons."

"I'd love to know what they are."

"I hope I can tell you someday," said Patrick, and then he hung up.

CHAPTER 43
UP IN FLAMES

Ellen felt the blood drain from her face, knowing full well Victor already knew the answers to his questions about Lisa and Patrick.

"Patrick and I had a long talk today," Victor said. "Seems you were pretty busy the day of the earthquake."

"I have no idea what you're talking about," said Ellen, crossing her legs and concentrating on staying calm.

Victor raised his eyebrows and shrugged. "Oh, really? Patrick told me how your fixer posed as a DEA agent to intimidate George Green, a respected member of the Portland business community, in his own home."

"George Green, respected? Please."

"Then there's your illegal search of Sheila Elkins's Airstream trailer."

"We entered the trailer because a massive Douglas fir had crushed it like a tin can. She was dying. We had to help her. Finding ten kilos of cocaine was pure coincidence. And I don't need to remind you that we saved Patrick's life too."

"He was only in that trailer with her because you coerced him into illegally recording their conversation."

"I don't know why he was there. Regardless, Sheila could wake up from her coma at any time. And then she and I are going to have a long conversation about who was really running the food cart drug ring."

"Right. Too bad about Sheila's coma. It's nice of you to keep checking up on her. All those calls to the intensive care ward. Everyone at the hospital talks about how interested Mayor Salder is in poor Sheila. How you call her doctor four or five times a day. I have a few buddies at the hospital too, you know. They might not be fancy doctors, but they're well informed and happy to keep me up-to-date on the condition of my former employee."

"She's under round-the-clock police guard," said Ellen with a warning in her voice.

"Of course she is," Victor said flatly.

Ellen clearly heard the threat in Victor's tone. "So you admit that Sheila worked for you."

"Of course. She managed my parking garages as an employee of All Star. Her extracurricular activities were her own business. You know, Sheila was at the parking garage the day they found your husband shot dead. Just a few blocks from here. Such a tragedy. My wife, she's still getting over it."

"You're going to cross a line pretty soon, Victor."

"By the way, I met her today."

"Who?"

"Your daughter. Lisa. Beautiful girl. She was all chummy with George Green. Seems like they're quite intimate." Victor smiled at Ellen's obvious discomfort. "I always heard she was a hellion."

"Keep my daughter out of it," said Ellen.

"I wish I could," said Victor helplessly. "But that's just not going to be possible, because the tastiest morsel Patrick shared was how you helped your daughter dodge a potential prostitution charge."

Ellen froze. That stupid boy.

"I see you're getting the picture. There are going to be some changes. You forget this run for governor, and I rebuild Portland the way I want to."

"I will run for whatever office I choose. And we had an agreement about the contracts; I stay out of your way as long as you rebuild according to my specifications."

"There's no more we. I'm tired of your meddling, and I'm done putting up with your LEED certification bullshit, your green roofs and bike lanes. It's cutting into my profits. This is my town. I just let you live in it—for now."

She held her ground. "You don't have any proof. Just the lies of a troubled boy."

Victor stood and stepped uncomfortably close to Ellen, looming over her. "You'll see soon enough. It won't take much. You're on such a high horse that pushing you off is easy. I'm so low in the dirt that I can get away with anything."

Victor took a last sip of his scotch, then threw the drink in the fire, the dregs of liquor flaring with the crash of breaking glass.

Alarmed by the sound, the bartender rushed into the library.

As Victor strode out of the room, he said in passing to the man, "You can put that on the mayor's bill too. And give yourself a nice tip."

CHAPTER 44
SHARING

Jamie looked at her phone, completely baffled by the whole exchange with Patrick. She hovered the cursor over the video, tempted to click and watch. But she held back. She left the computer unlocked and stepped out of Ellen's office, returning to her desk. She picked up her sandwich and took another bite just as Ellen opened the lobby door.

Ellen pointed an accusing finger at her. "Patrick is Victor Smith's son. Did you know? Did you?"

Jamie mumbled, "Ijustfoundouttoo."

"This is a disaster. An absolute disaster," said Ellen. She dropped her purse and coat on the sofa and started pacing. "Victor demanded to see me today. The man shows up late looking smug and more self-satisfied than ever, and drops this bombshell on me." She stopped mid-stride and turned her gaze on Jamie. "Why didn't you tell me? Why didn't Lisa?" Ellen continued pacing. "Patrick told him everything that happened the day of the earthquake. And the night of the party. All of it. And Victor will use every last bit against me. How will I protect Lisa now?"

"Mayor Salder, I just found out, and so did Lisa." Jamie stood up from her desk chair and tried to keep her voice calm. She couldn't believe that Patrick had confessed everything to Victor. She never thought her friend would betray them all like this. Ellen was right—this was a disaster.

"And Lisa is with George Green? I had to learn that little gem from Victor too. What is she thinking getting involved with that man again?"

Jamie shook her head emphatically. "No. She's not involved with him. Her temp job assigned her to Burnam & Green this morning. She didn't have a choice."

Ellen looked slightly mollified. "Oh. Well. That's a relief." Her eyes dropped from Jamie to the sandwich sitting vulnerably in its wrapping. "Dear, are you going to eat that? I'm recovering from a two-martini lunch and I really could use something solid."

Jamie thought longingly of the bread, the smoky roast chicken, and the myriad of toppings. "Of course, you're welcome to it." She protectively scooped up what remained of her half and handed the untouched portion to Ellen in its wax paper wrapping, internally vowing that she would absolutely refuse to share her chips.

"As usual, my dear, you are a lifesaver," said Ellen gratefully. She sat down on the sofa. "Now, what am I going to do about Victor?"

Jamie took a seat in one of the armchairs that flanked the sofa. She spoke quickly, feeling it best to relay everything she'd learned from Lisa. "I met Lisa for lunch. She told me about getting stuck at George's office this morning, and then going with him to a pitch at VSC. She said that Patrick was at the meeting, and Victor Smith introduced him as his son. Lisa couldn't believe it. I can't believe it. He never talked about his family. All I know is they dumped him off at the Academy and he never spoke to them again."

"Not the case anymore, apparently," said Ellen. "Patrick told Victor about our DEA ruse, about recording his conversations with Sheila and George. He even told his father about Lisa and George." Ellen gave Jamie a meaningful look and shook her head. "My daughter truly has atrocious taste in men. Victor's son. What are the odds?"

"I'm not so sure Patrick's all bad, Mayor Salder."

"Why is that?"

"Lisa said Patrick ignored her at the meeting. He didn't even acknowledge that he'd ever met her. That tells me he didn't want his father to know about their relationship. I think he was trying to protect her."

"So why tell Victor everything?" asked Ellen, though it was less a question than an accusation.

"Maybe he didn't have a choice."

"Maybe," said Ellen quietly. Having finished her sandwich, she crumpled the waxed paper and tossed it into the trash bin next to

Jamie's desk. "He's always a few steps ahead of me. I feel like I can't keep up. Call the hospital, will you? Make the nurse walk to Sheila's room and confirm there's an officer sitting at the door."

"On it," said Jamie.

Ellen picked up her purse and walked toward her office.

"There's one more thing," said Jamie. "Patrick called me a few minutes ago."

Ellen turned back to Jamie. "Patrick called? About what?"

"He asked me to look up a file on your computer, a video. He sounded really stressed. And since you still keep your password under your mousepad," said Jamie with a shrug, "I logged in and found it. I have no idea what it is, he told me to not watch it. He said he hoped it would help make up for a big mistake."

There was a knock at the door. "Shit. I totally forget about that reporter," said Jamie.

"Language dear," said Ellen.

Jamie ran to open the door and swore again. Instead of the reporter from the *Times*, it was her brother, Roderick.

CHAPTER 45
FOLLOWING

A steady stream of well-dressed professionals came and went from the Burnam & Green entrance. Patrick sat on his motorcycle wearing a black leather jacket and helmet. He watched as the oversized double doors opened and closed, emitting and receiving the greatest creative minds in Portland. None of them, so far, were George.

He remembered Lisa, when she first enrolled in art school, telling him that her dream was to join B&G. Their campaigns were the funniest, the most cutting edge. Everyone in her classes wanted to land a job at the agency. And apparently she had succeeded, thought Patrick glumly. Assigned or not, she could have just walked out instead of working for the asshole who'd almost ruined her life. Then he remembered he'd taken a job from someone who was currently ruining his.

To the right of the entrance was a wide rolling door that Patrick assumed must lead to an underground parking garage. He'd sit and wait. Green would have to emerge from the building eventually, he figured. He willed himself to concentrate on staring at the doors. To think only of them opening and closing, and not of his mother cheating. Cheating with Lisa's father. Sleeping with the mayor's husband.

The garage door began to lift and he saw a car approach the exit. He flipped up his kickstand and revved his motorcycle's engine, once, twice. His heart raced at what was to come next. The door slid slowly open to reveal a gray Honda Civic, driven by a middle-aged woman in dark glasses. Definitely not George.

Patrick took a deep breath, flipped the kickstand back down, and turned off the engine. Mom, he thought, what the hell. His thoughts went back to that day, years ago, when he and his parents drove up the mountain. A ski trip, his dad said. A ski trip for the whole family. They'd hit the slopes during the day, then spend the evening playing games and drinking hot cocoa next to the fireplace in their Mount Hood condo.

Patrick remembered thinking that spending time with his parents when his friends were waiting for him in Portland was total bullshit. Then his dad took a left when he should have taken a right. His father silenced his mother with a word when she asked where they were going. The feeling in the car changed. It grew tense and anxious as each unfamiliar mile passed by. Finally, through the trees, an opening. Then a compound. His father parked and made a call.

Patrick tried in vain to open his door, but it was locked. He tried the window, but it wouldn't budge. He braved a single question and asked, "Where are we?"

"You'll see," said his father grimly.

The men came for him then. Two, both dressed in puffy jackets and knit caps against the cold. They reached the car and finally his dad unlocked the doors. The smaller of the two opened Patrick's and the larger reached in, grabbed his arm, and pulled Patrick from the back seat. His father got out of the car and opened the trunk, removing an unfamiliar duffle bag and handing it to the smaller of the two men.

Patrick was so terrified he couldn't speak. He stared at his mother who sat paralyzed in the front seat.

Suddenly, she started screaming. "Victor. No, you can't. You've already taken so much. You can't take away my son too." She said it again and again, until finally his dad raised his hand threateningly, and she stopped.

His father then turned to Patrick. "Remember, she did this to you, son. Your mother did this."

Patrick had thought about his father's words for years. And finally, he understood. He remembered her panic in the car. Her protests as the men dragged him away. She didn't want her son taken. She didn't know what was happening. His dad sent him to the Academy to punish her for the affair. He used Patrick then, just like he'd used Patrick today. Had his parents ever loved each other? He thought about Christmas, his dad putting something expensive around his mother's neck or wrist, and her laughing and smiling at the extravagance. He thought of the nights hiding under the covers, as they screamed at one another in the dark hours, only to wake to his mother hiding a black eye behind sunglasses as she cooked him breakfast before school. He thought of acting out as a kid, gladly taking the brunt of his father's anger to protect his mother. Could Patrick blame her for looking somewhere else for love and compassion? Neither of them ever got much of that from his father. And Victor barely gave them room to comfort each other. Victor wanted all their attention on himself, whether it was love or fear. There wasn't enough space for anything else.

Patrick flipped his helmet's visor up and rubbed his eyes, surprised to feel tears. He shook his head, feeling empty and helpless. He wished now that he'd stayed under the radar and out of his father's life. He just hoped Jamie would show the mayor that video. Maybe Ellen and Lisa could at least get some closure out of this whole mess.

I need to talk to Mom, he thought. I need to hear the truth from her. He pulled his phone from his back pocket and scrolled to his mother's cell number. Just then, he noticed the Burnam & Green garage door lifting. He heard a terrible screeching sound and watched as a yellow Lamborghini laboriously made its way up the ramp. It was George.

CHAPTER 46
MEET THE PRESS

"Hey, sis. Surprise," said Roderick.

Jamie glared at him, then turned to Ellen. "It's just my brother. I'll let you know when the reporter arrives."

"Fine," said Ellen. "Don't forget to call the hospital."

Jamie waited until Ellen had closed her office door, then punched Roderick's arm.

"Ow!" he yelped.

"Why are you here?" Jamie asked. "I assumed you'd meet me at my apartment."

"Well, I . . ."

"Listen, some reporter is supposed to show up any minute now. We have about a thousand balls in the air and we need to deal with all of them at once. You need to leave." Jamie started pushing Roderick toward the door, then noticed that her brother, who invariably dressed in a T-shirt and jeans, was wearing a suit.

"Why are you dressed like this?" She gasped. "Oh my god. You're in town for a job interview? Are you moving back to Portland? Why would you do that? You're crazy."

"I'm the—"

"You can't move back here. I still haven't had a chance to visit you in New York. I never get to go anywhere." Feeling dejected, she sat back down at her desk and took another bite from her sandwich.

"I'm the reporter."

Jamie almost choked. "No, you're not. You're just an intern."

"Seriously. It's me. The other reporter got pulled onto a bigger story and she asked me to cover for her. Free trip home, right? I figured what the hell."

"Bigger story? Mayor Salder is going to be our next president."

Roderick didn't respond and just raised an eyebrow skeptically.

"Okay, maybe not next," Jamie said with a shrug. "But the next, next president."

"Yeah, right. Like any candidate from Oregon could ever make it to the Oval Office."

"Wait till you meet her. She's way impressive."

"And I guess you'll be her chief of staff?"

"Maybe I will," she said boldly, then stuck out her tongue.

Ellen's door swung open and she stood clutching the doorjamb for support. Her face was ashen. "Where did Patrick get that video?" she asked.

Before Jamie could speak, Roderick walked straight up to Ellen. He held out his hand and Jamie watched as Ellen shook it limply. "Mayor Salder, it's such a pleasure to meet you. I'm Roderick Kim from the *Times*."

Ellen kept her eyes on Jamie. "I don't understand. And why show it to me now? Jamie? Is it a trick? Did Victor put him up to it?"

Roderick continued, completely oblivious to Ellen's state of mind. He flipped open his bag, pulled out a voice recorder, and held it in front of her face.

Jamie stood and tugged on Roderick's arm, realizing whatever was on that video had shocked Ellen to her core. She needed to get her brother out of here. "We can reschedule the interview for tomorrow."

"I wish that were possible," said Roderick. "The story is going online tonight and it'll be in print nationwide tomorrow morning. I want to give Mayor Salder an opportunity to respond."

"Respond? To what?" asked Jamie with irritation. "I'm sure a piece about an earthquake that hit months ago can wait."

Roderick gave Jamie his most sparkling smile. She'd seen it before. It generally preceded his doing something truly awful. He turned back to Ellen. "Mayor Salder, you committed your daughter to the Lost Lake Academy, an unaccredited institution that staffed teachers and counselors who have since been accused of abusing students, both mentally and physically."

Ellen's eyebrows popped up in an uncharacteristic look of surprise.

Roderick continued. "I have it from a very reliable source—one of Portland's most respected businessmen and a concerned citizen—that you had your daughter kidnapped and kept against her will at a facility that is currently facing dozens of lawsuits by former students. My source was kind enough to anonymously share his personal experience as a father who sent his own son to the Academy. He's financed lawsuits by former students, many of whom I interviewed for this article. How can the city of Portland, the state of Oregon, or the nation itself have faith in a woman who would place her own daughter at such risk? Do you care to comment?"

Ellen stared at Roderick her face hardening. "There is no story."

"I have three thousand words filled with quotes from students and former teachers ready to file that say otherwise. I have shocking video footage from the school that will immediately go viral. And, I have personal anecdotes from Lisa herself."

"What?" exclaimed Jamie. "You can't use any of her stories. Those were told in confidence."

Roderick ignored Jamie's outburst and said to Ellen, "I thought I'd at least give you the courtesy of a response. Mayor Salder, if you want to stay off the record, that's fine. But your constituents are going to have a lot of questions."

Jamie was horrified, thinking of the late nights she, Lisa, and Roderick had spent at her parent's house after holiday dinners when Roderick was home from school. She and Lisa had talked freely of their Lost Lake horror stories over popcorn and endless games of poker. And that whole time, her brother had just been collecting potential material for a story.

CHAPTER 47
THE SHOOT OUT

Patrick crouched behind a dumpster and dropped his motorcycle helmet on the ground. Clutching his arm, he watched with shock at the blood that seeped through his fingers. He yanked off his tie and wrapped it around the wound a few times, then tied the ends, pulling the knot tight with his teeth.

Holding his injured arm as still as possible against the searing pain, he reached under the dumpster with his good hand and felt the ground for the gun. Every cell in his body screamed run, but he couldn't leave the weapon behind. Finally, he touched the warm metal with his fingertips.

He was such an idiot. How many rounds had he fired at the range? When it came to pointing a gun at another human being, even an asshole like George Green, he completely fell apart. Not that Patrick had ever intended to hurt George. He just wanted to ask if George had watched the video like Victor suspected.

Patrick had followed George from Burnam & Green, able to easily keep a safe distance on his motorcycle. The yellow Lamborghini stuck out like a sore thumb. George drove from the Pearl toward the Alphabet District, then turned down Twentieth toward Burnside. Patrick was surprised when George took a sudden right into the underground parking lot for the Relentless Rejuvenation Clinic. He followed as George pulled into an empty spot far from the entrance, near a line of dumpsters and recycling bins.

Patrick parked his motorcycle a few spots away. He looked around the dimly lit lot, noting how quiet it was for midafternoon.

Seems like as good a place as any for an interrogation, he thought. Patrick took off his leather jacket and draped it over his motorcycle seat. Keeping his helmet on, he quickly walked toward George's car and pulled on a pair of leather gloves. He pulled the gun from its holster and twisted the silencer into place, figuring he may as well make it look real.

The Lamborghini's engine was off, and Patrick could hear it ticking as it cooled. George remained seated, clutching a large bouquet of flowers stiffly in his hands, lost in thought.

Patrick tapped on the driver's side window with the gun. George jumped in shock at the noise, then seeing the gun, frantically tried to restart his car. Patrick shook his helmeted head no, then motioned with his index finger that George should roll down his window.

Clearly terrified, George pressed a button and the window opened.

"I just want to talk," said Patrick.

George swallowed, then spoke. His voice was unnaturally high. "This isn't a great time. Why don't you call my office? I'll give you my card." He reached toward the center console.

"Stop," said Patrick, and George froze. "Get out of the car," he commanded.

"I need to be somewhere," George begged. "You don't understand."

"What you don't seem to understand is that I have a gun, and you'd better do exactly what I say."

George nodded, rolled the window back up, and opened the door. Patrick motioned for George to step toward the dumpsters.

Still clutching the flowers close to his chest, George said, "Listen, if this is about money, I can get you as much as you want. Just let me go."

"Shut up." They reached the dumpsters, and Patrick pushed George against one of them. He glanced around but felt sure they were out of sight. Still, he didn't have a lot of time. Urgently he asked, "Did you watch the video?"

George looked baffled. "The video?"

Patrick waved the gun in frustration, and George cringed fearfully. "George, you know what I'm talking about. The DVD Sheila gave you for safekeeping the night of the party."

"What party? I go to a lot of parties. I'm a very important man."

"Jesus, dude. The night before the earthquake."

Patrick could see George struggling to remember, then suddenly his eyes lit up. "I completely forgot about that. I never had a chance to watch it. Some kid showed up the next day pretending to work for Sheila. I gave it him."

Patrick's shoulders dropped with relief, and he pointed the gun away from George. He could tell George was telling the truth. No one who watched that video could just forget it, not even a self-centered prick like George Green. Patrick loosened his chin strap and pulled off his motorcycle helmet with his free hand.

"Hey, do I know you?" asked George.

A car squealed into the parking garage. When Patrick turned to make sure they were still out of sight, George pushed him. Patrick fell to the ground, dropping the gun. He heard a loud pop, then a crack as the bullet ricocheted off a metal dumpster, and a shock of pain as it hit him. He whirled around, but George was gone.

And now he was stuck in this dank parking garage, probably bleeding to death, the cops presumably on their way. He pulled his phone from his back pocket and cursed when he saw the broken screen. Luckily it still worked, and he scrolled through his contacts for the only person he wanted to talk to right now—Lisa.

CHAPTER 48

THE CALL

Lisa sat at her desk at Burnam & Green playing a game of solitaire, idly clicking card after card, winning some, losing some. She wasn't sure why she'd returned to her seat outside George's office. No one had visited the sixth floor since George had left with his bouquet of flowers for Sue. At least she wouldn't get fired for bailing on the job. Not that she really cared. She'd lost the two most important people in her life—Jamie and Patrick. Her best friend was firmly on Ellen's side, and Patrick had chosen his father, Victor Smith, over her. Lisa hadn't felt this alone in a long time. Grief filled her chest and she choked back a sob, remembering the last time she'd lost someone precious.

$$\Y$$

Lisa lay curled up on the bed, a thin blanket twisted around her body. Her pillow was damp with tears, but her face had dried. Her father was dead. She breathed in and out. It was all she could do. Breath in and out. Like her father never would again.

"You should eat," said the counselor, obviously bored. The woman sat next to Lisa's bed, reading a magazine. Lisa didn't recognize her. She was one of a multitude of staff that circulated in and out of the school, all wearing identical Lost Lake Academy polo shirts and fleece jackets. A tray with a sandwich, an apple, and a carton of milk sat untouched on the bedside table, next to a sheaf of pamphlets on grief and a box of tissues.

Lisa dimly recollected that she'd been escorted to the small health center and was on suicide watch because of how she'd reacted to her mother's call. She'd screamed "I hate you, I wish I'd never been born," and "I want to die," over and over again.

She didn't mean it. She didn't want to die. Not in this horrible place. Lisa just wanted her mother to suffer for not letting her come home to say goodbye to her father. And as much as Lisa hated her mother right now, she needed her.

She heard the door open and glanced up. In spite of her sorrow, she smiled.

"Students aren't allowed in here," said the counselor cautiously. The woman set aside her magazine.

Jamie and Patrick stood in the doorway, their expressions calm.

"Dr. Nobile said we should check on Lisa," Jamie said. Her voice exuded confidence, though Lisa knew she was lying. Bob the Nob would never suggest such a thing. "We're in Lisa's peer group. He said some time alone with us would help."

Lisa sat up and pushed the blanket away.

"Dr. Nobile would have sent someone from the office," the counselor said.

"There was an incident at the lodge with one of the new students. All the other counselors are busy with that, so Dr. Nobile asked us to come," said Patrick.

Lisa cleared her throat. Her voice was still hoarse from the call with her mother. "I'm feeling better," she said. "And I trust Dr. Nobile. If he thinks talking with my peer group is a good idea, we should listen to him."

The woman glanced at Lisa and shrugged. "Fine." Looking back at Jamie and Patrick she pointed to the tray of food. "Try to get her to eat something."

"Absolutely," said Jamie.

"I'll be in the staff lounge if you need me." She grabbed her magazine and left, leaving the door ajar.

Jamie sat on the narrow bed next to Lisa and hugged her. "I'm so sorry."

"How did you find out?" Lisa asked.

Jamie and Patrick exchanged glances. "Some of the other students heard your call with your mom. Word traveled fast."

Lisa nodded and covered her face with her hands. "Yeah. It was pretty terrible."

Jamie handed her a tissue from the box.

Lisa wiped her eyes. "I'm so glad you came. Can we get out of here?"

"Yes," said Jamie enthusiastically. She grabbed the tray of food and tissues. "In case anyone stops us, we can say you wanted to eat outside."

Lisa stood and slipped on her sneakers. Patrick pushed the door open further and glanced up and down the hallway. He gave them a thumbs up and silently they hurried down the short corridor to the backdoor of the health center. Patrick opened it, once again checking that the way was clear. He waved them forward, and they quickly stepped outside and headed straight for the woods. The fall air was crisp and a little chilly. Patrick carried a backpack on his shoulder. As they walked, he unzipped it and pulled out a gray hoodie, handing it to Lisa.

"Thanks," Lisa said, pulling it on. It was oversized and smelled of woodsmoke and laundry detergent. She buried her hands deep in its pockets.

They walked into the forest for several minutes, toward a quiet spot with tree stumps to sit on. It had view of the mountain and was out of sight of any school buildings.

Patrick opened the backpack, laid out a blanket, and set up a little picnic of Lisa's lunch plus several contraband items—chocolate bars, string cheese, juice boxes, even a few tiny bottles of vodka.

"Where did you get this stuff?" asked Lisa.

"I shook down some of our classmates," said Patrick with a smirk.

Lisa laughed. For a moment, she'd forgotten her father was dead. Then she remembered everything and immediately felt guilty for enjoying a moment of levity. Tears spilled down her face.

"Oh Lisa," said Jamie. She scooted over to where Lisa sat. She kneeled and put her arm around Lisa's shoulder.

"She won't let me come home."

"Lisa, I'm so sorry. Maybe if you ask again?"

"You don't know her. Once my mom decides something, that's it. It's done." Lisa leaned against Jamie and sobbed. She'd never experienced true grief before, an emotion so raw and pure it came unclouded by any other thoughts. Her father was gone. She felt cut in half.

"Then forget her," said Patrick gently. "Let's talk about your dad. Tell us how much you loved him and your favorite things about him."

Lisa hung her head. "I don't know if I can."

"Okay," said Jamie. "I'll start."

Lisa looked at Jamie, confused. "You never even met him."

"I know him through you," said Jamie. She picked up a chocolate bar from the blanket and started unwrapping it. "My favorite thing about your dad was that he loved that blobby, rainbow-colored ashtray you made for him in second grade. He didn't smoke, but he always kept it on his office desk, and whenever anyone asked, he said proudly that his daughter Lisa had handcrafted it just for him."

Lisa saw the ashtray in her mind and imagined holding it in her hand, the rough earthenware covered in a dozen badly painted shades.

Jamie broke off a piece from the chocolate bar and handed it to Lisa. She took it, the candy melting slightly in her warm fingers. She put it in her mouth savoring the flavor and wondered if everything would taste and feel different now. Her life in two parts—the time before her dad died and the rest of her life now that he was gone.

"I'll go next," said Patrick. "My favorite thing about your dad was that recurring dream he had about picking strawberry pies in a field with his brothers. They'd pick whole pies and load them into the back of a pickup truck."

Lisa laughed softly. "He always had the craziest dreams."

"Lisa, how about you?" asked Jamie.

Lisa thought carefully for a long moment, and then spoke. "My favorite thing about my dad . . ."

Y

Lisa's cell phone rang.

CHAPTER 49
ANOTHER HIT & RUN

"Let's go, asshole!" yelled Sue out the open window of her Audi. She had lingered too long at Sheila's bedside at Good Samaritan and was running late.

Sue and Sheila's unlikely friendship was bound by blood, specifically the blood of a would-be mugger Sheila had knocked out cold when he attempted to steal Sue's Gucci handbag. Sheila had noticed the sketchy suspect on the security feed of the parking garage she managed and made it to Sue's rescue just in time. While waiting for the police, the pair realized they shared an obsession with exercise and often met for smoothies after working out.

Sue missed their two-way conversations, but had to admit that Sheila, in her comatose state, was Sue's dream therapist. No leading questions, no judgmental looks, only blissful silence while Sue talked and talked. And the doctors said Sheila could only benefit by hearing the familiar voices of friends and loved ones. It was a win-win situation. Today, in lieu of flowers, Sue had left Sheila a carton of her favorite cigarettes, Capri Menthols.

An old red Subaru sat at the intersection, giving everyone in the goddamn city the right-of-way. Eventually, the car turned the corner at a glacial pace, and Sue sped ahead, feeling a slight thrill as the sedan hit a small crater and briefly took flight. "Calm down, for the love of god. You'll make it in time," she spoke aloud to herself. As a birthday tradition, Sue was treating herself to a full regimen of treatments at the Relentless Rejuvenation Clinic, and she hated missing even a moment of the spa experience.

When Sue finally reached the entrance to the clinic's parking garage, her back wheel hit another pothole. Distracted, she glanced over her shoulder, then quickly swung her attention forward when she heard the soft *oof* of her vehicle making contact with a living thing. The sound was distinct—a tell-tale *whoosh* of breath being forced from a body. She knew it too well. "Not again!" she wailed. Sue slammed on the brakes and sat stunned, her hands grasping the steering wheel tightly. Maybe it was a deer, she thought. She realized how unlikely that was in the very urban Alphabet District, and frantically considered the other possibilities—a giant squirrel or one of those sixty-pound raccoons people were always going on about. Please don't let it be a dog, she prayed silently.

She opened the driver's side door and stepped out, walking to the front of the vehicle. A small dent now marred the otherwise pristine bumper, which had been replaced since Sue's encounter with the mayor's awful daughter.

Doesn't look too bad, she thought. Then she heard a groan coming from the sidewalk to her right.

A man lay on the concrete, covered in flowers and clutching his arm. He mumbled over and over, "He's trying to kill me. He's trying to kill me." The man's bright yellow sneakers looked disturbingly familiar.

Sue rushed over, ignoring the honks and curses as cars started to line up behind her. "Hey, it's going to be okay," she said, brushing the flowers away from the man's face.

He looked up at her with eyes that turned from fear to joy, and then burst into tears. "Sue, is it really you? Am I dead? Are you an angel?"

Sue, suddenly feeling far less concerned, pulled away from her estranged husband. "George, why did you run into my car?"

George wiped his tears away with his good arm and started ranting. "This kid. He had a gun. He tried to kill me in the parking lot." George pointed to the garage ramp. "We have to call the police."

"George, don't be an idiot. No one is trying to kill you. Except yourself, apparently. I'll drive you to the emergency room."

She helped George into the passenger seat and buckled him in, then got into her seat. As quickly as she dared, she took a right on Burnside, then barreled down Twenty-Third Avenue, honking at every pedestrian who dared to try and cross the street.

Finally they reached Good Samaritan, where she yanked the car into the ambulance lane and parked. She stepped out, then opened George's door and let him lean heavily on her as he stumbled to his feet.

An orderly rushed from the Emergency Room entrance. "Ma'am, you can't park here. This area is for emergency vehicles only," he said.

Sue turned her fiery glare on the hapless orderly, pleased by how he shrank back in terror. "My husband was the victim of a hit-and-run, which qualifies as an emergency, which makes my car an emergency vehicle, right?"

The orderly gulped and said, "Well, no ma'am. Technically, it does not."

"Well, what do I do about him?" she said, nodding toward George.

"I'll fetch a wheelchair and we'll get him right to the registration desk. Just give me a moment."

George panicked and turned to Sue, "No. You can't leave me. He could have followed me. He had a gun. A gun!"

"Do you see what I'm dealing with?" said Sue to the orderly. He'd reappeared with a wheelchair in record time. "He's having some kind of emotional breakdown. Trust me, it's not the first time. I need to stay with him. You park my car, I'll take him inside."

The orderly nervously looked back toward the Emergency Room doors.

"Please."

"Fine."

She tossed him the keys. Reaching into her wallet, she pulled out five twenties and handed them to him. "For your trouble. And please be careful with her. She's temperamental like her mother."

CHAPTER 50
COLLATERAL DAMAGE

"Roderick, why are you doing this?" asked Jamie.

He gave Jamie a puzzled look. "Sis, I'm doing this for you. And for Lisa. You both deserve to have your stories told."

Ellen crossed her arms. "I have a question for you, young man. This well-respected businessman you mentioned. Is it Victor Smith?"

Roderick looked thrown off guard, a rarity in Jamie's experience. "I can't reveal my sources," he said.

"You're looking a little twitchy, so I'm going to guess I hit the nail on the head. You are being manipulated by Portland's biggest crime boss. Smith is a drug trafficker, a known racketeer, and a man suspected of several murders here in Portland and beyond." She paused and looked away a moment, then cleared her throat. "I would expect the *Times* to have better standards." Ellen turned to Jamie. "Jamie, can you get Ed Salzmann on the phone?"

Jamie returned to her desk to search through the mayor's contacts.

Ellen said to Roderick, "Ed and I attended law school together. We meet for drinks every time I'm in New York. I believe he's currently the Deputy Managing Editor, which would make him your boss."

"Actually, he's probably your boss's boss's boss," said Jamie.

"I want to let him know what kind of naive and unprofessional reporters he has working for him. Coming to me hours before a story filled with fraudulent information is set to publish is not a way to make a name for oneself."

"I found the number, Mayor Salder," said Jamie, enjoying Roderick's panicked look.

"Okay fine, I lied," said Roderick. "The story isn't slated for publication. I just thought since I was in town, I'd try to get your side of the story."

"Jamie, please remove Mr. Kim from my office," said Ellen.

"It would be my pleasure," said Jamie. She grabbed her brother's arm and pulled him toward the lobby door. "You jerk," she hissed in his ear. "How could you do this to me? You are a genuinely terrible person. Did you have to ruin my life twice? I actually liked this job."

"You never said I ruined your life," he said. "I thought you were okay going to the Academy. That it was better than getting stuck in juvie."

"Did you ever actually listen to any of the stories I told you, or did you think I was making it all up? That I was exaggerating?" She shook her head in disgust. "I was holding back, you idiot. Think of every story I told you and multiply the shame and abuse and fear by a hundred. That was my life for a year and a half. I lost my high school experience. I lost prom, yearbook, dating, my friends. All the experiences you had, you stole from me. You went to Stanford. I had to get my GED, then go to community college before I could even get into Portland State. Do you have any idea how humiliating that was for me? And now you're here to ruin the life I just built back up. Then, there's Lisa. She will never forgive me if you publish this. She trusted me. To be clear—if you go ahead with this story, you'll lose a sister."

Roderick looked stunned. "I didn't know, Jamie. I'm so sorry. I really thought writing this story would help you."

Jamie stared him down till he looked away. He turned and walked out, quietly closing the lobby door behind him.

Behind her, Ellen spoke. "Jamie, can you come in here?"

Jamie walked slowly into Ellen's office, bracing herself for the dismissal that was sure to come. She'd have to move back in with her parents while she looked for a new job. Maybe Lisa could hook her up with the temp agency. "Mayor Salder, I'm so sorry about him. My brother is truly awful."

"At the least, very self-serving. Maybe we can use that to our advantage." Ellen looked thoughtful. "Is he still in the building?"

"Maybe. He just walked out a few moments ago. Do you want me to see if I can find him? Though I can't guarantee I won't push him down a flight of stairs or an elevator shaft."

"Please do. Find him I mean. I have an idea."

Jamie ran out to the hall in search of her brother. He was sitting just outside the office on the floor, his back against the wall.

"Roderick, what are you doing down there?"

He looked up at her warily.

"Listen, the mayor wants to talk to you."

Roderick didn't move. "I've been so selfish. I never realized Jamie, what it meant for you. I never put myself in your shoes before. Would I have survived what you went through? I don't think so."

"Empathy's a bitch," said Jamie.

Roderick just nodded.

"Come on, the mayor is waiting."

Together, they walked back to Ellen's office.

"Tell me what you know about Victor Smith," Ellen asked Roderick.

"I got in touch with Victor a few months ago after I saw his name on a lawsuit against the Academy. He was extremely helpful, to say the least. Gave me full access to his lawyers, who provided all their discovery documents and put me in touch with former students and staff."

"And what did you have to do in return?" she asked.

"He told me to dig up as much dirt on you as I could," said Roderick, looking sheepish.

Ellen pursed her lips. "And your moral compass was okay with that?"

"It's the news," Roderick said with a shrug. "Until today, I wasn't ever particularly concerned about collateral damage. But I don't want to lose my little sister."

"Glad you're able to use this as a learning moment," said Ellen sarcastically. "Regardless, you don't have to leave Portland empty-handed."

"Sure, what do you have?" asked Roderick.

"I've been trying to connect Victor Smith with the food cart drug ring I broke up six months ago, and so far, I've come up empty. With the contacts you've already made with Victor's organization, perhaps you can find something I've missed."

Jamie's desk phone rang. Irritated by the interruption, she grabbed the receiver. "Hello? Yes. Really?" Her voice rose in pitch with each word. "We'll be right there." She turned to Ellen and clapped her hands together in delight. Slightly mortified by her childish gesture, she eased her hands down to her sides and continued in what she hoped was a more professional manner. "That was the hospital. Sheila just woke up from her coma."

"Who is Sheila?" asked Roderick.

"A business associate of Victor Smith. I think we'll all be very interested to hear what she has to say. Are you up for a trip to Good Samaritan?"

"Absolutely," said Roderick.

Ellen picked up her cellphone and dialed. "Theo, Sheila's awake. Can you get to the hospital now? Victor has been having her watched. I'm concerned." Ellen paused to listen, then said, "Thank you," and hung up. She grabbed her purse and coat and headed for the door. Jamie and Roderick followed.

CHAPTER 51
GOOD SAMARITAN

As Jamie looked around the Emergency Room lobby, she felt a dizzying sense of déjà vu. It felt so similar to the night of the party when she'd brought Lisa in for treatment after her run-in with Sue Green, except that this afternoon, the hospital was far busier, and damage from the earthquake was still visible. Plywood panels covered broken windows, and workers on scaffolding were busy repairing the damaged atrium and rehanging light fixtures.

She looked for her old seat across from the mounted flat screen television and gasped.

"Jamie, what is it?" asked Roderick.

Jamie took a hard left at the registration desk where Ellen was speaking with an administrator and into a waiting area filled with dozens of people. She passed an elderly man with an oxygen tank, a stressed mother trying to sooth her crying toddler, and a young man in thick glasses tapping on his phone. But Jamie was only interested in a young couple holding hands.

"Well, hello there," she said to Lisa and Patrick.

The pair had been deep in conversation and looked away from each other reluctantly at the intrusion, but when they saw it was Jamie, they both smiled.

Jamie crossed her arms and kept her expression stern. "Patrick, you're bleeding."

Patrick glanced at his left arm. "It's just a flesh wound." A black leather jacket sat folded on the chair next to him.

"I will make it bleed harder if you don't tell me how it's possible that you are the son of Victor Smith," Jamie said.

"Yeah, about that."

"Hi, Lisa," said Roderick. "Are you going to introduce me to your friend?"

Jamie jumped in. "This young man is Patrick Smith. The son of Portland's most ruthless mobster."

Patrick nodded, "Guilty as charged."

"You have a lot to explain mister," said Jamie sternly.

"I know, I know," said Patrick, raising his hands as though to block Jamie's words, then wincing in pain at his injured arm.

Lisa took Patrick's hands as though to calm him. She held Jamie's eyes. "Jamie, he's told me everything. Patrick didn't have a choice. His dad threatened all of us. Patrick, me, my mom. His dad's been keeping tabs ever since we left the Academy. It's really scary."

"Speaking of scary," said Patrick. "Here comes your mom."

Ellen waded through the chairs to the small group. "Lisa, Patrick. What a pleasant surprise. Somehow this all feels very familiar."

"All that's missing are George and Sue Green," said Jamie in agreement.

Ellen shook her head. "Don't speak their names, Jamie. You might conjure them out of thin air."

"Who are George and Sue Green?" asked Roderick. Jamie just shook her head no, and for once, he took the hint.

"Patrick, I see you've been injured. Shall I call a doctor?" asked Ellen. "I know many of the staff personally."

Jamie and Lisa exchanged confused looks at how civil Ellen was being.

She should be attacking the devil's spawn, thought Jamie. Not trying to help him.

"It's nothing serious," said Patrick. "I might need some stitches."

Ellen just nodded.

Jamie was stunned. Why wasn't the mayor giving Patrick the third degree?

"Has she seen it?" Ellen asked Patrick.

"No."

"Good. Let's keep it that way."

"That's it, Mayor Salder? Patrick betrayed us all," said Jamie. "He's been lying all this time."

"True, but something new has come to light. And we need to adjust accordingly," said Ellen crisply.

"What has?" asked Roderick. Jamie could see him reaching into his messenger bag for his voice recorder.

"In good time," said Ellen in a way that made it clear the topic was off-limits. "Now, can you all head to Sheila's room? Patrick, unless you feel you need to see a doctor immediately, I'd like you and Lisa to go with Jamie and Roderick. I'd feel better if you all stayed together."

"Absolutely, Mayor Salder," said Patrick.

"Good. Ask Sheila if she needs anything that might make her more comfortable. I need to speak with the hospital administrator for a few more minutes."

"How do we find her?" asked Roderick.

"Jamie, you've been to her room. Do you remember how to get there?" asked Ellen.

"Third floor, first left, then a right?"

"No dear, two lefts, then a right. Now, Sheila is being guarded by an officer, so it's entirely safe. However, she is almost certainly being watched. Use your best judgement and be careful."

Jamie watched Ellen look meaningfully at Patrick. Dying of curiosity, she wished she'd ignored Patrick and clicked play.

CHAPTER 52
VITALS

Theo had walked this hall many times before, though never as the tattoo artist.

Before heading to the hospital, he'd pulled a set of scrubs from his locker at the back of the tattoo parlor. After kicking off his cowboy boots, he quickly changed, topping off his look with a white coat and a pair of pristine white sneakers. Finally, he pulled the silver caps from his teeth and neatly brushed his mustache, removing the western twist that was a signature style of Theo the tattoo artist, but was too bold for the infinitely forgettable hospital orderly.

The mayor had made an agreement with the hospital administration to give Theo clearance to all the nooks and crannies of Good Samaritan. Ellen knew Victor was biding his time, and she wanted an inside man in case he made a move. When Sheila was in a coma, this was less of a concern. No need to silence a woman who might never wake up. Now that she was conscious, Victor would almost certainly have someone on-site ready to make sure Sheila suffered a relapse, or worse.

Theo trotted down the long, wide hall. Blue vertical stripes with bold, white numbers announced rooms 385, 386, and finally 387, Sheila's home for the last six months. It was positioned on the corner within sight of the nurse's station, and easy to guard. But no bored-looking police officer sat on the chair outside.

Cautiously, Theo stepped through the open door. The curtain had been drawn around the bed. He ripped it open. Sheila was gone. In her place was an unconscious but still bored-looking officer, his shirt pulled open, the sensors that had been tracking Sheila's vitals now calmly tracking his. The man's wrist was firmly shackled to the bed's railing with what were likely his own handcuffs. Theo took in the rest of the room. A handful of cards from well-wishers had been swept to the floor, along with a cracked vase of roses, a dented bedpan, and a ripped open carton of Capri Menthols. He wondered vaguely what kind of lunatic would bring a coma patient a gift of cigarettes.

All this he'd absorbed in a moment, and then he rushed into the hall and to the nurse's station. "Where is Sheila Elkins?" he asked urgently.

A nurse looked up. "I checked in with Ms. Elkins before my rounds. She's awake and appears to be doing very well." The nurse glanced at a monitor. "Strong heartbeat today," he said, tapping on a screen.

"That's not Sheila's heartbeat. Call the police. We need to find her, now."

CHAPTER 53

GEORGE HIDES OUT

Sue couldn't stop laughing at the absurdity of George being assassinated. She clutched her aching sides.

"It's not funny," said George. Sue's future ex-husband sat on an examination table that was covered with a sheet of light blue paper. It rustled with his every nervous movement. He held his injured arm protectively against his chest and glowered at Sue.

At least he'd stopped crying, she thought. Safe on the hospital's third floor, Sue had finally calmed George down and she wasn't going to miss this opportunity to make fun of him. She rolled around on the doctor's exam stool, occasionally spinning, to George's obvious annoyance.

"You have to believe me," he said. "I'm not making this up. There really was a man with a gun. He threatened me."

Sue rolled over to a built-in shelving unit and started pulling cabinet doors open. They'd been waiting for the doctor for over twenty minutes, and she was getting bored. Another ten and she'd have to throw a tantrum. She dug through an array of bandages, cotton swabs, alcohol preps, wipes, ointments, rolls of tape, bottles of peroxide, alcohol, and K-Y Jelly. She flicked a tongue depressor at George.

"Stop it," he said. "Will you put all of that back? Someone might see."

Only a fabric curtain on a metal rod blocked the traffic and activity of the hallway and neighboring exam rooms. Sue had jerked the flimsy barrier closed as soon as the nurse left them with a promise of a doctor's quick arrival.

Sue glared at George and returned to her inventory of the cabinets. "Where do you think they keep the good stuff?" she asked as she snapped on a pair of latex gloves.

"Like what?" asked George hesitantly.

"You know, syringes and scalpels."

"Hopefully, not in here."

"If someone really is after you, we'll need weapons," she said with a wicked grin.

"I seriously don't understand why you find this all so amusing," said George glumly.

"Who would want you dead?" she asked.

"I don't know. Lots of people."

She started laughing again. "Okay fine, George. Did you recognize him?" she asked.

George continued. "All I know is some guy dressed all in black wearing a motorcycle helmet showed up out of nowhere. It was terrifying. I was just sitting in my car, and he tapped on the window. I swear, he had a gun with a silencer." He said these last words in a whisper.

"A silencer? It all sounds too crazy to be true. Were you up all night watching *John Wick* again?"

"No. Maybe."

The curtain was ripped aside violently and four people spilled into the room, making it suddenly feel very small. Clearly none of them were doctors or nurses, observed Sue.

"Patrick, this isn't Sheila's room," exclaimed a frustrated looking girl with jet-black hair.

"Jamie, I told you the mayor said to head down the hall and take the second left," said a tall young man with a necktie wrapped around a bloodied sleeve. He carried a black leather jacket.

"Or was it the first left?" asked a second girl with strangely familiar hazel eyes.

Behind them stood a handsome Asian man in a gray wool suit and bowtie. Sue thoroughly approved of his ensemble. He flashed a sudden and flirtatious smile at her. Involuntarily, she smiled back and wondered if he was too young for her or just right. Coming back to her senses, Sue glared at the quartet, and started to tell them to get out when George spoke up.

"Lisa? What are you doing here?" he asked.

"George? What happened?" Lisa blushed bright red when she saw Sue.

The little tramp is back, thought Sue, taking in the girl's terrible haircut and business casual office wear. She doesn't look so hot now without the sparkly dress and long hair, Sue thought with satisfaction.

"Well, I took your advice . . ." George started explaining, and then looked at the other three faces, landing finally on the tall young man with the injured arm. George leapt off the exam table and cowered behind Sue. He screamed, "Sue, he's going to kill me!"

"George, would you please calm down." Sue rolled her eyes. "Don't worry, I'll protect you."

Patrick put his hands up. "George, I'm so sorry about earlier. It was all a huge misunderstanding."

"Misunderstanding? You put a gun to my head. You were going to shoot me."

"I never actually put the gun to your head. I just waved it in your general direction."

George pointed an accusing finger. "You're Smith's kid. And you were at my house too, the day of the quake. Sue, look. Remember him? He's the drug dealer."

Sue glared at the young man. He looked vaguely familiar. Definitely cute. "Oh yeah! You burned a hole in my living room rug, you son of a bitch."

Patrick shook his head. "No. That was George. He dropped a lit joint."

Sue sighed audibly, then turned to her terrified husband. "George. I thought we promised, no more lies."

"Sue, you have to help me. He's going to kill me."

"Young man?" she asked.

"Yes?"

"Are you going to kill my husband?"

"No."

"That's good enough for me. Now get the hell out."

"Sue!" protested George. "You have to call the police."

She rolled her eyes and stood up about to yell police or fire or earthquake in hopes of getting the attention of someone official roaming the hallways of Good Samaritan. "Fire . . ."

"George, you are in danger," said Patrick cutting her off. "But not from me. From my dad."

"And who is your father?" asked Sue.

"Victor Smith."

"Really?" Sue was impressed.

Patrick nodded mournfully.

"I met him at a party once," said Sue. "He was wearing a gorgeous suit. Anyway, why on earth would Victor Smith want George dead? George is the least interesting person I know."

"My dad thinks you may have seen a video that could put him in jail for a very long time. And he won't hesitate to kill you both to protect himself."

"Both?" exclaimed Sue.

"That video again?" asked Jamie. "What's on it, Patrick? Mayor Salder watched it and I've never seen her so upset."

"Jamie, for your own safety, I can't tell you what's on it," said Patrick. He turned to George. "Sheila gave you a DVD the night of that party last summer, just before the earthquake."

"Yes. In the *Die Hard* case. You already asked me at gunpoint," snapped George.

"I don't have time to explain everything. You're in danger and need to hide. We'll ask Mayor Salder to send an officer."

George, still crouched next to Sue, looked around the exam room frantically. "Where exactly are we supposed to hide? This room has no door. We can't barricade ourselves behind a curtain."

"How about in here?" Lisa opened a small door to reveal a tiny bathroom. "It has a lock. We'll have my mom send the police to protect you. You'll only need to wait here for a few minutes."

"You're absolutely sure this is necessary?" Sue asked Lisa. "This isn't some perverse revenge for when I may or may not have hit you with my car?"

"No. Well, maybe. Of course, I did go home with your husband," said Lisa. "But nothing happened. Nothing, I swear," she said emphatically, waving her hands back and forth.

Sue nodded. "I'm not sure why, but I believe you." She paused for a moment, thinking about her recent therapy sessions and the psychologist's advice that in seeking forgiveness from others, she might have an easier time forgiving herself for her failed marriage.

"And Lisa, I am sorry. George and I should have stayed with you that night until the paramedics arrived. It was wrong of us."

Lisa looked at Sue with utter surprise. "Apology accepted."

"We need to get to Sheila's room," Jamie said.

Patrick turned to Sue and George. "Please get into the bathroom now. And don't open it for anyone except us or the police."

Sue shrugged in surrender. "All right, George. Listen to the man." She stepped into the tiny room and took a seat on the toilet lid, leaving George to cower in the shower stall. She shut the door and turned the lock, then called out, "You better hurry back, or if Victor Smith doesn't kill George, I might."

CHAPTER 54
THE LOADING DOCK

Theo grabbed his phone from his back pocket and hit the only number he had on speed dial. While the phone rang, he ran down the hall, looking in room after room. Nothing. The hospital was six stories high with hundreds of beds, he couldn't cover all that ground alone.

Ellen answered. "How is she?" she asked brusquely.

"Gone."

"What do you mean, gone?" she said, the undeniable sound of panic in her voice.

"The officer was handcuffed to her bed, unconscious, and Sheila was nowhere in sight."

"Was it Victor? Did he take her?"

He paused mid-stride, remembering the open carton of cigarettes with one pack missing. "You know. I don't think it was Victor. I have a hunch. Let me check something and I'll call you right back."

"Fine. Hurry. I'll alert security immediately."

He hung up and ran back to Sheila's room, then looked for the nearest stairwell. He realized, with the officer out of commission, she could have easily made it to the stairs without the nurse seeing. He followed what he hoped were Sheila's footsteps down three flights to an emergency exit door. He pushed it expecting to hear an alarm. There was none. Probably still damaged from the quake, he thought. He opened the door and found it led onto the sidewalk on Lovejoy between Twenty-Third and Twenty-Second. He took a chance and walked east.

Just ahead, he heard a laugh and a cough. A smoker's cough. He could see a narrow driveway carved into the sidewalk curb ahead. He peeked around the corner. It was Sheila. Dressed in a hospital gown and a white robe, she sat on the loading dock sharing a cigarette with Victor Smith.

He ducked out of sight, rapidly sent a text, then casually walked around the corner. With a smile he asked, "Can I bum a smoke?"

CHAPTER 55
THE HUNT

Patrick followed Lisa, Jamie, and Roderick as they rushed down the seemingly endless maze of third floor hallways, finally reaching Sheila's room. With dread, he saw that several police officers were at the scene, and a nurse was handing an ice pack to an officer with a large black-and-blue lump on his forehead.

"She was so strong," said the injured officer weakly. "I never imagined a coma patient would come at me like that. So strong . . ."

The four stepped back, not wanting to get in the way.

"What do you think happened?" asked Roderick.

"From what the officer is saying, it sounds like Sheila escaped on her own," said Jamie.

"So it wasn't my dad?" asked Patrick, relieved that his father hadn't committed yet another crime.

"Mayor Salder says Victor was having Sheila watched. We still need to find her first."

"Checking all the rooms is pointless. This place is huge," said Lisa.

Patrick nodded. "Agreed, we don't even know if she's still in the building."

Jamie's phone dinged, and she scanned the screen. "She's not. She's outside on a loading dock on Lovejoy."

"Let's go," said Roderick eagerly.

"Maybe we should ask one of these officers to go with us. You know, just in case. I mean, Sheila's already taken out one cop twice her size," said Lisa.

"We don't want to scare her off either. I say we should just go. Your mom is headed that direction too. If she wants back up, she can make that call," said Jamie.

"Okay, lead the way Jamie," said Patrick. He glanced back at the police, thinking how close he'd come to getting arrested today and wondered how long it would be before his father was led away in handcuffs.

"What about Sue and George? Shouldn't we send an officer to their room?" asked Roderick.

Patrick exchanged glances with Jamie and Lisa, and they all erupted into laughter at the thought of the Green's stuck in a tiny bathroom together.

"Let's give them a few more minutes," said Lisa. "They could use some alone time."

CHAPTER 56
TRUE LIES

Ellen leaned against a wall just out of sight of the loading dock. It was a mild day for February, but the cool air still made her shiver. Or, she wondered, was it listening to that monster Victor Smith talking so calmly with Sheila that chilled her to the bone?

Sheila laughed. "That stupid cop. He tried to cuff me, and I hit him over the head with a bedpan. He dropped like a ton of bricks."

Ellen could smell cigarette smoke as it drifted toward her.

"Feels like I haven't had a smoke in months," said Sheila, her voice hoarse from disuse. "What the hell was that yesterday?"

"Yesterday?" Ellen recognized Theo's voice and felt relieved to know that her ally was in place.

"Yeah. Was that an earthquake?" asked Sheila.

"What do you remember?" asked Victor. He sounded cagey.

"Not much. I was in my Airstream. Some kid was there. Can't remember for the life of me who it was. Then everything went dark. And now I'm here."

Ellen saw a black town car with tinted windows approach.

"This is us," said Victor. "Ready to go?"

"Am I ever. I'm dying to get out of here."

Theo spoke up. "Ma'am, are you sure you're ready to be discharged? That earthquake you mentioned was over six months ago. I think I should escort you back to your room."

"First of all, do not call me ma'am. And second, bullshit. The earthquake was yesterday. And third, Mr. Smith here has offered to let me rest and recuperate at his lovely home. Much better than a stinky hospital."

"No, it wasn't," said Theo.

"What are you talking about?" asked Sheila impatiently.

"The earthquake. It's February. Valentine's Day is next week."

"Bullshit," she said.

"Let's not worry about that right now, Sheila," said Victor. "The car is waiting. Once you're settled, we can take a ride on the yacht," said Victor smoothly. "I have it all gassed up and ready for a cruise on the lake."

It's now or never, thought Ellen. She took a deep breath, then stepped out from behind the wall. She stood at the top of the downward slope leading to the loading dock, just in view of the street. "He's telling the truth, Sheila."

"Who the hell are you?" asked the drug dealer.

Ellen took in Sheila's appearance, noting how pale and thin she looked. She wondered how the woman was able to take down a police officer single-handedly. "I'm the mayor of Portland. I helped save your life once, and I'm going to do it again today."

"Seriously? I'm at a hospital. How much danger can I be in?" asked Sheila. "Hey, Victor. About that ride." Sheila jumped down from the loading dock, then lost her balance.

Theo was by her side in an instant and put his arm around her shoulders to steady her. "Hey there, ma'am. I really think I should take you back up to your room."

Sheila leaned on him until her dizzy spell passed, then backed away. "Hands off. I'm fine. Victor, let's go." She started toward the car.

Ellen took a step closer. "Sheila, I'm going to have to ask you to stay. I have some questions for you. And if you leave with Victor, you won't survive the night. Trust me."

"I resent your allegations, mayor," said Victor with a smug look. "I'm simply here as Sheila's employer and friend. She called me for a ride, and I was happy to oblige."

"And I have nothing to say to you," said Sheila pointing at Ellen.

"Really? Nothing about the drug operation you were running for Victor?"

Sheila gave her a sullen look and tossed her cigarette on the pavement, crushing out the butt with a slipper-clad foot. "I don't know anything about that."

"Dad, are you okay?"

Ellen turned at the voice and saw Patrick, wearing a black leather jacket. Quickly taking in the scene, he stepped close to his father. Ellen noted that the loading dock felt very secluded for the busy Alphabet District. She quickly glanced around. The only security camera was broken and hanging useless from a wire, and she saw that in addition to the town car idling in front of them, two black SUVs had blocked the intersections on either side.

They were trapped.

CHAPTER 57
THE SILENCER

"What's going on?" whispered Lisa. She didn't like this at all. She could hear every word spoken, yet hated that she couldn't see the players.

Next to her, Roderick crouched as close as he dared to the loading dock entrance where Ellen had been standing moments before. He held his phone at an angle to record the scene. "Here, watch," he said.

Lisa and Jamie crouched next to him and looked at the small screen. Lisa could see everyone's faces except her mother's.

"Patrick, this doesn't concern you," said Ellen.

"You're threatening my father. Of course this concerns me."

"She's right, kid," said Victor, his voice flat. "Get out of here. Let the grown-ups talk."

"Dad, why don't we just take care of this now. I still have the gun." Patrick pointed at the broken camera. "And no one's watching."

Victor gave Patrick an appraising look. "Interesting idea."

Lisa watched Patrick pull a gun from a holster and a silencer from his jacket pocket. As he screwed the silencer on the gun barrel, every cell in her body wanted to rush forward to stop what was unfolding.

Victor rubbed his forehead thoughtfully, then retrieved a pair of leather gloves from an inside pocket of his overcoat and pulled them on. "I think a murder-suicide scenario works very well here. Sheila is unstable after waking up from her coma. She shoots the mayor, and whoever the hell you are," he said, pointing vaguely at an orderly in scrubs who stood just behind Sheila.

Poor guy, thought Lisa. He must be freaking out.

"Then Sheila offs herself." Victor finished his statement by miming a shot to the head.

"You wouldn't dare," said Sheila. She stumbled toward Victor with her arms raised to strike, then froze when Patrick pointed the gun at her.

"Stay where you are," commanded Patrick.

"Thanks, son," said Victor with a warm smile. He handed Patrick a handkerchief. "Wipe down the gun." He turned to Sheila and the smile vanished. He pointed at her. "You did this to yourself. This is your own fault."

"Patrick, stop this please," said Ellen. Lisa had never heard her mother beg before. "You don't have to follow in your father's footsteps."

"Sorry, Mayor Salder. Family first." Patrick finished wiping his fingerprints from the gun and handed the weapon to Victor.

Victor weighed the gun in his gloved hand, frowning. "You take care of Green?" he asked Patrick.

"George Green won't be bothering you again."

"How many bullets?"

"Don't worry. You'll have enough."

Victor nodded, then pointed the gun at Ellen. "Well, Mayor Salder, it's been a fun ride. But it's time it came to an end." He smiled. "And just think, this is the same gun I used to kill your husband. Sheila will be blamed for that murder too."

Lisa gasped as the revelation hit her. This monster had killed her father. Overwhelmed with rage, she stood from her crouched position and stepped forward to confront Victor. Strong hands pulled her back.

"Not yet," whispered Jamie. "I'm so sorry."

Knowing Jamie was right, Lisa forced herself to remain still, her anger silently thawing into grief. The rest happened so quickly, she barely took it in.

Victor pulled the trigger.

Click. Click. Click.

"Oops," said Patrick. "I guess I used more bullets than I thought."

Victor turned the gun toward Sheila and pulled the trigger again. Nothing.

The orderly dove at Victor, pinned him to the ground, and kicked the gun out of reach.

Sheila rushed toward Victor's car, but it was no use. Ellen had already signaled to the two black SUVs blocking the intersections. Lisa could see a dozen police officers converge on the scene, weapons drawn.

"You son of a bitch," screamed Sheila. She leapt at Victor, pushing the orderly out of the way with surprising strength, then scratched at Victor's face. "You were going to kill me? After everything I've done for you? Setting up the carts, selling your drugs, hiding your secrets. Well, it's all coming out, Victor. Everyone's going to learn where the bodies are buried."

Victor shoved Sheila away. He stumbled to his feet, then lunged, his big hands reaching for her neck, but the orderly swept his legs, and pinned Victor back down.

Leaning on Jamie, Lisa stumbled out from behind the wall, her heart pounding. Roderick continued to record everything on his phone. Together with Ellen and Patrick, they stood around a prostrate Victor, who glared up at them with hate-filled eyes. Deep gashes marred his face where Sheila's fingernails had made their mark.

"Like I said, Mayor Salder," said Patrick, putting his arm around Lisa's shoulders. "Family first."

CHAPTER 58
CRUCIAL CONVERSATIONS

Ellen sat across from Lisa in a quiet booth in the dining room at Jake's Famous Crawfish. It could have been the same table the Salder family had shared when Lisa was a little girl and she'd burst into tears at the sight of the restaurant's signature dish. As on that night, her daughter's eyes were red from tears, yet no simple remedy would ease her distress this time.

Only a few hours had passed since Victor and Sheila's arrests. Ellen had asked Lisa repeatedly if she wanted to go home and rest. But Lisa refused and insisted it was time she finally heard the whole truth.

From the front bar, sounds drifted in of patrons and staff celebrating the post-quake reopening of the restaurant. Ellen could hear Patrick and Theo cracking jokes, Jamie's infectious laugh, and Roderick's outrageous flirtations with the bartender. She longed to join them if only to delay this conversation for a few more moments.

"Lisa, what I'm about to tell you won't be easy to hear. Most of it you know. Are you sure you want me to tell you the rest?"

Lisa nodded.

Ellen began. "First, you need to remember how much your father loved you. Being a stay-at-home dad was the greatest joy of his life. And he did it for me too. He knew how much I loved my job, and he understood my ambitions."

Ellen placed her hand over Lisa's for a moment. Lisa's face blurred slightly as tears formed in Ellen's eyes. She blinked them back and cleared her throat. "It all started to fall apart when Ben went back to work and took on Victor Smith as a client. We didn't realize then what kind of a man he was. You were just eleven years old. Ben promised that the job would be part time, and that you would still be his main priority.

"At first, it was fine. We even socialized with Victor and his wife, Anne, if you can believe that. We'd meet out for dinner once or twice a month. Anne was such a sad thing, so nervous and timid around her husband. Ben always had a soft spot for damaged goods." Ellen couldn't keep the bitterness from her voice. She took a sip from her wine glass, wishing she had something stronger.

"After a few years, the part-time job turned full-time, and handling both his workload and your schedule started to overwhelm him. We managed at first, then, overnight it seemed, you turned into this moody, secretive teenager. Just when you needed him most, Ben wasn't there. And to my great regret, neither was I. You started skipping classes, you changed how you dressed, and left your old friends behind. Then came the drinking and drugs. When you came home from rehab, things were better for a while. You finished the school year, turned sixteen, and passed your driver's test. Ben and I thought you deserved a reward and so we gave you his old car for your birthday.

"Then, one night while Ben was away at a work retreat, you drove home drunk after a party. I tried to reach your father, to ask for his advice, but he didn't answer. He'd told me the retreat was at a resort in the mountains and that cell service would be unreliable. So, I did what I thought was best. I grounded you and took away your car keys. You were so angry with me. You locked yourself in your room and wouldn't talk to me. The next morning, I woke up and you were gone, and so was my car. I tried calling, but you didn't pick up your cell phone. When I saw you'd left it on the kitchen counter, I panicked. I had no idea how to find you. I spent hours calling your old friends, your teachers, your classmates. No one knew anything. I felt like I didn't have a choice, so I called the police and reported my car stolen."

Ellen paused and glanced cautiously at Lisa, but her daughter sat silent and attentive, for once not protesting or arguing over Ellen's interpretation of events. "And your father . . . I called and called. Still no answer. I tried his partners at the firm, and they said there was no business retreat and that Ben had taken a few days off. Finally, desperate, I called Victor. He said he had no idea. Then he asked when Ben had left. I answered, and he was quiet for a long time. He told me Anne had left town the same day.

"I hung up and a moment later my phone rang. I picked up, praying it was Ben. That he'd tell me he really was at a conference and not sleeping with his client's wife. But it was a police officer in Eugene. She'd found you. By this time, it was almost midnight, and she took you to that juvenile detention facility to spend the night.

"I tried to sleep for a few hours, but couldn't and just kept calling your father again and again. Nothing. At dawn, I drove south to pick you up. It broke my heart seeing you in that horrible place. I'd failed you. Ben had failed you. I realized I needed to take control. And I did.

"Your father finally called when we were driving back to Portland, and I didn't answer. I didn't want to give him the relief of knowing you were safe. When he returned home, I asked him if he was cheating with Anne. He nodded, like he knew an apology would get him nowhere. I was so angry and humiliated. He just stood there while I ranted on and on about how he'd destroyed our family, how he'd betrayed our marriage, and broken his promise to take care of you."

Ellen paused and closed her eyes, the moment replaying in her mind. She'd hoped to spare Lisa of any of this and let the girl keep her father on a pedestal. It was too late for that. And it felt good to say the words out loud, to share the burden. "He asked, what can I do? I told him to end the affair. He said it was already over. I told him that we needed to get you in treatment. If he refused, our marriage was over. He agreed to the Academy. I knew you'd never go willingly. I was sure that you would run away again, and the next time I wouldn't be able to find you. So, I took the school's advice, fool that I was. I had them stage the kidnapping. I'll never forgive myself.

"Months passed. Ben and I were in therapy, and I really thought we'd work through our problems. I visited you and you seemed to be doing so much better."

Lisa looked about to interrupt, and Ellen quickly said, "I know now that wasn't true. I only saw what I wanted to see." She took another sip of wine. She set the glass down and kept her eyes on the clear liquid, turning the glass slowly by its stem. "Then, he was found dead. There was no security footage. From the bruises, they could tell your father had fought back. As far as I knew, there was only one person who had any reason to hurt Ben—Victor—and he had an alibi. He was hosting a party at his home with a dozen guests who all swore he never left their sight.

"With Victor out of the picture, I looked at other enemies. My enemies. You probably wouldn't be surprised that I have quite a few. Did someone go after Ben to get to me? If you came home, would they hurt you? I tried to believe what the police told me was true. That it was a mugging gone wrong. But I couldn't take that risk. So, I refused to let you leave the Academy. God, I cursed Jamie's parents when they worked to have you released. At first, I was terrified. But weeks, then months went by and nothing happened. I convinced myself that the police were right. It was a random attack. Then, today I saw the video footage from the parking garage, and I finally learned the truth." Ellen took Lisa's hands in her own. She blinked back tears, not wanting to breakdown and lose her voice at this, of all moments. "I should have let you come home when your father died. I was so wrong. Can you ever forgive me?"

Lisa pulled her hands away. She slowly unrolled a linen napkin, setting the silverware aside, and wiped away her tears with the cloth. "Thank you for telling me the rest. I'm sorry Dad hurt you. Maybe if you'd told me what was going on, we could have helped each other."

Ellen nodded sadly. "Yes, maybe we could have." She noted that her daughter hadn't answered her question.

Lisa met Ellen's eyes. "Patrick is really important to me. I know he must be a terrible reminder of what happened between Dad and his mom. Can you ever look past that?"

"I can," said Ellen with a reassuring smile. She had conflicting feelings about the boy, certainly, but keeping Victor Smith's son firmly on her side seemed a wise move. As long as she never had to see Anne again. Seemed unlikely, she thought. Lisa and Patrick were young. They would never last.

Lisa nodded. "Mom, I don't want you to run for governor. I know I can't stop you, but what if I mess up again? I'll be under a micro-scope, and this time you won't be able to just hide me away."

"Lisa, this time we'll help each other. We'll take it one step at a time, together."

"Promise?" asked Lisa.

"I promise," said Ellen, meaning it.

"I miss Dad."

"Me too, honey. Everyday."

Jamie's laugh erupted again from the bar, and Lisa smiled. "Mom, let's go join the party."

EPILOGUE

The buzzer rang. Lisa navigated through a maze of packing boxes and opened the door. "You made it," said Lisa, surprised by how pleased she was to see her mother.

Ellen stood at the threshold holding a large potted plant in one arm and a brightly wrapped gift box in the other. Walking imperiously into the living room, she said with a tinge of sarcasm, "I see the unpacking is going well."

Lisa rolled her eyes, for once not taking the bait. "Mother, we managed to unpack the most important items," she said, pointing to a sofa decorated with throw pillows. In front of it sat a coffee table with a small stack of paper plates and napkins neatly arranged next to a wood cutting board covered in charcuterie.

Ellen laughed. "I'm glad to see you have your priorities in order."

"Hi, Mayor Salder," said Patrick as he relieved her of the plant.

"You'll want to keep that in a sunny spot and water it every five days."

"Yes, Mayor Salder. Sunny spot. Every five days. Can I get you something to drink?" he asked.

"White wine, please."

Jamie, armed with a utility knife, popped up from behind a tower of boxes. "Hello, Mayor Salder."

"Jamie, how many times do I have to tell you, please call me Ellen."

Lisa noted the invitation to be on a first name basis didn't extend to Patrick. She knew her mother wasn't happy about her new living arrangements, but Ellen would just have to get used to it. "Mom, let me give you the grand tour," said Lisa, gesturing around the large room. "This is the combo living room, kitchen, dining room, office, and art studio. The bedroom is down the hall."

"And there are two bathrooms," said Jamie, sighing with longing. "Can you imagine?"

The apartment was in the Southeast in a converted warehouse with views of the Willamette River and downtown Portland. When Lisa and Patrick had toured the building, there'd been another apartment available with a view of Mount Hood. Lisa had been tempted, but thought it was time to start looking forward rather than back.

As much as Ellen was against Lisa and Patrick moving in together, Patrick's mother Anne had been supportive and offered to cover the security deposit and first month's rent. Patrick's salary at VSC covered the rest, which freed Lisa to focus on finishing her degree at the reopened College of Art.

With Victor in jail awaiting trial and most of his assets frozen, Patrick and Anne had taken on sorting through the mess he'd left behind. Dozens of rebuilding projects were on hold, and Ellen made her frustration clear. Though today at least, it appeared she'd put that aside.

Patrick handed Ellen a glass of wine in a jelly jar and shrugged sheepishly at her look of dismay.

"In hindsight, I should have given you proper wine glasses, though I think you might like this better," she said, handing Lisa the gift.

Lisa sat down on the sofa and her mother joined her. Unwrapping the box, Lisa pulled out a misshapen object covered in a dozen garish colors. With a gasp, she clapped her hand over her mouth. "It's the ashtray I made for Dad. I thought you'd gotten rid of all his things."

"No, honey. I just stored them in the garage. After he passed, I just couldn't bear the constant reminders of what I'd lost. If you'd like, we could go through everything together."

Lisa gently placed the ashtray on the coffee table, then took Ellen's hand. "I'd like that." She felt some deep tension loosen in her body and wondered if this is what forgiving felt like.

The buzzer rang again. Lisa and Patrick exchanged looks. They weren't expecting anyone else today. Patrick walked to the door and pulled it open. An elegantly dressed woman with long dark hair stood in the doorway. Like Ellen before her, she held a potted plant and a wrapped box, yet other than this similarity, the two women couldn't have been more different. "Am I interrupting anything?" she asked.

Lisa felt her mother tense beside her, and she pulled her hand from Lisa's.

"Hi Mom," said Patrick.

ACKNOWLEDGEMENTS

Thank you to everyone at Ooligan Press, especially Alena Rivas and Kelly Zatlin for your brilliant editing, Robyn Crummer for navigating me through the publishing process, Claire Curry for keeping me on track with patience and grace, and Kelly Morrison for whipping my manuscript into perfect shape.

Thank you to Emily Chenoweth, the team at Portland's Literary Arts, and my delightful "How to Write a Novel in Eight Weeks" classmates: Alan Brickley, Pamela Larsen, Lisa Metcalf, Jim Reinhart, Gayle Seely, Jane Shapiro, and Dennis Steinman. Emily, you are an incredible and inspiring writer and teacher, and I'm forever grateful for your advice and support.

Thank you to Gabriel Reeve for your amazing editing of my very rough first draft, and helping me fill many plot holes.

I'm grateful to my early readers: Justin Graham, Renee Sreenivasam, Elizabeth Chapin, Faye Purdum, Jessica Outlaw, Catherine Statz, E.B. Min, Pamela Connors, Chris Burd, Becky Burd, Julia Latané, Robyn Sreenivasam, Jaqueline Statz, and Libby Carruth. You are all so generous, encouraging, and your thoughtful feedback means the world to me.

Very special thanks to Devin Ellin and Steve Dana for generously sharing their stories with me, and to Pamela Connors and Shoshanna Cohen for introducing me to so many inspirational people and places in Portland.

Thank you to my parents, JoAnn and Vince, and my siblings who instilled in me a farmer's work ethic, but always made sure we had time for books, movies and music.

And most of all, thank you to Justin Graham, my husband, my heart and my biggest advocate. This book wouldn't exist without your love, support, creativity, and encouragement. And Hooper, I don't care what anyone says, you're a good dog.

ABOUT THE AUTHOR

Pamela Statz grew up on a dairy farm in Wisconsin, the twelfth of thirteen children. She attended UW Madison earning degrees in Journalism and History. With four duffel bags and her goldfish Lucrezia swimming in a mason jar, Pamela flew to the West Coast at the cusp of the dot-com boom and never left. She's worked in media and advertising in San Francisco and Portland for Lucasfilm, WIRED, Nike, and Wieden+Kennedy. She currently splits her time between Portland and Manzanita, Oregon, with her husband Justin Graham and their giant dog Hooper. *Thorn City* is her first novel. Connect at pamelastatz.com.

OOLIGAN PRESS

Ooligan Press is a student-run publishing house rooted in the rich literary culture of the Pacific Northwest. Founded in 2001 as part of Portland State University's Department of English, Ooligan is dedicated to the art and craft of publishing. Students pursuing master's degrees in book publishing staff the press in an apprenticeship program under the guidance of a core faculty of publishing professionals.

PROJECT MANAGERS
Claire Curry

ACQUISITIONS
Alena Rivas
Kelly Zatlin
Amanda Fink
Jenny Davis

EDITORIAL
Kelly Morrison
Jordan Bernard
Tanner Croom
Sienna Berlinger

DESIGN
Laura Renckens
Elaine Schumacher

DIGITAL
Cecilia Too
Mara Palmieri
Anna Wehmeier Giol
Paige Brayton

MARKETING & PUBLICITY
Yomari Lobo
Sarah Bradley
Tara McCarron

ONLINE CONTENT & DEI
Jules Luck
Elliot Bailey
Nell Stamper

OPERATIONS
Haley Young
Dani Tellvik
Em Villaverde

BOOK PRODUCTION

AJ Adler
Rori Anderson
Chaz Akins
Corwin Benedict
Francisco Cabré Vásquez
Ryan Condon
Rachel Done
Amber Finnegan
Samantha Gallasch
Noraa Gunn
Angela Griffin
Janeth Hernandez
Julie Holland
John Huston
Maya Karkabi
Jackie Krantz
Isabel Lemus Kristensen
Ashley Lockard
Kaylee Lovato
Savannah Lyda
Rory Miner
Jazzminn Morecraft
Agi Mottern
Becca Moss
Tidari Pizani
Rachael Phillips
Claire Plaster
Abby Relph
Poch Saldana
Sarah Samms
Alexa Schmidt
Eva Sheehan
Brittany Shike
Annaliese Smith
Mackenzie Streissguth
Isaac Swindle

Kyndall Tiller
Emmily Tomulet
Shoshana Weaver
Phoebe Whittington
Isabel Zerr